The Staff and the Blade

Damien and Sari. Their union became pivotal in Irin history. But to understand their ending, you must go back to the beginning. A young singer and a hardened warrior meet and mate, but their life is torn apart by violence, betrayal, and grief.

Yet no matter how much pain and anger stain their lives, bonds in the Irin race cannot be abandoned. Damien and Sari will never truly leave each other, because those who are destined cannot be ignored.

> "She hates me as she loves me. Wholly and completely. Sari never does anything by halves."

The Staff and the Blade is a novel in four parts. It is the fourth book in the Irin Chronicles, a romantic fantasy series by ten-time USA Today bestselling author Elizabeth Hunter.

PRAISE FOR ELIZABETH HUNTER

The Staff and The Blade is a towering work of romantic fantasy that will captivate the reader's mind and delight their heart. Elizabeth Hunter's ability to construct such a sumptuous narrative time and time again is nothing short of amazing.

— CAT BOWEN, READEREATER.COM

Hunter does an outstanding job developing these characters and showcasing the events that have shattered their world. Terrific! 4.5 stars, TOP PICK

— RT MAGAZINE

Elizabeth Hunter's books are delicious and addicting, like the best kind of chocolate. She hooked me from the first page, and her stories just keep getting better and better. Paranormal romance fans won't want to miss this exciting author!

— THEA HARRISON, NYT BESTSELLING AUTHOR OF THE ELDER RACES SERIES

The Staff and the Blade is a beautifully-written, epic love story—a story of desire and duty, heartbreak and courage, and the ways love makes us both stronger and more vulnerable. This is Elizabeth Hunter at her absolute best, and it is breathtaking.

— COLLEEN VANDERLINDEN, AUTHOR
OF THE HIDDEN SERIES

A hauntingly beautiful tale of love, suffering, sacrifice, and ultimately forgiveness that spans centuries.

— WICKED SCRIBES

THE STAFF AND THE BLADE

IRIN CHRONICLES BOOK FOUR

ELIZABETH HUNTER

THE STAFF AND THE BLADE
Copyright © 2016
Elizabeth Hunter
ISBN: 978-1-959590-25-5

This is a work of fiction. Names, characters, places, and incidents are the products of the author's imagination or are used fictitiously. Any resemblance to actual persons, living or dead, business establishments, events, or locales is entirely coincidental.

Cover artist: Elizabeth Hunter
Illustrations: Chikovnaya
Developmental Editor: Lora Gasway
Copy Editor: Anne Victory
Proofreader: Linda at Victory Editing
Formatter: Elizabeth Hunter

YENE ANBESSA—
You are my favorite distraction

DREAMS

Damien of Bohemia was a legend content to live in obscurity. Weary from a century of human and Irin bloodshed, he took shelter among those who would not question his silence or the martial spells he wore over his body. Until an earth singer of raw power and no delicacy came to the village where he hid. Sari of Vestfold wasn't intrigued by the mysterious warrior or his moody silences. And she wasn't interested in listening for the whisper of his soul. Even when those whispers promised a connection that could tie them for eternity.

Mine is the fire. Mine is the blood.
Mine, her soft touch and her sharp tongue.
She that wields a strong hand
And a gentle embrace
Is my lover.
My own.
Mine is the need and the desire.
My witness, her song.
Daughter of heaven,
Beloved of my heart.
My Sari.
My own.

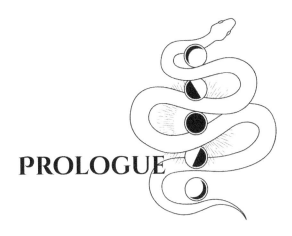

PROLOGUE

PARIS, 1314

SMOKE curled from the pile of wood stacked at the feet of the condemned. His brother stood, holding an elderly knight, a leader of their order whose hands were folded in prayer and whose eyes were lifted to heaven. The old knight didn't know what Damien and Otto were. None of the Templars did. The two men were knights of Bohemia, sent to serve the Christian god in the holy war. Nameless servants given to a cause greater than themselves.

They were Irin scribes, sent by their elders to protect those innocents—pilgrims of any religion—traveling along the roads to the Holy Land. Damien's company had watched over them, protecting them from a threat lost in legends. Grigori. Sons of the Fallen. Human legend had given them many names. Succubus. Vampire. Demon. They were the dark sons of angels who took and fed from vulnerable humans, especially women and children.

Despite that eternal threat, it wasn't supernatural forces that were killing his brother. The air was acrid with smoke.

The crowd jeered as scheming human rulers, fat with gold and titles, watched on.

No, it hadn't taken the sons of the Fallen to claim the silent scribe now standing in the growing flames. Plain human greed had slain him and those comrades he refused to abandon.

Otto. Damien mouthed his brother's name, standing on the edge of the crowd, his drab human clothes and cloak hiding his identity.

The tired scribe shook his head but kept his eyes on his brother even as the humans began to cry in fear. Gasped prayers and tearful pleas from the youngest. They were old men and frightened boys. Most of those condemned were innocent of any crime. All were innocent of the crimes they'd been accused of.

Every instinct in Damien cried out to save them.

A hand on his shoulder. "Brother, you agreed."

Stephen, the watcher of the Irin scribe house in Paris, held him back.

"This is not justice," Damien said through gritted teeth.

"No, Damien, this is human politics."

He clamped down a guttural cry as he saw Otto's head fall, the smoke taking his consciousness before the flames took his body.

"Hold, brother. Give him his peace." Stephen braced both his hands on Damien's shoulders and watched as, one by one, the humans around Otto also passed into unconsciousness and the flames grew higher. The crowd grew more volatile.

Otto could have escaped his human captors at any time. He had most of the same spells inked on his body that Damien did, but Otto's skills of subterfuge were even greater. Otto had tamed his magic so that he moved in shadow, barely a flicker of movement to the normal human eye. He could have passed from the humans' sight in front of their eyes, leaving them wondering what tricks their minds were playing.

Otto was the most feared of their order, the silent blade with eyes that had seen too much.

I am resigned, brother. I cannot return to life as it was. The thought of touching anything pure with these hands is abhorrent. I have found my peace with our human brothers-in-arms, many of whom are honorable men. There are worse ways to die. Send a message to my mother and father that I will see them in the heavenly realm. Do not tell them this was avoidable.

My dear brother, my eyes have seen too much to ever look on that which is lovely again.

You commanded us with honor, despite our orders. I thank you, but I am resigned.

"Otto." Old guilt overwhelmed him.

Damien's tears wet his cheeks as the flames reached his brother, licked up the tattered clothes that barely covered the intricate talesm inked on his skin. The dedicated work of hundreds of years turned black at the heat of human flames. It was those very markings that had made Otto's so-called inquisition a foregone conclusion. The quiet warrior had been accused of consorting with the devil and practicing magic.

Little did they know...

Red tinged the corners of Damien's vision. He felt the black rage rising. The ignorant humans around him jumped and craned to see the humiliation of the once-proud Templars as they were brought to their knees.

Stephen would not be able to hold him back when his rage broke. No one would if he—

A cool hand on the back of his neck. A soothing, delicate female scent and a whispered command in his ear.

"*Slemaa.*"

Peace. The familiar command of a watcher's mate. Jovana, Stephen's partner, pressed her cheek to his shoulder, whispering peace over and over as Stephen held Damien's other arm and shoulder. The Irina singer, as old and powerful as the mother Damien had left behind, worked her magic with her voice as Irin scribes worked theirs with pens and ivory tattoo needles.

"*Slemaa*, Damien," she whispered again. "Otto is gone now. At peace. Let us get you away from this place. You know you are in danger."

"Every Templar is in danger," he said woodenly as they led him away from the bonfire and the teeming crowds.

"You must leave," Jovana said. "Paris is not safe for you. There is a warrant out from the crown. Your name is known here, and your duke's connections hold no sway with someone as greedy and power mad as Phillipe."

He tried to turn, but their firm hands urged him onward.

"Stephen has made arrangements. You must go, Damien. Tonight. Immediately."

The rest of her words were lost in the memory of Otto's laughter around a campfire. Recollections of when Otto still smiled. When he held children who had been frightened, with an equal measure of gentleness and strength. Children had always trusted Otto. He could not touch them for long—none of their race could touch humans without hurting them—but his quiet presence had always brought comfort and confidence. Otto was safe.

Ironic, since Otto, like Damien, was a master of war.

Over the decades of the cursed Crusades, Otto laughed less in the camp at night. They all did. The blood, the loss, the waste had simply been too much. And then they had slain the angel.

I am resigned.

The only thing Damien felt anymore was guilt and rage. Rage and emptiness and a soul weariness he knew was leading him to the edge of madness.

DREAMS

My eyes have seen too much to ever look on that which is lovely again.

HOURS LATER, HE WAS PACKED ONTO A HORSE WITH THREE Irin scribes and one singer surrounding him, headed for the coast. Jovana reached up, took his hand, and pressed it between her own.

She clenched Damien's hand, and he felt her power as it flowed into him, jolting survival instincts that had long surrendered.

"You will go," she said. "You will heal. You are a warrior, Damien of Bohemia, but you are a scribe first. Find your peace, refill your soul, and one day you will fight again."

He looked down at the delicate brown fingers in his hand. "If I had a singer such as you at my side, I could have taken Damascus and slain every Fallen in the city."

Jovana smiled. "Then may you be blessed to find a mate as warlike as yourself, Damien."

Stephen stepped to his mate's side and patted the neck of Damien's mount. "Is that a blessing, my love, or a curse?"

"A blessing." Jovana's eyes lit with quiet humor. "As Damien knows full well."

"My lady." Damien bent down and pressed his lips to her fingers. Another pulse of magic. "You do me an honor. Thank you for your care. May the light continue to burn in your house."

"Return to us as a friend and a blessing." Stephen spoke the old words. "And may your path be safe before you."

Jovana and Stephen were smiling when Damien rode away, leaving the light of the scribe house in Paris burning, a warm safe haven to any Irin in need, tended by the scribes and singers who lived there with their families, caring for trav-

9

elers and keeping the humans safe from the demons that hunted in the night.

The scribe on his right said, "You haven't even asked where you're going."

"Away from here," Damien said. "Away from battle. And if heaven truly loves me, it will be somewhere warm."

The scribe smiled, the clean lines of his teeth bright in the waxing moon. "Well, brother, two out of three isn't bad."

CHAPTER
ONE

SOLBJERG, Denmark
1593

"SCOTLAND?" Sari's mouth dropped open. "You must be joking."

"The outer islands," her sister said. "Not the Scottish mainland. It's not official yet, but—"

"Well, let's make sure it doesn't become official." Sari stood and abandoned the stolen ivory she'd been practicing with.

"You know your mistress has the final say in your first assignment." Tala grabbed her arm when she rose and shoved up the thick woolen sleeve. "You've got to be joking. This again?"

Sari scowled. "If you don't try, you don't know."

"Only scribes can tattoo magic."

"We'll see when I try it." Sari rubbed the raised welts on her skin where the needle had scratched careful letters she'd practiced for hours. She hadn't tried it with ink. Yet. But she would. Her curiosity would not be satisfied until she'd attempted it. When she'd asked her old mistress, Greta had only given her a withering look and told her to concentrate on the soil. "I think I'll try my thigh first. Then if it doesn't work I won't have to listen to Mother nagging me."

"Do you ever just believe what you're taught?" Tala asked.

"No. Why do you think Mother was so relieved when I was ready for training?" Sari pulled on her wrap. "She'd had fifty years of my experiments. She would have shipped me off to Vinland if they would have taken me."

Tala laughed at her, and the tinkling sound filled the small room where Sari slept at Adna's House. Though the house was new, Sari's room was small and spare, befitting the apprentice she was. Tala's room was across the hall, decorated with soft touches and examples of the needlework she was so fond of.

The other rooms in the large farmhouse outside Copenhagen were taken by young singers who were apprenticing with the women of Adna's House. It wasn't a school. Only the careful scribes with their libraries of rules had actual schools or academies. But singers of every line lived in Adna's House. Some were widows. Others were unmated singers who had the gift of teaching. Singers who were mated to warriors in the Copenhagen scribe house often taught at Adna's House, giving the large hall a wealth of teachers from all over Europe.

When young singers around Scandinavia were ready for training past what their community could provide, they petitioned to Adna. If there was room in the house, they were accepted. If you were Tala, with a growing gift of foresight, you were taken automatically. If you were Sari, with robust but more common earth magic, you prayed there was an open room. Luckily, there had been. Tala and Sari would not be separated.

The sisters had giggled with delight when they'd first seen their rooms. It was the first time they hadn't shared a room or a bed since birth. For the first year, Tala had often crept into Sari's room, taking comfort with her twin. Now, after ten years of apprenticeship with her mentor, Tala had grown in confidence but lost nothing of her sweetness.

Sari, on the other hand...

"What on earth could Greta be thinking?" Sari marched down the hall. "Scotland?"

"Orkney," Tala soothed. "There has been an Irin community on the islands for hundreds of years, Sari, and they have never had an earth singer. For a long time it was only scribes, but so many have taken mates." Her sister's sky-blue eyes shone. "Children, sister. Like at home. The community is growing. Their farmers are struggling to grow enough to feed everyone. Greta thought you would be well suited to the position."

Sari racked her brain for anything she knew about the outer islands, but she couldn't think past her stabbing disappointment.

"And you?" she asked Tala. "Are they still sending you to Spain?"

Tala nodded. "The scribe house in Salamanca has been waiting for a singer of Leoc's line for many years, sister."

Sari stopped and put both her hands on Tala's cheeks. Though they were mirrors in appearance, no one ever mistook them for each other. While Sari was constantly out of doors, Tala was the softer sort. She enjoyed embroidery and reading. She loved to cook and mend.

"My sweet sister," Sari said, "living in a rough scribe house surrounded by warriors. What is Nienná thinking?"

Tala blushed. "I'm sure there are mostly mated couples. The Salamanca house is old and established. It's hardly an outpost in Vinland."

In fact, Salamanca was one of the most prestigious scribe houses in Europe. There was a scribe academy nearby and a thriving Irin community. Tala's appointment was an honor, but not surprising considering her skill and lineage.

Sari pinched her sister's cheek. "Of course, maybe you're not so reluctant to live among strong, virile warriors, eh?"

"Sari." Tala covered her blush with both hands. "Don't embarrass me. I'm hardly likely to find a mate when I'm so young. And I want to be taken seriously, not pursued by eager scribes." Her blush flared again.

Sari laughed. "Your face tells the truth. And who said anything about a mate? A lover, then. Someone to give that sweet face a kiss or two. Those Spanish scribes will fall over themselves to please you."

Tala turned away, wrapped her woolen cloak around herself and marched down the hall. "Didn't you want to talk to Greta about your exciting mission to Scotland?"

Sari smiled at Tala's back, but in her heart she mourned. Her whole life, her twin had been only a few steps away. Tala was her other half. Irin twins were attuned to each other since birth, and though their magic was often very different—as Sari and Tala's was—they had a bond akin to that which mates shared. Sari could sense Tala's feelings, knew her sister was equally excited and scared about her first assignment. But Tala would be heading to the heart of the Irin world, immersed in a land of culture and scholarship, while Sari…

Would be going to Scotland.

SPRING WINDS WHIPPED HER LONG BLOND HAIR FROM THE intricate knot she'd fashioned before she'd left Aberdeen. The boat from Copenhagen to Aberdeen had only taken a few days, but she'd boarded another smaller vessel to make her way to the outer islands. She'd been accompanied by no other singer. Hers was the only assignment on the isolated islands in the middle of the North Sea. The ship belonged to Irin merchants. The couple was transporting Sari and sacks of grain to the islands, then they'd be taking back a herd of sheep.

"Best lamb you've ever tasted comes from the islands," the friendly man told her. "You can ask anyone around here."

Though Sari had thoroughly studied the English language the man spoke, she had trouble deciphering his heavy accent. She was told the accent of the islanders was even more pronounced and many of them didn't speak English at all. Luckily, the language they did speak, Norn, was a variant of old Norse that she'd have an easier time navigating than English.

"Sheep and cows," she muttered. "So the islands have grass but no grain?" Sari kicked a bag of oats.

"Eh, it's harder, isn't it? The grass grows natural-like. The grain?" He shook his head. "That takes a singer's magic."

She leaned against the rough wooden board at her back. "I suppose that's why I'm here."

"And welcome you'll be."

A few hours later, the ship was docking in Kirkwall, the main port on Orkney. Sari bid farewell to the friendly Irin couple and waited for anyone or anything that looked familiar. She watched the sheep driven onto the boats, headed for the market in Aberdeen. There were humans all around her, but Sari had little trouble blending in. There was nothing outward that marked her as a daughter of angels. Unlike the heavily tattooed Irin men, Irina could blend seamlessly with the human population. She felt the whisper of their soul voices when she lowered her shields.

The Orcadians sounded like a peaceful bunch. Their features owed as much to the Norse as to the Scots, but their accent was unique, totally different than what she'd encountered in Aberdeen. But their soul voices…

Everywhere the same. Sari heard snatches of human thoughts and feelings when she lowered her shields, but nothing made her take notice until she caught the calm hum of an Irin scribe's soul voice approaching from dockside. It was low, resonant, and oddly familiar, sending an unexpected shiver up her spine when a gust of wind snatched her hair and blocked her vision as she turned.

She brushed the hair away from her face to see the scribe approaching from the walkway along the noisy docks. He was as tall as she was and wore dark breeches on his long legs with worn leather boots up to his knees. A brown coat whipped around him in the wind, but he wore no hat. Only a hood covered his head.

The scribe nodded politely as he passed the humans but didn't stop to speak to any of them. No one approached him. As he drew nearer, Sari was able to see his face. The unknown scribe was arresting in his visage. Damp, shaggy hair fell over dark eyes. His fierce gaze reminded her of the sea eagles who nested near her grandparents' land and hunted on the fjord. No wonder none of the humans tried to stop him. If she hadn't been expecting an Orcadian scribe to meet her, she would have avoided him as well.

Direct and unsmiling, the forbidding male approached her. "You are Sari?"

His voice called shivers up her spine, and Sari quickly shoved them down, embarrassed by her reaction to the somber man. "I am."

The scribe sent his gaze down her body, then slowly up again until their eyes met. Nothing about him looked Orcadian. His hair was rust brown and his face planed. High cheekbones led down to a jaw covered with a thick beard. His eyes were dark brown with flecks of gold and green. He caught her gaze for only a second before he looked away.

"Einar was expecting an older singer." His English wasn't Orcadian either.

"Are there many older singers longing to settle on isolated islands in the middle of the North Sea?" Sari asked, shifting the satchel that held her most personal possessions. "If there are, perhaps one of them might take my place."

He didn't smile, but she could see his eyes lighten in amusement. "Don't you find Orkney welcoming?"

"Not so far." She looked pointedly at the small chest near her feet. "I have been traveling for almost a week. If you'd be kind enough to—"

"The wagon will take us to the other side of the mainland." He bent down and hoisted Sari's chest onto his shoulder.

Sari was barely able to conceal her surprise. It wasn't a large chest, but she knew it was heavy. "Sir—"

"Damien," he said as he began walking. "My name is Damien."

Sari followed him with ease. She was a tall woman, like all those in her family, and she matched the scribe in height. If he'd asked for her assistance, she could have easily carried the other handle of the chest. "Would you like my help?"

"No."

The wagon stood waiting at the end of the docks, a rounded Irina sitting on the driving board. She held out her hand with a cheerful smile. "Hello, dear. You must be Sari."

Damien grunted and heaved her chest in the back of the wagon, then turned and walked back to the ship. Sari watched his retreating figure.

"Ignore Damien," the woman said. "I'm Ingrid. Welcome to Orkney."

Sari watched as Damien hoisted a sack of grain to his shoulder. "Should we help?"

"Oh no," Ingrid said. "He prefers working alone. That's just his way."

The scribe had the strength and bearing of a warrior. An old one. So why was he carrying sacks of grain to isolated islands in the middle of the sea?

"Come join me." Ingrid patted the board beside her. "Damien will ride in back."

"Won't he drive?" Sari climbed up behind the horses and set her satchel by her feet. If there was one thing she knew of all men in her village, they were always keen to be the one driving the wagon or sled.

"Damien?" Ingrid shook her head. "He doesn't drive at all. Enough about the male, dear. Tell me about yourself! What brought you here? I'm sure Einar was expecting someone older, but I'm certain Greta wouldn't have sent you to us if you weren't a skilled singer."

"I am," Sari said. "I'm very good. It will take me some time to acclimate to the soil and vegetation here, but once I'm settled, your crops should be much more successful."

Delight colored Ingrid's features. "I do like a confident young woman! Very pleased to meet you. I cannot wait to see what Einar thinks of you." Ingrid laughed. "This should be lively."

CHAPTER

TWO

T HIS was going to be a disaster.

Damien brought another bag of grain to his shoulder and lifted it, catching traces of the women's conversation as he loaded the bags from the Aberdeen boat. The new singer was hardly more than a girl no matter how confidently she walked. And she wasn't the kind of docile creature Damien associated with Ariel's line. Earth singers were usually the calm, quiet sort, content to work their magic in the fields and woods, not quick-tongued women with eyes that cut through the comfortable cloak of numbness he'd worn for the past three hundred years.

He was too old to notice her so keenly. And Einar would dislike her immediately. If he had to, he'd put his foot down. Though Einar was the undisputed leader of the village, it was actually Damien and Henry who had been there the longest. Henry was ancient; all he wanted was to be left alone with his books. Damien had taken on the mantle of Henry's guardian, so all *he* wanted was food, beer, plenty of work… and for Henry to be left alone with his books. It was a comfortable partnership.

Sadly, Einar was a brash sort and often let his own delusions of grandeur get in the way of the good of the village.

It was a small commune on the north end of the mainland. The humans on the island tolerated them and their secretive ways because the women were excellent healers and midwives and the men were handy and always willing to help on neighboring farms. It was a restful place that often had Irin warriors passing through for a few months or a few years. Orkney was, on the whole, isolated and accepting of the odd and wayward.

Damien had made the outer islands his home for two hundred years and had no plans to return to the mire of politics and war, not when he'd finally stopped dreaming. But Einar dealing with this new girl could be trying.

Damien glanced up to see her watching him and hoped she wasn't the fanciful sort. She didn't look fanciful. She looked... direct. Intelligent. Her height was both disconcerting and attractive.

He had no desire to be attracted.

At one point or another, it seemed that all the unmated women of the village had flirted with him. He ignored them and eventually they lost interest and found other men. Or they left the island if they were restless. But none had interested him as more than a passing curiosity. He was sure the new girl would be the same, though he couldn't imagine one like her settling on the island for good. No, that one had restless eyes.

Three more sacks of grain and he climbed in the back of the wagon, slotting in the backboard so nothing fell out.

"All right there, Damien?" Ingrid asked.

"All right."

She snapped the reins and the wagon jerked forward, throwing Damien to the side. The girl's sea chest slammed into his knees and he cursed quietly. He glanced up to see the girl watching him. Her eyes were laughing, and Damien felt compelled to speak.

"Your chest bruised my knees, earth singer."

"Do you expect an apology? You're the one who loaded it."

He narrowed his eyes and watched her, but she didn't look away like most girls did.

Fearless.

Heaven help her, she reminded Damien of himself at that age. Brash. Confident. Ready to take on the world.

He was the one who looked away.

"Ingrid says you don't like to drive," the girl said. "Why? Do you not like horses?"

"I like horses just fine." But the old nags pulling the wagon and the plow frustrated him. If there was one thing Damien did miss from his old life, it was the feel of a horse racing beneath him. The speed of galloping along the rolling fields surrounding his father's castle or the empty deserts where he'd once fought. There was no thrill to compare to it except the touch of an eager woman in bed.

Damien shoved that thought to the side as well.

He wasn't a monk like Henry. On his few trips to Aberdeen, there was a woman he visited, the widow of an old friend. But sharing a bed with Marie was more about friend-ship and comfort than excitement. He hadn't seen her in months. And now he couldn't banish the thought of an eager young partner warming his bed.

Disastrous woman.

He'd dump her in the village and be done with her. Maybe Henry needed to make a pilgrimage somewhere. That would take his mind off things. Ingrid took a sharp left and the sea chest slammed into his knees again. Damien winced but didn't say a thing.

"Damien?"

He was copying a manuscript in his room when he heard Henry's nervous voice. "In here, Henry."

"Dami— Oh, there you are." The scribe's round face poked around the door. Even though Henry kept up his longevity spells, there was something about the man that screamed old age. Maybe it was the bald head or the squint that no amount of magic was able to cure. Whatever the cause, there was no scribe in his acquaintance that reminded Damien more of the Christian monks who had first sheltered him after the Crusades, and for that, Henry would always have his loyalty.

Henry was utterly kind. Completely faithful. He worshiped scholarship as much as the Creator it came from. There wasn't an unkind bone in the man's body.

"Did you need me, Henry?"

"Not precisely. I was simply curious what you thought of the new earth singer. She already seems to have rubbed Einar the wrong way, so I'm predisposed to like her."

Damien gave him a short laugh.

Henry continued, "Though I'll try to smooth things over a bit. Einar can be… Well, you know Einar."

"I do."

"So?"

Damien put down his pen carefully. "So what?"

"What do you think of the new singer?"

"She's…" He searched his brain for something noncommittal. "…tall. She's quite tall."

"She's tall?"

Damien shrugged. "And has very blond hair. You've seen Norse women before, Henry. She looks Norse."

"Is she intelligent?"

"It would seem so." He picked up his pen and turned back to his page.

"Is she humorous?"

"Possibly."

"Is she—"

"Henry!" Damien huffed a sigh. "Go introduce yourself to the woman. She doesn't strike me as shy. She was more than happy to speak to Ingrid."

Henry waved a hand and his cheeks colored. "Well, I don't want to bother her."

Damien blinked. "Henry, are you... are you interested in this woman?"

That was a first. Damien couldn't remember Henry showing any interest in any woman. Ever.

"I must confess that I am, brother."

Oddly enough, Damien wasn't sure how he felt about that. He would hardly put the vibrant, fearless woman he'd met with someone of Henry's personality. But though she'd been in the village for nearly two weeks, he'd managed to avoid her except in passing. Perhaps she'd shown Henry some encouragement or interest.

"That's... wonderful, my friend." There was no one more generous of spirit than Henry. If he was truly interested in the woman—

"Did you know Orsala of Vestfold is her grandmother?" Henry's expression was one of near wonder. "I wonder if she will visit her granddaughter during her time here."

Damien frowned. "Orsala of Vestfold?"

"Surely you've heard of her." Henry sat on the bench by Damien's door. "Her singing of 'The Lux Cycle' was considered transformative by Vienna."

"'The Lux Cycle'?"

Henry nodded with enthusiasm.

"Henry, are you interested in this woman because of who she is or because you admire her grandmother's scholarship?"

His cheeks colored pink again. "Well, I'm sure this young woman—"

"Sari. Her name is Sari."

"I'm sure Sari is lovely. I am simply curious." Henry's eyes grew wide. "Do you think my curiosity would offend her? Perhaps she came here to escape recognition. I should not say anything, should I?"

Damien couldn't hold back his smile. "Henry, I doubt your interest in her grandmother would offend her. And as to why she's on Orkney, I think it has more to do with grain production than escape."

Henry wasn't listening. He tapped his foot against the bench in rhythm. "I should write to the brothers in Edinburgh. They might know more about why she's here."

"Or you could ask the girl."

"I thought you said her name was Sari."

"It is." He just avoided saying it. His hand reached for a piece of blotting paper, and he wrote out her name as it would appear in the Old Language, unable to resist his curiosity. He let his pen linger, carelessly spreading ink where it touched the page.

Beautiful. *Sari* was beautiful.

CHAPTER

THREE

S ARI nodded politely to the young man who brought
porridge to the table. She gave him a half smile in
thanks as Einar continued to ramble.

"—obviously something you're not understanding. I'd not
expect you to so quickly of course, but seeing as the growing
season here is so short—"

"It's similar to some of the land where I grew up." Sari
interrupted him, tired of his monologue. She took a drink of
the excellent milk the village dairy produced and set down her
mug. "Greta said you'd not had an earth singer here in many
years. But I don't feel any residual magic. Have you ever had
one?"

Einar shrugged. "Not since I've been here. Before that?
Who knows. Does it matter?"

Sari took a bite of porridge to avoid the sharp retort
sitting on her tongue.

Henry, the friendly scholar who'd been peppering her with
indirect questions about her grandmother for the past week,
sat down on her left. He glanced between Sari's carefully silent
face and Einar's complacent expression.

"Good morning. What are we talking about?" Henry asked.

"Henry," Einar started, "you've been here a long while."

"Indeed." His bald head bobbed. "In fact, I've been here the longest, if you recall, Einar. Perhaps you'd forgotten that."

Einar's eyes narrowed, and Sari bit her lip and took another gulp of milk.

"I'm sure it's easy to forget," Henry continued, seemingly oblivious to Einar's irritation. "You do have so much on your mind in the village. But in fact, I have been on Orkney for over two hundred years. And before that I was in Scotland. That's where I met Damien, you see," Henry said to Sari. "I met him in Scotland and we both came to Orkney. So you see, both Damien and I have been here far longer than Einar. But of course it's very hard to remember those things when you are very busy."

Sari managed to stifle a smile. "Thank you, Henry."

"Of course," Henry said. "But I'm reminded of my question: What are we speaking of?"

"Earth singers," Einar grumbled with a curled lip. "The girl was asking if the land had felt an earth singer recently."

"Oh." Henry's eyes went wide. "Probably not ever, Einar. Didn't you tell the scribe house in Edinburgh this was untouched land?"

Sari sighed and closed her eyes. No wonder she'd been feeling stymied. She'd been searching for traces of old magic on ground that had never felt its touch.

"No," Einar said. "What does it matter?"

"It matters quite a lot," Sari said. "Land that has never known earth magic is like land that has never been plowed. It will take longer—much longer—for it to reach its full potential." She took another drink of milk, emptying her cup before she banged it down. "You should not expect a full harvest this year. Petition to Aberdeen for a greater share of grain this winter."

Einar looked ready to erupt. "Listen, girl, if you're not up to the task—"

"No single singer is up to the task of breaking virgin ground in a short season's time," Sari said. "If you'd told my mistress at Adna's House the truth—"

"Are you calling me a liar?" Einar growled.

"I'm calling you ignorant," Sari said. "They should have sent three of us to break ground. I'll need three times as long to do it on my own."

She ignored the stubborn scribe on her right, now fuming in the near-silent room. Through their argument, the bustle of the longhouse had ceased and all eyes had turned toward them.

"You're an arrogant chit, aren't you?" Einar said. "I take it your father never used the back of his hand on that mouth."

Henry sat silently next to Sari, watching the argument but making no move to interrupt. He glanced at her, and she could see the curve of a smile at the corner of his lips. It gave her a surge of confidence.

"My father didn't need to raise his hand to me," Sari said, continuing to eat her porridge like her heart wasn't in her throat. "He is a wise man, and I was happy to listen to him and take his counsel."

Einar was the worst sort of petty tyrant. She'd seen his type before, scribes or singers who gained prominence in a small community only to forget the true meaning of leadership, which was—her father had taught her—sacrifice.

His nostrils flared, and he looked seconds away from erupting in anger as the door banged open and a gust of the ever-present island wind blew into the room followed by the dark form of Damien.

Sari's gaze swung toward him without thinking. In her weeks on the island, the man had been a ghost. She'd see him for a moment at the end of the common hall, then he was gone. People spoke of him, but he never appeared. They'd passed in the village once, but he'd had his hood pulled up and she didn't even know if he saw her. Ingrid told Sari that it had been Damien to ready the small cottage where she had taken residence. It was stocked with wood for the fire and as clean as Adna's House.

She wondered if he'd been the one to cut the clutch of wildflowers sitting cheerfully on the kitchen table.

Probably not.

Damien paused when he closed the door and turned slowly. Dark eyes swept the room as he pulled his hood back.

"Brothers. Sisters. Good morning." He took the offered bowl of porridge and inclined his head in thanks. Then he walked to the table as if his joining them for breakfast was a daily occurrence and sat across from Sari at the table. He met her eyes briefly, then looked away. "Good morning, earth singer. Henry. Einar."

The common hall, which had been silent, felt void of sound. Sari had never seen Damien take his meals with the rest of the village. Ingrid, who was the village cook, said he often took his meals with Henry in the library, but other than the old scribe, he didn't appear to have any friends.

"Damien," Henry said with a smile. "Perhaps you can clarify something for us. Has the ground around the village ever been worked by an earth singer?"

Damien paused and pursed his lips. "Not one formally trained."

"Ah!" Henry said. "There you go, Einar. Damien has a far better memory than I do for practical things. With books, of course, I am far superior."

Sari saw the corner of Damien's mouth move up slightly.

He looked up when Einar made a huffing sound. "Problem?"

Einar glowered, but his volcanic mood had been tempered by the gust of cold and the new company. "The earth singer says we're to order more grain. We won't have a full harvest this year, even with her here."

Damien grunted. "I could have told you that if you'd asked. On her own, she'll need two or three seasons at least."

Sari felt vindicated, but she didn't say anything. She might have been bold, but she'd also listened to enough of Greta's lectures to know when to keep quiet in front of her elders. These three scribes had been on the island far longer than she had. Sari had no desire to look foolish by talking too much.

Sari spoke to Damien for the first time since the wagon ride into town. "Which grain does best?" She'd seen him plowing the fields south of town with some of the other men yesterday.

"Barley," he said. "There's a variety that's adapted well to the islands. The growing season is short, but it's a rougher taste than wheat."

"If we're looking for sustenance, we don't worry about taste," Sari said. "We'll focus on planting the barley and working to strengthen the soil in those acres."

Henry perked up. "And if we have excess barley, we might have enough for brewing."

Damien smiled at his friend but said nothing.

Sari said, "Your winters are milder here, I think."

Damien nodded.

Sari turned to Einar. "Then I'll be able to work with the soil through the winter. By next spring, you'll have a better season. And a better season after that."

Einar sniffed. "If that's the best you can do…"

She reined in her temper and was surprised to hear Damien speak.

"Sari is an earth singer of Adna's House," he said. "The island is fortunate to have her."

It was the first time he'd spoken her name since their meeting, and Sari found the impact of his low voice wrapping around it more potent than she would have liked. She lowered her shields and listened. In the confusing murmur of soul voices in the room, his rang clear.

"Ya safeerta—"

Sari raised her shields before she trespassed on any more of his thoughts. It wasn't her place to eavesdrop on Damien's soul, and if he knew she'd been listening in, she suspected he'd be offended. It was very bad manners.

"But if you want her to have some help," Damien continued, looking down at his porridge and stirring it without eating, "then you can let her borrow Mirren and her daughter."

"The healer?" Sari asked.

Damien nodded and finally took a bite of his porridge.

"Oh!" Henry said. "Why didn't we think of that? Mirren is a very talented herb singer of Rafael's line, but her gardens bloom all winter. Of course she has some of Ariel's blood. Good thinking, Damien."

Einar grunted. "Healing gets precedence."

"Of course," Henry said, "but she's not needed that often, Einar. She could easily help Sari with the songs for the fields. We should at least ask her. And as her daughter is already apprenticing with her, their magic must be similar."

Damien said, "It is."

"Well then," Henry said. "This has been a most illuminating breakfast. Sari"—he stood and offered his arm—"I'd be happy to take you to Mirren's cottage and introduce you. You might not have met her yet. She's been helping a human village with an outbreak of fever the past week, but I'm sure I saw her back yesterday.

"Of course. Thank you, Henry." Sari stood, only to see Damien's shoulders straighten as she did. He didn't stand with her, but it was as if his body came to attention when she rose.

A warrior, she thought again. He is a warrior.

A man of his bearing could only be a warrior, and his manners told Sari he was old. What was he doing in the middle of the North Sea? And why did his ferocious gaze settle on her like a brand? She felt Damien's eyes long after she'd walked away.

THE NEXT DAY WAS FILLED WITH LAUGHTER AND TEACHING. Mirren and her daughter did have earth magic. Quite a lot of it, though their primary talent lay in healing. They were herb singers, and though neither had ever worked with grains or cereal crops, they were more than happy to learn. She took them to the edge of a barley field where seed was just springing up. The men were still plowing the field across the lane, and she could hear their shouts and laughter in the distance.

"Tell me," Sari said, "how do you make your garden bloom in winter?"

Mirren smiled. "It's not anything extraordinary, I suppose. Part of it is knowing where to place certain plants. It doesn't snow often, but the winds are biting cold."

"And the soil?"

"The soil is rich here," Mirren said. "But cold. We know it must be coaxed."

"Exactly," Sari said. "It's no different for barley or wheat. Just larger scale. But you have a step up on me. The island already knows your voice. You just have to learn how to speak a bit louder, eh?"

The women both laughed, and Sari proceeded to teach them a few spells that would coax the soil in the small field to feed the roots of the young barley. Taught them a variation on a song Mirren already knew that would help the soil hold on to the heat of the sun, even when the temperature dropped at night.

It was instinctive, easy work, but tedious at the same time.

Teaching songs was like Tala's needlework. It took concentration and precision when Sari craved a burst of power. Mirren and her daughter Kirsten were quick students but obviously struggled with the scope of the field. They were also like Tala, detailed and precise, but they lacked the raw power needed to sing a field.

Still, they could help. It would be far better than singing on her own. Once they learned the proper spells, they could sing along with Sari, adding their own power as she led.

They stopped for lunch when the sun was high, and a young man from the village delivered a basket of bread and fresh milk.

"Sari," Kirsten said, "have you traveled much?"

She shook her head. "Not much. My parents' home is near Oslo, and I studied in Copenhagen. I've traveled along the coast of Norway quite a bit, but nothing too grand. My grandmother has been all the way to Vienna though."

Kirsten and Mirren's eyes both went wide, so Sari didn't share that Orsala was serving a term as an elder singer. It took more explanation than she wanted to give during a midday meal.

"That's exciting," Mirren said. "For myself, I've traveled only in England and Scotland. One day I think I'd like a short trip across the water to France, but I prefer staying near home."

"No, you prefer Father." Kirsten teased her mother. "And Father likes to stay on the islands."

Mirren laughed. "Well, that's no lie."

The girl was full-grown, so the two women looked more like sisters than mother and daughter. They reminded Sari of her mother, her sister, and herself. The three looked so similar they always drew glances, even in Oslo where tall blond women were common.

Mirren patted her knee. "You look like you're missing someone."

"My sister," Sari said immediately. "And my mother a little. But my sister is all the way in Spain. I-I can't imagine it. She left for Spain at the same time I left for Orkney, so I haven't received a letter from her yet."

"I'm sure you will," Kirsten said. "How lovely to have a sister. You two must be very close. Are you twins?"

"Yes." Twins were as common as any other siblings in their world. Irin didn't have many children, but twins happened with regularity.

"A blessed family," Mirren said, her eyes drifting across the field to where the men were plowing. "I think Henry mentioned once that Damien had been in Spain."

"Oh?" Her eyes wandered across the lane and she tried to smother her quick inhalation of breath.

All the men had stripped their shirts off, and sweat shone on bared shoulders and chests. Among the pale, tattooed chests of the Orcadian scribes, Damien's golden skin glowed. He was walking behind the horses, digging the plow into the soil. His ink-swirled arms flexed when he tugged or snapped the reins. His whole torso twisted with the effort of working the soil and preparing it for seed.

His talesm…

She'd never seen their equal. It wasn't just the sheer number, it was the beauty of his hand. Her father's glyphs were straight and economical, almost utilitarian in their neatness. Sari supposed they reflected the Norse influence of his forefathers.

Damien's script spoke of Eastern heat. Intricate and twisting, his spells curled from his wrists up his left arm, across his shoulder, and down his right. His torso was similarly covered from the right side down his abdomen, covering the sharp cut of his muscles before the ink dipped below his waist. His left side was bare—he wore no mating mark—and dark hair dusted his chest and trailed down the center of his stomach until it too disappeared beneath his breeches.

Sari tore her eyes away from his harsh beauty before others caught her stare.

"Damien has traveled more than anyone on the island," Mirren said. "I remember when I first came here. He seemed so mysterious."

Kirsten laughed. "He's still mysterious. All the girls try to talk to him though."

Sari smiled. She had no problem seeing the allure of a silent, mysterious warrior on a small island like Orkney.

"I think he only confides in Henry," Kirsten continued. "If he confides in anyone at all."

When Mirren spoke, her age reflected in her eyes. "I think Damien saw many battles before he came here. Often those so wounded don't seek the company of others."

"He's quiet," Sari said. "He's barely spoken to me."

"That he speaks at all to you is notable," Mirren said.

"Has he ever come to you for healing?"

"No." Mirren rose and held out her hand to help Sari up. "The kind of wounds I suspect Damien carries are not the kind I can heal. Those can only be healed by the touch of a mate, and he seems to have no interest in finding one."

Kirsten said, "Not that any number of singers haven't offered!"

"Including you, daughter?"

"I'd have to be blind and dumb not to notice a scribe like him," Kirsten said. "But I'm not content to bash my head against the rocks. Damien has no interest in women."

The women got back to work for the rest of the afternoon. Sari forgot the time during the summer when the sun stayed high and there was so much to do. She taught Mirren and Kirsten two more songs before the older woman raised a hand.

"Sari," she said with a laugh, "enough. I don't know where you get your energy, but I am exhausted."

She paused in the middle of explaining the warming spell. "I'm sorry, Mirren. I forget the time."

The sun had sunk, but there was still plenty of light. With nothing else to do and no one to socialize with now that Tala was gone, Sari had been working late into the evenings. Glancing across the lane, she saw that only Damien and another scribe remained plowing. All the others had taken themselves back to the village.

"I can see the chimney smoking in our cottage," Mirren said. "Bernard is probably cooking already, and I don't want to make him wait to serve supper. Would you like to join us for the evening meal?"

Kirsten nodded. "You'd be more than welcome!"

"Thank you." The invitation meant much, but Sari felt like she was bursting at the seams. Hours of fine magical work with none of the intense expulsion of energy she craved. She eyed the heavy plow across the lane and the horses that plodded along the rough ground. "I do appreciate it, but I need to work a bit longer or I won't be able to sleep tonight."

"Understood." Mirren patted her shoulder. "Thank you for your patience, sister. Kirsten and I have learned much today."

"No." Sari grabbed her hand. "Thank you. It means much to me that you'd be willing to help with this. I know it's not your true responsibility."

"Always good to learn new things," Kirsten said. "But I'm with Mother. I'm exhausted. I hope you don't mind if I abandon you and Father for the common room tonight."

"Of course not, dear." Mirren brushed Kirsten's chin with dirty fingers. "Enjoy the time with your friends."

The two singers bid Sari good night and walked back to the village while Sari paused and finished the water in the drinking jar. She eyed the slowly plodding horses and the rough, gritty soil.

Taking a deep breath, she strode across the lane and

straight out to Damien, who was clucking at the animals as they pulled the plow. His arms were outstretched and gleaming. His hair was tied back with a fine leather strap, and she could see the straining muscles and tendons in his neck.

"Damien," she shouted, striding across the rough ground.

He halted, and his whole body turned toward her. She felt branded by the force of his attention, though he said nothing as she drew near.

"Let me take the plow," she said.

He frowned. "No."

"Let me." Her skin felt as if it would burst. She crackled with power. The awareness of his strength and physical appeal was not helping. "Please," she forced out, hating the word. "Let me take the plow for a while."

"You're not—"

"For heaven's sake!" she shouted, stepping closer. "Don't you know that I'm perfectly capable of plowing this field? I could plow five fields in the time you men have plowed one. Let. Me. Take. The. Plow."

He left one hand on the handle and put the other on his waist. Slowly he stepped back as she stepped forward.

"Fine," he said over her shoulder as she took the reins, "but don't take your frustration out on these animals or you'll answer to me."

It might have been the longest statement he'd ever spoken to her, but she rolled her eyes and snapped the reins, letting the horses surge forward as she raised her voice in song.

It was an old song, one that she remembered hearing her mother sing as she walked in front of her mate. Sari's parents had plowed their fields together, her father steering the plow and her mother walking beside the horses, singing at the top of her lungs in a laughing voice, easing the path of the horses and the metal as it worked the ground. Sari sang the same song now, letting the raw force of her power shoot down her body and release into the earth. The ground softened under the force of her magic, and the horses sped up.

She walked the length of the small field and turned to walk back. By the time she reached the end, she noticed that Damien was the only scribe standing there, arms crossed as he watched her silently. She smiled and met his eyes on the turn, then her voice rose again in a different song. It had the same purpose as the last one, easing the ground before the plow, but Sari liked the tune more. She loosened her collar and felt the sweat on her neck cool in the biting wind.

The earth's soothing energy crept up her legs, and Sari wished she could strip her shoes and stockings off. She wanted to feel the earth between her toes and the mud on her ankles. Instead, she focused on the pair of horses, starting a new song just for them. They raised their heads proudly and snorted as Sari laughed.

Joy. Peace. Utter and complete rightness in the world.

Her song rose and carried across the field. She didn't care who heard. She didn't care who listened. Her power flowed out of her like water down a worn stone, soaking the ground beneath her, softening the soil until she could hear it whisper to her. Damp, rotting roots and leaves, green hopes for the season ahead. The tiny creatures that lived in the earth rose to feel the warmth of her power.

She didn't know how long it took her to plow the small plot, but when she got to the far corner, the sun was still up. She took a deep breath, felt the soothing energy of the soil and the water and the green hedge surrounding her. She let out her breath and her shoulders finally relaxed.

For the first time since she'd arrived on this isolated island, she felt peace.

Until a hand planted on her shoulder, a dark, tattooed arm swung her around, and Damien took her mouth with the force of a winter storm. Sari barely had time to catch her breath before his lips took hers. She heard the needy groan work up from her throat when he clutched the homespun wool at her back. He gripped the fabric between her shoulders in his fist and pulled her close, his tongue driving into her mouth as if he would consume her.

Sari plunged her fingers into his thick brown hair, tugging and twisting the leather strap until it fell free and she could feel the dark warmth of it brushing her cheeks and shoulders, surrounding her with his scent. His lips were as fierce as his visage, biting and tasting hers with abandon. He was hungry, and he made her hungry too. She could smell the clean sweat on his neck and the dust that coated his shoulders. His skin burned beneath her palms.

And his mouth…

Hard then soft. Generous and greedy. Sari had been kissed, but she'd never been kissed like *this*.

Her shields fell, and a clear word rang in her mind, low and resonant, like a bell struck at daybreak.

Reshon.

Reshon.

Reshon.

Abruptly, Damien pulled away from her, panting. His eyes looked angry and his lips were flushed. He took the reins where they lay on the plow handle and quickly unhitched the horses from the machine. Without a word, he swung up on the back of the grey mare with a warrior's grace and tugged at the gelding's reins.

Before Sari could raise her shields, Damien left. He rode over the fields and out of sight while she stood on the edge of the field, her mouth hot from his kiss and the echo of his soul voice ringing in her mind.

CHAPTER
FOUR

DISASTROUS woman.

It wasn't her fault. Damien was the fool. A fool taken in by the joy and light of her. Walking across the land, power and magic pouring off her, she'd been intoxicating. The single most beautiful sight in four hundred years of life.

She was an innocent.

My eyes have seen too much to ever look on that which is lovely again.

Otto's words convicted him, and Damien hid from the world.

He took his meals in his room or the library for the next two weeks. He used the excuse of his current manuscript to occupy him and begged off his usual meetings with Henry. The manuscript recounting the tale of Melaku's journey had only three known copies in existence. Damien had been working on a precise copy for the past five years, but he'd been letting the business of the village and Henry's stories distract him.

Damien worked until late at night, taking advantage of the long days and his guilt. He visited the bathhouse in the middle of the night when no others would be partaking of the ritual bath. Ingrid's son delivered his meals, and he avoided everyone but Henry.

He never should have touched her. Her taste had entered his blood, the knowledge just one more painful memory in a lifetime of painful memories. His father's disappointment. His mother's anger. The rage and helplessness of battle and the blood of his brothers and friends.

Isolation would save him. He took comfort in it and the quiet understanding of the village. Ingrid and Henry were accustomed to his moods. Einar could bite stone.

Damien wondered if the village leader was giving Sari any more grief. Hopefully not. She was an extraordinarily gifted singer. Her power, with training, would be enough to put Einar on his backside. Added to that, she had the spirit to back up her power with action.

Part of Damien, the part that couldn't resist tasting her mouth under the spring sky, wanted to take her vibrant presence and hide her away. Wrap her in lamb's wool so she could never be bruised. Her light would never be dimmed by tragedy or grief. But he knew that Sari wouldn't stand for it. Like Damien when he'd left home on a fool's mission, Sari would break any bond and throw off any stifling mantle. The singer was no tame thing.

A firm knock at the door let him know when Ingrid's boy brought his tray for the night. Damien put down his pen and rose, stretching so that his raised arms touched the bare ceiling. His rooms were cold; it was better that way. It kept him awake. Focused. When he was warm, he dreamed.

He walked to the door and opened it, only to slam it shut when he saw Sari's defiant face on the other side.

Fuck.

His stomach growled at the scent of the lamb stew. He didn't move. Didn't say a word. If he was lucky, she'd leave the tray and abandon him to his mood. He closed his eyes and bit out a silent curse when she remained unmoving on the other side of the door.

"Coward," she said simply. She didn't whisper. Didn't even sound angry. She was just stating fact.

Coward.

He was. Damien opened the door again, pulling the familiar mask of indifference over his face. He held out his hands for the tray. "Thank you for bringing my meal."

Sari ignored him and marched into the room, glancing for a place to put down the food. Dismissing the table where his manuscript and inks were spread, she set the steaming bowl and mug of ale on the end of his narrow bed before she turned. Her hands were on her hips as she surveyed his small room.

"Cozy," she said.

"It suffices."

"It's freezing in here." She raised a judgmental eyebrow at the cold hearth in the corner of the room.

"I prefer the room cold when I'm working."

"Apparently."

He shared a large house with Henry and the village library, but his room in it was small. Henry and Damien shared the responsibility of tending the sacred fire of the village and the ritual room where the scribes inked their talesm.

The library was silent that night. She stood in his room, magic casting a glow around her, angry and powerful. She was, quite simply, the most beautiful thing he'd ever seen. Damien felt dirty and small next to her.

"What do you want?" he asked.

"You have the gall to ask me that?"

He paused. "You're correct. I offer you my sincere apology. I should not have kissed you."

"You shouldn't apologize for kissing me. You should apologize for walking away."

Damien finally managed to look her in the eye. She didn't look angry or coy. Her face, as always, was direct and open, her blue eyes clear as the sky.

"No," he said. "I should apologize for kissing you."

"Why?"

He paused again. "I don't want to tell you."

"Because I won't understand?"

"I'm not so foolish." His voice was quiet. "I don't want to tell you because I think you'll understand too much."

She raised her chin. "Thank you for not patronizing me."

"If you were the kind of woman I'd patronize, I never would have kissed you."

He walked to the table and put his quill in the stand; then he capped his ink and set the manuscript to the side.

"Why did you kiss me?" she asked.

Damien closed his eyes and took a deep breath. His fingers pressed into the rough oak of the table. "I kissed you because your song was the most beautiful thing I've heard in three hundred years."

She was silent for a moment. "I doubt that. My voice isn't very good."

"Then my ears are better than yours," he said quietly.

"Are you sure it wasn't because you thought I might be your *reshon*?"

He spun and glared at her. "What?"

She said nothing.

"I never took you for a foolish girl," Damien said, "but the fact that you'd joke about something like that—"

"I'm not joking. Your soul was whispering it before you walked away."

Damien froze. He could not hear as she did. Had no idea if she was lying or not. If she wasn't...

It changed everything.

"I wasn't trying to listen," she said quickly, looking flustered. "I promise. But... you surprised me. And then I couldn't *not* hear it. Your soul voice is just... It doesn't matter! I came here tonight because I want you to know that you're not allowed to kiss me like that and walk away. If you want to kiss me again, then—"

"Why doesn't it matter?" Damien asked, ignoring her words about kissing. He'd kiss her if he damn well wanted to. In fact, maybe he'd make sure she did the kissing from now on and he'd be the happy receiver of her attentions.

Reshon.

The word hung in the air. A mad hope and a foolish dream.

She frowned. "What?"

"Why doesn't it matter if you heard my soul say *reshon?*"

It mattered to him. It mattered more than anything.

Her cheeks were an angry red. "Because I don't believe in fate. I make my own fate. My own decisions. And I didn't come to this village to find a mate. I came for a purpose, and I have no intention—"

"Maybe I do." He stepped closer, and suddenly her heat felt like a promise he wanted to wrap his cold heart in. She *was* a disaster of a woman. Breaking into his life and bashing at the comfortable numbness he'd spent three hundred years cultivating. She was a disaster, and if she was telling the truth...

He dismissed the thought of her lying. There wasn't a deceptive bone in the woman's body. She couldn't even perform polite deceptions from what he'd observed. She was honest to the point of rudeness.

Which meant she was telling the truth. His heart jumped in his chest.

"Maybe you do what?" She backed away from him, but he didn't stop. "Believe in fate or have intentions?"

"Both."

She stopped near the door but didn't cross the threshold. Thank heaven for stubborn, face-saving females. Damien stepped close enough that he could feel her heat warming his skin. He let his eyes drop to her lips and suppressed the urge to take them again. The next time they kissed, he wanted Sari to kiss him. He bent so his lips were only inches away. He didn't have to bend far. He loved that she was so tall; he'd never had a lover nearly as tall as he was.

"Both?"

"It's cause and effect, Sari." He let his voice wrap around her name, tasting it. Teasing it between his lips.

"What are you talking about?" Her pulse thrummed in her neck.

"I *do* believe in fate. Therefore..." He let his voice drop to a whisper. "I have *intentions*."

Her chest rose and he let his eyes fall to her breasts. Her skin would be soft and pale beneath her dress. Her gold hair would spill over her shoulders when he unwound it. Would spill over his body when she—

"You can keep your intentions to yourself," she said tartly. "I'm not a silly girl, besotted with the dark, mysterious warrior who kissed me, then ran away."

"I rode away. And I won't be doing that again."

She scoffed, and Damien allowed himself a smile. There was a lightness in his chest he couldn't describe.

Hope. He thought it might be hope.

"I only told you that because I thought it would unnerve you," she confessed. "I wanted the upper hand because I was angry with you."

"Were you lying?"

Her eyes flashed. "Of course not."

"Do I seem like the kind of man who is easily unnerved?"

Her mouth opened and closed again.

"Lesson learned, *milá*. That's only your first lesson about me."

"I hope you enjoy your supper," she said. "I scraped the bottom of the pot, so there should be a few burned onions in it. You're welcome."

And with that, Sari turned and walked out the door. Damien tucked that bit of knowledge about his future mate away.

Sari was a woman who liked having the last word.

He could handle that.

DAMIEN TOOK HIS BREAKFAST IN THE COMMON ROOM THE next morning. He'd woken early and visited the ritual bath, then spent an hour in meditation before he inked a new spell.

He needed clarity.

The resulting punch of magic left him restless. He took the bowl of porridge Ingrid handed him and looked for Sari.

Ingrid asked, "You finished with your manuscript, Damien?"

"No."

"Ah." She smiled. "I didn't think it was the work keeping you away. Mistress Sari has been up and out already. She took her breakfast to the fields with Kirsten."

He narrowed his eyes. "Is that so?"

"Maybe it's her turn to avoid *you*, eh?"

He leaned over and kissed Ingrid's plump cheek. "Do you really think that will work?"

The cheerful cook gaped at him. "Who are you? And what have you done with my sour friend?"

He allowed her a smile before he took his breakfast to one of the long tables. Instead of focusing on finishing his food as quickly as possible, he let his eyes roam around the room.

While many mated couples took their meals in privacy, the majority of the village ate their morning and midday meals together in the longhouse in the center of the village next to the library. It was built with community in mind. Ingrid, the village cook, and her mate lived in the back, but the common room was the site of everything important in village life. Meals. Sings. Meetings about problems or welcome ceremonies.

It was a long room with just a few high windows. A fire burned from a stone hearth in the center of the hall, the community kitchen was at the front, and smaller benches and rugs were strewn at the end for the children. Damien saw one mother nursing her babe near the fire while her mate spoke to her quietly with a hand on his son's small foot.

It was a good village. A safe place. There were probably a million Irin villages scattered like this over the world, but this one had been his home for two hundred years. He still felt like an outsider, and he had to admit it was entirely his own doing.

Henry sat down across from him. "What are you doing out of the library?"

"Eating breakfast." Damien stared out the door near the hearth. If he followed the path out the door, taking it out of the village and toward the grain fields, he would find her. He could drink in her presence and soak in her light.

"I scraped the bottom of the pot…"

Damien burst into laughter. By the time he composed himself, every eye in the hall was on him.

Henry's eyes were the size of saucers. "Are you feeling well?"

"She'll have no patience for gentle wooing."

"Who won't? What are you talking about?"

"Sari."

"The earth singer?" Henry frowned. "You mean… I thought you didn't like her."

"She may be my reshon."

"That… would be surprising. Are you sure you're well? I

know you were in the ritual room this morning. Do you think—"

"I think…" Damien narrowed his eyes. "I need a plan."

"For what?"

"For wooing Sari, of course."

"I don't even know what's going on." Henry put his head in his hands. "You are indifferent to women. You always have been."

"Not true."

"Fine. You've been indifferent to them the entire time I have known you."

"That *is* true." He poured himself a mug of milk from the pitcher on the table. "But I am not indifferent to her."

"Why?"

"Why does it matter?" Damien asked.

"My friend, consider this." Henry put his elbows on the table and leaned forward. "You say you need a plan to woo her. I propose that a good beginning to this plan would be to identify the reasons you are pursuing this woman. This woman, and no other, in over two hundred years."

"She heard my soul whisper *reshon*. She told me this."

"And you believe she is being truthful?"

"You've spoken with her. Does she seem like a woman who would lie?"

Henry's eyes were pained. "More than one in the village can attest she is not."

Damien nodded and took a drink of his milk. "So she speaks truth. My soul recognized hers."

"Brother, you know her hearing that could mean any number of things. Your soul could have called to hers, or it could simply be the *desire* for a reshon. The longing for connection. Loneliness—"

"No." Damien shook his head. "As soon as she said it, I knew she was right."

"I ask you again, why? What about this woman calls to you?"

Damien's gaze drifted out the door again. "Sari said she doesn't believe in fate."

"Fate is a conundrum. If she truly is your reshon, there is something in her soul—and something in yours—that can only be fulfilled by each other. But either of you may choose to turn away from that. If she doesn't believe in fate, she may reject your connection even if it is compelling."

Damien scowled. "Why would anyone choose to do that?"

"Personal goals. Family obligations. There are any number of very good reasons."

Disastrous woman. He craned his neck, trying to catch a glimpse of her in the fields. "I'll make her see it. I've lived alone too long."

"Yes, *you* have," Henry said. "But *she* is young. Many singers do not want the obligations of family and mate so early in life."

Damien turned back to his friend. "You asked me why I know it is her."

"Yes."

"Because she is my equal."

"*...may you be blessed to find a mate as warlike as yourself...*"

The words, spoken almost three hundred years before, came back to him. His equal. That was what his soul was looking for. A woman with the spirit to stand at his side. Not follow him, but stand beside him and fight as long and as hard as he would.

"Damien." Henry dropped his voice. "You are a battle-hardened warrior of Mikael's line. Both your mother and father were of the guardian's blood. You were commissioned by the Elder Council and pledged to one of the most feared human orders in the world because of your skill in battle and strategy. You have slain hundreds of Grigori and killed one of the Fallen with your own hand." Henry paused. "You know the council will call you back someday, and you will be given charge over a house. Most likely a significant one."

"I know all this."

"This girl is an earth singer of the northern people and barely out of her training."

"Yes," Damien said. "And she is my equal."

CHAPTER
FIVE

I RRITATING man. Sari saw him in the longhouse as she entered to take her morning meal. The quiet scribe had taken to eating breakfast as early as she did. Prior to what she was now thinking of as their disastrous conversation, he rarely spent time with others of the village. He was a loner, which didn't surprise her. He was polite to everyone, spare of speech, and only truly smiled at the children.

Ever since she'd made the mistake of being truthful, he'd dogged her. If she was eating breakfast alone, he would join her and ask her how she had slept. If she was sitting by the fire, he'd sit across from her and draw in a leather-bound journal he always carried with him. If she asked for volunteers to work a field, he was always the first to step forward.

It was maddening.

She hadn't been lying. She wasn't a silly girl to find his quiet ways intriguing. The men in her life were bold men who spoke their mind, often without being asked. Her father was loud, possessed of an infectious laugh and a raucous sense of humor. Sari absolutely adored him. Her grandfather was quieter but always had a story ready for his loved ones. Her first lover, *only* lover, had been a sweet scribe from a neighboring village who had shared her passion for learning and debate. They were still fast friends who would meet for meals and stories when they could.

Damien's mysterious history and taciturn demeanor did nothing but irritate Sari.

That morning she hadn't been sitting long enough for her oats to cool before he sat across from her and put his own bowl down.

"Mirren mentioned that your sister is in Spain," Damien said without preamble. "Would you like to know of it?"

"Yes. But I want to know it from her."

He nodded. "Yet she is not here. I am."

Sari paused. "You have been to Spain."

"I have been many places," he said quietly. "Spain is one of them."

Sari *did* want to learn of Tala's new home from her own sister, but no letters had yet reached her. She ached for knowledge of the strange world her twin now lived in.

"What is it like?"

A slow, fond smile spread across Damien's face. "Warm."

"Warm?"

"In the summer, almost too warm. The earth bakes as if the sun was its oven, and the dust can spread everywhere. Sometimes weeks or months will go by with no rain."

"No rain at all?"

"None." He pulled out his leather journal. "But the summer is also when the grapes grow sweetest and the orange trees blossom."

"Oranges?" Sari was entranced. She'd heard of the sweet fruit that grew in warm countries but had never tasted it or smelled its blossom. She'd only seen pictures in books.

"The wind is filled with the scent of them," Damien continued. "Some days it feels as if the sweetness coats your skin because the air is so laden."

He opened his journal and paged to the front. Sari tried

not to crane her neck when she looked. Each page was filled with intricate drawings and words in a flowing script she recognized from his tattoos. Coins and scraps of paper were tucked into the seams along with some leaves and faded blooms. He found the page he was looking for and turned it toward her, lifting a pressed flower from the book.

"Here." He held it out. "This is what the blossoms look like. They're pure white on the tree."

Sari took the delicate flower and held it to her nose, but no hint of scent remained. Still, she examined it, noting the size and shape of the petals. The leaf. The stem. "Do you have others?"

"Other flowers?"

She nodded, eying his journal. "How many places have you been?"

The flicker of a shadow in his eyes. "Many places."

"So you said."

He took the dried bloom from her hand and folded it carefully in the paper before he placed it back in the book. He said nothing for minutes, so Sari went back to eating her breakfast and tried to ignore her burning curiosity.

"The world is full of beautiful, wild places," Damien finally said softly. "Sadly, it's also full of violence and danger."

She set down her bowl. "Which is greater, the beauty or the violence?"

He shook his head. "It's not that simple. Sometimes the beauty is violent. And sometimes the violent is beautiful."

Sari understood him. "An eagle hunting the fjords is beautiful."

"But does the fish he snatches think so?" He gave her the edge of a smile.

"So you were the eagle?"

"Sometimes." He closed his eyes and let out a long breath. "But so was I the fish."

Sari couldn't help herself. "How old are you? Where do

you come from? The writing in your journal, what language is that?"

"Slavic mostly. Some Latin. I spoke both as a boy."

"Slavic?"

"I was born in a place called Bohemia. Do you know it?"

Sari shook her head, and Damien opened his journal to another page where a map had been drawn. Damien pointed to the top left. "Here are the northern lands where you are from."

"I recognize them."

His finger inched down. "And here is Orkney."

"Yes."

He trailed his finger down and over a large peninsula in the south. "And here is Spain, where your sister lives now."

"I cannot imagine the journey." Sari watched his finger trace up and over to settle in the heart of the map. The center.

"This is Vienna, where the elders preside."

"I know. My grandmother is an elder singer, though she does not reside in the city more than a few months at a time."

He inched his finger to the side. "And this is Bohemia, where my family is from."

Sari looked at the map. There were far more lands that he had drawn in. The whole of the right page was filled with his hand.

"But have you been everywhere on this map?" She glanced and caught him watching her. "All these places?"

He nodded.

Sari hadn't known it was possible to travel so far. She thought Orsala's tales of Vienna were exotic.

"How many years?" she asked.

He hesitated.

"I know you're much older than me. I've seen your talesm."

"I spent two hundred years training, fighting, and traveling," he said. "And I've been here two hundred."

"Four hundred?" Not as old as she'd thought then. She gave him a crooked smile. "Barely out of your foolish youth then."

His eyes were warm. "Older than you."

"Oh, everyone knows that scribes take far longer than singers to master their magic."

"I have a new study now." The smile at the corner of his lips was wickedness. "I'm looking forward to mastering something far more interesting then magic."

Irritating man.

"Well"—Sari stood and picked up her bowl, trying to ignore her pounding heart—"it's good that you're four hundred years old. I'm sure you've learned to handle disappointment."

THE WHOLE OF THE VILLAGE CAME TOGETHER TO READY THE breeding ewes for pasture. It was midsummer and all the fields had been planted, so Sari and the other women of the village were trimming hooves while Einar and his mate, Agnes, walked through the flock, picking the hardiest to breed with the new ram that Einar had traded for in Kirkwall the week before. Others checked the flock and tied a red string around the necks of the ones whose hooves were overgrown.

Sari had to admit that, faults aside, Einar knew his sheep. It was probably the reason he was the leader of the village. While grain provided sustenance, it was sheep and wool that provided funds for trading off the small island. Orkney sheep were well known, even in Scotland, and their wool was valued.

The flock had been sheared months before, but the spring ewes Einar chose would be trimmed and put in richer pasture close to the village. Shearing was never a pleasant job—especially in the height of summer—but Sari had to admit Damien took on the task without complaint.

Damien and Matthew, Ingrid's mate, had been chosen to do the more delicate job of shearing the ewes for breeding. It had surprised Sari at first. Damien hardly seemed the type to master animal husbandry. But as she watched him, she saw his calm demeanor settle over each animal he touched. He hummed under his breath, using firm, gentle pressure to hold each ewe before he clipped it quickly. Passing near him, Sari realized the song was one of her own.

Sari held the sheep's hooves and cut, slicing her hands more than once during the process. The ground of the island didn't wear the hooves the way the rocks in her homeland did. Here the land was soft and damp throughout the year.

"Oh, thank you, Damien!"

Sari looked up, blowing away the hair that had fallen into her face, when she heard Kirsten's voice. The young woman had been holding each sheep while Sari worked.

"What?" Sari asked Kirsten, pausing in the middle of a trim.

Damien was walking toward them as Kirsten said, "Didn't you hear me? I need to get back to the village to help Mother ready a bundle of herbs for the humans. Damien offered to take over helping you. He and Matthew are finished with the shearing."

"Of course he did," she grumbled.

Kirsten smiled. "He must like you. No one holds sheep for trimming by choice."

"Go on." Sari nodded toward the village with a grimace. "Leave me with the irritating male."

"You mean fascinating?" Kirsten whispered with a wink. "You can't fool me, Sari." She spoke more loudly. "Thank you, Damien. Mother will be grateful to have me back."

"You're welcome." His low voice washed over her and Sari

couldn't help herself. She lowered her shields just to catch a whisper of Damien's unique resonance. The depth of it went straight to her stomach, though she didn't catch anything meaningful. Sari slammed her shields up again and bent to her task.

"Careful, she's ornery," Sari said, lifting up a hoof.

"I have her." Damien hummed and held the ewe. "Ornery females like me. Even when they won't admit it."

Sari rolled her eyes but kept her mind on her task. The flock's hooves weren't terrible, but they were overgrown and she was worried about rot.

"Why did he wait so long?" Sari muttered.

"Einar waits until the ground is driest. Here, that means almost into June."

She grunted and went back to her task.

"You have a steady cut," he said. "Strong hands."

"Do you have an opinion about my mannish hands?"

"You mistake me, Sari. I've never held anything but admiration for a woman with a good strong grip."

She glanced over her shoulder as she let the ewe's leg down. Damien's eyes were dancing though he didn't smile.

"Bedding humor, scribe?"

"Forgive me. The sight of a fine woman's legs does move the imagination. Do you always wear breeches when you're with the animals?"

"Skirts are cumbersome. And why does no one ever remark on *males* wearing breeches?" She glanced at him as he pulled another ewe up the low platform. "Perhaps women's imaginations are as prone to wander at the sight of a man's fine thigh?"

"Wonder away, *milá*. Let me know if you'd like to inspect my thighs more closely. I am more than happy to satisfy your curiosity."

She said nothing for a time and concentrated on her task. They weren't the only couple in the field trimming. The pasture was filled with the sounds of laughter and joking, along with an occasional curse or the bleating complaint from a sheep.

"Speaking of your thighs…"

Damien barked out a short laugh. "Were we? Please continue."

Sari offered him a reluctant smile as she lifted the back hoof of a particularly noisy ewe. "You wear many talesm for a scribe your age. Your torso is covered. How far down do they go?"

Damien was suddenly quiet.

Sari was surprised. Most scribes, in her experience, were happy to speak of their talesm. More than happy, some bordered on gloating. A man who wore talesm such as Damien would be the envy of others.

She had no capacity for delicacy. "Did I offend you in some way?"

He shook his head and bent to hold the sheep. "Continue. We've hours of work yet."

"And here I thought it would pass quickly while we talked of thighs." Sari bent over again and lifted the right hoof. "If I offended you, I apologize."

"You didn't offend me. I do carry a heavy number of talesm for my age."

"It's a testament to your strength, I'm sure."

"More a testament to my breeding."

She stood and untied the red yarn from around the sheep's neck and slapped it away, snagging another marked with red. "Breeding?"

"Yes."

Sari paused, but he didn't continue. "You can't say something like that and then—"

"Why don't you believe in fate?" Damien put a fist on his hip. "That is like me saying I do not believe in the sun. Or in the earth. Fate exists. It moves us all. The happiest unions I have known have been reshon."

"Matings do not have to be reshon. Hold her." She bent and picked up a front hoof as Damien put strong arms around the ewe's neck and shoulder. His hold meant that she could feel his heat. Feel his breath against her neck when he spoke.

"They don't *have* to be reshon," he said, "but the best ones are."

"I don't agree. My parents are not reshon. They chose each other when they mated. They loved each other and they chose each other." Her cheeks were red, but she refused to be embarrassed. She was a grown woman. There was no shame in stating her desires. "That's what I want. To be chosen, not swept up in a mystical inevitability."

"What if your reshon chose you? Would you deny him?"

"There is no choice in fate."

"So what you're saying is that if your soul mate found you…" He paused until she stopped in her task and looked at him. "If he met you, Sari. *Loved* you. *Chose* you. You would still deny him because you think he had no choice?"

"There is no choice in fate." Her heart pounded, but she could not look away.

"Do you know what my fate was?" His voice was low and intimate. "My fate was to be another male in the breeding line of Mikael's warriors."

"Breeding line—?"

"For centuries, my family has searched for the strongest warriors, male and female. The ones they deem the purest of Mikael's line. They search the world. Language and homeland do not matter. When they find the strongest warriors, we are expected to mate and breed to produce warrior offspring. Like Einar choosing and breeding the best in his flock."

Sari's mouth fell open. "Irin families do not breed their young like livestock."

"*Your* family does not. My family does."

"But—"

"We have no choice. We have only duty. I have never known any of my family to find their reshon. It is a luxury we are not allowed."

"And you?" Sari's heart pounded.

He leaned back and took the clippers from her hand. Sari shifted so that she held the ewe for Damien as he focused on the task. Despite the boil of emotions she felt from him, he was still firm and gentle handling the animal.

She finally said, "You have been away from your family for two hundred years."

"Yes."

"They have not found a woman for you? In all that time? Or do you have a mate half a world away while you make bedding jokes with me?"

"They found a woman for me," he said. "But I refused to return home. I was no longer content with my *fate*."

"So you don't believe in it either."

He glanced up with burning eyes. "I believe in fate. The fate the Creator chose for me—a mate chosen by heaven—not the fate of my family."

"And you have not seen them or written to them in two hundred years?"

He looked down and continued working. "My mother writes. I do not answer. The singer they chose for me mated with another, but my mother has not given up. They will call me back to service soon."

"Who? Your family?"

"The Elder Council. My family has more than a little influence in Vienna. Once they call me back into service, my family believes I will accede to what they want for me."

"And what do you want?"

His shoulders slumped a little. "I want… peace. To be valued for more than my blood and training. Perhaps we're more alike than you think, Sari. I suppose I want someone to choose me too."

PERHAPS WE'RE MORE ALIKE THAN YOU THINK.

Sari stared into the small fire in her cottage, the brewing manual she'd been reading forgotten on her lap. Damien had not joined the village for the evening meal, though several lambs had been butchered and Ingrid and Matthew had celebrated the hard day of work with a feast.

She had a feeling the cost of Damien's honesty might be paid in isolation.

Next to his age and experience, she felt like a child. And while she'd never been a sheltered girl—her parents believing industry and independence were more important than manners—she had been surrounded by love. Rich with it. Her parents loved her. Her sister did too. Her grandparents doted on them all. They were loud and raucous, and some might find them coarse compared to the fine manners or sophisticated parlors of the city scribe houses. But Sari knew they were fierce and generous with their affection.

I want someone to choose me too.

She suddenly wanted to give Damien a very long, very hard hug.

Never one to deny an honest desire, Sari decided she would. She set her book to the side, carefully marking her place, and found her wrap. The warm woolen cloak had been a welcome gift from the women in the village, and she treasured it. It had been dyed a deep blue that matched her eyes. Her hair was long and wild. She'd taken it down when she returned to her cottage and had no desire to put it up again. She stepped into her boots, wrapped her cloak around her shoulders, and walked to the library.

It was open. It was always open and available for reading or meditation by the sacred fire. She heard Henry reading aloud and followed his voice down a long hallway. She passed his room on the left and walked farther down to a small chamber where a light flickered under the door. She hesitated for only a moment before she knocked.

Her stomach dropped when she heard his footsteps, but she didn't run or wilt like a ninny. Damien opened the door. The light was at his back, so she couldn't read his expression.

"Sari?"

Why hadn't she rehearsed what she wanted to say? Because even she wasn't capable of embracing a man who'd stated an interest in her and then just stomped off. That would be… unseemly.

"Sari, are you all right?"

"I like your voice," she blurted out. Then she waved a hand. "But that's not why I came here."

She stepped closer and slid her arms around his waist, pulling him close until his arms came around her shoulders. They stood in silence, and Sari felt his heart beating in his chest. Again she noticed the smell of his hair and the fine scent of clean sweat at his neck. Blended with that, the smell of ink, incense, and oils from the ritual bath. She took a deep breath and felt his arms tighten.

"I'm not saying it is me," she said softly. "I am not saying it isn't. But you deserve to be chosen, Damien. I think you are a good man, a scribe who knows honor and sacrifice, and you deserve to be chosen."

He didn't say anything, but his arms pressed around her and he didn't let go.

CHAPTER
SIX

SUMMER flew faster than Damien had ever remembered. The barley fields were shorn and the flocks ready for breeding. Summer gardens had given up the last of their bounty and cellars were full.

And the new beer that Sari and Henry had brewed was ready to be shared with the village.

It was an impromptu feast, but no less cheerful for it. Damien sat in the corner watching his old friend and his laughing girl as they danced down the center of the lines while the fiddle, lute, and pipes played cheerfully by the fire. One song flowed into another, and Damien couldn't remember the last time he'd felt so content. Their race couldn't truly become intoxicated by anything other than magic, but beer and liquor did allow a certain mellowing of their normal faculties.

Henry and Sari were the heroes of the evening. Their first batch of beer had not turned out well, but the second batch did. The nights were growing longer and the wind colder, but that night voices were raised and dancing filled the longhouse as the whole village enjoyed the fruits of their labor and the feast Ingrid and Matthew had prepared. Three children ran past him, laughing and tripping over each other while they chased a dog that had run into the party. He was so distracted by the spectacle that he didn't notice Sari approaching.

She plopped down on the bench next to him and sat astride, leaning forward as he rested his back against the wall.

He was completely in love with her. Of course he was. Days flew by and weeks had turned to months. Damien's initial admiration and fascination had turned into something far deeper the longer he knew her. Sari was strong and honest and beautiful, and he wanted her. Mostly he wanted her to admit that she had feelings for him as well.

Damien smiled. "Hello, *milá.*"

"You refuse to tell me what that means."

"It means… my little cabbage." He told her something different every time she asked.

Sari threw her head back and laughed. "Who would call someone a cabbage?"

"The French."

"Truly?" She shook her head, still smiling. "You're not dancing."

"No."

"Are you bad at the steps?"

He shrugged. "I am a fair dancer."

"So why don't you join us?"

"Because I can watch you dance sitting from here, and I prefer that."

Her smile fell. "Why?"

"You're a good dancer. And I like imaging those long legs—"

"Damien." She squeezed her eyes shut and shook her head. "Not that. Why me?"

"I don't understand."

"You've been… all around the world." She flung her arm out. "Seen ancient cities and modern ones. You've fought in wars I can only imagine and met important people."

She pressed forward until she was nearly lying on his

chest, and Damien fought—and failed—to keep his hands at his sides. He reached up and tucked a lock of her hair behind her ear. It fell around her face, wild and as untamed as she was.

"Are you playing with me?" she asked.

He shook his head.

"Then why?"

"Do you not believe my soul calls to yours? You told me we were reshon."

"I said we *might* be. And that's not enough."

"No?" He caught her chin with his fingers and tilted her face up, a spike of anger making his movements and his voice sharp. "What do you want from me? For me to lay my heart bare so you can step on it?"

"Why do you think I would step on it?"

"We *might* be reshon?" It stung. He released her and leaned back. "Maybe you're not as honest as I thought."

It wasn't that Damien thought Sari would be dishonest on purpose, but her willing ignorance of their connection was driving him mad. They *were* reshon. Months of knowing her, nights spent arguing and laughing, heated moments that never resolved. They all confirmed his mad hope. She just refused to see it.

Sari stood and moved away from him, but he caught her arm and pulled her back.

"You have a fierce heart, *milá*."

"Don't—"

"Someday…" He pressed her palm to his cheek and took a deep breath as she froze. "Someday you will love a man, and the fire of it will be a violent, dangerous thing."

"Why do you say this to me?" she whispered. "Am I not also worthy of choosing?"

"Because there is beauty in your violence. Like the eagle over the fjord, Sari. You will love a man, and if he is a wise scribe who knows what life is, he will cling to it and treasure it even as it lashes him." Damien closed his eyes and let the heat of her palm sear him. "He will treasure it, because within your love a man would never feel more alive. Even if he had lived a thousand years, he would burn from it."

He kept his eyes closed, expecting her to pull her hand from his and walk away. She didn't. She stood next to him as the music rose and shifted. A singer stood and opened a song, calling to her sisters to add to the old ballad of Adelina's doomed love. Voices took turns as they sang the ancient rhyme, but Sari still stood beside him, her hand resting against his cheek.

Then silently she turned her hand and clasped his fingers in her own, drawing him to his feet.

Damien blinked. "Sari?"

She said nothing as she led him out the nearest door, away from prying eyes in the hall and into a night barely lit by the new moon.

Sari turned when they were out of the hall and cloaked in the shadow of the library, raised her face to his and kissed him.

It was a soft kiss. Merely a brush of lips over his own. She grew bolder, kissing him over and over, pressing more firmly each time. Damien brought his hand up and cupped the back of her neck, reveling in the heat of her skin as he drew her closer. He fought his instinct to take control and let her explore his mouth. When she slid her hands around his waist, he was reminded of the night she had come to him and embraced him.

Generous. Heaven above, her heart was so generous. He wanted her desperately. She nipped at his lower lip and let out a frustrated sigh.

It was the sigh that did him in.

Clasping her cheeks between his hands, Damien angled her mouth and dove deep, then he gripped her hair in his fist and held on with everything in him. Their passion roared to life, like brush thrown on a bed of coals. Hot and sharp and flaring. Her mouth was demanding; she bit the edge of his tongue as he drew back. Then Damien's mouth plunged down her neck.

He plumped her breast beneath her bodice and slicked his tongue over the soft flesh that swelled along the edge. Her back arched and she clung to his shoulders.

"Damien!"

He said nothing, starving for the taste of her skin. He pulled down her dress and cupped her breast as his other hand threw up her skirts until he could feel the firm curve of her bottom in his palm. He squeezed hard and felt her gasp as his mouth closed around the rosy red blush of her nipple.

Sari was no delicate female but a strong, lush woman. He feasted on her breast, even as his other hand explored between her legs. She was wet and slick, and his body was already hard as a randy lad's. She had stripped him bare of his control. When she spread her legs for his exploring fingers, he did not hesitate.

My eyes have seen too much to ever look on that which is lovely again.

He pushed the thought away, along with the guilt of touching Sari's body with blood-stained hands. She was eager and hungry and he could satisfy her. He was made to satisfy her. He would do anything, be anything, sacrifice anything to give her what she needed. That was his only thought as he teased her flesh with his hands and tongue.

"Ah!" Her soft cries of pleasure fed a deep longing within him. "Damien… Damien, *please.*"

He lifted his lips to her mouth and caught Sari's cries as she came in his arms. His fingers were slick as he softened his touch and eased her down from the height of her pleasure. He slid his hand back and cupped her again, smoothing his palm over the supple skin of her buttock and thigh. Furious kisses turned lazy and languid. Her heart was still racing. He closed his eyes and pressed his ear to her chest, listening to the sweet rhythm, then turned his head and feathered kisses over her breast.

"Sari," he whispered, "you are so lovely. In every way, lovely."

"Take me home." She leaned against the wall of the library as Damien rested against her breast. Her fingers threaded through his hair. "Warm my bed."

He ached with wanting her body, but he wanted her heart more. "Are you ready to be mine, Sari? Completely and utterly?"

She paused in her caresses. "You mean…"

"You can try to deny it, but I *know*. We are reshon. Once I have taken you, you will have no other," he said. "I will not let you go. You know what I want, so be sure, Sari."

She wasn't sure. He could tell by her stiff posture and the pounding of her heart. Damien stepped back and carefully covered her breasts before he eased her skirts down, smoothing them until they fell to her feet. But he didn't let her go. He put his arms around her and held her close, kissing her forehead before she buried her face in his neck.

"I am patient, *milá*," he whispered. "My lovely one. My dearest."

DAMIEN WAS CHECKING ON THE FLOCKS THE NEXT DAY, watching the dogs round up the stragglers to move them closer to pastures near the village. His mind wandered to the night before and the taste of Sari's mouth. The feel of her flesh under his hands. He frowned and examined his palms.

Sari was no shy girl, so he doubted he'd been the first to put his hands on her body, but he wondered if her other lovers had been scribes of learning or men like him. Warrior. Farmer.

Damien's hands were rough. They had always been rough, ever since he'd held his first blade at ten years old. His palms were callused and his nails ragged and gritty. Some nights Damien stared at them in the candlelight as he held his quill and saw them dripping with blood. He would wash them— soak them in near-boiling water—but the blood lingered. It lingered because he knew these years were only a reprieve. It had taken the council fifty years to find him in Scotland, but they had.

Then the letters had started. The enticements that felt to him more like veiled threats. Henry was right. He was no Rafaene scribe needing peace and meditation. He would be called back into service. Perhaps to Vienna or Rome. Perhaps to Damascus or Salamanca.

Then his hands would drip with blood again, just as they had for one hundred years.

My eyes have seen too much to ever look on that which is lovely again.

If he were less selfish, he would leave her alone. Leave her safe in the northern lands where Grigori were scarce and the twisted politics of Irin and Irina power trickled to rumors that little affected the daily life of their kind.

But he wasn't a saint. He hadn't been innocent for centuries. If Damien was going to be forced back into the Irin power structure, he wanted Sari at his side. Mated to him. Loyal to him. He would always know truth because Sari would never tell him sweet or gentle lies. He wanted to be everything to her. He wanted her to desire him desperately, because the heat in his dreams tormented him.

He was so lost in his thoughts he almost didn't see the girl. In fact, he didn't see her at first, he heard her. A whimper like a pup. A catching breath and a hiss of pain.

Damien caught sight of her as she crested the hill.

"Kirsten?"

The young healer stumbled when she heard her name.

"Brother Damien…" Her voice caught in a soft sob before she could say more.

Damien ran to her, catching her before her legs gave out. "Sister, what has happened?"

She'd been attacked, but by what, Damien could not understand. Her clothes were torn and her face clawed, but he could see no bites on her legs when he lifted her skirts. Her ankle was bruised and swollen, but no other mark was on her. There were no predators on the island to speak of. Even a wild dog didn't seem likely.

"Kirsten, what did this?"

She started crying and her tears mixed with the claw marks on her face, causing her to wince.

"Not what," she said. "Who."

"Who?"

Still crying, she forced out the words between hiccuping breaths. "Ann. Ann and her sisters. In the human village. I was… I was checking the baby. She only gave birth two weeks ago, but everything was normal. I was just there to check the baby. I've been to the house with Mother before."

Damien lifted her and whistled for the dogs. They trotted over, their tongues hanging out, and followed him as he walked swiftly to the village. The sheep would have to wait. "Was the babe healthy, Kirsten?"

"She was fine. Fine! But then Ann, she… I don't know what happened. Her sisters blocked the door and Ann said cruel things. She called me unnatural. That her milk was dry and it was my fault. That I wanted her babe to die so I could seduce her husband. It was madness."

No, it was a poison that he'd hoped the islands would escape. He'd heard the humans whisper in Aberdeen, but on Orkney they called his sisters *spae-wives* and wisewomen. The Irina still practiced their healing arts among the humans when singers in other parts of Europe had drawn back from their

calling years before for fear of human ignorance and super-
stition.

"Damien, Ann and her sisters called me…"

"A witch?"

She nodded.

He forced himself not to curse. Cursing wouldn't solve
anything, but something needed to be done and he doubted
Einar was up to playing politics. No, this would be a job for
Henry.

"They clawed at my face," she said, touching her cheek as
if she still couldn't wrap her mind around the violence that
had touched her. "I think they wanted to blind me. Why
would they do that, Damien?"

"Because they're ignorant and afraid."

"Ann was sweet to me before. She thanked me for coming
to help deliver the babe. It was her first." Kirsten winced
when he shifted her.

"Almost home, sister."

"Why would she do this?"

His heart broke. Kirsten was such a little thing and had
lived a sheltered life. She'd never seen an Irina burn or drown
at the hands of humans. Never seen a scribe out of his mind
with grief taking vengeance in the worst way. This was why
the calls for isolation were growing louder. The days of
peaceful coexistence with the human population of Europe
were coming to an end because of the fear of witchcraft and
of any women of learning.

"Almost home," he said, hoping his calm would seep into
the girl. He brushed a spell over her sweaty forehead,
watching the faint gold glow as her breathing evened out.
"Easy, Kirsten."

The last thing they needed were otherwise peaceful scribes
and singers of Orkney making out for the humans in anger.
Relations could be salvaged. Their haven could remain. But
only if cool heads were in charge.

"Kirsten?" Mirren's voice rose from the doorway of her cottage. "Kirsten!"

"Remember," Damien whispered. "Calm."

The brave girl nodded and took a shuddering breath.

"What's happened?" Mirren came running. "Did she fall? Why isn't she walking?"

"Twisted ankle." Damien ducked under the doorway and searched for a place to put the young woman. "Her bed?"

"Here." Mirren parted a curtain that divided the room. "She's not here much anymore. She has her own cottage. What happened?"

Kirsten said, "It was Ann." She glanced at Damien. "I think she must be unwell, Mother. She accused me of witchcraft. Her milk has dried up, and she might be running a fever. I checked on the baby, but I couldn't check her because she and her sisters…"

Mirren's eyes blazed. "She did this to you? The scratches? The bruises?"

"I twisted my ankle trying to get away. I fell on the way back. It hurt so much, but I didn't want to ask anyone in the human village for help. Damien found me on the road."

Mirren was cursing low under her breath, and Damien put a hand on her shoulder. "You know the moods that sometimes strike new mothers. Ann could be ill, Mirren."

"And her ignorance would be fed by her mother," Mirren spit out. "The girl's mother didn't even want us to help her give birth. But the husband's family is traditional. I delivered him myself—well, they assume it was my own mother, of course. The young man—"

"He wasn't there, but Ann accused me of seducing him." Kirsten looked confused. "Why would I seduce her husband?"

Damien put a hand on her head. "Don't try to make sense of it, sister. The woman wasn't well in her mind."

Mirren heaved a sigh and poured boiling water into a deep pan. "This hasn't happened in many years."

"But it has happened before," he said quietly. "We must keep calm heads."

Mirren nodded and set to tending her daughter. None of the cuts on her face were serious and with Mirren's tending would heal quickly. Her swollen ankle would mend. Kirsten's father, Bernard, was a sensible, steady scribe who would listen to reason and not overreact.

It was Einar whom Damien was worried about. Einar had been making noises lately about the Irina working so closely with the humans on the island. He tried to keep Sari in the village instead of letting her help the local farmers. Tried to keep Ingrid from trading her herbs in Kirkwall.

He would say it was for safety, but Einar wasn't a man who trusted females. His mate, Agnes, was a capable woman, but the clinging sort, and Einar made the mistake of thinking his woman was the model of all others.

Bypassing the longhouse, Damien walked to the library and hoped Henry would have some ideas. Because Einar needed to be controlled, and Damien's memories were still too stained with horror to have much perspective about humanity.

CHAPTER
SEVEN

B Y the time Sari heard about the attack on Kirsten, the episode had taken on the ring of legend. Like any news in a small, peaceful village, details were exaggerated until Kirsten hadn't faced three angry women but a whole village of rioting humans bent on her destruction.

> *They want to burn the singers.*
> *The humans are going to try to take the village.*
> *Einar has a heavenly blade stored under his house.*
> *Someone from the Irina Council is traveling to Orkney.*
> *Damien is scribing talesm to ready himself for war.*

Sari pulled off her work gloves and tied her hair back in a quick knot before she walked to the library. Rumors of her friend's ordeal had come to her in the fields where she was working on the barley harvest with half the village. Mostly the non-gossiping half.

Still, news had come at midday with the meal, and Sari had run to Mirren's house, then left in relief when she learned that Kirsten was sleeping and the worst of her injuries were nasty scratches and a sprained ankle that was already healing.

Sari was hungry, but she didn't want to hear gossip in the longhouse. It was likely Henry would have some kind of rations in the library, so she decided to go there.

The fact that Damien would also be there only briefly touched her mind.

My lovely one. My dearest.

She could still feel his hands. Feel his mouth at her neck and on her breasts. Sari shoved the thought away. Trouble like Kirsten's could quickly spiral if the right steps weren't taken to smother rumors about witches and curses. She didn't need to think about Damien's mouth just then.

"Henry?" She pulled open the door of the library and walked into the dim room. Her eyes had barely adjusted when she saw Damien walking toward her. "Oh Damien, I—"

He stopped her words with a deep, thorough kiss that bent her back and stole her breath. He wrapped an arm around her waist and put his other hand at the side of her neck, brushing his thumb over her hammering pulse as he tasted her. He took his time, and when he drew away, her eyes were crossed and her knees were weak.

"Hello." He licked his lips as if tasting the memory of her mouth. "I thought you were in the barley fields today."

"I was." Sari was still wrapped in his arms, and Damien showed no intention of letting her loose. "I heard about Kirsten."

"She'll be fine. Henry and I need to speak to Einar before he does something foolish."

"Good luck with that." She glanced down at their bodies pressed together. "Are you going to…"

"Kiss you again?" His hands rose to her cheeks. "I'd be happy to, *milá*."

And he did, teasing her mouth playfully with the tip of his tongue and nibbling at her lower lip. She could feel him smiling against her when she put a hand on his chest and pushed him back.

"I was going to ask if you were going to let me go," she said, trying to sound cross. "Don't you need to speak to Einar so we don't have a riot?"

"I like kissing you more; the day is suddenly much brighter." Something fell in a crash from down the hall and Damien shrugged. "And Henry is putting on his boots."

Something crashed again.

"Does he need help?"

"If he does," Damien growled, "someone else can help him."

Sari wriggled out of his arms and started toward the hall, but Henry emerged, his spectacles askew but his boots on.

"Ah, Sari!" He smiled. "Isn't it awful about Kirsten? Poor girl. We're going to talk to Einar. Try to calm the situation."

Sari straightened Henry's spectacles. "Try to talk sense into your friend. Tell Damien he can't grab me whenever he likes and kiss me. Especially when the village is in crisis."

Henry looked confused. "Are you doing that now?"

Damien said, "As often as possible."

"I thought you were trying patience. You said something about a campaign of attrition."

Sari's mouth dropped open. "What?"

Henry's eyebrows rose. "Damien did point out—quite correctly—that it worked well against the Mongols in Hungary."

Damien said, "I decided that a more direct forward assault was called for."

Sari narrowed her eyes. "And how did that work against the Mongols?"

"Not well."

"There's a lesson to be learned there."

Henry patted her back and made for the door. "This is entertaining, but we really need to go stop Einar from riding to the village without us. That man is not known for his tact or discretion."

Damien swooped down and stole one more kiss before she could respond.

"That was a stealth attack," he whispered, biting her earlobe. "In case you were wondering."

"IT'S NOT BEEN SO BLATANT AS WHAT HAPPENED TO KIRSTEN," Ingrid said later that night in the longhouse after the evening meal. "But it's been there."

"Talk of witchcraft?"

Ingrid nodded. "I hear it in Kirkwall. At the market. The humans here… they're a traditional sort. They've not felt the conflict between their human faith and our magic in the past. Wisewomen were always here. The men, they don't notice as much."

"Too dangerous?" Sari had come in from the harvest to hear that Henry, Einar, and Damien had gone to the neighboring village where Kirsten had been attacked. They had not yet returned, and Sari was trying to distract herself from worrying.

Damien didn't need her worry. He was a warrior.

"Weakness invites violence," Ingrid said. "These villagers see us the same as their human women and they dismiss us. Don't understand why we speak up with the men or sit on the village council here. We're strange to their eyes. Add our magic to that as well, and…"

Sari nodded. She wasn't ignorant of the growing unease between humans and the Irin people. There was a reason she'd been raised in a small village in the country. Even in larger cities, Irin families kept to themselves. It wouldn't do to have the men questioned when they went out hunting Grigori. It wouldn't be wise to have the healers and scholars scrutinized.

"Our mandate has always been to help humanity," Sari said quietly. "Protect them."

Ingrid shrugged. "At the risk of our own safety? You know what has happened in the Catholic countries. The fear overwhelms reason."

"They speak of locking us up," Sari said. "I had a letter from Tala that said there is talk in Salamanca of forcing singers, mated or not, into communities away from humans. Locking them out of scribe houses and libraries."

Ingrid scoffed. "Madness. The elder singers would never permit it. The scribe houses are mostly staffed by Irin warriors, but who do they turn to for counsel and healing? Who would take the place of our singers who support them? Not to mention how many mated Irin fight together. Mated warriors are far stronger when they work in tandem. That has been our way since ancient times."

Sari didn't share Ingrid's confidence. "I fear the twisted thinking of humans influences our people. Humans see their woman as less."

"Then they are foolish to deny half their race." Ingrid patted her hand. "Besides, there simply aren't enough of us to survive without singers and scribes working together. We'd be in a sad place indeed if all the singers were sequestered in villages. Heaven would weep, Sari, to see their daughters hidden away."

HOURS LATER SHE RESTED IN THE LIBRARY. SHE DIDN'T WANT to return home, and she was worried about Damien and Henry. The sun was long set and the crisp fall wind had turned biting. She built a fire and put out a bottle of whisky for when the men returned.

She was dozing in front of the warm hearth when she heard them stomping and speaking in low voices.

"Sari?" Henry called. "You didn't have to wait for us, sister, but thank you so much for doing so."

Sari blinked and rubbed her eyes. "Henry, where's——"

"I'm here." His voice came from the door. He took off his cloak and hung it on the hook by the door. "What are you doing here, Sari? It's so late."

He sounded exhausted. They both did.

"I didn't want you to come home to a cold house," she said, rising and clearing her throat. "I'm sure you're tired, so——"

"*Milá.*" Damien sighed walked to her, pulling her into his arms and wrapping her up. "Thank you."

The relief was instant. Something tight and angry uncurled in her chest and she hugged him back. His rough chin scraped her cheek, and he took a deep breath as if inhaling her scent.

"I'll take the whisky to my room," Henry said quietly. "Good night. Thank you, Sari. It's lovely coming home to a warm house. That was very thoughtful."

"You're welcome, Henry."

Damien didn't let her go.

"I didn't like that you were gone so long," Sari said. *I didn't like that you went without me.* "What happened?"

"Much blustering and puffing of chests. Be glad you missed it."

"Did they apologize?"

"Not in so many words, but they were clearly chagrined that Kirsten was hurt. And afraid."

"Of Kirsten?"

He drew back, smiling a little, and tucked a piece of her wild hair behind her ear. "No, Sari, not of Kirsten."

She blinked when he kissed her forehead. *Oh.* Him. They were afraid of Damien. Her dark, hooded warrior was rarely seen in human villages. The sight of him on horseback, visiting at dusk after a woman of his people had been attacked, must have filled them with dread.

"Come," he whispered. "Don't go out into the cold tonight. Come with me."

Her body heated despite her exhaustion. "You said I needed to be sure."

The corner of his mouth turned up. "I'm too tired to bed you properly. Keep me warm. That's all I want from you tonight."

Sleep with him? "In your bed?" It was an intimacy she'd shared with no man, not even her first lover.

"Yes, in my bed." He steered her down the hallway. "I'll even wear a tunic if you like."

"Do you not normally? Even in winter?"

He stopped and spoke against her ear. "I prefer nothing on my skin when I sleep. When I was at war, I had to sleep in armor."

"Oh."

"But I will make an exception for you."

Sari walked past him and into his room. She'd lit a small fire in the hearth there as well. "Wear what makes you comfortable, Damien. You know I will." Sari unbuttoned her kirtle and slipped it off, leaving herself in the long chemise she wore against her skin. Without a backward glance, she slid under the covers of the bed and wished she'd thought to heat a few bricks to warm the linens.

No matter. When Damien slipped in behind her, his chest was a furnace. He wrapped a bare arm around her waist and pulled her back into his chest.

"Relax," he said, pressing a kiss to the curve of her neck. "Just sleep, Sari."

"I don't know if I can."

"Have you never shared a bed before?"

"Only with my sister."

"Hmmm." His hum held a satisfied note as his chest rose and fell in a deep breath. "Sleep. And dream of me."

It should have been impossible, but she did.

THEY WERE IN THE FIELD WHERE HE FIRST KISSED HER, BUT the sun wasn't shining as it had been. The moon was full and the hills rose in black waves around them as the night wind rustled the barley.

He stood alone in the center of the field, staring down at his outstretched hands.

She stood in front of him, but he did not see her.

"What do you see?"

"Blood." He spoke and the wind ceased. "So much blood."

She curled her long fingers around his and lifted his hands to her mouth.

"No." He tried to pull away, but she held on. "Don't."

She kissed them, and he fell to his knees. He wrapped his arms around her waist and pressed his head to her belly.

"Love me." His voice was no plea. He commanded, even from his knees. "Love me, *milá.*"

"I do."

SHE WOKE. THE NIGHT WAS PITCH-BLACK SAVE FOR THE glowing coals in the hearth, but Sari felt no cold. Damien rested at her back, breathing deeply, his arms still tight around her.

Love me.

I do.

Oh, she did. So deeply it scared her. For the first time, Sari lowered her shields and let the unguarded thoughts of Damien's soul flow over hers. She reveled in the way his voice caressed her mind. It was nonsense, a tumble of impressions and words in the old language. Feelings more than thoughts.

Happy. Peace. Warmth. Love.

So much love.

Reshon.

She turned in his arms and lifted her mouth to his, softly kissing his unguarded lips until his eyes blinked open.

"Sari?"

"Shhhh."

She kept kissing him, whispering kisses that trailed over his face. His soft lips. His rough jaw. Her fingers followed her lips, tracing the hard planes and arching brows. He said nothing, watching her cautiously until he gave in and closed his eyes, surrendering to her attentions. His chest rose and his hand skimmed down her side, sweeping along the curve of her breast and over her hip until he reached her thigh. He pulled up her chemise under the woolen blankets and stroked the soft skin behind her knee before he pulled up her thigh and hooked it over his hips.

Bare. He wore nothing against his skin. Sari could feel the heat of his body and the heavy weight of his erection pressing against her. With a soft groan, she put her mouth at his neck and sucked, tasting the salt of his skin where he was warmest. His hand gripped her thigh when she used her teeth. She licked down his neck and across his collarbone, her tongue tracing the ink on his skin. She could feel his magic rising and reaching out.

She was not his mate. Not yet.

But she was his reshon.

She should have told him, but her mouth was doing other things. More essential things. She wanted to know every inch of his skin. A strange, feral possession rose in her when she remembered her dream. She reached for the hand that wasn't gripping her thigh, the hand that lay against her cheek, the rough pads of his fingers resting lightly, almost delicately, against her flushed cheek.

He tried to pull away, but she brought that hand to her lips and touched the knuckles with her mouth.

"I love your hands," she whispered when he stiffened. "I do."

It broke whatever resistance had been holding him back. Damien tilted her chin up and crushed her mouth to his, holding her almost painfully against his chest. He stole her breath, then stole it again when he bit teasing nips along her chin. Sari wriggled against him until he cooperated and tugged the chemise up and over her head so she was naked against him.

The shivering overtook her, and Sari trembled against his chest, but Damien took her mouth again and drank her in. As he did, a wave of deepest peace settled over her. It was as if her soul rose up, settled against his, and came to rest.

"Sari," he whispered her name over and over again. "Sari…"

"Yes." She turned her head to the side and let him put his mouth where he was wont.

Her neck.

"*Milá*, do you like this?"

Her breasts.

"Tell me."

His whispering mouth at the crease of her elbow. Her wrist.

"Tell me what you want."

"Everything." She sighed out and pressed her hips to his. "I want everything."

She was swollen and aching and wet. Her body was like a raw nerve, and she felt every inch as he turned her to her back and settled between her legs.

"Look at me," he commanded.

Her eyes rose and locked with his as he eased inside. Her mouth fell open in a soft gasp of pleasure at the aching fullness. His strength and control. He braced his arms on either side of her and lowered his body, the solid weight pressing her into the bed.

"Am I dreaming?" he whispered against her mouth. "I think I am."

"We both are." She kissed him and lifted her knees to hold his hips. "Love me."

"I do." He reached back, wrapping her legs around his waist with a determined glint in his eye. "Sari, you feel…" He groaned when she lifted her hips.

"Good?" she asked with a smile.

"Mine." He thrust once, then drew back and thrust harder as she gasped. "You feel like you're *mine*."

MORNING LIGHT TEASED HER EYELIDS AND SHE COULD HEAR someone moving around the room. A blaze of crackling heat when peat was added to the coals. A low murmur of voices at the door.

"Sari," he whispered and brushed a finger over her cheek.

"Hmmm." She sighed and rolled over, enjoying the decadent slide of her bare skin against sheets that smelled of Damien. "Come back to bed."

She hoped he wasn't shy about gossip. There would be more than one tongue wagging in the village, but Sari didn't care. She never had, and it would surprise her if Damien did. He certainly hadn't been shy in the dead of night. A secret smile tugged the corner of her lips.

"*Milá*, I can't."

His voice didn't carry the lazy timbre of a man well satisfied. And Damien had been very well satisfied.

Sari sat up and rubbed her eyes, pulling the blankets over her shoulders in the chilly room. Damien was already dressed.

"What's wrong?"

He sat on the edge of the bed and put a letter on her lap.

"What is this?" Sari didn't touch it. Something about that letter made her skin crawl.

"Henry slipped it under the door this morning. It arrived yesterday from Aberdeen. I didn't see it before I went to the human village with Einar."

"What is it, Damien?"

He trailed a rough finger down her neck and over her shoulder. "I am called to Edinburgh."

The tight angry thing that had relaxed in her chest when he arrived safe the night before tightened again. "Why?"

He gave her a patient look. "To hunt, of course."

"They have scribes in Edinburgh. More in Aberdeen."

Damien walked to the corner and lifted a heavy woolen blanket from the oak chest sitting like a quiet sentinel in the austere room. The chest was solid and scarred. It bore no outward decoration except a worn crest. A blood-red shield with a dragon curled in front of it and words in the Old Language: *Ours is the blood.*

Damien opened it and took out a smaller box, this one wrapped in worn leather.

"Why do they need you?"

"Because I have skills they do not."

"Every scribe is taught to hunt Grigori."

He opened the box and withdrew a black-handled blade. It was barely over a foot long and made of a type of metal she had never seen before. Sari felt the magic pulsing off it and she shivered. "What is that?"

Damien secured the long knife in a black scabbard before he strapped it to his waist. "It is a heaven-forged blade."

The cry caught in her throat. There was only one reason that Damien would carry a heaven-forged weapon.

"You're hunting an angel."

"Yes."

No no no no no. She wanted to scream, but she couldn't. *This is what the warriors do*, an ancient voice whispered inside. This was their mission. If one of the Fallen was terrorizing Scotland, only a warrior with a heaven-forged blade could kill it. Whether that warrior would survive the effort was a moot point. It had to be done.

"How long?"

"Sari—"

"How long?"

He paused. "There are Grigori in the city. More in Stirling. Too many for it to be random attacks. There have been reports from the interior that make the watcher certain one of the Fallen—he is guessing one of the lesser—is in the Highlands. From the report, I would estimate six to eight months."

She nodded woodenly. She refused to cry. Grigori in the city. A Fallen in the Highlands. Damien would kill them, or they would kill him. He would be hunting and fighting for six months, and she would be on the islands harvesting barley and making sure the animals stayed fed.

"Sari, do you—?"

"Is the boat that brought the letter waiting for you?"

He paused. "It is waiting in Kirkwall. I was supposed to be there at daybreak, but I just received the letter this morning."

She nodded again, her eyes never leaving the letter.

"I have already delayed too long," he whispered. "But I could not bear to leave before you woke."

One night. One perfect night and then he was gone. Her body already ached for him. Her heart...

Damien leaned forward and grabbed her by her shoulders. "Look at me."

She looked up and his eyes were on fire. He was so beautiful in the morning light—his eagle eyes devouring her as his thick hair spilled over his shoulders—that Sari wanted to weep. She wanted to cry and rage and bite him. She wanted to wrap her arms around him and beg him to stay.

"This is what I do," he said. "Do you understand? This is *always* what I will do."

She forced her lips to form the words. "You are a warrior."

"I was bred for this. I am trained for this. They will not kill me."

She couldn't speak. If she did, she would scream.

"I am coming back, *milá*. I am coming back after I have hunted these monsters, and then you will have to decide."

"Decide?"

"Will you have a warrior for a mate? Decide if you are mine, Sari, and be sure."

With one more hard kiss, Damien threw on his black cloak and walked out the door.

CHAPTER
EIGHT

D AMIEN did not think of Sari laying warm in his bed when he boarded the merchant boat to Aberdeen. He did not think of her when he mounted a fast horse and rode south. He did not think of her until he stepped up to the door of the scribe house in Edinburgh and felt the empty space where she should have been beside him.

He wanted her with him.

It was no place for an earth singer, even a fierce one. Sari had probably never handled a sword in her life. She'd never killed a monster and watched its dust rise in the air. Never had to close her eyes to the blood or the gore.

He still wanted her with him.

Damien knocked and waited only a minute before he saw the candlelight flicker through the covered window. A pause and a brush of curtains, then the door was wrenched open.

"Brother," the grateful scribe said. "We did not expect you so soon."

"I rode through the night." He drew back his cloak. "I am Damien of Bohemia, son of Veceslav Custos and Katelin of Vértes. Does the fire still burn in this house?"

"It does, and you are welcome to its light." The man opened the door wider. "We are grateful you were able to come. I am Harold, the watcher of Edinburgh scribe house."

Damien frowned. "I need food and rest. My horse is in the stable."

"Of course. I'll rouse the boy to tend to it."

Harold ushered Damien into a lower room near the kitchen before he went to call a groom. A fire was lit and the room heated quickly. The watcher, whom Damien had never met before, did not bother him with many questions after he sat but cut him a hunk of rough brown bread and poured a mug of ale while Damien stowed his light leather armor and blades in the bedroom he'd been shown.

As he ate, Damien felt the gnaw of hunger ease and his manners reemerge.

"Where are Diana and Monroe?"

"In a village near Stirling. They were the first pair I sent. They took four of the scribes here and are attempting to organize the Irin in the outer villages."

Damien glanced at the man. He was young for a watcher and sounded English. A political appointment? The house had changed hands fifteen years before, but Damien had not visited Edinburgh in much longer. The little news he got was via Diana and Monroe, a mated pair of warriors who had been in Scotland nearly as long as Damien had.

"I expected Monroe to be given the watcher's post here," he said. "How did you end up in the position?"

To his credit, the scribe seemed to take no offense. "It wasn't a popular decision. But Monroe doesn't care much for Vienna's opinion. He's made that clear."

Damien grunted. The watcher spoke only the truth.

"There was talk of appointing you," Harold said.

"I wouldn't have accepted."

Color rose in Harold's cheeks, as if the man was embarrassed by Damien's defiance.

DREAMS

"There was also the matter of Diana." The young watcher took a drink of his own ale. "But Monroe knew that would be a complication."

"Why?"

"Because she fights alongside him."

"And?"

The young scribe's mouth reminded Damien of a fish. "It's not... seemly. Watcher's mates are healers or seers. They support the mission of the scribe house. They don't bloody themselves in battle as Diana does."

"Since when?" Damien asked. "How old are you?"

Harold's lips thinned. "Old enough."

"Since when have our elders cared more for manners and fashions than expediency in battle?" Damien grumbled. "God help them if Katelin catches wind of that nonsense."

"You call your mother by her first name?"

"Everyone calls my mother by her first name. Or *praetora*. If you ever have cause to meet her, remember that."

Damien's mind raced. Just how out of step was he with the council? Had things changed so much since his retreat? Two hundred years ago, Monroe having a warrior for a mate would have made him a stronger candidate politically. It wasn't common for Irina to fight beside mates, but it wasn't "unseemly." Most Irina simply considered warrior's work a waste of time when they could be doing more productive things.

His family, of course, excepted.

"I'll ride to Stirling in the morning."

"Morning is already here, brother. You should rest a day at least."

He wasn't going to rest. Damien knew when he closed his eyes, he would feel the void where Sari's presence should be. "I'll rest a few hours and start again. I will need a new horse."

Harold watched him with narrow eyes. "I could command

91

you to rest, you know. You'll be no good in battle if you're exhausted when you reach it."

Damien ignored him and took another bite of bread. "You're not my watcher, boy."

He probably shouldn't have called the scribe a "boy." The man's voice was acid when he spoke again.

"Technically, I *am* your watcher."

Damien's eyes rose to meet the young watcher's.

"You have never been released by the council," Harold said. "I am the senior scribe in the area where you live. I asked you here to battle one of the Fallen, not prove your mettle."

Damien chewed deliberately and cleared his mouth with another gulp of ale. "I will rest a few hours. Then I will start again. I require a fresh horse. Am I understood?"

Harold's eye twitched, but he said nothing else. He rose and left the kitchen while Damien finished his ale and sought his bed. When his body hit the woolen mattress, he slept and he did not dream.

THE TRIP TO STIRLING TOOK ONLY A DAY. THE IRIN community there was small and integrated with the human population. Damien followed the groom's directions to the old farmhouse where Monroe was residing, but when he arrived, he was told that both Monroe and Diana were still on a scouting trip in the Highlands. They were expected to return in the morning.

Forced to be patient, Damien settled into the small room the Irina matron showed him and took out pen and paper.

Milá,

I wish you were here. You would likely be annoyed and restless, for the whole of hunting seems to be a game of rushing to wait. I am waiting now, and I wish you were here. Have you ever held a sword? I will teach you. Your arms are long and strong. When you wrap them around me, I think I feel the broken parts of myself mending. You will have excellent reach. A woman's center of gravity is lower than a man's. Given the proper training, Irina can be experts with a blade.

I want you to lie over me in the dark with the fire burning while your gold hair is loose and falling around us. I think it would feel like being embraced by the sun.

I am in Stirling waiting for old friends. Monroe and his mate Diana are no untrained initiates. If they have called me here, they have already planned how they wish to use me. This is good. I prefer walking into a battle that has already been planned. If I am very fortunate, this will be over before winter truly sets in. I wish to be back to you by spring. I hope that is possible.

Yours, Damien

"WE DON'T HAVE A PLAN," DIANA CONFESSED. "WE CALLED you here because we're having trouble locating him."

Damien shook his head. "I am no seer, and I do not know this land nearly as well as you do."

Monroe said, "But you understand pattern. There are too many places to hide in the Highlands. We're missing something—perhaps because we are *too* familiar. We hoped you'd be able to see it. I mentioned your skills and your blade to Harold and he agreed to summon you."

"Who is that one?"

Monroe snorted. "Not a bad sort, but young. Trained at the scribe academy in Oxford. His father and mother are very well connected."

"So much learning," Diana said. "So little battle sense."

"Be kind, love. Not everyone was raised at your father's table."

Damien sat back and crossed his arms, staring into the fire. The mates sat across from him. Diana propped her feet up near the fire and rested a hand on her belly while Monroe watched her. The Irina warrior had been born in France and reminded Damien of the dark-eyed women in the south. Her body was as compact and muscled as Monroe's was tall and wiry.

Damien glanced at her hand. "When will the babe come?"

Diana smiled. "Spring." She looked at her mate. "I think she will be a giant like her papa. I'm already so big."

Monroe smiled and squeezed her hand, but Damien could see the stress around his eyes. The silver around his temples and sprinkling his beard was more pronounced than the last time Damien had seen him.

The Highlander and the French warrior had been mated for over one hundred years, but this was the first pregnancy that Damien knew of. Irin did not breed as the humans did. Children were rare and valuable. It was unusual for their women to be lost in childbirth as human mothers were, but it did happen. Damien wondered if Monroe had encouraged Diana to stop riding. If he had, she'd ignored him.

Damien said, "They're attacking in the towns now. Stirling and the outer villages."

Diana nodded. "It took a long time for us to detect them. People can be so easily lost when traveling here. Then we started to hear about human girls going missing in town. People blamed a wolf first. Then a bandit. The worry became worse when both young men and elders started disappearing too."

Monroe sighed. "The old women say it's a kelpie. The younger ones worry me more."

"Are they calling it a witch yet?"

Monroe nodded.

Damien glanced at Diana. She was staring into the fire, her lips pursed.

"I know," she said in a low voice. "All the Irina are being careful. We're part of the community here. We take care to appear as common as possible."

Damien stated the obvious. "You wear breeches and ride like a man, Diana. You're wearing a blade while your belly swells. Are you telling me the humans haven't noticed?"

She rolled her eyes and shrugged. "I am French. They expect me to be odd."

Monroe's hand squeezed hers. "Please don't jest, love."

She turned and put her hand on his cheek. "I'm sorry. I know you worry. But I cannot be other than I am. You know this as well as I do."

"Have I asked you to be?" His voice was tense. "I only ask for caution and you ignore me."

Damien wished he could leave them to their fight, but unfortunately they had a fallen angel preying on the Highland population and Damien had no desire to be in Scotland longer than necessary.

"Friends," he said softly. "The Fallen?"

Diana looked abashed. "I should not be so flippant. A dozen young people have gone missing. Another six have been found dead. It appears from falls or exposure, but we believe they are Grigori kills."

"And if that many have been found, how many others are undiscovered?" Damien asked. "As you said, the wilderness here is dense."

"This might have been going on for months and we were oblivious," Monroe said. "The abductions in Stirling have only been noted in the past few weeks."

"Edinburgh?"

Diana said, "Most Grigori activity in Edinburgh comes from the south. Grigori usually prefer the cities were they can blend in. The Highlands?" She shook her head. "This hasn't happened before."

"And yet communities are so isolated that one of the

Fallen could be hiding within a day's ride of Stirling," Damien said. "Hunting in the country and recently in town. A girl here and there. A lost traveler. No one would connect them."

"Until there became too many."

"Which means their numbers are large enough that they need to take a noticeable amount."

Diana said, "The Grigori could be moving into the towns because winter is coming. Not as many travelers in the mountains."

"It's possible." He scratched the whiskers on his chin. "Let me sleep on it. Monroe, I'll need whatever maps you have."

"The scribe house here specializes in maps of the Highlands," Monroe offered. "Their collection is excellent. I'll find the information you need tomorrow."

"We'll need a small, swift group." Damien stared into the fire, mulling over the terrain they'd be searching. "Monroe, get me five scribes not including yourself. I want endurance, not speed. No grumblers. At least one good game hunter and two good archers. Diana, I won't be taking you, and don't argue. One, you'll be needed here at the scribe house to maintain discipline and watch the town. And two, this could take months, and I won't have you birthing in the mountains."

Diana narrowed her eyes but nodded. "Get my mate back to me by spring, Damien of Bohemia, or you'll feel the edge of my sword. I won't be birthing our babe alone either."

Four months into the mission, Damien knew he wouldn't make it back to Orkney by spring.

We have tracked the Grigori farther into the mountains, he wrote Sari, *and we have killed as many as we could find. Human deaths are lessening as the winter drags on. The Highland trails become ever more impassable. We must find the Fallen before spring comes. His sons will be starving, and I do not want to imagine the terror they could bring. Many of the villages are isolated. They could wipe out entire communities before a report reached us.*

Damien tried to write a letter to Sari each night—there was blessed little else to do when the nights were dripping and cold—but he had no way of sending them.

I try not to grow angry with my summons here. A week's delay would have made little difference to the human population, but a week in your arms would have made me a far more contented soldier. Likely I fool myself to think a week would have made me any less reluctant to leave.

At night he often dreamed of the barley field where he had kissed her. He wandered in his mind, searching for her, but Sari was not yet his mate and Damien searched in vain.

"THERE. JUST OVER THE RISE OF THAT HILL."

"Are you sure?"

Damien wiped the water and a smear of mud from his eyes. "As sure as I am of anything in this place."

Six months of winter in the Highlands had done nothing to make Damien familiar with the area. These were some of the most treacherous and inhospitable mountains he'd ever traveled. The snowfall was mild, but the near-constant rain made the mountain passes almost impossible for tracking. He no longer had any sense of direction other than north, west, and up. He, Monroe, and the Edinburgh scribes had gone north and west from Stirling, tracking each attack and abduction of humans they could find. This path had led them farther into the Highlands and away from anything Damien might have considered familiar.

They'd come across a small party of Grigori three nights before, lurking on the edge of a remote village, and they'd dispatched them. Their fear was the first clue that Damien and his fellow scribes might be on the right track to finding their angelic sire. The lack of any living humans was the other. Damien and Monroe tracked that pack of Grigori back to an even more remote mountain village where a crumbling ruin of a castle dominated a narrow valley.

When they reached the rise of the hill, they lay in the brush and watched. Damien called on the magic he'd scribed when he'd been young, heightening his vision in the early-evening light.

"Nothing," Monroe whispered. "You?"

"Crofter's huts and cottages in seemingly good repair," Damien said. "But no cooking fires. No animals."

"It's deserted."

"Or emptied." Damien eyed the crumbling ruin. It was a small fortification with no flag flying. "Whose land is this?"

"MacNab? Probably MacGregor. I can't say for certain."

Damien rolled over and scooted back down the hill, his back sliding down the muddy ground. "Why here?"

Monroe followed him. "I'm not sure."

"It's isolated."

"Maybe that's all he wanted."

Damien thought about the men they'd brought with them. Faraz, the best hunter in the group, tracked game deep into the mountains, and Monroe said the man often went roaming for months into the Highlands on his own. He was the most familiar with the terrain, though it was nowhere near his homeland.

"Let's ask the hunter."

Damien and Monroe jogged back to the small cave where their men had taken shelter. Faraz was feeding a smoky fire at the edge of the cave, just out of the falling mist.

"There's a village in the valley," Damien said.

Faraz cocked his head and thought. Then he ducked out of the cave and returned a few minutes later. "Yes. I was here last spring and it was not deserted, though the castle was."

"Could the Fallen be here?"

Faraz shrugged. "I don't feel that level of magic. Do you?"

"No, but he could easily be cloaking his power. If he is here, why?"

"There's a game trail that runs down the east side of this valley that smuggler's often use. It would give him access to the river and the lowlands but without attracting attention from some of the larger settlements. That could be it."

Monroe folded his long legs and leaned against the cave wall. "I say we investigate the castle in the morning. Early. I'm ready to go home, Damien. If you make me miss the birth of my child, we'll both be feeling Diana's blades."

"Morning," Damien said. "And let us pray that we have finally cornered our quarry."

THE GRIGORI SENTINELS AT THE EDGE OF THE WOODS WERE their first clue. Faraz and Monroe silently took them out while Damien led the four other scribes through the deserted village and toward the ruined tower. Six months of hunting with these men had given him confidence in Monroe's choice. They were hardy, silent warriors who followed orders well and were sure of hand and foot.

Monroe and Faraz circled back to them silently, and Damien sent his two archers away to take position and watch for any Grigori returning to the valley. Whatever soldiers they met inside they would have to take care of themselves.

They used hand signals to communicate, a common warrior's language that had been taught to Damien before he could speak. He moved silently toward the tower, listening for any sound that would signal life.

There was nothing. No sheep bleated. No hog snorted. Not even the birds were calling in the early-morning rain. Their feet were silent as they approached the moss-covered ruin.

The hinges on the old oak door were rusted, but Monroe signaled that there was a window that might give access. The scribe boosted himself on the shoulders of his brothers and reached for the narrow window. He managed to squeeze through, then held his hand out for the next scribe. One by one, they made it through the tight opening without making a sound. Damien was the last to climb. For a moment he wondered how he would boost himself up the first few feet, until he heard one of his archers chirp from the bushes.

Stepping back, he let the man fire two arrows into the crumbling wall, then using them as footholds, he boosted himself up to the edge of the window and pulled himself in.

The stench of death hit him immediately.

The scribes were wrapping cloths around their mouths and trying not to gag at the smell. The window had dropped them into a small sentry room where bodies had been piled. From the clothing, Damien guessed they were the men of the village. Old men and boys mostly. No women. The women would have been taken to the Fallen or saved for his Grigori spawn.

Grim eyed, the scribes spread through the first level, sneaking into a large hall where a dozen Grigori slept on straw mattresses. They had taken the winter stores from the village and used them for themselves. Animal bones were strewn on the floor, and furs were piled in alcoves where the Grigori were sleeping.

No bodies here, but Damien could almost taste the death

in the room. One by one, Monroe and the other scribes spread out and silently slew the Grigori as they slept. Damien and Faraz moved farther in.

Finally a faint noise reached his ears.

Then another.

Groaning and panting.

Damien's lip curled when he realized what he was hearing. Was it a Grigori taking his pleasure from one of the humans or the Fallen himself? He looked over at Faraz, the scribe's face revealing the same disgust Damien felt. Fallen would enthrall a woman with power, then plant a child in her belly, not caring that the angelic spawn would drain her life even before she bore it. Women did not survive once they'd given birth to a Grigori child.

Damien and Faraz followed the noises to a tower at the back of the castle yard. They'd taken only a few steps into the open when the wind and rain came, lashing them and breaking the dead silence that lay over the valley. With a shout, Monroe ran out of the hall, two of his brothers at his sides.

"I think the stealth part of the mission is over, brother!" he shouted.

"Are the Grigori dead?"

"All we could find."

A screaming voice echoed on the wind.

"Mikael's blood spoils my air," the voice said. "Begone, scribe, or meet your death."

Damien halted for a second, observing his brothers and examining his mind. Other than a piercing pain from the screaming voice, his mind was not affected. His movements were not hindered. It was a Fallen, but not a powerful one.

Monroe nodded toward the tower. "Any other option?"

Damien shook his head and put his hand on the black heaven-forged blade at his side. "He knows we're here. We go in force and pray he does not have many weapons."

He caught movement from the corner of his eye. With the speed and skill of a spider, Faraz was scaling the outside of the tower, his boots kicked off and his toes and fingers clutching the rough stone. Within moments, he was at the top of the tower, peeking in then ducking his head back when a burst of fire shot out the narrow window.

Women screamed inside and the wind grew more violent. Faraz tried to climb down the side but fell the last twenty feet, landing on his back as his brothers gave a shout. Monroe and Damien ran to him.

"No Grigori," Faraz said through gritted teeth. "I only saw women. No weapons that I could see but his fire. He looks intoxicated. Go now while he's weak. I can't move my legs." A gasp as he tried to rise. "Brothers, I cannot move my legs."

Cursing himself that he hadn't found an Irina healer to make the trek with them, Damien said, "Monroe, stay with Faraz and do what you can."

"No!" Faraz yelled. "The Fallen first. Then deal with me."

"Brother—"

"Go. Kill the bastard and come back for me."

Damien and Monroe did not hesitate another moment. They ran toward the door of the tower, calling their brothers to their back as Damien saw his two archers take up position, one on the wall of the castle, the other running to his fallen comrade.

They rushed up the tower, almost tripping over two human women with dead eyes and swollen bellies. Damien could not care for them. He had only one goal. Monroe ran ahead as all the scribes activated their talesm. Their bodies glowed with magic as the ancient runes lit with power. As one, their magic rose and filled the air with a smell not unlike lightning after a storm. Monroe was the first through the arched door. With a shout, he doubled over and rolled to the side just as two other scribes ducked low and entered the room.

"Where is Mikael's blood?" the angel shouted, his voice filling the air. "I grow tired of weaklings."

Damien came in low and braced himself for the wind. For once, the Scottish weather had been a boon. Though Monroe's clothes smoked, they did not burn. No, they'd been soaked with damp for weeks. Damien drew his wet cloak around him and rose, hand at the heavenly blade at his side. He could not draw it until he had a clear angle on the Fallen's neck. Any cut from the blade would be lethal for his brothers or himself so far from a ritual fire.

Two scribes were wrestling with the angel, who had shifted into an otherworldly eight-foot-tall monster. Light and fierce beauty poured off him, and he would not be wrestled down.

"Quick and dirty, brother!" Monroe barreled past him and into the Fallen's legs, the three scribes finally managing to bring the angel to his knees. One of the brothers started screaming and blood streamed from his ears, but he did not let go. Damien leapt into the fray, keeping the heaven-forged blade at his waist, waiting for a clear target.

The tangle of scribes and angel rolled across the floor of the tower, fire shooting from the hands of the Fallen. Every time one of his brothers screamed, Damien felt it. But fighting an angel was dirty and taxing. They wrestled with the giant creature who continued to pierce them with what magic he had, which mostly consisted of fire and mental blades. Wind filled the tower, making even a scrap of cloth a weapon.

A clay bowl bashed Damien on the temple and he went down, but Monroe grabbed his arm and yanked him up.

"Now!" Damien saw four scribes, including one of his archers and a pale Faraz dragging himself on his elbows, holding the roaring angel down. Arrows littered the angel's back and blood dripped from multiple gashes and wounds, but none of them would kill the creature. Only Damien could do that.

"Damien!"

He leapt on the back of the Fallen, adding his weight to the mass of scribes restraining the monster. Climbing up the back of the angel, he used his elbow to pummel the creature's proud head.

"I will kill you, Mikael's blood!" it yelled.

But it wouldn't. Damien grabbed a handful of the angel's golden hair and yanked up. Then he drew the black blade and stabbed it into its neck as the angel screamed and fire filled the room.

CHAPTER
NINE

S ARI watched the ships bob in the harbor in Kirkwall as
Ingrid and her mate loaded the bags of grain. They
wouldn't need wheat by next year. The fields were
already bursting with crops, though the season was early.
She'd worked tirelessly all winter to prepare the ground,
working two seasons of magic into one mild winter because
she was desperate to keep her mind occupied and her body
exhausted.

There had been no word from Damien in months, though
Sari rode into Kirkwall with Ingrid every time she met the
ship from Aberdeen. No word except that he and his brothers
were hunting an angel in the Highlands and he would not be
back before spring at the earliest.

It had been eight months since their night together. She
cursed his memory. Searched for him in dreams. She missed
him. She loved him. She was furious.

This is what I do. Do you understand? This is always *what I
will do.*

Curse him.

Of course it was what he did. From the moment she'd seen him, she'd known Damien was a warrior. Known he was simply biding his time on the small island in the North Sea. Had that stopped her from falling in love with him? Of course not.

But she'd be damned if he left her behind again.

"We're finished," Ingrid said, climbing onto the front of the wagon. "Did you want to drive home?"

This is not my home.

"Unless you or Matthew wants to drive."

"No." Ingrid waved a hand as the wagon lurched and her large mate, Matthew, climbed in back. "Go ahead."

With a quick flick of the reins, Sari nudged the team into motion, ignoring the stares of the humans at the docks. The Irina were still the subject of suspicion, and more and more they avoided going into the human villages without an Irin escort. It was starting to drive Sari mad. She felt like a child, but Einar was insisting. There had been no more incidents since Kirsten's attack, but more than one singer felt uncomfortable around the humans. Sari couldn't blame her sisters, but it was frustrating to feel as if other's fear was hemming her in.

They drove back to the village and unloaded the grain. Sari decided to spend the day tending her own household garden. Weeding was a constant challenge. Earth magic was an equal opportunity fertilizer, which meant though her garden was lush and fruitful, the weeds were also attracted to her magic and grew quick and eager alongside her vegetables.

She took her evening meal in the longhouse with Henry. The friendly scribe was the only one who seemed to be able to put up with her sullen moods most nights.

Nights were the worst.

He chatted and told stories, even sang a few songs by the fire after they'd finished their meal. Henry poured her a mug of ale and sat at her side, throwing a brotherly arm around her shoulders and soothing her with his easy affection. The anxious energy that had been building since she'd met the ship in Kirkwall eased a little.

"Thank you, Henry." She squeezed his hand and stared into the fire.

"I know it's not the same," Henry said. "But sister, come to me any time you have need."

"It's been eight months."

"Little goes according to plan in battle," Henry said. "Damien knows this better than anyone."

"Which is why he said six to eight months when he left. He was being conservative. He would have tried to hunt this fallen before winter set in. Something is wrong."

"If he had been injured, the watcher of Edinburgh would have written."

"Unless he doesn't know they are injured. The last letter I received said they were going into the Highlands."

"A slow hunt in winter." Henry rubbed her shoulder and let his magic flow out, soothing her. "Damien is a very skilled warrior, Sari."

"I know."

"You realize that if he kills this angel, it is likely the council will call him back into service."

She blinked. "You mean this is a… trial? A test of some sort?"

"There are scribes in London who carry heaven-forged blades. They could have sent another. I suspect the council wanted to test Damien's skills to see if his years of seclusion had dampened his strength in battle. They're ready to call him back."

Sari's eyes hardened. Bastards. What if he wasn't ready? What if sending him into battle *against an angel* as a test killed him?

"Sister." Henry shook her. "You have no need to worry. Do you truly think anything could soften Damien?"

She shook her head. It might have been more out of hope than assurance.

"Even loving you has only made him fiercer, sister."

Gabriel's fist, she hoped so.

"'Iron sharpeneth iron,'" Henry continued. "'So a man sharpeneth the countenance of his friend.' You sharpen him, Sari. Give him direction and purpose."

She closed her eyes. "He needs to come back to me, Henry. He needs to come home."

SARI HEARD WHISPERS IN HER SLEEP. AN URGENT VOICE whispered in her mind. Hoofbeats and driving rain. Shouts and—

She jerked awake at the pounding at her door.

"Sari!"

She yanked open the bolt and threw herself into the arms of the muddy, rain-soaked scribe at her door. She couldn't speak. She clung to him as he stumbled inside and slammed the door shut. Damien locked his arms around her and lifted her off her feet. Sari wrapped her arms around his neck and brought his mouth to hers. Their kiss was desperate and hungry. Hard lips and sharp teeth. He bit her lower lip when she tried to pull away. Sari gripped his hair and forced his head back.

"You will never"—she choked on her tears—"*never* leave me behind again! Never, Damien."

"I promise." He kissed her over and over. "I promise."

"Never again."

"I love you."

Sari burst into tears of relief, and he buried his face in her neck. "I'm so angry with you."

"I know." He turned and set her on the edge of the bed, kneeling between her legs. "I love you."

"I love you so much," she whispered. "And I'm still angry with you."

He pulled away and looked at her in wonder. His thick hair hung in wet ropes around his face. His beard was wild, but his eagle eyes glowed with fierce joy. "You love me."

"Reshon," she whispered, drawing his mouth back to hers. Her face would be rubbed raw by his whiskers, but she didn't care. "You are my reshon, Damien. I love you. I choose you. I have decided."

"*Reshon.*" He let out a hard breath and pulled her closer. "*Milá*, you are my own."

She began to peel off his mud-caked cloak, but he stilled her hand with trembling fingers.

"A bath," he whispered. "I have been in battle, Sari, and it was… Take me to the ritual bath that I may cleanse myself."

Sari nodded, recognizing the soul-deep weariness in his voice. She threw a few more bricks of peat on the coals to heat her cottage, then stood and took Damien's hand.

HE SAT IN THE ROUND POOL HEATED FROM THE FIRE SARI continued to stoke. She had poured buckets of cold water over him to cleanse his body of the mud he'd collected on the hard ride from Kirkwall. Damien told her he'd missed the Irin merchant ship and been forced to sail with humans to get to her. The boat had arrived just before dark, but he couldn't stand to wait. The moon was full, so he'd ridden through the night despite the summer storm that had swept in from the sea.

Sari stripped down and wrapped herself in her ritual linen robe before she scrubbed him with a soapy rag. She ignored his body's reaction to her and bathed him head to foot, scrubbing the months of dirt and grime from his hair and neck. She silently trimmed his beard as he watched her with tired eyes. When his body was clean, she led him to the warm pool, sitting behind him as she took oils and anointed his back and hair. With strong hands, she massaged his shoulders and felt the magic rise on his skin as if reaching for her.

When his shoulders began to unknot and his arms fell around her knees, she spoke. "Tell me."

"It was a long hunt."

He told her of his months in the wilderness and the humans who had been lost. About his brothers' determination and strength in battle. Though he didn't say it, Sari heard the pride in his voice when he spoke of the men he'd led. Heard his appreciation and respect for Monroe, the Scottish scribe who'd sacrificed months of time with his pregnant mate to accompany Damien on his hunt. His sorrow for Faraz, who was healing from grievous injuries.

When his story reached the dead human village, she wrapped her arms around his shoulders and pressed her cheek to his back. Whole families had been killed by the Grigori. Young women and girls enthralled by the Fallen.

"There were pregnant women there," he said quietly. "Girls carrying Grigori babies."

Sari tensed. "What did you do?"

"Nothing." He paused. "Monroe tried to get them to return to Stirling. He thought one of the healers might be able to rid them of the Fallen's offspring and save their lives. They wouldn't go. They were distraught when we killed the angel."

"Their minds had been turned by magic, Damien."

"There was some food there. We left them with what supplies we could, but…"

Sari knew that the women were probably already dead. Even if they survived the birth of their Grigori children, they would die in isolation. And the Grigori babes would as well. It was evil, but an evil caused by the Fallen, not by her reshon, though Sari knew he still carried the weight of it.

"We are supposed to kill human women carrying Grigori," he said. "They will die anyway after their children are born. It is considered a mercy to kill them swiftly instead of letting them starve and fade."

"But you didn't."

His voice was barely audible. "I could not."

"Damien—"

"I have…," he said. "I have killed an angel before. That is how I obtained the heaven-forged blade. It was the only other time when I saw surviving humans carrying Grigori children. Usually we would only find bodies. But when I was young, I followed orders. We let them fall into a deep sleep with our touch and then one brother killed them quickly."

Her arms were tight around him. "They would have died anyway."

"*My eyes have seen too much to ever look on that which is lovely again*," Damien whispered. "Otto followed my orders. I believe that is why he wanted to die."

"*Slemaa, reshon.*" Sari murmured a spell to give him peace. "We did not start this war. We can only fight it with as much honor as we own. You have fought hundreds, Damien. Protected thousands. Do not let guilt eat our joy."

He clutched her hands over his heart. "You choose me?"

"I do."

"Then be my mate, Sari. Take my mark. Walk my dark nights with me and call me your own."

"I will."

He warmed the ink by the fire, and when the sable brushed over Sari's skin, it was as if the brush was an extension of her lover's own body. Warm lips kissed her shoulders as Damien painted the mating marks on her shoulders and down the center of her back. She could see the glow of gold in the dark cottage where they had returned after the cleansing bath. Felt his hand tremble even as he wrote ancient spells and vows over her body, tying them together.

When he finished one portion, she sang softly to him. Old songs of joy and binding and love. Songs given to her mothers by the Forgiven and passed down in joyful whispers from grandmother to mother to daughter. Sari felt the old magic rise in her heart, suspending her joy as Damien wrote again. She felt his tears against her shoulder, but he kissed them away and returned to writing.

When he finally turned her to write his mating vow over her heart, the heat and desire for him took her breath away.

"Soon," he whispered, his lips flushed and swollen. His eyes locked on her breast as he wrote his vow over her heart, speaking it so Sari would know the words he had written just for her.

"So many years," he murmured. "I dreamed, but I never truly hoped... How could I have imagined this love I feel for you now? Love did not exist for me until I saw your face."

"Damien." She wanted him so badly it was an ache in her belly. She had only her last song to give him after he wrote his vow on her. The vow that would glow each time they made love. "Hurry."

He dipped his brush and started, whispering as he wrote:

> "Mine is the fire. Mine is the blood.
> Mine, her soft touch and her sharp tongue.
> She that wields a strong hand
> And a gentle embrace
> Is my lover.
> My own.
> Mine is the need and the desire.

My witness, her song.
Daughter of heaven,
Beloved of my heart.
My Sari.
My own."

She felt his power and heard his voice, sharp and martial, rise in her breast and flood her mind. Felt his ravenous need and heady possession. Threaded through the wash of sensation and magic was an aching tenderness, a gentleness and surrender that she did not expect. She opened her eyes and met his, unashamed of her joyful tears.

"Hear my own vow, Damien of Bohemia:

I choose you.
Through ages you have come to me,
And I choose you.
Because you wandered many roads alone
And this body has bled and shed blood in
    honor,
I choose you.
The one who sees me and challenges me,
My warrior, my lover. Friend, protector, help-
    meet, mate.
As iron sharpens iron, I will ever be your own.
I choose you, my love."

Sari leaned forward and pressed her forehead against Damien's, their hands linked together as her song died to a whisper. "I choose you."

They stayed like that, hands locked together as the ink dried on her skin and the fire crackled in the hearth. The next day, Damien would tattoo her vow on his skin and ink her magic permanently onto his body. Until then, Sari would sate months of hunger and longing. Nights of aching for his body and missing his touch. She opened her mind to his voice and heard the longing and desire mirrored in his soul. The night birds sang, but the air was laden in magic, like the moment after a lightning strike.

Their skin glowed in the low light, Damien's talesm a deep burnished silver. Sari's new marks were a bright gold that lit her pale skin as if she'd been painted by the midsummer sun.

"Reshon." Damien's mouth found hers, and his lips were trembling. His hands shook as they locked around her wrists. "Sari?"

"M-my ink is dry," she stuttered, barely in command of her body.

"Good." He took her down to the bed in a controlled rush, shoving her hands over her head and his tongue in her mouth. Damien groaned and thrust his body between her thighs. "I have waited so long. So long for you, my singer."

"Don't wait anymore." She arched against him, but his muscled weight pinned her down.

Bracing himself over her, Damien kept control of her hands and arms, pressing them over her head as his mouth descended and tasted her neck. He spread her legs apart and settled his body in the space between her thighs, resting his heavy length against her as months of desire spiraled into a barely controlled tangle of need. She *ached* for him.

"Please, please, please," she sobbed. "Damien." Wresting her hands away from his own, she gripped his hair in one hand and reached for him with the other, guiding him into her body and arching up as he slid tight and deep.

He thrust into her with a groan, and Sari cried out as her body and magic recognized him. *This* was true union. No other physical pleasure could compare.

She clutched Damien tighter as he began to move. She kept trying to get closer, and the dried ink cracked against her skin. She reveled in the friction of their bodies together. Pressing and giving and taking. Push and pull. They rolled on her narrow bed and didn't stop, even when they crashed to the floor. They landed on their side in the pile of linen robes smeared red with sweat and ink.

His magic heightened her senses. She smelled the ash from the fire and the sweat on his body, the sweet almond oil she'd used against his skin. His talesm shone brighter than the firelight.

Damien was no quiet lover. He growled and twisted her hair in his hand, wrapping the golden blond in his fist as he whispered in her ear. "Love you. Need you, *milá*."

Come for me.

I want to feel your flesh tight around me.

More, Sari.

Bite harder.

I love you.

His words and touch intoxicated her. He reached down and played with her body, eliciting the most delicious thrill. His strong hands gentled her and drew out her pleasure as she locked her legs around his hips.

"Take me," he whispered against her mouth. "All of me."

"Yes," she panted. "Always."

The hand in her hair twisted painfully as his movements turned rougher, balancing on the edge of control. Sari's mind and body were a whirl of magic and pleasure. She came under him, surrounded by him, over him. Damien's hands were fierce and gentle, commanding as he coaxed her to release over and over again with his hands and his voice. He drew teasing spells across her thighs and bit her knees, tasting her in ways Sari had only heard of in rumors. He was wild for her, demanding in his appetites and greedy for her satisfaction.

Her head was spinning and her body was flush with heat and magic by the time Damien found his own release. He shouted her name as he arched up, and Sari rocked over him, her hair curtained around them, red-gold in the light of the fire and their mating marks. He pulled her mouth down to meet his lips, kissing her deeply as his body shuddered in climax. He rolled them to the side and pressed her face to his chest.

"Every night, Sari. I will have you like this every night."

She shivered against his chest, her skin a living thing under his command. "We'll never get any sleep."

"I can survive on very little sleep. I was bred for war."

Her laugh was sharp but her eyes were heavy. She wanted to burrow into him and sleep for days. Wake up, make love for a few more hours, then fall back to sleep.

"That, my Sari, sounds like a most excellent plan."

"Did I say that aloud?"

"I have no idea." Damien rolled to his knees, picked Sari up and lifted her into bed, covering her with a light blanket before he crawled beside her. "Sleep, mate. I have plans for you when we can both walk again."

She closed her eyes and felt his arms come around her. "I never want to be parted from you, Damien."

"Then we won't," he whispered, playing absently with her hair, spreading it over his chest as she lay boneless across him.

"Never, Damien."

"Sleep, *milá*. I will see you in your dreams."

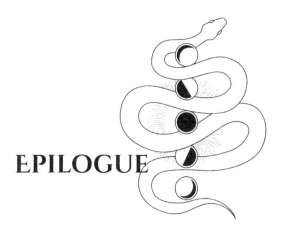

EPILOGUE

Nordfjord region, 1596

"HIT me again," she said. "Harder this time. You're going too easy on me."

"Sari..." He let his head fall back and looked at the clear blue sky cut with streaks of white clouds. "I'm pushing you harder than I would a scribe newly out of the academy."

"Then push me harder! How am I supposed to learn if you won't teach me?"

Sari was proficient with a short staff, but Damien was better. Though it was considered an Irina weapon, his mother had trained him on it even before he picked up a sword. Sari wanted to be able to best him, so instead of making love out of doors—which was how Damien would much rather be spending a summer afternoon—he was beating up his mate with a short staff and barking orders at her.

As expected, the council had called him back into service after his hunt of the angel in Scotland. It had been a test, just as Henry suspected. Damien had received the letter from

Vienna only weeks after he'd returned to Orkney and Sari's arms. When he had written back and requested a year of bonding time with his new mate, the response from the elders had been more than enthusiastic. After all, mated scribes of Mikael's line were even more desirable than unmated ones. The fact that he'd mated with the granddaughter of Orsala of Vestfold had even placated his parents. Not much, but some. Sari was a powerful singer, but one of Ariel's line. His mother worried for their offspring.

Sari's family, on the other hand, was happy if she was happy. And Damien did everything in his power to make her happy. His young mate was eager for travel, so Damien's upcoming posting to the scribe house in London was welcome, though Damien knew she would have preferred to go farther south.

Her sister, Tala, was still in Spain. London would put him and Sari closer to Salamanca than they had been in Orkney, and it was possible that Tala would even be granted time for a visit once they were there. If not, they would travel to Spain.

Sari needed to see her twin, and Damien gave Sari what she needed.

Which at that moment was a sharp strike to the back of her knee.

"Too slow!" he shouted. "We're the same size. I should have no advantage over you with the staff. You need to be faster. Tomorrow we start running more."

Her angry red face preluded a flurry of blows.

She was getting better.

Not long after they mated, Sari announced her determination to become a warrior. Though she had made up a very logical list of reasons why it was prudent for her to have martial training, along with relevant arguments and counter-arguments, none of those had been necessary.

Damien wanted her with him. She needed to be able to defend herself. And Damien gave his mate what she needed.

So they would spend their bonding year running and training in the wilderness where her family had often taken refuge, with Damien drilling Sari on Irin military history and battle tactics along with knives, staffs, swords, and archery.

He parried her, spinning around and flipping the staff from her grip. As she lunged toward it, he tackled her to the dirt and ground his hips against her.

"Enough," he panted. "I have other plans for you, earth singer."

"Oh?" Her blue eyes narrowed. "You did promise to introduce me to swordplay this week, but I wasn't expecting the *long* sword."

"Bedding humor, Sari?" His mouth curled into a smile. "I thought only unsophisticated warriors played at that."

She arched up and kissed him. "As I will be a warrior, I guessed that I should practice it also."

"You already are a warrior," he said. "*My* warrior."

She was. Sari battled back the darkness that threatened to envelop Damien some nights, chasing it with her laughter and her wit and her sharp tongue. He grew less and less somber. More and more optimistic. He imagined a future, not only of duty but of happiness. Children and grandchildren. Long centuries of life with his mate at his side.

…may you be blessed to find a mate as warlike as yourself.

She was. Thank heaven above, she was.

Damien had found his mate. As unlikely as it had once seemed, he'd found his equal and his other half.

And he was never letting her go.

End of Book One

GHOSTS

A new posting in Paris during Napoleon's reign leads Sari and Damien back to familiar faces and the council politics Damien has tried so hard to avoid. But the Irin world has changed in the two hundred years since their mating. The singers have become more isolated. The scribes are more martial. And the Grigori flood growing cities and lay in wait. When Sari's sister envisions the future, she sees emptiness, chaos, and a darkness that threatens to overtake their world.

OH MY CHILD, how I grieve for you!
My empty arms ache with longing.
I cry, "Come back to me," but you cannot hear.
The light of my heart is extinguished.

Take me, O heaven, and silence my voice
For my soul is black with pain.
I wander among the rocks and trees
And hide from my beloved.

I am barren in the wilderness.
The child of my heart is no more.

—From *Adelina's Lament*

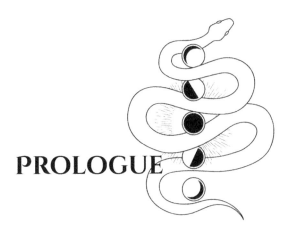

PROLOGUE

PARIS, 1807

TALA knew she was in a vision when she opened her eyes. The air was cold and a bite of cedar flavored the air. She walked out of the forest of her youth and toward the simple farmhouse where she and her sister had been born.

Her visions often started like this, walking out of the woods and into her childhood home. When she opened the door, it could open to her mother or grandfather baking. Or it could open into a ship on the ocean or a woman giving birth.

In this seeing, she opened the house to what it always had been. Water bubbling on the glowing stove. The smell of bread and salt. Ocean air and smoke. Her home appeared as it had in her childhood, except…

Empty clothes were piled in front of the fire. More clothes at the table. A bowl of uneaten soup with the spoon dropped to the floor. No people. Only clothes. Shoes. A forgotten staff lying on the ground.

The cold tugged at Tala's belly, and a scrambled voice whispered in the distance like a voice from another room.

She walked through the cottage and opened the back door to enter the meeting hall of Adna's House. She glided between the tables, cloaks and kirtles crumpled on benches before open books and mugs of steaming broth. She walked slowly, taking in the smell and temperature of the room. She opened the side door to find the sun on her face.

Tala stood in the doorway of her room in Salamanca, the courtyard of the scribe house stretching hot and dusty in the summer air. The fountain in the center of the small plaza bubbled happily, and Tala noted the bright skirts and colorful wraps lying empty on the ground around it where water jugs had been dropped and baskets of flowers lay abandoned. In one corner, children's toys lay deserted beside tiny dresses and shoes. An empty cradle rocked in the wind, no hand stirring it to motion.

Empty. Everything was empty. No one breathed or played or sang.

A quiet scream whispered in her mind.

The smell of lemon blossoms filled the air as Tala walked across the silent courtyard and opened carved double doors.

Stepping down a small flight of stairs, the sounds of battle rang in the air. Smoke and gunpowder clogged her nose. She saw humans rushing past, some pushing cannons and others writhing in pain on the muddy, bloody ground. A ghostly human, his bayonet fixed, ran past her, his soul voice desperate and crying.

She walked through the battle, soldiers running and scattering from her path. An even road ran through the torn field and toward a grand house at the end of an alley of trees. Looking up, she realized the house was a modern confection of a mansion, fronted with ornate columns and bright flower borders. In the smoke-filled battle, it lay undisturbed, an island of beauty amidst blood and sickness.

Tala walked up the steps and halted at the massive double doors.

Voices drifted from inside.

They were familiar, but she could not recognize them. The doors opened on their own, and Tala forced herself to step inside. The entry hall was grand, a double staircase curling up to the second-floor landing. Stained glass decorated the walls; colored sunlight painted the room. It was beautiful and eerie. She heard children laughing somewhere in the house and the sound of slamming doors.

More laughter behind her.

Tala spun, but no one was there.

She turned slowly in the entry hall, a thick Persian rug cushioning her bare feet. There were shouts, but they came in echoes and whispers through the corridors of the empty house.

Empty. So empty.

It's all gone.

Walking down a wood-paneled hallway, Tala reached out and touched the walls, feeling the house breathe with her as she searched. She saw nothing, only heard the memory of scuffling and muffled shouts. A child was sobbing somewhere. Another child. And another. Tiny voices started to crowd her mind. Whimpers and sniffles and pained crying.

The house, once a beacon of light and warmth in the raging battle outside, grew dark and cold. The farther she walked down the hall, the more children she heard. All were crying. All were in pain. A woman screamed, and she started to run.

"*No! Tala, no!*"

The shout came from behind her, but she could not turn back. A blood-red door came into view.

"*No, no, NO!*"

She reached for it, and the shouting turned to screaming behind her. Deep, guttural howls of agony that pierced her temple and kicked her gut. Sharp pain flooded her body, and her mouth filled with bile a moment before her vision went black.

"*TALA, NO!*"

SHE SAT UP STRAIGHT AND FELL TO THE SIDE, RETCHING OVER the edge of the bed, vomit splashing on the floor as Tala emptied her stomach and groaned. A sharp pain pierced her temple as her body convulsed in the wake of the vision.

"Tala?" Gabriel's rough voice at her side. "Oh, my love." A soft hand soothed the small of her back. "Just your stomach or your head too?"

"Both," she managed to say, her mouth bitter with sick.

Gabriel rolled out of bed and walked down the hall. In a few minutes, he returned with a cool cloth he put on her forehead, a candle to light the room, and one of his brothers who helped him clean the floor. Gabriel lifted Tala and held her cradled in his arms as the young scribe quickly changed the sheets and smoothed the bedclothes.

Tala would have protested, tried to help, but her head was still spinning and her whole body felt weak. She often entered a seeing state between her first and second sleeps, and she usually woke with her stomach twisted in knots. Headache and nausea were typical symptoms when a seer had a vision, but these were worse than usual. Her stomach felt bruised. Her temple felt as if it had been jabbed with a knife.

Her mate whispered soothing words to her and rocked her like a child. Though Tala was a few inches taller than him— she'd been taller than almost everyone in Spain—Gabriel's powerful body and broad shoulders easily held her when she became ill.

In a few more minutes, they were alone again. Quiet thanks to the brother who had helped them, the promise of a cold pitcher of water, and Tala was back in bed, the cold sheets cutting through some of the lethargy from the vision.

"A bad one this time." Gabriel helped her to sit and gathered her hair, twisting it into a loose braid to keep it out of her face. Gabriel adored her golden hair, begging her to keep it long no matter how much the Spanish summers burned. And Tala adored him, her quiet, sardonic mate whose calm exterior and mild manner concealed a passionate protectiveness toward the singer he had pledged himself to.

They had met in Salamanca only twenty years after Tala had arrived. Spain was finally starting to feel familiar to her, and Gabriel had been returning to his childhood home after a long assignment in North Africa. He was tanned and dark as a Moor, his hair grown past his shoulders and his cheeks rough with weeks of travel the first time Tala had seen him throwing water over his neck and shoulders by the fountain. A deep rasping voice had woken her from an afternoon siesta, the summer heat still unbearable to a woman bred in the cold north. She walked to the door in a daze and opened it, squinting into the glare of the midday sun.

The low voice halted when she opened her door. Tala blinked and held her hand up to shade her eyes and discovered the unfamiliar scribe who had disturbed her rest. The dark man was staring at her, his mouth open and his black eyes fixed. She'd closed the door quickly, unnerved by his silent stare.

It had taken months for Tala to understand that the fact Gabriel was quiet didn't mean he was shy, as she was. Gabriel didn't speak unless he had something to say, but he was always thinking. He was a mapmaker by training. A scholar. At first Tala hadn't been able to tell when he was being serious or teasing her.

She had become accustomed to the brash warriors who filled the Salamanca scribe house. Most of the unmated scribes had flirted madly with her until they realized she was not a bold young woman eager to play as most singers were when freed from the apprentice house. After weeks of determined attempts to court her, the warriors' innate protectiveness had taken over. Most saw Tala as a younger sister. Others ignored her. But male attention toward Tala was firmly discouraged by the Salamanca scribes if visitors attempted it.

Gabriel, familiar to most of the residents of the scribe house, was the subject of cheerful ribbing when he did not play their battle games or train with them, but he had earned their respect in different ways. His keen mind and observations were valued by the watcher and the chief archivist.

He was not a social man. He sat apart at mealtimes, usually reading a book or drawing silently, until one day Tala realized that he was sitting across from her and had been for weeks. His courtship was quiet, persistent, and focused. Gabriel silenced Tala's usual guardians with a single look. Within months, he'd made her his lover. And one morning, Tala woke in Gabriel's bed, realizing that she was in love with him and had been for weeks. When she told him, he smiled with not a hint of surprise.

"Tala?"

Nearly a century and a half mated, and Tala still shivered when he said her name in that low, rasping voice. At home, they mostly spoke Spanish, though they'd been assigned to Paris five years before. She had fallen in love with the language when she fell in love with Gabriel.

"I'm fine." She pressed a hand to her stomach. "Can I have some water?"

He held a glass to her lips. "Do you want to talk about it?"

She shook her head. "Not yet."

"Is it about the war?"

War had been raging among the humans of Europe for years, led by a brilliant French general by the name of Napoleon. From the ashes of the revolution, he had risen to domination in France. War was always a difficult time to be a seer. Visions came fast and furious but often were hard to interpret. Attempts to intervene could cause more harm than good. Tala had made the mistake when she was younger of thinking every vision had to be acted on. Now she knew that some knowledge could only cause pain. Some events were inevitable.

And some were not.

The strange vision of the house felt like a storm gathering. There were so many layers. It was different from the random flashes she usually received.

She frowned. "I'm not sure what it was about. I need to think about it. Try to remember everything. It's all muddled right now."

"Sleep." He tucked her into his side. "Let me know if you want to consult with Anabel, and I'll make arrangements to go to Lyon."

"Thank you, love." Tala pressed her ear to Gabriel's side and listened for the steady thump of his heart. She closed her eyes and focused on it. He was her rock. Her anchor. Tala had thanked the Creator the moment she realized Gabriel would be her mate and her partner. She could not have asked for a better man.

He blew out the candle and the room fell into deep darkness. As Tala drifted to sleep, a thought slipped into her head.

"Tala, no!"

Gabriel. It had been Gabriel's voice. And the scream had been his own.

CHAPTER
ONE

S ARI felt like singing. It didn't matter that they'd been
forced to take a tiny smuggler's craft to the French coast
because of the human war. It didn't matter that she'd
had to leave the majority of their household things in London.
Sari felt like singing because finally, after years of requests and
subtle pleas to Vienna, Sari and her sister, Tala, were going to
be together again.

Damien's assignment to Paris had come only weeks before
when his replacement had been confirmed by the Watchers'
Council. Sari had shouted with excitement, then made her
pleasure evident when she pulled her mate into their room to
celebrate privately. Playful ribbing followed them, lifting the
spirits of their brothers, most of whom were unhappy to see
the leading scribe and singer of London move on.

When Tala and her mate Gabriel had first been sent to
Paris, Sari had rejoiced. The journey to Paris was much
shorter than the one to Spain. But when Napoleon had
mounted his war steed, visits to her sister had become few and
far between.

Sari knew the Elder Council in Vienna had worked tirelessly to call on old allegiances, hefty bribes, and sometimes

ancient promises in order for their people to remain neutral. A few Irin warriors had been conscripted into battle, but the majority of the Irin scribes and singers were able to live normal lives. Or as normal as they could be while the Irin world struggled with its own demons.

Damien glanced at her in the carriage, a small smile flirting at the corner of his lips. "You do realize most of the other singers will be living in one of the 'damned and cursed retreats,' do you not? I tried to overrule the previous watcher, but my request was denied."

"I don't care."

He chuckled. "Never in a hundred years would I have imagined I'd see the day my Sari said that."

"It's not forever."

He stared at her hard, then looked away, focusing his eyes on the passing scenery.

Sari sighed. "Damien—"

"Is it so bad a thing to be near a place that is safer?" he asked quietly. "A place where a child… Never mind."

A twist in her gut. "I haven't said no. I've just said I want to wait."

"You've wanted to wait for thirty years."

"We should have had twice the number of guardians in London. We couldn't spare me with the increase in Grigori activity, and we definitely couldn't spare *you*."

The growth in British naval power over their time in London and the increase of international trade had meant a stunning uptick in Grigori activity. Britain was still an island, but it was no longer isolated or visited by raiders who came and left. No, the sons of the Fallen found easy prey along the growing waterfronts and busy ports. More and more humans lived on the margins as cities grew, which made those individuals ripe for Grigori picking.

"There are thousands of Irin warriors, Sari. I am not

indispensable. And taking a few decades to start a family is not unreasonable. It is expected."

"There is only one *you*," Sari said. "You wouldn't leave London until they found a successor you found worthy enough."

"Of course I wouldn't. I'm not irresponsi—"

"And how long did it take you to find a successor to present to the council? A successor you found merely *satisfactory?*"

He snapped his mouth shut, but Sari finished for him. "Fifteen years. You've been scheduled for reassignment for fifteen years, and it took you that long to find a watcher to replace you."

Damien was silent because he didn't have a rebuttal. It was an argument they'd been having on and off for almost fifty years. Damien wanted to start their family. Sari wanted to wait. Damien wanted a child. Sari wanted a child too, but not when there was so much to do.

She knew that the moment she became pregnant everything would change. Two hundred years before, her friend Diana had hunted through her pregnancy at her mate's side, only returning to the scribe house to bear their child. Their son was raised among warrior scribes and singers, then sent off to the academy in London when he was thirteen. After that, Diana and Monroe returned to hunting and patrolling the highlands unless their son was at home.

But over the past three hundred years, Irin communities had come under more and more scrutiny, becoming ever more isolated. Now, the minute an Irina was with child, she and her mate were shipped off to a "retreat."

More like a penal colony in Sari's mind.

They were guarded by the scribes, but the singers were isolated. No longer could an Irina practice her healing or study a new agricultural practice in a neighboring territory. No longer could a pregnant singer hunt with her mate. No longer could an artist take a commission directly from a human patron or a singer compose music for a human church. Mothers were cosseted and pampered "for their safety" while children grew up isolated from the human world they were supposed to protect.

More and more, the Irin were withdrawing from the world around them. Sari had grown up isolated by geography, but nothing like the Irin children born now. It was a troubling time to think about raising a family.

As for the scribe houses...

As a watcher's mate, she was granted special permission to live in the scribe house that had once housed multiple warriors' families. Tala lived there as well, but only because of her position as seer. The Irina librarians and archivists had been sent away, along with the female healers.

Scribes were put in their place while singers were forced to live in an isolated rural retreat one hundred miles southwest of Paris. After a number of frightening incidents where singers were targeted by the French church, the scribes' council would hear no arguments to the contrary, and the singers' council had been divided. The Irina of France were hidden away; the rest of Europe followed suit.

"How far is the retreat from the scribe house?" she asked. "How are the roads?"

"Two days' ride." He squeezed her hand. "I know. I don't like it either."

There would be no jovial camaraderie among new Irina sisters, no cheerful songs in the house. Scribes without small children would only see their mates when they could be released from patrol and training. In Sari's mind, it was a recipe for disaster. She knew Damien did not approve of the practice, but he also understood why so many Irina chose to enter retreats and so many Irin males encouraged it.

"Is it so bad a thing to be in a place that is safer?"

Sari squeezed his hand and felt him squeeze back. They

might never agree, but she knew his concern came from a place of deep love. The only thing Damien truly feared was losing her, yet he had never held her back, even as his superiors encouraged him to do so. It had become "unseemly" for a watcher's mate to patrol with her scribe. Proper Irina pursued creative or intellectual pursuits, not war.

Sari no longer had any patience for science and soft magic. She had worked for a hundred years to be her mate's equal, but she knew he still outstripped her in the field. Since he was older, she could accept it, but Sari longed for more spoken magic to use in combat. According to her grandmother, the Irina had once been as feared in battle as the Irin. But then the world had gentled and much martial magic had been lost.

Why would the Irina need martial magic? She could hear the voices already. The scribes were there to protect them. Irina magic was meant for healing and building. Growing and creating. Martial magic was ugly and hard, not nearly refined enough for the tongue of heaven's daughters. The ignorance was rife among singers and scribes both.

Gabriel's fist, she thought with a growing scowl. *What have we done to ourselves?*

"Sari!" Tala barreled out of the house and into Sari's arms as soon as she jumped out of the carriage. "I missed you. I missed you so much."

"I missed *you*. Has it truly been seven years?"

"Eight." Tala sniffed and wiped her eyes, one arm still hanging around Sari's neck. "I can't believe you're here."

"I can't either." Sari laughed through her own tears. "Grandmother must have had to intervene."

Tala laughed but didn't let go, even as the sisters turned to walk into the house. Sari glanced over her shoulder to see Damien's fond smile and warm eyes. He quietly instructed the young scribe driving the carriage and grabbed Sari's valise from the interior. As they approached the house, Tala's mate came to the door.

"Well met, Watcher." Gabriel held out his hand, grasping Damien's at the wrist before he pulled him into a hug. "Well met, brother."

"Does the fire still burn in this house?" Damien asked.

"It does," Tala said, her arm squeezing Sari's waist. "And you are welcome to its warmth. You and your own."

As the seer of the house, Tala was subordinate only to Damien as watcher. She and Gabriel had been in charge of the Paris house until Damien could arrive, the previous watcher having already departed for his new post in Hamburg.

Tala finally released Sari and went to embrace Damien. "Brother, it is so good to see you."

Sari went to Gabriel, and the quiet Spanish scribe pulled her into a tight hug. Sari hadn't been sure she would like her sister's mate, but she did, as did Damien. They both had great respect for Gabriel's character and devotion to Tala. It wasn't easy being the mate of a seer. No mate could protect Tala from the demons that sometimes whispered to her, and there was little Gabriel could do at times except guard her body while she wandered in her mind.

"She is so happy," Gabriel whispered. "I think you are as well."

She patted his cheek. "Now we are as we always should have been. Tala and I were never meant to be apart."

"I'm glad you're here." Gabriel turned to Damien. "And you! I have a stack of letters for you to answer. Welcome to Paris."

"The blessings of leadership," Damien said. "I await them after we've taken rest."

"And a bath." Sari pulled off her cloak. "The crossing was safe, but I've slept in caves that were more comfortable."

"But secure." Damien put an arm around her and kissed her temple. "Safety is more important than comfort."

"So you say." They entered a large, well-appointed scribe house that felt empty without the bustle of singers and children. Sari saw the library open and a few younger scribes wander out, curious about the new watcher and his mate. But no songs rose from the kitchen. No children ran underfoot.

Damien's thoughts must have mirrored her own. "It's different than I remember."

Gabriel said, "The previous house was torn down when the ritual fire was moved to this one. It doesn't have the age or magic that the old house did, but the location is better to keep an eye on the city as it grows."

"And the retreat?"

"Farther than we would like," Gabriel said. "But secure. The landowner who controls the area has an understanding with the council. The roads are good. I've worked out a rough schedule for the mated scribes so that they're not long from their families."

"We'll talk about how to rotate some of the unmated scribes into the retreat as well," Damien said.

"The unmated?" Gabriel asked.

"It's not healthy for our younger brothers to be long away from their Irina sisters," Damien said. "Mated or not, our men need the influence of Irina."

Tala smiled. "I hadn't thought of that," she said. "But you are right."

They chatted for a few more minutes, Damien and Sari greeting the scribes that were in the house and hearing reports of those who were patrolling, along with two more who were investigating rumors of a highwayman north of the city whom Gabriel suspected was a Grigori in truth.

By the time they were able to retreat to their new quarters,

Sari was nearly dead on her feet. She sank into a large copper tub filled with steaming water and let her eyes close. Damien came to her side, crouching down and running a finger across her cheek.

"You speak Norse with her."

"Norwegian," she corrected. "Do we really?"

"You do."

"I suppose it's a good thing you've learned it then."

"Does Gabriel speak it?"

"I think so. I've lost track of all the languages he knows." She leaned her head on his shoulder. "Even more than you, I think."

Damien picked up the pitcher on the floor and dipped it in the tub. Then he tipped her head forward and poured the warm water over the golden hair he loved.

"Modern houses…," Sari murmured. "I could become accustomed to this comfort."

"Don't linger too long unless you want company, *milá*. Or a stinking man in bed."

Sari laughed and put her hand on his cheek. His jaw was rough and stubbled. She missed the beard he'd once had, but her mate had learned long ago to blend with modern human fashion as a means of camouflage.

"Come in the bath with me."

He pressed a kiss to the curve of her neck. "We're too tall. I was jesting, Sari. Take as long as you like. Enjoy your bath." He stripped off his shirt before he knelt next to her again and poured another pitcher of water down her back as Sari enjoyed the rose-oil soap someone had placed by the tub. She scrubbed at the grime of their journey as Damien washed the suds away.

Sari sighed and leaned forward on her knees. "I promise I won't leave you with a cold bath. Just a few minutes more."

Damien ran the soap up her spine. "I shall endeavor to amuse myself."

Clever fingers she never tired of. He traced her spine with his knuckles and dug his thumbs into the tight muscles at her lower back. He brushed the wet strands of her hair to the side and kneaded her shoulders until Sari felt boneless.

She blinked awake when she felt the water cool. "You let me fall asleep."

"You were exhausted."

Sari stood and reached for a linen wrap hanging nearby. "You should have woken me. The water will be cold."

Damien's eyes caressed her form even as she wrapped the clean linen around her body.

"I have other plans now," he said. "Forget the bath."

Sari laughed and tugged at the breeches he was still wearing. "Bathe yourself. I promise I'll make the cold water up to you in a warm bed."

He caught her laughing lips in a kiss, opening her mouth with his tongue and teasing a delicious shiver from her. He commanded her. Her heart. Her body. Sari was almost embarrassed by how she let him rule her.

Nipping at her lower lip, Damien said, "Go. Warm my bed, mate."

"Who will wash your back?"

"I'll manage." He tugged at her wrap. "Go before this comes off you and you get wet again."

"Is that a promise?"

"Yes."

SARI WOKE IN THE MIDDLE OF THE NIGHT TO THE SOUNDS OF retching down the hall. She sat up and swung her legs over the edge of the bed.

"Sari?"

"I think it's Tala," she whispered. "Go back to sleep. I'm going to help Gabriel."

"Need me?" he murmured.

"No, love." She brushed a kiss over his cheek. "Sleep."

Sari wrapped her dressing gown around her and slid her feet into warm slippers she'd placed by the bed. The house was new, but the floors were still freezing. She lit a candle and opened their chamber door. Quiet voices and a soothing song drifted down the hall.

"Tala?"

The voices stopped, but Gabriel came to the door. "Sari? I'm sorry we woke you. Tala is fine."

"Can I help?"

Gabriel opened the door wider and ushered her inside. Tala was pale and resting on a chaise by the fire while two young scribes cleaned the floor and changed the linens.

"Such a bother," her sister muttered, a hand pressed over her eyes. "If they'd wait for me to feel better—"

"Don't be silly," Sari interrupted her. "You have to bear the visions. Let others care for you in our way."

Gabriel gave her a conspiratorial wink and handed her a cool cloth. "For the headache."

"I remember."

Sari went to Tala and scooted her sister forward until she could sit behind her and draw her head back. Tala sighed and rested her head on Sari's shoulder as she had when they were girls.

"Cloth?"

"On my neck."

"Your temples?"

"Like spikes."

Sari placed the cool cloth around Tala's neck and began to rub her temples as she hummed a healing song their mother had sung when the visions first started to wake in Tala at age twelve. She finished one song as Gabriel and the brothers cleaned the room, then segued into another as the tension started to leach out of her sister.

They were alone when Tala let out a long sigh. "It's the same vision. Over and over."

"Do you want to talk about it?"

"No." She shifted in Sari's arms. "Maybe."

"The same vision. That's significant, isn't it?"

"Yes."

"Time?"

"It's past. I wake up in the forest near home. It's present. I see the war. Whatever battles we've most recently heard of, I'm seeing them. But it's the future that scares me."

Sari combed her fingers though Tala's long hair. "War is always a frightening time. And this war has come on the heels of revolution."

"It's not the war, it's the silence," Tala murmured.

"The silence?"

Sari could tell that Tala was drifting off. "No one is there. All the children…"

The hairs rose on the back of Sari's neck. "What about the children?"

"Gone." Tala turned her face to Sari's shoulder. "They're all gone."

Her sister's shoulders relaxed into an exhausted sleep, but Sari's eyes rose to the doorway. Damien had roused himself, his hair and nightclothes were rumpled, but his eyes were narrowed and keen. He watched Tala as she slept, his eagle eyes distant. Sari could almost see the thoughts shifting in his mind.

He was the blood of Mikael's line.

Sari looked down at the pale woman in her arms. Her sister had never been a warrior but had seen visions of death and violence when her cheeks still carried the roundness of youth.

Tala was Damien's sister, but she was also his seer. Part of the reason the council had transferred him to Paris was because they needed his expertise. Meager their possessions might have been, but among them was wrapped the black knife that had killed the angel in Scotland and brought her mate back onto a warrior's path.

When she looked back up, Damien was watching her.

"We'll talk in the morning."

Sari wrapped her arms more tightly around Tala and nodded before he walked away.

CHAPTER

TWO

IF there was one thing that Damien hadn't missed during his time of isolation in Orkney, it was record keeping and correspondence. The Irin could be a singularly pedantic race. They loved their records and journals, letters and ledgers. As a scribe, Damien knew he should love them too. But while translation and research filled something in his soul, the rote transmission of information did not.

And damn if there wasn't an abundance of information in Paris.

"As you can see"—Gabriel shuffled through piles of papers on Damien's desk—"Ensel decided that many of these needed to be answered by the new watcher, not the old."

Damien lifted an eyebrow. "A bill for the stonemason he hired needed to be paid by me?"

"Let us say that he was not pleased to be leaving this post."

"He had been here for seventy years."

"And he enjoyed the lights of Paris." Gabriel tossed another letter on the pile. "His transfer to Kiev was not something he anticipated."

"His mate?"

Gabriel shrugged. "Many a watcher has a mate who is an asset to the house. Who are, in fact, essential to its health."

"And there are some who are not."

"Patricia will not be missed by either the scribes of the house or their families. She was the one who urged Ensel to move the house singers from Paris to the retreat not long after they came."

Damien steepled his fingers. "Why?"

"She said for their safety. Abra—who was the healer here —will tell you Patricia was a jealous woman who always resented that she and Ensel were not *reshon*. She was insecure in their union."

Damien snorted. "Ridiculous. You and Tala are not, and I have rarely seen two people more suited for each other."

A smile touched the corners of Gabriel's lips. "Thank you, brother."

"Do you think we could get a reversal from Vienna?"

Gabriel's eyebrows rose. "About the singers in the retreat?"

"Yes."

"Doubtful. The council has become intractable in the matter. Exceptions such as mates and seers like Tala are one thing, but a baker, an archivist, or a seamstress? What need is there for them to be in a scribe house instead of a guarded retreat?"

"A healer then," Damien said. "None of the scribes here is a trained healer."

"We didn't need to be with Abra around. But then Patricia…"

"Enough," Damien said. "Do you think she would come back?"

"Abra? Farrin is here. Of course she would."

Farrin, the healer's mate, was a capable scribe who served as the weapons master of the house. Damien had already met and spoken with the man. He liked his brusque demeanor and quiet steadiness. Abra was a small singer from North Africa who had mated with Farrin when he was learning to forge blades in Spain.

"There is no excuse for not having a healer in the scribe house. Frankly, I think it was foolish to move her to the retreat, but I don't know if the village can spare her at this point."

Gabriel scratched his chin. "There is a family with child at the moment, but it is their second. They may not need a healer so close if the singer has had an easy birth in the past."

"Ask. And Abra should have an apprentice anyway. Suggest it to her as a way to lighten the load. If none is available in the village, call one from the nearest Irina training house."

"The closest house is in Brittany."

"That will work; just get me a healer."

He shuffled through more bills regarding the house and a few that were legitimate items for him to deal with as the new watcher. Correspondence from nearby houses in Lyon and Brussels. A transfer request from one of the scribes in order to be closer to a sister who had lost her mate. A request for seclusion in a Rafaene house for another scribe. The list of tasks went on and on. He would spend weeks just answering letters.

"Are we going to request permission?" Gabriel said.

"For what?"

"For moving Abra back to the house if she is able to come."

Damien scowled. "Who would we ask?"

"The council."

"The council has no need to dictate how I run my scribe house," Damien said. "They moved me here and I will run it as I see fit."

Gabriel snorted.

"What?"

"Tala said that you and Sari are equally ill-tempered when others question you. No, I told her, Damien is a quiet, steady sort. He's not a troublemaker."

He had to smile. "If you thought that, then I'm doing my job correctly. Once I've gone through these papers, I'll expect a report from you too."

Gabriel had been assigned to the Paris scribe house because Tala was there. Seers and their mates were never separated. Luckily, the geographic position gave the mapmaker access to an extensive network of contacts from his days as an explorer. Damien was thrilled to have such a skilled spy working with him. The Spaniard could slip in and out of conversations with ease, lulling most Irin into thinking he was merely an academic. Those who discounted him did so at their peril.

A tapping sounded at the door, and Tala poked her head in. "A moment of your time, Watcher?"

Wondering if this had anything to do with the vision she'd suffered the night before, Damien nodded.

Gabriel rose and walked to the door. Kissing both his mate's cheeks, he said, "Am I being banished, *amor*?"

Sari's face broke into the smile of a well-loved woman. "Only for a little while."

Gabriel whispered something in her ear that made Tala's cheeks flush, then turned to Damien. "I'll send a message to Abra about moving back."

Tala's face lit. "Is Abra moving back?"

"We can hope." He brushed a hand over her cheek and left, closing the door behind him.

Damien waited for Tala to sit before he spoke. "Does this have to do with your vision?"

"Yes," Tala said, a hint of steel in her soft golden eyes. "But before I tell you, you must promise me that you will *not* tell Gabriel."

"You're certain it's his voice?" Damien asked after Tala had related her dream. "His specifically?"

"Yes."

"Is that common?"

She shook her head. "I don't think I have ever heard his voice in a vision before. Usually they are very... vague. I rarely recognize exact details. But this was definitely his voice."

Damien flipped a dagger end over end, thinking. "Just at the end."

"Yes."

"In the new house. The mansion."

"Yes."

"But the battle changes?"

Tala nodded. "None of the other elements change but the battle. I don't see the reports in detail, but it sounds as if whatever battle is happening most recently is what I'm seeing. The uniforms change, but other than that..." She shrugged helplessly. "I'm not a strategist, so I could not tell you more than that."

"If that is the part changing, then it seems the least important." He kept flipping the dagger. "The beginning is in your home. Familiar, but not familiar."

"The empty clothes," Tala said.

"And the Salamanca house..."

"Again, something from my past. Familiar, but not familiar."

"The past cannot change," Damien said. "The present— the battle you walk through—is constantly changing."

"And the mansion?"

He scowled. "I can't help but think of this house. It's new. In the same style—"

"But it is *not* this house. Nothing about it is the same. The exterior. The interior. The house in the dream was far more

ELIZABETH HUNTER

fashionable. Like those in Saint Germain. Large and airy with many windows."

"Is it a real house or a representation?"

"I have no way of knowing that," Tala said. "Experience tells me it could be either. It doesn't feel as if anyone lives there. It feels…"

"What?"

"Empty and crowded at the same time."

Damien gave her an incredulous look as Tala threw up her hands.

"I know! This is the way things appear in my head. I know it doesn't make sense to others."

"The house is empty but crowded." Damien paused. "Silent, but you hear voices. Including Gabriel's shouting *no*."

"Yes." She twisted the handkerchief on her lap. "It is."

Damien took a deep breath. "It goes against my instincts not to tell your mate these things, sister."

"I do not command you any more than you command me." Tala's face was pinched. "But please don't. He would go looking for it."

"And what if he did? Your mate is a formidable scribe." Something in Damien's stomach tugged at him. "Are you telling me everything?"

"As much as I can remember."

She was lying. Damien recognized the steady look that Sari sometimes gave when she was deceiving people. He recognized it, though his mate had never used it on him. He decided to keep quiet. For now.

"If you see this house, you will tell me," he said. "And if anything about the dream changes, you will keep me informed."

Tension eased from her shoulders. "Of course, Watcher."

"You're my sister, but you are also my seer. And you and I both know that seers are targeted by the Grigori. I have too much respect for you to set a guard on you, but I'd appreciate if you were cautious. If you're uncertain about anything, take Sari with you."

Tala smiled. "She would like to lock me in a retreat for my own good."

"Lock a singer up for her own safety?" Damien raised an eyebrow. "Where would she get that idea?"

"I can't imagine," Tala said. "But do not fear for me. I know my sister and I know my own strengths. I am no fighter. Sari, however, is as fierce as most of the scribes here."

"No, she's fiercer."

"I *love* you for her." Tala's voice softened. "I always worried that we would find our mates and one of us would dislike the other's. But I don't. I think you're perfect together."

"That's because you haven't seen us fight," he said. "Once you live with us for a time, you won't like me so well. Of course, you might not like your sister as much either."

Tala laughed. "I'll take my chances."

DAMIEN WAS WATCHING THE MEN DRILL IN THE COURTYARD behind the house when Gabriel joined him. The knowledge that he was concealing something from Tala's mate sat like lead in his gut, but he had to respect Tala's wishes.

Seers held special rank within the scribe house. If Damien broke her trust and Tala hesitated to come to him with another vision because of it, the warriors under his command could suffer.

"She's as fast as the younger men." Gabriel nodded at Sari, who was practicing with the scribes.

"She's faster with the staff," he said. "It is only with the blade that she struggles."

"The weight?"

He gave a short nod. "She will never be able to carry a blade as easily as a scribe, though she is better than a human."

"Does it bother her?"

"Yes." He watched Sari put one of his new men on the ground by spotting a weakness in his stance and exploiting it. "But she knows her strengths and plays to them."

Sari used her body far more than Irin males. Used balance and cunning. He'd trained her that way, mirroring some of the early lessons from his mother when he was a child. She would never be able to heft a blade as he could, but she could beat him with the staff. And the staff could be a far more useful weapon as it could be concealed in plain sight.

Gabriel said, "You'll never progress politically with her as a mate. Not in the current climate."

"That makes me love her more. Not less." Damien smiled. "I don't see you being called to the city any day soon either, my brother."

Gabriel shrugged. "Tala's parents' views are out of favor at the present time, but these things change."

Damien looked at Gabriel with new eyes. "Do you *want* political advancement?"

"Tala will advance within the hierarchy." Gabriel's jaw was set. "That is no vision. That is reality. No matter how much her parents voice their dissatisfaction with the present state of Irina autonomy and the growth of the retreats, Tala's grandmother is an elder and Tala's reputation as a seer is growing. She will be in Vienna eventually."

Damien began to see his brother's mind. "And she'll need a mate who can navigate the political waters better than she can."

"She has no interest in politics." Gabriel gave him a rueful smile. "Her heart is too generous. Others would use her and her talents for their own ends, given the chance."

"Then it is a good thing that she has you as a mate," Damien said.

"Indeed."

"Did you find the answers you were looking for within the court?"

Gabriel handed him a sealed report. "Four."

"That many?"

"In the chaos of the Napoleonic court"—Gabriel clearly wasn't fond of the term—"four Grigori are easily concealed. The only humans who might notice a threat are consumed by their emperor's latest campaign."

"He's brilliant," Damien said. Tyrant or not, he had to admire the French general's military acumen. His mother would be convinced Napoleon had Mikael's blood if it were possible.

"The Frenchman overreaches."

"Says the Spaniard."

Gabriel grinned. "Says the spy."

"These Grigori in the court… they must be circumspect in their habits."

"According to the humans I spoke to, they take many lovers and appear to be quite popular with the society wives and actresses, though they are also known for not spending more than a single night with a woman."

Damien raised an eyebrow. "Not generally a trait to recommend them to a human lover."

"It doesn't matter," Gabriel said. "These are sons of the Fallen. The humans are enamored with them. Men and women both."

"Who do they belong to?"

"I cannot say for certain, but I believe they belong to the archangel Volund."

"One of the northern angels?"

Gabriel nodded. "Volund and Barak are at odds. Volund stayed in the Russian territories for centuries, but he has recently been moving into the Baltic region, which puts him in conflict with Barak."

Damien narrowed his eyes. "So what is he doing in Paris?"

"According to my predecessor, Volund is curious about this new regime. His sons fled during the revolution, but he's sent some back to explore the political climate. See if it might be worth Volund's attention."

"And no human deaths?"

"One, but it was discounted as natural, and I cannot say otherwise." Gabriel shrugged. "The young lady was known to be of weak constitution."

Damien nodded and watched the men and Sari sparring. "So there are four Grigori in Napoleon's court, but they seem to be... behaving. Does this have anything to do with the surge of Grigori present in the city?"

"I don't know." Gabriel was obviously irritated. "They're in the city, but if they're hunting, they're doing it so discreetly we hear no rumor of it."

"And the news from Belgium?"

Gabriel dropped his voice. "The rumors are true. It wasn't human violence. A retreat *was* attacked. A massacre. Only a few scribes were present because a majority had been called to Brussels to deal with a surge in Grigori attacks there. The retreat was fortunate that two of the Irina there were trained in offensive magic and were able to hold off the worst of it."

Damien felt the chill in his bones. "Deaths?"

"A dozen singers. Five children."

"Heaven above, Gabriel." Damien closed his eyes and took a deep breath. "Did they have any warning?"

"No." Gabriel's face was grim. "I'm telling you, if there hadn't been two combat-trained Irina there, the whole retreat could have been devastated. If they had been populated as most retreats are—with scholars and untrained singers—they would have been."

"Is this a new Grigori tactic?" Damien asked. "To attack our women and children?"

"They never have before, but anything is possible. It's

equally possible this was a freak occurrence. The Grigori involved were hunted and executed too quickly."

"They were not questioned?"

"The scribes who killed them were enraged."

"Hardly surprising," Damien said. "But not helpful for the rest of us."

"Agreed."

Damien thought long and hard, but the choice seemed obvious. "The human wars are not our concern. Grigori numbers in the city are up, but attacks on the population are down. We move more of the warriors to the retreat for now. I'll write to the elders in Vienna—"

"It could take months to hear back from them with the Austrian campaign starting."

"That's why I'm not waiting. Guarding our families is more important, and the men will be distracted anyway once word of the Belgian massacre spreads. We reassign scribes for at least a year to make sure this was a random attack and not a new pattern."

"I agree," Gabriel said, turning back to the men training in the courtyard. "What a time we live in, brother."

Damien's eyes lay only on Sari. They lived in a dangerous world, no matter how well-trained they both were. War was a way of life for the Irin. Would this cloud always hang over them? Sari's decision to delay bearing a child seemed reasonable, but…

A dark thought swirled in the back of his mind.

What if she was taken from him? What if Damien was one of the grieving scribes in Belgium mourning the loss of his mate? Would he curse every moment they delayed their life together to answer the call of duty?

CHAPTER
THREE

One year later

S ARI strolled through the retreat, the quaint streets of
the Irin village humming with life and growth. She was
walking barefoot, feeling her newly sprung magic in the
ground twining with older paths and appreciating the easier
country fashions that freed her body.

It was spring, and war seemed far away, at least in their
region. The crops had been successful the year before—
helped along, Sari was sure, by the extra hands of the scribes
who were spending more and more time in the retreat. Even
Sari and Damien had a cottage there. When the weather in
Paris was sweltering, the fresh air of the country held more
and more appeal.

The village was isolated but flourishing. Fifty families now
lived in the community along with a group of scholars who
tended a growing library and had become known for their
translation of Irin folktales. Two children had been born that
year, and Sari knew the longing she tried so hard to ignore was
only growing stronger.

She turned toward the sound of laughter in the distance.

The children of the village were playing with the new lambs in the pasture.

Despite Sari's initial misgivings about living in the retreat —which had felt so much like a prison before—the peace and community soothed her and fed the elemental magic in her soul. It was easy and comfortable to be around other singers and scribes.

Life in Paris could be stressful, particularly when human scrutiny became too intense. In the village, there were children shouting. Teachers and scholars talked about ancient interpretations of obscure scrolls while the more pragmatic of their race conversed about crops and horse breeding, which was one of the few trades that involved them in the human world. The community sang and ate together, reminding Sari of the tiny village where she and Damien had first fallen in love.

Speaking of love…

Sari spotted Gabriel and Tala sitting under a tree on the edge of the forest. Her sister was straddling her mate's legs, speaking animatedly as Gabriel smiled up at her and braided pieces of her hair. Occasionally his lips moved, but mostly his eyes rested on Tala.

His adoration was so open, so honest, Sari almost looked away. But she didn't.

Watching her twin bloom under Gabriel's love was one of the most beautiful things Sari had ever seen. Tala had always been the quiet, less vibrant twin, despite her enormous talent. She paid an awful price for her "gift." Growing up, it had been Sari who flourished in their rowdy, affectionate clan while Tala lingered on the edges.

Gabriel's love transformed her.

He caught Sari's eye and sent her a smile across the lane. Then he interrupted Tala's tale and helped his mate to her feet, though not before he gave her bottom a pinch that had Tala laughing and blushing.

"How long have you been waiting for me?" she asked.

"Not long," Sari said. "I didn't want to interrupt."

"It wasn't anything important," Tala said, waving a hand. "I was telling Gabriel about the novel Miriam sent me."

Sari hooked her arm in her sister's and gave her a squeeze. "That's important."

"Not really." She smiled. "But he's a good listener."

"I know." Sari heard the children's laughter again. Both she and Tala turned to look, letting their eyes rest on the merry sight.

"The war seems to be waning," Sari said.

"My visions come less and less." Tala raised a hand to shield her eyes. Her eyes were fixed on the pasture, as were Sari's.

Sari's sister didn't tell her what the visions were. Tala told Damien, and sometimes Damien told Sari. But often Tala's visions were elusive, nascent things needing weeks or even years of contemplation. Leoc's daughters had always seen this way. No vision came without sacrifice and pain, but the wrenching dreams were fewer these days than they ever had been before.

"You're feeling healthier."

"I am." Tala's eyes—so filled with joy a moment before—took on a shadow of sadness despite the bright spring day.

Sari put her head on Tala's shoulder. "What is it? Why are you sad?"

Tala paused, her eyes lost in the distance, her words almost a whisper. "I want a child, Sari. I want Gabriel's child so badly it is an ache in my gut worse than any vision I've experienced."

Sari wasn't surprised. "We cannot retreat from service right now. Even if the human war ceases."

"We will never be able to retreat from service," Tala said. She put her hand down and turned to her sister. "I will never stop seeing visions. You and Damien will always fight."

"I know this."

"Does that mean we will never bear our own children? We are not destined to sing the songs of our grandmothers and feel new life growing within us? Never give our mates the joy and honor of fatherhood? Is that what this life means now?"

"Tala—"

"I know you want a child too," her sister said. "I have seen the way you watch the children and new mothers."

She did want a child. Like Tala, Sari felt the pain of empty arms. Unlike Tala, her longing was tinged with anger and bitterness. Who were the council to deem that pregnant Irina could not fight the Grigori? Had her race become so fragile?

"Damien wants a child," she said. "He's wanted a child for so many years."

"You do too. At least admit it."

Sari nodded. "I do."

They walked a little longer in silence. When they reached the edge of the forest where the protection spells shielded them, Tala finally spoke.

"I'm going to sing Uriel's Petition," she said. "I'm going to talk to Gabriel, but I know he feels the same. He has waited for me to be ready."

Uriel, one of the oldest of the Forgiven, was also the one who granted the gift of life. Unlike the humans, who could become pregnant easily, Irina rarely conceived without magic. Though it did happen, an Irina most often sang Uriel's Petition before she and her mate wanted to conceive. One of the most ancient spells, it called on the magic of the Forgiven to bless a union with a child. Most couples only had one or two children, though mates could be together for hundreds of years. It was the blessing and the curse of their long lives.

"Sing it with me." Tala's face shone. "We are here. Together in this place. Who knows when either of us could be moved by new orders. Think of it, Sari. We could share this joy as sisters."

Sari's heart ached. She could see Tala and her, swollen with child, laughing with shared joy and expectation. Damien and Gabriel, proudly presenting the new babes to the elders of the village, brushing spells for newborns over their soft skin. Cousins born close together were rare and treasured.

"Please, Sari."

Tears threatened her eyes. "I'll think on it, Tala. I promise."

"You said that last year. You've thought about it long enough. I know my sister. We might never get another reprieve like this. Grigori attacks are rare. The retreat is stable and flourishing. The Paris house has more than enough scribes to cover the city and patrol the village. Even the humans make noises about truces and peace."

Sari's heart sped when she considered Tala's words. Could she? Should she? "I can't just... decide like that. I have to think."

"You think too much!" her sister said. "You debate every decision like you were on the council itself. You argue with Damien. Argue with Gabriel. Argue with *me*. For once, Sari, what does your heart say?"

"Yes," she blurted out. "My heart says yes."

Tala's smile glowed like the sun. "Then don't you think you should follow it?"

Her heart raced. Nerves? Excitement? "Yes?"

"Sing with me," Tala said, gripping both her hands. "Let us share this joy. Don't let duty rule everything in our lives, sister. We deserve happiness too."

"Yes." Now that Sari had said it, it seemed so much easier to say it a second time. And a third. She felt peace. Her own smile grew, though it couldn't be as incandescent as Tala's. "Yes, I'll... I'll talk to Damien tonight."

Tala threw her arms around Sari's neck. "He won't say no."

"You know this could take years, don't you?" Her pragmatic mind couldn't help but creep in. "There is no guarantee that you and I will be pregnant together."

"I know." Tala wiped her eyes but couldn't stop smiling. "But I hope it doesn't. I hope we can share this. Even if our babies are a few years apart, they will grow to be the best of friends."

SARI LAY IN THEIR BED IN THE VILLAGE, WATCHING DAMIEN undress and perform his ritual prayers. He carefully washed his body in the small basin and dried himself with clean linen, his talesm glowing faintly with magic as he spoke. A few drops of water lingered on his back, rolling slowly down the hard ridges of muscle on either side of his spine. She read the ancient magic of the family marks his father had tattooed on him, dark and elaborate with medieval grandeur. Damien's family was old and his line one of Mikael's purest blood. The dense spells covering his body seemed to move and surge as he prayed.

Sari closed her eyes and smiled.

Her mate's low voice murmuring prayers had become Sari's nightly lullaby, as soothing as the songs her mother and grandmother had sung through her childhood. She loved Damien's voice and often thought it was a tragedy that his magic could not be sung. When he joined his voice with hers, it brought her to tears. When she closed her eyes and listened to his soul, she knew what heaven sounded like.

"What has brought that smile to your face, *milá*?" Damien sat on the end of the large bed he'd made especially for their home in the village. Both of them were tall. Here, they had a bed they could roll in, and Sari and Damien took full advantage of it. "Hmm?"

She kept her eyes closed and felt the bed dip as he crawled

up to her, biting her thigh, brushing his lips over her belly, nibbling at her throat. Neither of them slept in nightclothes except in the coldest of winters, so every inch of him was exposed to every inch of her. She tried not to giggle, but he teased her neck mercilessly.

"What has given my Sari laughter today?" he said.

"You."

He stretched out next to her, leisurely reacquainting his mouth with the soft skin he knew so well. "If I have given you joy, then my day was well spent. But please, acquaint me with this success so that I may repeat it."

She put her palm to his rough cheek and pressed him closer, her heart suddenly seizing with the depth of love she felt for him. He was everything she'd never been able to dream. The desire of her heart. Her true mate. On days she wasn't able to see him because of duty or travel, she felt half alive.

"I love you so much, Damien."

He lifted his head and his eyes were soft. "What is it, love?"

They'd talked of it endlessly, but on the night she let her heart surrender, Sari felt shy. What if he'd changed his mind? He hadn't brought up the subject of children in almost a year. Because he'd given up on her or had decided that waiting was wise?

"I know the words," she said softly. "I think I've known them forever. But will you sing Uriel's Petition with me?"

For a moment his whole body froze, then his mouth was on hers with such passion, such raw desire, that Sari felt like she'd been transported back to the barley field where they had first kissed.

"Truly?" he asked when he came up for air. "Truly, milá?"

"Yes."

"You're certain?" He didn't seem to believe her.

Sari knew in that moment how much he'd held back his own desire for a family.

"Truly, truly, truly." She pushed him to his back and knelt over him, peppering his face with kisses. "I want a child so much, Damien. *Your* child. Tala and I spoke today, and she's right. There will never be the perfect time, but we are more than duty. Our life, our family, should not stop."

"My love." He brushed her long hair back from her face and twisted it around his fist, drawing her down to meet his mouth. He had tears in his eyes. "I am blessed by the heavens to call you my mate."

"I kept you waiting long enough." She put a finger on his mouth when he opened it to protest. "Not that I have decided this because you pressured me. You have been the picture of patience, and I am grateful."

He put a hand low on her belly. "Sari of Vestfold will carry my child." He smiled, and she saw a hint of the arrogant warrior he sometimes allowed to peek through. "Our child."

Damien should rightly have been arrogant—he was a warrior of fierce reputation, legendary bloodlines, and meticulous training—but he'd never carried himself as such. She asked him once why he pursued humility, and her mate told her he'd seen far greater warriors die when it should have been him. He was too grateful, he said, to be proud.

"I will carry your child, Damien of Bohemia"—the corner of her mouth curved up—"but you'll have to bed me first."

He rolled them over and pressed his hips between her legs. She could feel him, already hard and eager. Damien hooked her long leg over his forearm and spread her thighs wider.

His voice was rough when he spoke. "Sing, then."

She was breathless with wanting him. "Like this?"

"Just like this." His mouth hovered over hers. His teeth nipped at her lower lip. His voice whispered decadence. "*Sing.*"

Sari took a deep breath and felt her breasts press against his chest. His low rumble of a voice joined hers when she began the ancient song. She felt the magic swell and grow between them, and their mating marks lit.

> First of the forgiven
> Giver of life
> Father of our people
> We pray...

The heat remained in his eyes, but Damien's hand was soft at her cheek. He was propped on his elbows, his body covering hers like a blanket. Sari was reminded of the Hebrew poetry of the great King Solomon: "He brought me to the banqueting house, and his banner over me was love."

> As heaven's waters meet the earth
> Let our union reflect creation
> Let us bring forth life

She felt him between her legs, tormenting her, arousing her. She was panting for him when she finished the song.

> For the glory of heaven
> Uriel, father of heaven,
> First of the Forgiven
> Bless us with new life.

At the final words of the song, Damien thrust into her, sealing their union with a savage kiss. He rose up and surged forward, the magic lighting the talesm on his arms until they glowed like twin columns of silver fire. Sari threw her head back and closed her eyes, letting the power of his possession overwhelm her senses. The scent of magic and sweat. The taste of his skin and touch of his mouth. Their love had never been a soft thing. Though his tenderness could overwhelm her, theirs was a union of blood and bone.

I will carry his child.

Her heart grew until it ached in her chest. The love she held for Damien, a love she had thought consumed her, grew impossibly bigger. Deeper. Sank into her bones as she contemplated a new life growing from their union.

Uriel, give us this life, she prayed.

And give us eternity.

Six months later

THE PARIS SCRIBE HOUSE WAS HUMMING WITH ENERGY AND the sounds of happy brothers. Two of the warriors had been given permission to bring their mates into the city for the month, and Sari and Tala had welcomed the sisters, who were both easy, cheerful women. One was an excellent cook and the other was an earth singer like Sari who was determined to bring the neglected kitchen garden back to fruitful life.

Tala leaned over to Sari at breakfast. "You're pregnant."

Sari's eyes widened. "I'm not."

"You are."

She shut up when she heard the determined tone. Sari had stopped arguing with Tala about certain things when they were ten years old. Anytime Tala used that tone, it wasn't a time to argue.

"How do you know?"

A smile flirted at her sister's lips. "Because I had a dream last night."

Sari leaned forward. "I didn't hear you. Are you well? Did Gabriel——"

"I wasn't sick." Tala's face was glowing. "Not even a little. Maybe Leoc knows that I am with child too."

Sari's hand shot out and gripped Tala's wrist. "Truly?"

Her sister laughed. "Now you sound like Gabriel when I told him I wanted us to try."

"I cannot dare to hope. Are you certain? I feel no different, though I watch for signs every month."

"I'm certain." Tala knit their fingers together.

It had only been a few months. Her courses were late, but they had never followed a strict schedule. Though she and Damien had been spending themselves like new mates, Sari hadn't expected anything to happen so quickly. But Tala wouldn't tell her such a thing if she wasn't sure.

She let the smile break through. "I should tell Damien."

Tala laughed. "Wait until he's finished his meeting with Gabriel, and then we will both steal them away from their duties. It's been quiet lately, and Gabriel has just returned. His watcher will not begrudge him a few hours of celebration."

Sari glanced at the locked door of the library. Gabriel had returned from Spain last night, his face grim with worry or exhaustion. Sari couldn't tell which. He and Damien had been cloistered in the library before dawn broke.

"Did he tell you anything?"

Tala shook her head. "He had ridden all day. He fell into bed without even taking a bath. I do think there was something troubling him, but he wanted to speak to Damien first."

When the door to the library finally opened, Damien was the one at the door.

"Seer," he called to Tala. "Sari. A moment with both of you."

Damien calling Tala by her title told Sari the business of the scribe house waited. She and Tala took seats in the library, though Gabriel was quick to pull Tala onto the chaise beside him. Sari sat in the chair across from Damien at the table.

"What has happened?" Sari asked.

Damien looked at Gabriel.

"You know I spent the past month traveling," he said. "I've noticed a growing trend that troubles me, and I don't know what to make of it."

"Tell us," Sari said. "Perhaps another perspective may help."

When it came to strategy, Sari was an amateur compared to Damien. But often her mate's vast experience left him closed-minded to unexpected moves.

"We know what has happened in Paris. A growing Grigori population, but with none of the subsequent attacks on the humans. This has left us… stymied."

Because the stated mandate of the Irin Council was that no Irin could take action against a Grigori unless that son of the Fallen was threatening humans. It infuriated Sari. Did one wait until a fox broke into the chicken coop to drive the predator away? Nevertheless, the mandate had been the governing rule of their race since before Sari had been born.

"We have watched them, suspecting the worst," Gabriel continued, "but even our closest observation reveals no direct attacks. These Grigori are being particularly patient and feeding from enough humans that they are draining and killing none. Or none that we can prove."

"Have they suddenly grown a conscience?" Sari scoffed. "There must be attacks we're missing."

"There aren't." Damien's voice was final. "And I do not think conscience is at work. There is some other motive we have not guessed yet."

Tala took Gabriel's hand. "What did you discover on your journey?"

"The same thing is happening elsewhere," Gabriel said. "Madrid. Salamanca. Bordeaux. Tours. All are seeing an influx of Grigori, but no subsequent rise in attacks."

"They are setting the board," Sari said. "Like in chess, Damien."

Her mate had been teaching her the game of strategy, and she might have enjoyed it more than he did. Damien had been taught a variation of the modern game as a boy and drilled relentlessly in it to practice strategic thinking. For Sari, it was only a game. But a helpful one.

"That is my thinking as well," Damien said. "But for what? This slow rise has only increased Irin presence in each of these cities. As the roads improve, it becomes easier and easier to move about. Just in our house, we've taken on five new scribes in the past year."

Gabriel said, "And each of the houses has had a similar increase. All are working at full capacity. Some are building on to their houses in order to bring more."

Tala's head cocked to the side.

Sari said, "What do you see, Tala?"

"Nothing yet. It's more of a feeling. I have to think more."

Damien's eyes were locked on Tala. "Have you had any more visions? Abra said you were awake last night."

"Meddling healer," Tala muttered. "Nothing. Well yes, something, but not related to what we're talking about." A faint blush rose in her cheeks.

Damien said, "Whatever the vision was, I need to know it."

"I'm not sure this is the best—"

"Tala, I need to know."

Gabriel ran a hand down her back. "What is it, love?"

"Gabriel…" She halted and looked at Sari, her mouth hanging open. "Tell me what to do."

"Not this time." Sari tried to contain her smile. "And you're the one who is so certain."

Gabriel sat up straighter. "Tala?"

"I'm pregnant," she blurted out. "That's what the vision was about."

"I am too," Sari said. "At least according to my sister."

"*Amor.*" A stream of joyful Spanish fell from Gabriel's lips as he pulled Tala into an embrace.

Sari turned to Damien.

"Is it true?" he said, his eyes hopeful.

Sari nodded. "According to Tala, though I have not seen the signs yet."

Tears welled up, but he stood and walked around the table, folding her into his arms, tucking her face into his neck and gripping her hair with his fist.

"*Milá,*" he murmured. "My child."

"Our child."

"Sari of Vestfold is carrying my child," he whispered in her ear. "And she tells me this when I cannot thank her properly."

"You're the one who pushed Tala about her vision."

She felt the tension take his body. His arms tightened around her before he raised his head and forced her eyes to his.

"Damien?"

"You're moving to the retreat. Both of you. Today."

CHAPTER
FOUR

"DID you really think I would be rational about this?" He paced around their bedchamber. "Truly, Sari?"

"Did you think I would meekly trot off to the village without a word?" she asked him. "*Truly*?"

"I will not argue about this with you. In the end, I am your watcher as well as your mate."

Rage filled her eyes. "And if it was Abra who was with child? Your house healer? What then? Would she be packed off without a thought?"

"I *am* thinking. And it is not Abra! It's you."

"And I am your mate. Not your faithful soldier."

He rounded on her. "I know you're not my faithful soldier, because if you were, *you would do as I am commanding you!*"

"You do not command *me*," she yelled. "We agreed—"

"We agreed if you had a disagreement with one of my orders, you would speak to me in private, not storm out of the library in full view of my men, shouting that I was a dictator. Sari, I *am* your watcher. If you want to be treated as a warrior—"

"I am a warrior."

"Then act like one."

"Accord me the same respect you would give your men."

He threw his hand toward the door. "This is not because you're a woman. Didn't Marcel leave for the village last year when his mate was with child?"

"Because he asked to leave," she said. "Not because you commanded him."

"I would have commanded him if he hadn't asked. His mate needed to be protected."

They stood a foot apart, chests heaving. They both could explode when they were roused; this was hardly their first fight. Though Damien was usually the more even tempered, today it didn't matter. The moment Sari had told him she was with child, he felt it. Fierce, wild joy. And heart-gripping fear. He couldn't lose her. He wouldn't. It would destroy him.

"And you?" Angry tears were in her eyes. "Will you be coming to prison with me?"

"It is not a prison," he said. "And you know I cannot."

"It is a prison if I am forced to be there," she said.

He saw the light slipping from her eyes. The wild independence that had lured him from the beginning. It was like watching a falcon's wings clipped in front of him.

"Sari, please." He wouldn't relent. He couldn't. But he hated seeing that wild light flee. "You knew this would happen. You knew it. We've talked about it before."

Her voice was wooden. "I know."

"Then why—"

"Because now I know something is coming." She crossed her arms and turned her back to him. "And whatever it is, I will not be there to protect you if I am in the village. You will be here and I will be there. And if something happens, we will not be together."

"Sari…" He put his arms around her and hugged her back into his chest. His hand slipped down to her belly where their child was growing. He knew it was just his imagination, but he could feel the spark of the babe's soul. His and Sari's child. It was a dream he'd almost given up. "I survived many years without you, my love."

"But you weren't mine then," she said. "You didn't hold my heart in your hands, Damien. Now you do."

If there was anything he loved more than her spirit, it was the honesty of her emotions. Sari never held back. Happy or angry, he would know it. How often had he wished he could speak his feelings as easily as she did?

"I will take care of your heart," he said. "But I need you to take care of our child. And yourself. If you are here, I won't be able to concentrate. I'll only be thinking of you. The retreat is isolated from Grigori violence. Protected. You and Tala will be safe there."

He honed in on the mention of her sister. If there was anyone Sari was more protective of than even him, it was Tala. Did he feel guilty taking advantage of her protectiveness? Not if it kept her safe.

"The Grigori know who she is, Sari. They have always targeted seers, and once they learn of her pregnancy, she will be even more at risk. The only reason Gabriel doesn't go mad about her leaving the house and going into town now is because you always go with her. She needs to go to the retreat, and you need to go with her."

She finally clutched his hands, and Damien felt her soften. "I hate this. I hate the thought of being parted from you."

"A matter of months, *milá*. And then our child will be here. I will come to the village as often as I can. Farrin and Abra will be here. Gabriel and I can take turns visiting. We will not be parted for months. Only days, my love."

"It won't be the same."

"I know. Who will challenge my every command and question my every decision when you are gone?" He pinched her waist.

She sniffed. "You like it."

"I do." He kissed her jaw. "You make me better. Sharper."

"What will you do without me?"

Go slowly mad. Only the thought of their child calmed him. This was but a season of life, her grandmother would say. Damien had already decided he would request a sabbatical as other expecting fathers did. He did not want to miss a moment of his son or daughter's life.

"I'll write to the Watchers' Council tomorrow," he said. "I want to be with you. Not in the city."

Her hands clutched his. "They won't approve it."

"They'll have to. I'm not the only watcher whose mate has become pregnant. It is expected for warriors to ask for leave to raise children. I'm not the only one."

"But you're the only *you*."

Damien laughed. "I do love that your opinion of me is so elevated."

"It's not elevated. It's true."

He would admit the request would not be welcome, especially coming on the heels of the letter he knew Gabriel and Tala had sent that morning. For one house to lose both a seer and a watcher was not ideal. Damien wasn't going to ignore his elders, but he *would* be with his mate, even if he had to call in political favors from his family to be released from command.

"Sari, you do what you must to protect our child now," he said. "And I'll do what I must to protect both of you as soon as my request is granted. And it *will* be granted, if I have to ride to Vienna myself."

"Damien—"

"Enough." He held her tighter. "Enough fighting for now. We are having a child, Sari. A *child*. We've waited so long, *reshon*. Now is the time for joy."

He was writing the letter the next morning when Tala walked into his study.

"Sister." He rose and went to embrace her. "With all the fighting yesterday, I did not get the chance to congratulate you and Gabriel."

She smiled and hugged him back. "You didn't expect her to run off without an argument, did you?"

"No. I used you to convince her to go. Do you mind?"

"It's nothing I didn't expect," she said. "Gabriel and I have already sent a request to the singers' council."

"I'm writing my letter to the elders now."

"Good." She shivered and hugged her arms around herself. "I know something is coming. I can feel it. But we cannot stop living because a battle is on the horizon."

"A battle is *always* on the horizon."

"Exactly."

"You must promise me to send word if the vision starts again."

The disturbing vision of the empty house and Gabriel crying out had lessened in the past year and a half, but it hadn't ceased. She still mentioned it. Mentioned any changes. Mentioned the things that stayed the same. She'd even tried to draw the house she saw in detail, convinced it was a real place and not merely symbolic. He had the sketch in his desk, though he'd never shown it to Gabriel. Tala had made him promise.

"Sari says we leave tomorrow," she said. "When will you come to visit?"

"I told Gabriel to accompany you both to the village this time. I should be down next week. Farrin and Abra have been told, though they've promised not to breathe a word to the men."

"They'll know she is with child as soon as Sari tells them she's moving permanently to the retreat."

He grimaced. "Do me a favor, sister. Do not say the word 'permanently' in regard to the retreat."

Tala laughed. "You know what I mean. Only a child could tear her from a warrior's life."

Damien paused. "Did she do it for me?"

If she had, Tala would be honest. Kind, but honest.

But Tala shook her head. "She wants a child as much as you do."

He took a deep breath. "Are you sure?"

She gave him an impish grin. "All this doubt. Honestly, it's as if you think I do not see the future."

"Tala," he warned.

"Stow your temper, Damien. I'll have enough with just hers for the next few months."

"You're nothing but trouble."

"That's why I'm the little sister," she said. "But you love me anyway."

Damien couldn't stop the smile. He did. He would have loved Tala, if for no other reason than she made Sari so happy. But she was also a delight. Bright, cheerful, and funny. She was the calm balance to Sari's fiery personality. Damien had never had a sister, but that didn't matter to Tala. She'd loved him as an older brother from the start.

"She'll be sad," Tala said. "But don't worry. I'll keep her from brooding."

"See that you do."

THEY LEFT THE NEXT MORNING, SURROUNDED BY FARRIN, Gabriel, and five of Damien's fiercest men. Sari and he had taken their farewells in their room, unwilling to let the rest of the house see their bittersweet kisses. He was still their watcher. She was still their watcher's mate. Though he felt as if his heart left in the carriage with her, Damien was unwilling to show how keenly he already felt her absence.

He would see her soon. He knew that. It didn't make the parting easier.

"Watcher?"

Damien turned to see Auguste, one of the new scribes recently returned from the Near East, holding a report sealed in gold wax.

"A missive from Vienna?"

The young scribe nodded. "It arrived early this morning, but I did not want to disturb you or your mate before she took her leave."

"Thank you, brother."

He took it and retreated to his study. He'd only written to the council requesting leave that morning. The letter had left with the same courier that must have brought this one, so he knew it couldn't be a response to his or Tala's petitions. He broke the seal, recognizing the figure of a rearing horse that was the symbol of Attila, an elder scribe and distant relative of his mother's, who had always treated Damien as a nephew. He scanned the letter quickly before he began to read between the carefully composed lines.

...series of attacks...

...troubling trends in the east...

...shifts in power among the Fallen...

Damien felt his heart race. The beginning of the letter was a summary of recent findings from the council that warned European scribe houses about a power shift. The intelligence was based on rumors among the Fallen regarding happenings in the East. It matched many of the same patterns Gabriel had seen in their part of the world.

The end of the letter was a personal note from Attila to Damien.

"I cannot tell you what steps to take, Damjan. I can only tell you that the seers in Esztergom have seen visions of death and emptiness that match the reports you sent me from your own seer. The shift of Grigori into the cities of Western Europe has been matched to a lesser degree in Eastern Europe, and indeed in the East and Northern Africa as well. Inquiries to Southern Africa and the Far East have not yet been answered. The New World remains a mystery.

Take care. Be watchful and ready. I do feel the change in Fallen power indicates a growing threat of some kind. Though your father and I have argued in the Library, we are seen as tired old warhorses starting at threats where there are none. Too many of the elders are convinced that our future is secure in the retreats and we have no need to worry. I do not agree."

Damien closed the letter after reading it no less than five times. He felt Sari and Tala's absence keenly. He would have to wait five days for Gabriel to return. He was tempted to leave for the retreat himself but could not justify it when his mapmaker and weapons-master were away.

Brooding accomplished nothing. He locked the letter away and went to join his men. Grigori attacks might have become rare, but he had no intention of letting his scribes become soft. If long life had taught him anything, it was that change was inevitable and that while luck was fleeting, fortune favored those who were vigilant.

CHAPTER
FIVE

S ARI closed her eyes and pretended to sleep. Damien
was stretched out next to her, his long, graceful fingers
trailing over the swollen skin of her belly. It was only a
small bump, but he had not been able to keep his hands off it
since he'd arrived on Sunday. Now it was Wednesday, and she
knew he only had a few hours before he needed to return to
the city.

She smiled when she felt the tickle of his beard on her
skin.

"I know you're awake," he whispered.

"I'm not."

"No?"

"When I wake, you will need to say good-bye. So I am
very sure I am still asleep."

He sighed and laid his head on her belly. "*Milá.* I wish I
could stay forever."

"I hate being apart from you, Damien. Hate it."

"It will not be forever."

"Have you heard back from the council?"

"No."

Of course he hadn't. Sari knew they would not want to let

him go and would use any excuse in the world to retain him. Whatever this growing darkness was that Tala and Gabriel predicted, she knew the council would use it.

"Write them again," she said.

"I will."

Sari reached down and slid lazy fingers through the thick hair at his neck. "They cannot keep us apart. Our child needs you. I need you."

"And I need you." He stretched under her petting. "I don't sleep well without you. If I didn't want to see you in my dreams, I wouldn't sleep at all."

"And I sleep all the time." She laughed. "You would not believe how I laze in bed most days."

He kissed her belly. "Your body is working hard."

"I've been feeling better lately. More energy."

"And Tala?"

"Better. The visit from Gabriel last week was important. She has been sicker than me. Abra helps."

Indeed, the healer had become not just a trusted sister but a dear friend. Abra and Farrin had taken over guarding the village since Tala and Sari were in residence.

While there were many scribes living in the retreat, the majority were boys in training at the library and older men who had not chosen a warrior's life. Farmers and traders. Blacksmiths and millers. All scribes knew how to fight, but not all chose to keep their skills honed to a sharp edge. There were only two trained warriors in the retreat, who were there because their children were young.

"Have you felt the quickening?" Damien asked, his fingers still tracing her belly.

"Not yet. Abra says in a month or a little longer I should expect to feel it."

He kissed the small bump again; his breath was warm on her skin.

"When will you be back?" Sari asked.

ELIZABETH HUNTER

"Two weeks."

Her hand gripped his hair a little harder and he grunted. "So long?"

"But I'll be back for a full week. Gabriel is coming on Sunday, and he'll be staying until Saturday. Then he'll ride back and we'll have a week in town together to coordinate before I'm down for the week. If we're lucky, the scribes' council will have responded to me by then with an answer."

"The baby will be born before they agree to release you from your post."

He slid up and kissed her very awake lips. "Such a cynic, my Sari."

"I'm a realist. They don't want to let you go."

And Damien wouldn't abandon them. The very thought of betraying the mighty Irin Council and the men under his command was anathema to her mate, a man raised on honor, duty, and sacrifice. His loyalty was inviolate.

"They will have to let me go." He shrugged. "After my daughter is born, they cannot keep me away. And they know I am needed for the birth."

She smiled. "It could be a son."

He shook his head. "Impossible. Heaven would not deny me. I have prayed for a stronghearted singer with eyes like her mother's. I have petitioned Uriel and Ariel both. It must be a daughter."

"Or a son. With his father's courage and great heart," she said, brushing his long hair back over his shoulders. His talesm shone where she touched. "A son to fight at his father's side and win this war. Perhaps I will petition Mikael for this."

"You will start a war in the heavens, my love."

She sighed. "It only seems fair, as we've had war on earth for so many years."

"Hush." He put a finger over her lips. "Kiss me. And do not tempt fate."

"Come back to me, my Damien."

180

"As soon as I can."

TALA WAS UNUSUALLY PALE THAT AFTERNOON WHEN SARI MET her in the meeting house for the midday meal. Most of the singers and scribes of the village chose to eat together. It was a motley settlement, with as many wanderers as native French. While Irin families often moved, the tumult from revolution and war had made everything worse and driven many of their people far from home or kept them from returning as planned.

There were North Africans like Abra and her sister's family, and two brothers and their families from Damascus who'd been waylaid on their way back from sojourn in Ireland. The rest were a mix of paler faces from all over Europe. French and Belgian. Dutch and Spanish. Sari had never lived with such a diverse group. Her natural curiosity loved it. As did her palate. That afternoon, Abra's sister was cooking a lemon-scented lamb stew spiced with cumin and nutmeg. The scent made Sari's mouth water, but Tala only looked ill.

Pregnancy exhausted her sister. Sari was beginning to recover her energy, but Tala, a month further along, was not as fortunate. She had only grown thinner, more wan. Her blue eyes were red and swollen many mornings, and her hair was limp. Abra told Sari that some mothers simply took to pregnancy worse than others but Tala was healthy enough. Both the healer and Sari suspected separation from her mate was more to blame than actual sickness. Sari would be glad when Gabriel arrived. Perhaps Abra would order him to stay. In her capacity as healer, she had the authority to override the watcher and even the council.

A large dish of the spicy stew was set in the middle of the table along with long loaves of bread.

"Shall I ask if there is something milder?" Sari reached over and grasped Tala's hand.

Tala shook her head. "I want mother's bread and fresh butter. That's all I crave. And no one can make that but mother."

"There is bread here. I can get you some butter if you wish."

"*Mother's* bread, Sari." Tala shook her head. "I am fine. I am well."

"You were sick last night. Why didn't you wake me?"

"It was your last night with Damien. Of course I would not wake you."

"He loves you too. You know we would have helped you."

A faint smile crossed Tala's face. "I'm not strong like you, but I can survive a little vision sickness. I've been doing it for years. I sent someone for Abra, and she brought back those ginger sweets her sister makes. They helped."

Sari hesitated. Normally if a dream was for sharing, Tala would offer. Sari knew that not all visions were meant for everyone, even for family. But with Damien gone…

"The vision," she asked. "Should I write to Damien about it?"

Tala shook her head. "It's one I've had before." A dark look crossed her face. "I don't think it is pressing, but I promise I'll consult Gabriel about it when he comes."

"Promise?"

"Yes, sister. Now eat. Enjoy the meal." Tala smiled. "It really does smell lovely."

Sari insisted on sleeping next to Tala that night. She'd abandon her twin's bed when Tala's mate came, but not before. Sari was worried about her. Tala was muttering in her sleep. Sari didn't know if it was a vision or simply a dream. It was often impossible to tell. Then Tala sat bolt upright in bed; her eyes flew open.

"I know where it is."

Sari blinked and rubbed her eyes. "Where what is?"

"The house. The house, of course. I know where it is. The clothes are mine. I can see them there, but this time everything is silent."

A chill stole up Sari's spine. "What are you talking about, Tala?"

"The clothes…" A moment later she bent over the side of the bed and retched into the ever-present basin.

Sari jumped into action. She threw one of Damien's linen wraps around herself and got out of bed, pouring fresh water into a mug for Tala to drink after she emptied her stomach. She wet a clean cloth and wiped her sister's forehead as Tala spat out the remnants of sickness into the basin. Then Sari covered it and took it to the hallway to dump in the morning. She went to the kitchen and brought some soft white bread along with a few of the wrapped ginger sweets.

When she got back, she roused Tala and made her drink more water and eat the bread, but her sister waved off the sweets and fell back into a deeper sleep before Sari could ask more about the vision.

I know where it is. The clothes are mine.

In the years since she and Damien had moved to Paris, Sari had often felt like there was something her mate and her sister had held back from her. She knew some secrets related to Tala's visions were not for her ears. Some related to nothing Tala or Damien could share, even with their mates. They both reported directly to the elders in Vienna.

But this vision…

The clothes are mine.

This related to Tala. Sari knew Damien must know what the vision was—Sari suspected it was the same one that had plagued her sister for years—but he had not told her. Was he unable or unwilling? Had Tala forbidden it? Or had the council?

Thoughts of her sister and her mate circled Sari's mind until the sun rose. She drifted into a fitful sleep just as the rooster crowed.

◆ ◆ ◆ ✦ ◆ ◆ ◆

SHE WAS MENDING SHEETS WHEN SHE HEARD THE HOOFBEATS. Shouts and panicked cries filled the air. Sari put down her needlework and picked up her staff. She might be slower, but she could still defend her—

"Sari!"

She turned toward Damien's voice. "What are you doing here? What has happened?"

"The Grigori." He kissed her swiftly. "They are finally moving. Gabriel sent a messenger to us on the road. There are cries of plague amongst the court. Men and women dying in their sleep. Prominent generals. Wealthy men of trade. Well-known men and women in society. Inexplicable deaths, Sari. They are even going after the children. The city is in uproar. It must be the Grigori."

"The humans, are they looking to blame someone?" Panic closed her throat. Visions of Irina burning. Cries of "witch" rising over a crowd.

"*Milá*, no." Damien grasped her shoulders. "Think, Sari. Who would they blame?"

She took a deep breath and relaxed. There were no Irina in the city. They could not be targeted. No Irina had been in

French society for one hundred years, at least. Her sisters were safe, even if the humans were not.

"Of course. I am sorry, Damien. The human deaths are awful enough." She frowned. "But why—"

"I need your touch, mate." He looked stricken for even asking. "But it is up to you. I go into battle and you cannot come. I have forbidden Gabriel from touching Tala as she is so ill, but the rest…"

Sari finally looked at who was in the company with him. She'd been so focused on Damien the other riders hadn't even caught her attention. They were all there. Every mated Irin in the Paris house. Even the warriors of the village were readying mounts, kissing their mates and children good-bye.

"Then this is truly war," she whispered. Mated Irin only asked for their singers to loan them power when they were going into battle. A simple patrol or strike was not deemed important or dangerous enough to weaken a mate.

"Sari, if you're not feeling strong enough—"

"I am." She took his hand and led him to their cottage. "Come, Damien. We must get all of you back to the city."

"I am taking Farrin with me."

She halted. "No."

"Sari, I must. He is my weapons master. I need his arm."

Something roared in her head. Some inner voice screamed alarm, but she tried to be rational. "But that will leave every warrior absent. Damien, I don't think—"

"Sari, I don't have time to argue with you. I need them in the city. Especially Farrin."

"And we need someone here. The only able scribes will be the older men and apprentices."

"What of the other townsmen? What of you and Abra? Sari, you're making this worse than it is. The Grigori are not *here*, they're in Paris. That is where we need our forces."

"The men here have plows, not swords. The women…" She almost cried from frustration. "They know nothing of defense." The other Irin mates retreated to their homes, but she and Damien stood on the path to their cottage, still arguing. "These men will not follow my direction like they will Farrin. If Farrin tells them to fight, they will without question. If I tell them, they will argue with me."

"I will instruct them not to."

Sari snorted. "Of course! I'm sure that's all that is needed."

"I am their watcher."

"And you will be hundreds of miles away should something happen."

"A hundred, if that. Don't exaggerate, *milá*."

It felt like hundreds. Felt like thousands some days. Thousands of miles away from her hardheaded, stubborn mate.

"Do you think I would leave you unprotected if I thought a threat existed here?" he continued. "The Grigori are in the city. Attacking there. Not here."

She dragged him to their cottage and closed the door, pushing him toward a chair as she stripped off the top of her shift so that her mating marks were exposed. They already glowed gold, roused by anger, hunger, and her mate's addictive scent. Damien removed his shirt and sat, holding his arms out for her.

"Sari, please."

She went to him in silence.

"I don't want to fight," he said.

"I don't agree with your taking the strongest scribes here."

He held both her wrists. "We have kept the Grigori away from the village. They don't even know this place exists. We have watched for any sign of them for years, *milá*."

"They are evil, not soft in the head."

He kissed her. "Then I will depend on my fierce mate to protect her sisters."

There was no arguing with him. He'd made up his mind, and Sari could not change it. He was most likely right, she just hated to feel vulnerable, especially when she was far from her fighting best.

"Leave your sword."

He nodded. "If you wish it."

He had others in the city, but Sari knew if Damien was hunting, he would use his black, heaven-forged blade. He had no need of the short, silver-tipped sword that Sari used for training.

He put one hand on her belly. "This won't hurt the child, will it?"

"Of course not, Damien." She softened toward him. "Loaning you power could never hurt him. I can hear his little voice already. The baby is fine."

"Her voice." The ache was in his eyes. "I don't want to leave you here."

"But you must." And he was taking all his warriors with him. For a moment, Sari felt relief. She wanted her mate surrounded by his fiercest in battle. If she couldn't be with him, Farrin would have to do.

Damien pulled her forward until their skin pressed together. "Sing to me, *reshon*. Strengthen me that I may return to you whole and unbruised."

Sari lifted her voice and poured her power into her song.

It wasn't until hours later, after she'd slept away the worst of the exhaustion, that she realized Tala could not be found.

CHAPTER
SIX

D AMIEN approached the small rider trailing behind the company when they stopped to water the horses an hour outside the city. He didn't recognize the stride of the young man, but was not surprised that one of the youngsters had joined them. He'd been eager for battle himself when he was that age. If the young scribe proved skilled, he'd put him with Farrin and let him feel his first battle blood. If he was useless, Damien could always leave him at the house.

"Brother." The cloaked figure tried to dart away, but Damien caught his arm. "Hold, son. I'm not sending you back, I just need to…" His voice died when he saw who he was holding. "Tala?"

Her face was even paler than it had been at the beginning of the week. She was wearing men's clothes and her hair was tied back. Dark circles were under her eyes. Carrying a child had not been easy on her. He hadn't truly commanded Gabriel not to ask for his mate's power. The scribe had insisted he would *not*, even on pain of discipline. Damien had not argued because the man was right. Tala was not hearty enough to loan her power.

But she was hearty enough to sneak onto a horse and ride with them.

"Gabriel's *bloody* fist, Tala. What are you doing here?"

"I've already had this argument with Abra. I am a good rider." She turned back to her horse. "It will not harm the baby. Not for months."

"That's not what I'm talking about!" He strode after her.

"I need to go with you. If you send me back with a brother, you will be one warrior less and I will sneak away again." Her voice was quiet but firm.

"Tala—"

"I have seen more, Damien. I know where the house is."

Damien paused. That cursed house. The vision had plagued her for over two years, but Damien had never been certain. Tala was convinced the place was real and not symbolic. Was it coincidence that this new vision came just as the Grigori of Paris started to move? Could it be the heart of the conspiracy?

"How? You and Sari looked for it everywhere."

"I had another vision last night. Almost the same, but with more detail. There is a linden tree I recognize. It leans at an odd angle, and I've seen it at the end of a lane we walk regularly. I did not think any houses were built there. Perhaps it has just been completed or renovated. It could be—"

"It could be many things, but humans are dying right now. The Grigori offensive is already underway. Whatever they have been planning, they are attacking now, Tala. I cannot investigate this."

"You can if it means finding out what their plan is," she said firmly. "Think, Damien. There is no sign of a Fallen in the city, your knife is not needed, therefore others can fight as effectively as you. This is more important. I'm certain of it. If we can find their base, perhaps interrogate whichever Grigori is in charge, we could warn other cities. We need the intelligence, Damien. It is not only Paris at stake."

He debated silently. Sari would be furious. Gabriel would be enraged. But Tala was superior to both of them. As seer, he could not ignore her. This vision had been tormenting her for two years, and the location of the house had only now been revealed. There must be a purpose in it, though Leoc himself might be the only one who knew what it was.

"I will go with you," he said. "Keep hidden. If Gabriel sees you, he won't be able to think of anything else. Stay behind at the house when I send the teams out. I will keep a small company back and then we will search."

"We don't have to look. I know where it is. The neighborhood is only a few miles from our own house."

GABRIEL MET THEM AT THE DOOR.

"Is Tala safe? The retreat?"

Damien avoided the first question. "I left my sword with Sari, along with instructions for the village. There was no sign of Grigori anywhere on the road. All the movement seems to be in the city. What news since last night?"

They had ridden to the village and back in three days. Damien was exhausted and the horses were spent. But night was falling and his men, flush with borrowed power, needed to be set to hunt.

Gabriel didn't notice the slight figure lingering in the hallway, her eyes huge and aching and fixed on her mate. Damien pulled Gabriel into the library and toward the spread map of Paris on the table, giving Tala time to hide.

"We already identified five of their safe houses," Gabriel said, his fingers pointing toward five chess pieces he'd used to mark the targets. "I've sent scouts out and all appear to be empty."

"So they're hunting."

"They're doing something." Gabriel scratched his jaw, rough from days and nights spent poring over missives from his many informants. "The Grigori we'd identified who were previously so popular in the society pages seem to have disappeared, but the deaths continue. They are hunting in stealth now."

A silent, awful part of Damien screamed, *Finally*! It had been torturous to watch their enemies grow and build in numbers without a single obstacle. The mandate of the council was sacrosanct. No Grigori could be killed unless he was attacking a human. Which meant, though Damien knew they had to be feeding somehow, they had not been killing, and he had not been able to attack them in their lairs.

"How many?"

"Sixty so far. One a cousin of the general himself. She was healthy two days ago. Napoleon's people are in a quiet panic and the physicians have no answers. There are beginning to be rumors of poison and murder. I've sent men around to the priests, but we know not all have been reported."

The poorest, the indigent, and the prostitutes usually made up the bulk of Grigori prey. Those deaths would always be overlooked.

"They're moving in force," Damien said. "It's enough to justify our actions. Have you divided the men into teams?"

Gabriel nodded. "I haven't made any changes to the plan you laid out. Every scribe is able and ready."

"And those just back from the retreat are eager for combat. Make sure at least one is on every team."

"Yes, Watcher."

"I will stay behind for now."

Gabriel looked up sharply, as Damien knew he would. It was unlike Damien to avoid a hunt.

"I have some intelligence I must act on," he said quietly. "I cannot tell you more."

Gabriel paused. "Is it related to her vision?"

"Yes." That much Damien could confirm.

Gabriel nodded but didn't press. "Very well. Farrin and I will take the lead in the field for now. If you are here, you can coordinate runners as they come in."

"I'll need a small team of men. Five or six should do. Men who know what it means to be quiet."

"I'll choose the most suited and shift the teams accordingly."

"Good hunting, brother."

Gabriel grasped his shoulder and squeezed. "And to you as well."

DAMIEN OPENED THE DOOR TO HIS AND SARI'S CHAMBER. "I do not like lying to your mate."

"I doubt you lied to him," Tala said. "If you had, he would have known."

"Avoiding the truth, then."

She blinked hard. "Every night. I hear his voice crying out every night, Damien. He cannot come. If he does, I fear it will be his end."

"You do this to protect him, but he would not want it."

Her eyes glinted. "We protect the ones we love, even if it means holding back the truth. Would you ask Sari for permission?"

"No. But I would be willing to brave her wrath when she learned of it."

"As I am willing to face Gabriel's. But he cannot come. I know it in my heart."

He took a deep breath and nodded. "I have sent the teams out. When they are away and the men Gabriel chose are left, we will depart."

"Thank you for trusting me."

"You can repay me by staying safe and listening to my orders."

"You are my brother, not my commander."

"In the field, I am both."

Tala did not look appeased.

"Sister." He gentled his tone. "You know you are a target."

"We have always been targets."

"Then have mercy on me and allow me to command you. This once, please do what I say."

He knew by the angle of her jaw she would relent.

"I agree," she said. "But you must listen to my counsel when I insist."

"I can agree to that." He handed her a loaf of bread he'd taken from the kitchen. "Please eat something. I know you're unwell."

"I'll be better when I can rest."

"Resting is for later, sister. Tonight we hunt."

CHAPTER

SEVEN

ABRA was speaking, but Sari was only half listening to the healer. They were in the meeting house for the evening meal, but the mood was grim. Even with a night's rest, the mated singers were feeling the effects of the power exchange, including the healer.

"You know she went with Damien. He will keep her safe. She's been pining for Gabriel for weeks now. He'll tuck her into the house with a guard and she'll be fine, Sari. It's useless to go after her. And frankly, neither of us has the energy."

"I could send Gaston." The blacksmith wasn't the brightest of scribes, but he was strong and an able rider.

"It's too late. Besides, sending Gaston would deprive the retreat of one of its few defenses. There have been no signs of Grigori, but we're already weakened and missing Farrin. Losing another strong scribe would be ill-advised."

Sari knew Abra was right. For the thousandth time, she was grateful for the calm reason of the older singer. She reached over and grasped the woman's hand. "Thank you."

"You worry. She is your twin. It is expected. But trust your mate to keep her safe."

"I wish he'd simply sent her back."

"Perhaps he could not have," Abra said quietly. "She is a seer, sister. Near equal in rank to your mate. He cannot ignore her wishes if she insisted. And Tala would only insist for good reason. She's not reckless."

"I know."

I know where it is. The clothes are mine.

Sari was afraid Tala did have good reason to follow Damien into Paris. She just didn't want to imagine why.

Dinner that night was a simple soup of barley and beef that some of the older scribes had prepared to give the singers a reprieve from preparing the evening meal. Sari accepted her bowl with thanks and set it down just as a cry rose from down the lane.

Sari and Abra both turned toward the door, but the sound was faint, cut off swiftly in the gathering dusk.

"Did you—?"

"Yes."

They waited, but no other sound came.

Abra rose and reached for the staff behind her. Sari rose and reached for her blade. They walked toward the door. The rest of the village watched them. Sari turned and said, "Gather the children. Make sure they're all inside."

The old scribe by the fire stood. "Yes, sister."

It was light enough that lamps would only hamper their vision, so Abra and Sari opened the door and headed down the lane with their staff and their sword held ready.

"I'm trying to think who was missing at supper," Sari said.

"Terese? She was particularly moody this afternoon. I don't think I saw her."

Terese was intended for Randel, a young warrior in the Paris house, but they were not yet mated, therefore her young man had not been in the company that had visited the village. The girl had a tendency toward the dramatic, and Sari could easily imagine her brooding.

The lane was empty and silent. The setting sun cast deep

195

shadows in the forest. Even the birds were mute. As they reached the turn that led to the main road, Sari saw something on a path leading toward the fields.

"Abra."

"I see it."

Something brown and white on the path. A cloak? Had someone taken Terese and left her cloak? Sari began to run.

Abra reached the cloak first and knelt down beside it. It was more than just a cloak. It was… a whole set of clothing. Dress. Jacket. Cap, cloak, and shoes. Familiar clothes that belonged to an impetuous young singer. Empty clothes lying on a path. They were stretched out as if the wearer had simply…

Abra's hand came away from the cap, golden dust sticking to her skin. She turned to Sari in horror.

"Grig—" Her voice was cut off by a silver spear through her neck. Abra's eyes widened for a second before the healer's face dissolved in a gold mist.

Sari dropped to the ground and screamed as loud as she could as the woods came alive.

"GRIGORI!"

GABRIEL TAPPED A STEADY FINGER AGAINST HIS THIGH. HE'D returned to the house after the second report came in. No trace of Grigori in the usual haunts. No slinking parasites near the docks or in the parks. Every death they were called to left no trace. They were behind their prey, not in front. There were reports from a few scattered confrontations that only led to minor kills.

Damien had disappeared on his mysterious errand having to do with Tala's vision, and Gabriel's teams had been searching for hours with no luck. It was as if the sons of the

Fallen had fled the city at once, but none of the scribes set to watch their homes had reported anyone fleeing. All their possessions were intact. Their horses were in the stables and their servants asleep.

He smoked his pipe and tried to untangle the threads in his mind.

They had gathered numbers. Lain quiet. Antagonized them until the Paris scribes were looking for any excuse to attack, but… none came. Not even a hint of provocation until three nights before when forty humans—

A shout from outside the gate, then two men burst through the door, carrying an unconscious Farrin between them.

Gabriel bolted to his feet. "What happened?"

"Nothing!" The young man's eyes were panicked. "He wasn't attacked. We were headed back to the house because we'd found nothing but a few young Grigori, barely able to fight at all, and Farrin was waiting for a report from another team. Just like that, he fell over. He sounded as if someone had knocked the breath from his chest, then he fell."

"Help him to bed."

The next hour saw five more scribes brought in, all completely unconscious as Farrin had been. Gabriel had tried to wake the powerful man, tried drawing spells for healing across his skin. Burned prayers before the ritual fire.

Nothing.

The house was in chaos. The few men who'd seen combat had pushed away any attempts at healing to focus on those who had collapsed. As more and more unconscious scribes came in, Gabriel realized what they had in common. He finally recognized the connection.

"Heaven above…"

"Brother Gabriel?"

They had been fooled.

The scribes who were collapsing were all mated men. Men with singers in the village.

Gabriel grabbed the sleeve of a man rushing by, one who had been sent with Damien.

"Rene? What are you doing here? Where is Damien?"

"At the house, I assume. I only brought Randel back when he became sick. Damien said he was no use like that."

A faint hope lifted the weight in Gabriel's chest. Randel was not mated. "What happened to Randel?"

"He began to vomit and his head ached. Like daggers piercing him, he said."

"He is unmated, is he not?"

Rene's face grew pale. He looked around the house, seeing the same connection Gabriel had. "Randel is unmated, but he and Terese have made promises. She wears his mark on her forehead. As he wears hers."

"'Daggers piercing him...'" Gabriel muttered.

"Brother Gab—?"

"This has been a ruse!" Gabriel shouted and the room came to a deadly quiet. "Get to the village. Immediately! Take every man you can and ride as fast as you are able. Leave the wounded. Leave everything but your weapons. Go now!"

The room erupted in movement, every scribe able to ride a horse leaping into action.

A voice inside Gabriel roared, *Too late!*

They would be too late.

Fear threatened to unman him. He reached along the bond he felt with his mate but felt nothing. No panic. No fear.

"Brother Gabriel?" Rene was almost in tears.

"What?"

"Damien is at the house with the seer."

"With who?"

"With your mate, Brother Gabriel. I thought you knew."

Twin spears of rage and relief rose in Gabriel. He grasped Rene's arm and shoved him toward the library. "You are going to show me this house where Damien has taken Tala." He grabbed a confused scribe who was rushing one of the unconscious who was just beginning to wake. "You! Forget the sick. Go now and find the others who are still hunting. Gather as many as you can and ride hard for the retreat. Grigori are attacking the village."

SARI HAD RAISED THE ALARM, BUT THE MONSTERS WERE already pouring in from the forest. She yelled for the village to arm themselves but had to fall back to escape another silver-tipped spear. Grigori surrounded them, moving like deadly locusts from house to house.

The sheer horror of the sight made Sari want to scream, but she could not. Her mind went blank. The only thing she remembered was Damien's voice as he drilled her with the sword.

You cannot think of the blood.

Keep your eyes moving.

Keep your blade up.

She crept through the woods, taking cover in the bushes and grabbing Grigori as she came upon them. A few had dragged women and children out of the village and were feeding in the woods. She killed the monsters as swiftly as possible and urged the survivors to flee.

From the village, she heard the voice of the old scribe. "Fall back to the bathhouse!"

Sari's faint hope rose. If they could take shelter there—if she could come at the Grigori from behind as others held their attention at the front— She cut down another monster grasping the body of a child. The little boy's eyes were blank as his body began to dissolve before Sari's eyes.

Do not think of it.

Two small shapes shot through the bushes, fleeing into the forest. A young mother holding an infant bound to her chest ran into the shadow of trees. Sari cut down soldier after soldier, but there were too many.

A glancing blow off her shoulder and Sari turned and hurled a spell at a Grigori not even as tall as her shoulder. "*Shanda vash!*" Her spell threw him into a tree where he crumpled.

Sari ran behind the meeting house, determined to cut through it and surprise the mass of Grigori that must have followed the villagers to the bathhouse. She was exhausted. Weary of body and mind. A low, silent scream threatened to claw its way up her throat. This was everything she had feared. Every nightmare brought to life.

Do not think of it.

When she opened the door to the meeting hall, it was empty of Irin, but five Grigori were searching under tables. When they spotted her, wild hair and blood splattered across her dress and face, their inhuman eyes lit with glee. Sari lifted her sword, letting the gore that marked it speak for itself.

"Look at the Irin cow," one said, laughing. "She's stolen her master's sword."

"With a body like that, I'd give her my sword," another joked as they began to stalk her.

Sari could see her people fighting through the windows of the meeting hall. She just needed to make it through these five monsters…

"Look, brothers, she's carrying a little angel get," one sneered as his eyes narrowed on her belly. "I'll rip the babe from her womb with my teeth. Then I'll devour *her*."

Sari ignored them and opened her mouth, the ancient words filling the room. "*Shanda vash!*"

Three of the Grigori fell to their knees, the other two swaying and holding their stomachs. She lunged toward them in a fury, taking off the head of two before the others could react.

She didn't think of her sisters or her mate or the child in her belly.

She thought only of the monsters in front of her.

Behind her.

Dead men before her blade.

"Get the bitch!" one screamed.

"*Shanda huul,*" she hissed, stabbing another in the neck as he tried to twist away.

She cut and hacked around the stumbling Grigori, hating her skirts but grateful for the simple spells her grandmother had taught her, even more grateful for the sword drills from her mate.

Damien, where are you?

The bitter question burned in her mind, but she had no time for anger. She'd almost killed the last one when another Grigori burst into the room.

"Preston, we've found— Oh hell!"

Sari reached for a dagger from one of the fallen Grigori and flung it at the man coming through the door. She caught him in the neck. He fell but did not turn to dust. She concentrated on parrying the remaining opponent, who was proving more wily than his mates.

She was so tired. She was weak from loaning Damien her magic. She could not do this much longer. The smell of blood and piss was working its way past the mental walls she'd erected. Something in her belly felt torn and twisted. Her hip was bruised and her shoulder bloodied.

Knocked off balance by nausea, Sari saw a young scribe, no older than fifteen, huddling under one of the tables. Tears were streaming down his face and he was trembling.

Have to protect...

She barely felt the blow to her knee. As she toppled over, she saw the Grigori with the dagger in his throat holding a board ripped from one of the benches. He stood over her, his friend gasping and puking in the corner. They'd knocked the wind out of her, and Sari couldn't find her voice. As she opened her mouth to hurl another spell, the Grigori kicked her head, cutting her off.

Black stars flashed in front of her eyes. Everything began to spin. She barely felt it when they began to kick her body. She curled up, protecting herself and her babe as much as she could. With the last of her strength, she shoved her blade across the floor toward the boy under the table who was biting his lip so hard blood was pouring down his chin.

Please, she mouthed at him before her world turned black.

CHAPTER
EIGHT

"SOMETHING is wrong," Tala said, pausing at the entrance to the house.

"You mean other than Randel turning ill?"

"There was something wrong with that too," she said. "I can't see…"

Damien paused. He knew by now that pushing Tala when she was muttering over something in her head accomplished nothing. He was grateful for his own mate. He loved his sister but didn't know how Gabriel had the patience for Tala's rambling sometimes. It had taken far longer to find the house than Tala had imagined. And once they'd found it, they had to wait and make sure no Grigori were around. They only had five men, and Damien was cautious.

Cautious and edgy. He was full of magic and ready to hunt. His senses were almost *too* alert as he tried to hold still in the shadows.

"This is the house," she said. "I'm sure of it. But it feels… wrong."

Damien watched the large, empty house at the end of the lane. It was brand-new. Tala had been right. It looked barely finished. No lights illuminated the interior, and no servants moved in the windows. The moon was full, and an eerie silence filled the night. Damien could hear a dog barking in one of the neighboring houses, but no signs of life came from the house where Tala had led them.

Five scribes lingered at his back.

"Tala?"

"We should go in," she said.

One of his men asked, "Should we scout around the back?"

Damien nodded and two of the men took off, three staying with the watcher and the seer. They walked slowly up to the front door, but no light greeted them. No servant peeked out. No sound of any kind met their ears. A house this grand would always have a resident, even if it was only a caretaker.

"No one is here," Damien said. "We should go back to the scribe house."

"But they have been here," Tala said. "Can't you smell the sandalwood in the air? There will be something inside. Some intelligence that could help. Try the door."

It opened when he pushed, which only made the grim feeling in the pit of his stomach heavier.

Damien spoke to his men. "Stay close."

"Yes, Watcher."

Tala waited for Damien and the young scribes to clear the entryway. They lit the sconces hanging on the walls and the space shone with mirrors and tinted glass. Tala was right. The smell of sandalwood surrounded him, but he could sense no movement from the adjoining rooms or the floors above.

"It's exactly as I saw it," Tala said.

"But no voices," Damien said pointedly. "No screaming."

"No." Tala wandered around the room, climbing halfway up the stairs as Damien examined the dimensions of the entryway and the hallways. There was something off about the structure, and not just because it was empty. It felt smaller on the inside than the outside, but it could have been a trick of the light.

Tala halted on the stairs. "The hallway."

Damien nodded toward a young brother who took one of the lit tapers to make his way down the hall. Slowly, a long wood-paneled passage was revealed. Leaving two of his men to guard the entry, he took Tala's arm.

"Are you getting anything?"

"Yes. And no. There is a feeling at the back of my mind, but nothing has become clear yet. There are so many echoes… I'm blocking everything but my vision pathways, but your voices are *shouting* at me." She gave him a wry smile. "Someone is losing patience."

"I am at your service, Seer. Take your time."

"Liar. You're dying to fight."

Damien knew he was not an ideal companion for mystical pursuits. He liked hard targets and clear plans. If Tala weren't his sister, he probably would have refused to work with her despite her rank in the Irina hierarchy. It made strategic sense to take her into this situation—confronting the subject of her vision could trigger some insight into it—but at the moment, he just wanted her curiosity satisfied so he could leave and hunt Grigori.

"There!"

Tala lurched forward, but Damien held her back. "What is it?"

"There. On the ground."

Damien nodded at the young scribe, but Tala said, "Don't touch it!"

There was a room at the end of the hall, glowing as if lit from within. As Damien entered, he saw that glass had been built into the ceiling, allowing the full moon to shine through.

When he first glanced down, he thought it was a body. It wasn't. Someone had laid out an intricate feminine dress—

stockings, jacket, and all. Even the shoes and bonnet were placed in neat order.

"I don't understand," he said. "Women's clothes?"

Tala reached out and touched a ribbon on the bonnet. Her face was blank. "My clothes."

Damien and his man exchanged a look. The young scribe drew his dagger and walked down the hall.

"Tala, explain."

She knelt down. "These are mine. It was a present from Gabriel. He had the dress made for me when I became pregnant. I teased him because it was so beautiful, but I wouldn't be able to wear it when I grew heavy with child."

"I've never seen it."

"No, of course not," she murmured, rubbing the ribbon between her fingers. "It's a town dress, but I didn't want to leave it here. I keep it at the retreat."

Icy fear clawed his heart. "You keep it at the village?"

"They've been in the village." Tala looked up. "They've been in my house." Her gaze drifted past him, down the hall where Damien's soldier had taken position. Her eyes lost focus. "How clever. Of course I would come."

"Tala?"

"Someone would have fetched me, but I came myself."

A low warning churned in his gut. "Tala, we need to leave. Now!"

"We can't." Tala's eyes widened. "They're here."

Damien turned, realization mixing with horror as he heard scuffling in the walls. Something far bigger than rats.

Every night. I hear his voice crying out every night.

Panels slid away or were kicked through as Grigori burst from hidden passages. They flooded the room, surrounding Tala before she could lift her voice. Before Damien could reach her.

He reached for his blade a second before a Grigori bent over and sliced Tala's throat. Blood splashed over the flower-strewn silk lying on the floor. Her mouth fell open, but no sound would ever come again.

"NO!"

SARI WOKE IN A POOL OF VOMIT AND BLOOD. HER EYES WERE crusted shut. Her body was in agony. But she was alive. She felt every bruise. Every cut. Felt the wetness of blood leaking between her thighs.

Do not think of it.

She tried to open her eyes, but a trembling hand reached out and held a wet cloth to her face.

She rolled over, swinging out her arms to defend herself.

"Sister, wait." It was a young voice. Whispering. Male. "P-please."

"Who...?"

"I killed them when they were beating you." A hiccuping sob. "I aimed for their necks and they dissolved. One was almost dead from your magic."

"Are they gone? Who are you?"

Another cry. "I'm so sorry I hid. I didn't know what to do."

She reached out and felt for his hand. Felt for anything. Her body screamed, but the urge to comfort the child was innate. "You killed them and saved my life. What is your name?"

"Bassel." One of the Syrian boys.

"You did well, Bassel." Her bruised hand closed around the wet cloth, and she brought it to her eyes to soak the crust of blood that covered them. "They are gone?"

"I think so."

Silence lay over Sari like a leaden blanket. There were no cries of pain or wails from scared children. When she finally cleared her eyes, she could see that Bassel had dragged her over to a corner of the meeting hall and turned tables and benches to surround them in a feeble barrier. Damien's blood-crusted blade lay at the boy's side. Her dress was soaked in scarlet, and Sari knew the tiny life inside her had been extinguished. A keening sorrow threatened to overwhelm her, but she forced it back and focused on the child who lived.

"Have you heard anything?" she asked him. "Anyone else?"

Bassel shook his head.

"I want you to find a lamp and light it." Sari struggled to her feet and reached for the heavy sword. "We must check the houses."

He nodded, his own face covered with blood and his lower lip red and weeping where he had bitten it.

They cautiously made their way out the side door and crept around the back of the meeting house. The first cottage they checked held nothing.

"Maybe they all ran into the woods," Bassel said hopefully.

"Maybe." She didn't tell him of the dust she'd seen rising in the setting sun. Didn't tell him of the bodies that had dissolved before she could rescue them. Sari limped to the next house where an empty set of clothing lay bloody on the ground. She flashed back to another set of clothing.

Terese's clothing.

Abra—

Do not think of it.

The pain was a blade in her chest, but she kept moving forward.

The minute she let herself bleed, the wound would be unceasing.

More houses. More empty clothes. Small pants and dresses pointing toward the woods where the children had tried to run.

There was nothing but empty dresses at Bassel's house

where his sisters and mother had fled. She left the boy sobbing in the ruins of his home and started for the bathhouse at the center of the village. Bloody linen robes lay kicked in the dust in front of it. The door was cracked open and steam escaped into the moonlit night.

Someone had stoked the fire.

Sari held the lantern up and walked forward. The screaming had already started in her mind, but she wouldn't let it escape. If she let it out, she would scream forever.

She limped up the stairs and pushed the door all the way open. It swung smoothly, lovingly maintained by the old scribes who tended the library and fed the ritual fire. More steam escaped, clearing the room, and Sari raised the lantern in the red-gold mist.

Tiny piles of clothes lined the walls where the children had sought refuge behind the benches. Dripping blood sprayed the room. Scarlet-stained dresses and caps lay in front of the benches. Other robes, crumpled and piled near the door.

At the end of the room, slumped next to the ritual fire, was the old scribe who had stood in the meeting hall. His guts spilled out of his robes and his hands were drenched in blood as he tried to hold his innards in his own body.

His eyes were glazed over, but he turned toward the sound of her gasp. "Sister?"

The feral moan rose from her throat when Sari knelt in front of him, placing the lantern on an empty bench. She felt her body rocking back and forth.

Do not think of it. Do not think of it. Do not—

"The fire still burns," the old scribe muttered. "It still burns…"

Hoarse sobs worked their way up Sari's throat and took hold of her body. Wretched cries crawled up her throat and escaped before she could shove them back.

"Sister…?" For a moment the scribe blinked and his eyes

cleared. He met Sari's agonized gaze before his eyes fell on a small red-stained cap lying near his hand. His wrinkled fingers reached out and rested on the bloody fabric.

"Release me," he whispered. "Let me join them." He let go with the hand at his belly, and his intestines spilled onto his linen robes. He took the ritual knife at his waist and handed it to Sari, his eyes pleading. "Release me."

He let his neck fall forward. Sari took the blade and placed the point at the base of his spine. She hesitated.

"Thank you, sister," he whispered.

She pushed the dagger in, and his dust rose like the steam filling the room.

Sari fell to the ground and screamed until the blackness took her.

* * * * * *

"TALA!" DAMIEN ROARED AND LUNGED TOWARD HIS SISTER, but it was too late.

A Grigori grabbed Tala's golden hair and pulled her to her feet, a river of blood coursing down her breast. He plunged a silver dagger into the back of her neck before Damien could reach her. Tala's blue eyes went wide with sorrow and confusion as her face shimmered gold. Damien reached out, but all he felt was dust. She rose before his eyes, swirling in the moonlit room as her clothes fell empty to the floor. He felt the punch of pain in his own chest.

No.

He reached out, grabbed the Grigori who had killed his sister, and dug his fingers into its throat.

No!

Rage took him. He gripped the monster's neck and twisted, snapping the creature's neck before it fell to the ground. Damien spun and drew the black blade from his waist, throwing himself into the mass of Grigori as he called on the ancient magic that flowed in his veins.

Ours is the blood.
Ours is the bone.
Ours is the vengeance of heaven.

Old rage rose up, an armor as familiar as the talesm that covered him. The Grigori continued to attack, unaware of the beast they had roused. Damien moved as one with his sword, grabbing and embracing his enemies, not waiting for them to attack. A single cut from his black blade was enough to fell them, poisoning their blood and causing them to fall to the ground in writhing agony.

The warrior held the blade of heaven close, grabbing each Grigori and sliding the knife into their guts. Their necks. The sweet, soft ease of flesh under their ribs. A few were wiser than their brethren. They lurked in the corners of the room, waiting for Damien to tire.

He did not tire.

Damien sliced through them, his talesm a glowing shield as his body moved on instinct. He would cut down every monster in the room.

Kill them all.

Never stop.

If he stopped, the pain would start.

Damien felt their blades pierce his skin, but he did not halt. A slice on his shoulder. A near miss at his neck. Both his legs were bloodied by the mass of attackers. His world narrowed to the glint of eyes and the flashing sneer of his enemies. They blinked out, one by one. He heard a rush of feathers over his head.

Kill another.

And another.

Until all he heard was silence.

"Damien!"

A voice rose outside the house.

"*Watcher!*"

He shook his head, trying to clear the bloodlust, and realized there was nothing left to kill. He was standing in a pile of dust; the air was thick with it. The walls were ashen grey and spattered red. Two of his soldiers stood at his side, arms hanging loosely, blood and tears in their eyes. Their brothers' dust rose with the Grigori they'd slain.

Damien fell to his knees, digging for his sister's clothes. Tears pouring down his face, he lifted them and pressed them to his chest as the truth of Tala's vision finally became clear.

"*Every night.*"

Gabriel's voice at the entry hall.

"Watcher?" he shouted.

"*I hear his voice crying out every night.*"

Damien's eyes rose to see his brother stumbling down the hall, pale and trembling, held by two other scribes.

"Where is she, Watcher?"

"Tala." Damien breathed out her name like a prayer. "I didn't see."

I'm sorry. I'm so sorry.

Gabriel roared. "*Damien, where is my mate?*"

He spotted Tala's bloody clothes clutched to Damien's chest.

Agonized screams rent the air.

"TALA, NO!"

CHAPTER
NINE

S HE didn't speak because there was nothing to say.
Sari woke in her bed at the scribe house. As soon as she opened her eyes, the brothers tending her called for Damien.

When he came, she closed her eyes and turned away.

If she looked at him, her heart would force itself to beat again.

If her heart beat again, the pain would return.

"Sari? Sister?"

Kind hands tended her, but she refused to acknowledge them. From listening, she knew that not everyone was dead. Some of the young singers had fled to the forest and escaped, taking as many of the children as they could and leaving the old ones behind. They had hidden in caves until the scribes from the Paris house had come to find them.

A few had survived.

Most had not.

Of the fifty families that had lived in the village, ten women, five young men, and three children were all that survived. Everyone else had been slaughtered by the Grigori who had snuck out of Paris after laying a careful trap for the hunters there.

Abra was dead.

Farrin was dead. He'd died in his sleep, his body giving up soon after his mate had been killed.

Tala was dead.

Her baby was dead.

Her child was gone.

Sari closed her eyes and let sleep take her.

IN HER DREAMS, HE WAS THERE. HE HELD HER SILENTLY WHILE she wept until the mist fell over them and the day came again.

GABRIEL RETURNED A MONTH LATER TO COLLECT HIS AND Tala's possessions. He found Sari in the library. His eyes were dead with repressed pain that matched her own.

"He won't come," Sari said when Gabriel glanced at the door. "I told him to leave the house while you're here."

"You think I would try to hurt him."

"I know you would."

Gabriel sat next to her, silent for long minutes.

"Reports are coming in from all over the world. It happened everywhere, Sari. Everywhere."

"How?"

"Just like it did here, I think. Draw the attention of the scribes in the city. Attack the retreats while attention was diverted. We thought the attack in Belgium was a fluke. It wasn't. They've planned this for years. Almost all the seers…"

Sari closed her eyes. "Did they find the retreat outside London?"

"Yes."

Do not think of it.

"Oslo?"

"Yes."

"Vienna?"

"Even Vienna."

"My grandmother?"

"I don't know. Everything is confusion right now. People are disappearing all over the world, and no one knows if they are alive and hiding or dead."

Sari stared into the fire. Sitting near it was the only time she felt warm.

The fire still burns. Still burns…

The old scribe's dust still coated her skin no matter how many hours she scalded her body in the bath.

"How many?" she asked.

Gabriel's voice was barely a whisper. "How are we to know?"

Sari didn't look at him. If she did, she might start feeling again. "Where will you go?"

"Vienna. I want answers."

Sari's heart clutched in her chest. "Gabriel, I need you to take me away from here."

He looked at her long and hard. "I hate him, you know."

"I know."

"He should never have taken her there. Never. We were in battle, and she was untrained."

"I know."

"She never stood a chance against so many."

"Gabriel, I know."

"I hate him for lying to me."

Some days Sari thought she might hate him as well.

Gabriel continued. "But you should not leave him."

"I cannot be here anymore." Sari shook her head. "I cannot even look at him."

"If Tala were alive, I would hate her too. For putting herself in harm's way. For lying to me."

"You have a right to be angry."

"But I would never…" His voice choked. "Never *leave* her. Especially not right now."

"If I stay, I will do something unforgivable." She closed her eyes so the tears wouldn't escape. "I don't know who or what to trust anymore. I need you to take me away from here. Hide me. Hide the girls who are left. I know you can."

"He will find you. You know he will find you, Sari."

"I know he *can*. I am hoping he will not."

Gabriel waited for a long time, staring into the fire as he sat next to her.

Finally he reached out and took her hand. "Where do you want to go?"

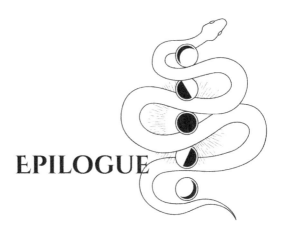

EPILOGUE

Paris, 1811

I cannot stay here. I cannot see you. I have lost everything—

"You haven't lost *me*!" Damien stood and threw another book against the wall of their room, but he didn't throw the letter. He'd read it so many times it was creased with dust and tears. He folded it carefully and put it back in Sari's copy of *Adelina's Songs*. The same place he had found it months ago after she had disappeared with Gabriel, a few warriors, and the surviving women and children from the village.

She'd placed it there deliberately, the letter bookmarking the lament Adelina sang after her angelic lover had killed their child.

> Take me, O heaven, and silence my voice
> For my soul is black with pain.
> I wander among the rocks and trees

And hide from my beloved.
I am barren in the wilderness.
The child of my heart is no more.

His child had died too, along with his dreams for the future. What was the future anymore? Their people were a remnant who fought against each other as much as they fought the monsters who had rent them in two.

Damien had been the one to gather the clothing in the bathhouse, carefully folding each piece and whispering prayers before he placed them in the meeting house where his men sang the old verses to lift their sisters' and children's souls to heaven. The songs sounded wrong in the voices of his brothers, but there were no singers left to offer their songs. The few who had survived had fallen silent in horror and grief.

Damien and his men burned the village to the ground, but no comfort came.

The survivors returned to Paris, heartsick and aching. Most of the warriors who'd lost mates had woken, though many wished they had passed like Farrin. Some had lost everything. Not only mates but children. Damien watched his men closely, but two died by their own hand within weeks. No one could condemn them. Too many families had been destroyed.

They called it the Rending.

The council was in chaos. Anger was hurled in every direction. More than one watcher had been killed when scribes blamed their superiors for the deaths of their mates and children. All over Europe—all over the world—the Irin were in chaos.

Damien remained in Paris, trying to put the pieces of their world back together while Sari hid.

A tiny voice whispered at the back of his mind. *You could find her.*

He *could* find her. If Damien turned the full force of his

skill to it, no hiding place in the world could conceal her. He would rip apart the earth itself to bring her back.

I know you can find me. Please, give me time. You hid from your pain for hundreds of years, Damien. Allow me the same respect.

Not that long. Heaven above, he couldn't wait that long to see her again. His only consolation was his dreams. In his dreams, he held her. In his dreams, his mate let him comfort her. She let him weep. She didn't push him away. She held on as tightly as he did. She didn't turn hate-filled eyes on him. In his dreams, his guilt didn't eat him alive.

I love you. I will never stop loving you. We are reshon. We will be together again. But please give me time. I don't know what to believe anymore. I don't know what our world has become.

"*Milá*, neither do I." Damien fell back on the bed, clutching the thin book of poetry to his chest. His bed was empty. His heart was full of sorrow. And his guilt ate him alive.

He couldn't close his eyes without seeing the spray of blood across silk flowers. He couldn't look at Sari without seeing her sister's shocked gaze.

He hadn't protected Tala.

He hadn't protected any of them.

Damien had beat his chest before the sacred fire, weeping as he burned prayers to Mikael.

Send them back. Take me. I will gladly give my life for a single child.

The heavens were silent as the blood of Irin women and children soaked the earth. Somewhere, Damien knew, the sons of the Fallen were laughing. Not in Paris. The Grigori had wisely fled from Irin rage. Damien did not know where they were hiding, and for the moment he didn't care. He wanted his mate back. He wanted his family back.

Nothing will ever be the same. I don't know what the future will look like. But know that I love you. I will never stop.

"You promised," Damien whispered, holding her book to his chest. "You promised, my Sari."

I never want to be parted from you again, she had whispered once. *Never.*

Tears burned hot on Damien's cheeks as he remembered her whispered vow the night she had taken him as her mate. He fell asleep with Sari's letter still clutched to his chest. He fell asleep and opened his eyes to dreams.

• • • • • •

London, 1815

SHE STALKED THE GRIGORI FROM THE TAVERN, FOLLOWING AT a distance while he ushered the woman toward the street. The human, laughing coyly, didn't hear the hunter. She didn't turn, not even when the Grigori led the prostitute away from the bustling dockside and toward the room he'd taken in a dirty boardinghouse where no one would look too closely.

No doubt this woman thought the man she'd met would only be another paying customer. She didn't notice his hands, carefully kept at his sides until he could isolate his prey.

Sari followed them, her heavy cloak pulled up to cover the gleaming blond hair she'd chopped off at the shoulder. With her stride and height, she was often mistaken for a male as long as she kept her face concealed. The humans cared about such things. Would note that a woman wore men's clothing. Would worry that a female would traverse the dirty streets of London at night without a male to protect her.

Sari needed no guard. She wanted none.

She followed them and waited. She heard the woman's

cries of mindless pleasure. Heard the monster's grunts and sighs of satisfaction as he fed from the human's soul.

And still Sari waited, her silver-tipped daggers concealed beneath the cloak.

Hours later, when the dense fog of London had covered the moon, she walked up the stairs. This one was a solitary beast. From what she'd observed, he didn't kill his prey. He lived quietly, away from others of his kind.

She didn't care.

He was Grigori, and she was no scribe. She was Irina. The council's mandate had died with her sisters.

As she walked, she let the nightmares come. Let the anguished sound of crying children touch her mind. During the day, she pushed the ghosts back. She cared for the ones who had sought protection with her. But at night, she let the dead steal into her mind and rage.

She tested the lock and found it secure. Bending down, she used the tools she'd brought to release it, then she eased her way inside. Noted the crumbled bedclothes and glowing coals in the fireplace. The simple valise by the small chest in the corner. Boots removed and set by the door.

The monster wasn't sprawled across the human but had fallen asleep at her side, wrapped in sheets stained yellow with age. The human was bare, exhausted by her inhuman lover. Sari knew she wouldn't wake until morning.

Sari drew her daggers and stood over the monster, who continued to sleep. She examined his face but saw nothing familiar. He possessed an unearthly beauty, like all spawn of the Fallen. In sleep, he almost looked innocent. Dark lashes brushed perfect, uncreased cheeks. His hair was a tumble of black silk around his shoulders.

The sobs grew louder. A boy mourning his mother and sisters. Old men praying. Women muffling infants too young to be wise.

To the bathhouse!

Abra!

The fire still burns…

No, no, no, no.

Sister, release me.

"Release me."

Sari's whisper woke the Grigori, whose eyes flew open, horrid recognition flashing on his face a second before he rolled to the ground and reached for something under the bed.

"*Yah domem*," she whispered, paralyzing him where he lay. She turned him with the toe of her boot, then put one foot on his chest.

His beautiful, terrified face stared up at her.

"I didn't take part in it," he managed to say through clenched teeth. "I ran."

"Do you think I care?" Sari stared at him and let the dead rise.

She flipped the monster over and drove her dagger into the base of his spine, letting out a long breath as the blade sank into his neck. She felt it pierce the wood of the floor and she twisted it, let the warm blood gush over her hands. His body began to dissolve in the silent room, the dust rising and choking her as it searched for the cracks around the window where cold air sucked it into the night. Within minutes there was nothing but traces of dust, one bloodstain, and an empty set of clothes beneath her.

Sari found the Grigori's purse and put it on the small table nearest the bed. Then she gathered the monster's clothes, his valise, and his boots. Dragging the rug over the bloodstain, she glanced at the human woman once more before she left the room, carefully locking it behind her. The woman was alive and would be paid for her services. It was more than could be said for most Grigori prey.

She dropped the monster's belongings at the door of the nearest church, then straightened her cloak, making sure her hair and weapons were concealed. She needed to return to the safe house, but there would be another hunt. Another monster. Another kill. It didn't matter. No matter how many she executed, the voices in her memory refused to let her rest.

Sari walked into the dark fog, the ghosts of her sisters screaming in her mind.

End of Book Two

MEMORIES

Hidden from Irin society, the Irina have learned to take their revenge on the Grigori. They answer to no one. They ask for no mercy. And forgiveness? That's the last thing on anyone's mind. Two hundred years after the Rending, Damien and Sari are thrown together to face a new threat, a girl who might be key to the healing of the Irin race. If they can survive the anger and grief that has separated them for two hundred years.

Now rest in the power of heaven, my love
Forgive me for my absence
I long for the jewels that live in your eyes
And the golden touch of your hand

—from *The Song of Uriel's Fall*

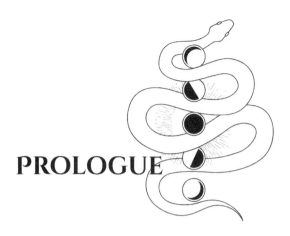

PROLOGUE

Helsinki, 1816

"YOU need to stop looking for me," she said. "It's more than just my own safety at risk."

"If you come back, I can protect you."

Her caution was a wound she opened every time he found her. "Like the haven outside Rome was protected? Thirty Irina. Five children. Slaughtered. Gone because a singer sent a letter to her lover. They're still hunting us. We cannot reveal ourselves. And every time you look for me, you could potentially lead Grigori to our door."

He stood, anger coursing through him. "Do you think me an untrained youth? That I would lead assassins to my mate's door?"

Sari refused to look into his eyes. For forty years, she'd averted her gaze, even the few times they'd come together. She only met his gaze in their dreams. There, she could not look away. It was the one thing he clung to. The one thing that gave him hope.

Her face that night was pale and cold. It grew colder with

every year that passed. "There are too many Grigori. They are everywhere."

"Why do you think we hunt them day and night? We want you back, Sari."

She shook her head. "Not all of you."

Damien was silent because he knew it was true. In the six years since the Rending, the Irina Council had broken, and now the elder scribes ruled the Library. Laws were set and protocols handed down with little debate. The Irin had become ever more militant and structured. While some on the council were actively petitioning to find the Irina and reform traditional Irin society, the more pedantic of their number seemed content to drive their race into an ever more isolated and militant position. The Irina, they claimed, would come back when the Grigori were fewer in number. When Vienna was safe again. When the threat from the Fallen was no more.

Damien knew it would never be safe enough.

"Come back to *me* then," Damien pleaded quietly. "Come to Istanbul. The house there—"

"Do you think it is only me that matters?" she broke in. "I am one of the few who can safeguard them. Would you have me abandon the vulnerable who look to me for protection?"

"But you ask me to abandon my mate!" His voice rose. "You ask me to live without you beside me? To see you only in my dreams and be content?"

Her face betrayed nothing. "How long did you retreat from the world, Damien of Bohemia?"

"Two and a half centuries." The words were bitter on his tongue. "Would you have me wait that long again?"

"Wait or don't wait," she said. "I am your mate—you know I have no other—but you must stop this mad hunt. Stop, or I will stop meeting you here or anyplace. Give me that, Damien. Give me time. Give *them* time. Most of them lost everything."

"But we did not. We lost Tala. We lost our child. But we still have each other when so many do not."

"Damien—"

"Gabriel's fist!" He lost his temper completely. "Can you not be grateful that we are both still alive?"

She stood silent, a pale statue of the vibrant woman she'd once been. Then she turned and walked out the door.

London, 1860

HE STOPPED HUNTING. SHE GAVE HIM NO CHOICE. HER MAGIC had grown with frightening speed, honed and sharpened by trauma and sheer will. He knew she'd joined forces with her grandmother, Orsala. Against the two powerful singers, even Damien's skills could not compare. He could have found her, but not without exposing those under her care. Not without hurting her.

It must have been mercy that led her to find him in London.

Their home there had never been sold. It had remained in the possession of one Irin scribe or another since they'd abandoned it before they left for Paris. Damien rarely checked on it or visited except for one week every year when, by silent agreement, he met Sari in London. The current occupant would leave, and the house would be their home.

For one week.

I miss you. He didn't speak the words as he watched her dress. For this one week, she was his again. One week, then she would disappear. She met him here for one precious week, and he agreed he would not hunt for her.

I miss you so much my bones ache with it. Your absence is a hole in my spirit and a wound on my soul. Only our dreams keep me sane.

They didn't speak of the past here. Or the politics of the present. For one week, they ate and drank together. Made love with furious frequency. Saw a play or a concert as if they were ordinary citizens of London. They laughed together. Slept tangled in each other. For a few days, they were as they had once been.

But inevitably Sari's eyes would grow dark again. Her face would lose its light. He would catch her staring into the distance, her head cocked at an angle as if she were listening for a voice in a distant room. Slowly she would withdraw into silence.

And then she would be gone.

Was it madness to keep meeting her like this? Damien wondered if her healing would come faster if he could somehow banish himself from her life. If he was gone completely, would her pain lessen? Would the wall between them grow weak?

It didn't matter. They were mates. Every night, her bitter-sweet presence kept him company in his dreams. In them, she laughed and she wept. She rested in his arms and kissed his lips. Their souls were still one. In dreams.

And in the morning, she was the absence in his bed and the ghost that haunted his days.

"I miss you."

He said it aloud, but she was already gone.

London, 1960

"I CAN'T DO THIS ANYMORE."

Sari looked up and for a moment their eyes met before she looked away.

What did she see in him, after all these years? Damien

had realized that morning that they had been apart almost as long they had been together. Theirs was a union marked by absence. In the decades since the Rending, they had fallen into a rhythm not unlike the few Irin mates who remained. They saw each other infrequently. They walked in dreams. When they were together, they avoided any argument because who wanted to fight when you had so little time?

Damien felt as if their life was in a holding pattern neither knew how to break. And every year that passed saw his mate, his wild girl, grow harder and darker and colder. Her eyes had lost their light, and Damien didn't know how to bring it back. He didn't even know if it was possible.

"What do you mean?" she asked.

"Come with me now. Or let me come with you. But I cannot do this anymore."

She straightened from untying her shoe. "You would abandon your men?"

"Yes."

"Defy the council?"

"Yes."

She paused. "I don't believe you."

Something in him died, and in its place, an angry root took hold. "I always knew you thought I was a liar," he said softly. "At least now you don't feel the need to shield me."

"That's not what I meant."

"Yes, it is. When I told you about Tala, you didn't believe me. When I told you she insisted, you didn't believe me." He glanced up. "You still don't."

She flinched, and Damien knew he was right.

"The plan made the best strategic sense at the time," he said quietly.

"Is that your excuse for letting her die?"

"You weren't there!"

"No, I was fighting for my life. Watching my sisters and

our children be slaughtered by Grigori," she said. "Where were you?"

Where were you?

The weight of guilt would never ease. He had been in the city. Doing what he thought was right. Following orders. Despite Tala's dream. Despite the attacks in Brussels. He'd been blind and proud, convinced the Grigori were thinking as he was. Convinced his council was right.

Where were you?

He had been flush with his mate's power, leaving Sari weak against the enemy who had attacked her, attacked their unborn child. He'd left her to fight alone, so she had pushed him away.

I wasn't there.

She didn't need him anymore. She was as hardened a warrior as he had ever been. Hardened by anger and terror and survival. Hardened by the choices she'd made and the ghosts that haunted her.

"What can I do?" he asked. "There is no making this right. What would you have me do, Sari?"

She sat alone on the bed, her face blank. "I don't know."

Damien closed his eyes in defeat. There was no forgiveness. There might never be. For a moment he thought of Otto, his brother too haunted by the past to envision a future. He thought of his men who had taken their own lives and left this horror of a world for the peace of eternity with their mates.

But Sari was alive. Leaving this world would bring him no peace. His death, even if she hated him, would wound his mate, and everything in Damien revolted at the thought.

"I will never leave you," he said. "Never. But I will not come to you again. I cannot."

She was livid. "You do this to punish me. Because I won't—"

"Do you want me to hunt you?" His voice rose. He tried to

tamp it down, but the predatory instincts in him were on a very tight leash. "Because I will, Sari. To the ends of the earth, there would be no rest from my pursuit. Is that what you desire? I *would* hunt you, my love, and I would find you."

Her eyes grew cold again. "You would try."

Proud. Stubborn. Combative. Her will was honed steel.

May you be blessed to find a mate as warlike as yourself.

Should he laugh or cry at his fortune?

Damien hung his head. "I can't do this. When you are ready, *milá*. When you can find forgiveness in your heart for me, come to me. Knock on my door, and I will always open it. Always. Come to me when you are ready to take me back. I love you, Sari. I chose you, and I always will."

That night it was Damien who left the house. He left, and he did not return.

CHAPTER
ONE

Sarihöfn, Norway
2013

"THE risk is minimal for the reward," Sari said. "I vote we allow her to continue on the continent for now."

Mala, her first lieutenant, didn't agree. *She's becoming a liability,* Mala signed. *For her contacts and, more importantly, herself.*

"I know you're attached to her," Sari said, "but you can't argue with her success. She's taken out five nests of the monsters in the past two years. And she's done it under the watchers' noses."

Sari caught Astrid, the haven's healer, biting her lip.

"You agree with Mala," Sari said.

"I do," Astrid said quietly. "I love her, but we all know what Renata is like. This past decade, we've seen her spiraling out of control. It's one thing when she's risking her own life, but when she's careless with others…"

The fearsome singer had come to them, barely out of her training as an archivist, from a village outside Rome. Renata's family and her intended mate had thought they'd escaped the ravages of the Rending, but the Grigori stalking them had only been lying in wait. Renata was the only survivor of that massacre. She'd made it a point to hunt down Mala—renowned for her ferocity—and demand training as a warrior. Mala had led her to Sari. Renata had been taking her revenge on Grigori ever since.

"Do we know where she is?" Sari asked.

Mala shrugged. Astrid said, "I know how to find out. I'll get the message out. It could take a while."

"Fine. Until she's back—"

Karen burst into the library. "Sorry! Sorry, sorry, sorry. I was baking and lost track of time."

Mala signed, *Sari just agreed to call Renata back.*

"Good," Karen said. "It's about time. She's going to kill herself and someone else at this rate. She needs to be home for a while."

"That's all you've missed so far," Sari said. "We were just going to go over news from the other havens."

As Astrid began to read some of the correspondence from singers' havens around the world, Sari thought for the thousandth time how much had changed since the Rending. Would mobile phones and e-mail have prevented the slaughter of so many? It was easy to forget as communication became instantaneous how confusing those months had been. Everyone was traumatized. Added to that, reports of other attacks were so muddled and contradictory that no one knew what was going on.

In the centuries since, the Irina had become masters of communication. When the Internet was developed, they'd learned its secrets early. They wouldn't survive in the modern world without it. While the scribe houses stagnated among their ancient scrolls, the remnants of singers had become adept at communication and obfuscation in the modern world. Havens like Sarihöfn existed all over the world, and they were all connected. Silent assassins were sent out to eliminate threats. Careful contacts were cultivated to maintain anonymity.

It was a new world.

A new world still carrying the corpse of the old, Mala had told her once.

It was true. The world had moved on, and the Irina had moved with it. But in many ways, they were still the walking dead.

"I've had word from Patiala," Astrid said quietly. "Anamitra has surrendered to the heavens."

Sari felt the slow intake of breath. A pause before the exhale. "Have you told my grandmother yet?"

"I only got word this morning. Her niece said she had been in silence for over a year now."

Anamitra, one of the eldest of the Irina. Older even than her grandmother Orsala, and a dear friend who had served on the Irina Council at the time of the Rending. For decades, rumors said she'd been killed with her daughter and her granddaughters. Then the word had come that the singer had been in seclusion since the death of her mate, who had died in his attempt to defend their village. She'd stopped her longevity spells and had been slowly fading for two hundred years.

Mala put her fingers to her lips and lifted them to heaven. Karen closed her eyes and smiled.

"May peace find her," Sari said. "Is there anything else?"

"No."

"I'll go tell my grandmother." Sari rose and walked to the door, leaving her three most trusted advisors in the library, quietly talking about the passing of a legend. When Sari reached the edge of their small commune, she toed off her shoes and dug her feet into the soil, letting her magic reach down and twine with the ground that fed it. It pulsed with life and heat despite the chill in the air.

She felt more than the changing of the seasons. Something in the rhythm of the earth had changed. The death of one of their elders marked something. Some shift was happening in the heavens perhaps. A change in the wind off the sea.

Sari turned her face to the sun and walked to Orsala's cottage.

"You're very affectionate tonight," Damien whispered to her. "Talk to me."

"I can't."

"You won't."

The sea tumbled behind them, and the sun warmed their bodies. They were on the coast of Brittany. A short holiday after they'd first moved to Paris. The golden time when their family surrounded them and dreams felt like promises.

Damien held her on the blanket, his shirt stripped off, as was hers. They lay skin to skin as the sun and the sea surrounded them.

It wasn't the same as feeling his arms. Nothing was the same as that. Dream-walking with her mate was like smelling and tasting the finest food but never being able to swallow. It fed her soul enough that she could function, but she never felt full.

"The past feels very heavy tonight," Sari said, resting her head on his chest. Two hundred years of dreams, and she most often spent them like this. Resting her head on his chest while he held her. Sometimes passion filled their thoughts, but they were not new lovers. Most often, it was his presence her soul needed. That night she ran her hands up and down his torso, feeling every dip and scar. Every raised line of his *talesm*. Every battle-hardened muscle. He was her personal homeland, and she mapped him inch by inch.

"Sari," he said. "Something has happened."

She blinked as the dream began to grow muddled. He

lived in Istanbul and often woke before her.

"What?"

"Something has happened." His voice was foggier.

"Damien." She held on to him even as his body grew faint beneath her. "Please, go back to sleep. I need you tonight."

"I need…" His voice came from a distance. "…come to you."

She shook her head. He wouldn't come to her. He'd walked away. Part of her couldn't blame him. Part of her was incensed. Another part of her lived in the fury and didn't know how to break from it even when she desperately wanted to. She'd made Damien her world, and then he'd failed her. She'd put her faith in him, and his feet were made of clay.

"Damien?"

She opened her eyes, and the beach where they'd been lying was cold and dark. But as she turned to look for him, she felt his warmth at her back and his voice came to her ear, as clear as if he were lying in the same bed.

"I am coming to you."

SHE WAS STILL THINKING ABOUT THE DREAM A WEEK LATER. For days, Sari had expected to hear word of her mate in Oslo or even Bergen.

He wouldn't, the logical part of her argued. He'd promised, and Damien did not break his promises. A tiny part of her whispered in hope. After a week, that part fell quiet again.

Sari was weeding the gardens, clearing the raised beds for winter planting. They would put the hot frames over them the following week so modern technology and Irina magic could keep their commune in vegetables through the winter. But before then, every errant sprout must be eliminated. It was good work. It connected her to her magic and distracted her from the itching in the back of her mind.

Damien was not coming to her. He was busy in Istanbul. Busy obeying the gaggle of old men who still held his leash. Busy following rules that had led to the slaughter of half their race.

He could have been on the council if he'd wanted. With his family and connections, the appointment would have been an easy one. Or he could have worked from behind the scenes, like Gabriel.

He did neither.

"Sari?" Astrid called from behind one of the permanent greenhouses.

"Back here!"

Astrid walked over the even ground, her hands in her pockets. She was an even-tempered healer, with just enough humor to keep Sari from killing her. Her hair was normally a light brown, but it glowed golden in the sun that day.

"I heard from Renata," Astrid said as she approached. "She wasn't happy about it, but she agreed to come back."

"Where was she?"

"She didn't say."

Sari grunted and went back to pulling weeds. "Here's hoping she's home before it snows."

Astrid looked up at the sky. "Do you think a storm is coming?"

She shook her head. "Why?"

"I don't know," Astrid said. "Something in the air. Karen mentioned it this morning too."

That hopeful whisper started again. Sari shoved it back as Astrid walked back to her cottage.

She worked four more hours before she noticed a figure standing at the edge of the greenhouses, watching her. It was her grandmother, Orsala. Sari pushed the hair out of her dirt-smudged face and straightened. "Grandmother?"

The old singer said nothing, simply turned her face to the west. "Magic on the borders."

Sari stood and reached for the staff that was always within reach. "Where?"

"Coming up the old road."

The road that had existed before the modern highway had been built. A footpath still linked the old road and the haven, though few ever used it.

"Who?"

Orsala shook her head.

"Grandmother?"

"I can't see them. I only feel... I have not felt this magic before."

Sari didn't wait for more. If it was anyone familiar, anyone with a right to visit the haven, Orsala's magic would have recognized them. Her grandmother was a singer of Chamuel's line, empathy her greatest weapon. While singers of the past had not seen empathy as an offensive ability, Orsala had honed her magic in the fire of the Rending. She'd learned to use other's emotions against them. Any unwelcome visitor with angelic blood would feel an inescapable urge to run.

But this visitor was not running.

She felt him as soon as he crossed the boundary line she'd marked with her magic half a century before.

I am coming to you.

Damien was here. But so was another. Soft, feminine magic whispered over the land. Foreign heat and the smell of sandalwood came to her senses. Old magic. New magic. Sari didn't know what she was sensing.

Every nerve went on alert.

"Mala!" She yelled for her most trusted. "Astrid!"

Both singers came running as Sari left the clutch of buildings in the small valley, crossed the gravel road that led to the modern highway, and strode up the path her mate was following. Mala had her sword, but Astrid carried nothing.

"What is it?" the healer asked, her eyes wide and worried.

Sari couldn't speak.

He returned to her like this? No word of warning, with an unknown singer at his side? There was something so strange about the woman's magic, so foreign, fear rose up and clutched her throat. What was happening? Could someone have coerced her mate? Could the Fallen be playing a trick? Was it truly Damien at all?

She thought of the dozens of families in the haven. Orsala would be moving the children into hiding places while each rogue scribe and singer took defensive positions drilled into them over decades of preparation.

"*Ya kazar,*" she whispered into the wind, letting the air carry it over the land she commanded. *Turn back.*

"Sari, who is coming?" Astrid asked again.

The magic kept coming. It raced over the earth and leapt to her senses. The magic tasted of him. Of Sari's mate and lover. It knew his scent, recognized his step, and welcomed him. And that welcome enraged her. This was *her* land. *Her* safe haven. He had no place here. He'd abandoned her for his precious council. Abandoned it when he'd abandoned her.

Unlike foreigners, Damien had come to the valley before Orsala's safeguards were in place. He had loved her here. The earth would not turn him away even if Sari commanded it with her magic. Damien's soul was too old. Too familiar.

She felt Orsala's voice on the wind, knew that whoever was coming with him would feel the cold rush of air from her grandmother's power.

The strange magic did not turn away. And neither did her mate's.

Sari turned her face to the sky and called down the rain. "*Vared gesham!*"

If she could not make him stop, she'd at least slow him

down.

Mala and Astrid followed her as she raced up the hill, stopping at the top of a rocky outcrop that overlooked the old trail. Sari saw two figures, both struggling up the hill. Damien's form was achingly familiar. Her heart leapt in her chest and her pulse pounded.

But the small woman with him held out her hand and cried out, "You're hurt!"

The woman was beautiful and delicate, reaching for Sari's mate with both hands. Their words were muddled in the roaring wind of her anger. Her heart stopped, and the wind died down.

Damien's eyes rose and locked with hers. She could barely stand the pain of it. Beautiful and wild, his eyes pierced her. After decades, she heard her mate's true voice.

"Now you'll see why they are feared," he said.

Icy claws dug into her heart. *Fear this.*

"*Kazar vash!*"

Damien flew from his feet and tumbled backward, rolling down the hill.

Leaving Mala and Astrid to deal with the female, she strode down the mountain, anger eating up the ground between them. Decades of abandonment, and he returned in the company of a foreign woman with magic unlike anything Sari had ever felt? She raised her staff without thinking and struck out, realizing that Damien had grabbed a branch when she felt it strike her own.

Why? her heart screamed.

He was her *reshon*. The mate of her heart. They walked in dreams together.

She swept him from his feet and brought her staff down next to his head.

Fear that, my love.

He had returned after decades apart, but not for her. She saw him glancing at the woman over and over, even as he rolled to his feet. His care for her was as clear as the eagle eyes that had once looked on her as if she was his world. Had this been why he'd stayed away? Had he found comfort in another's embrace?

She whispered a command to her old staff, and the wood split in two. She tossed half to her mate. Sari was not finished venting her rage. He was holding back. Damien was not allowed to hold back. She was as much a warrior as he was.

As they fought, she remembered his first lessons. Here, on the land where her grandmother had been born, he'd taught her to hold a sword and use it to slay their enemies. Insisted she never pull a punch. He had made her a warrior, fought beside her, but left her when she needed him most.

Flashes of training exercises and hunts together. Night after night of fighting. Passion. Release. Joy. Camaraderie. Then the sight of his horse leaving the retreat in the gathering dusk. Leaving her behind. His last kiss before the world had turned to nightmares and her sister turned to dust.

She fell. He fell.

Where were you?

She rose and struck again.

Where were you!

She was crying and fighting in the mud. He was everything. Her mate. Her teacher. Her lover and her betrayer.

The rain continued to fall around them as he fended off her brutal attack. She had become a creature of raw emotion. She hated him and she loved him. She saw her opening and struck. Damien's knee bent to the side and he came down, kneeling before her.

Where were you?

He held out his arms and looked up, rain tracing through the mud that marred his noble face.

Here.

Eagle eyes met her own.

I am right here, they said.

I am coming to you.

Take me.

Sari dropped her staff and went to her knees before him. She pulled his mouth down to meet her own. She was hungry, and he was half her soul. She didn't care how or why he had returned. She only knew that she'd been starving for decades and her mate was before her. No other existed. She was lost in the memory of his body; his arms embraced her, and she felt whole again.

His hands were at her back; she could smell his skin.

A hint of sandalwood at his neck.

Sari shoved Damien away, reality wiping away the strange spell that had overtaken her. She had allowed her rage to rule her and struck before asking questions, too stunned by his appearance to form words. She'd reacted like a scorned lover instead of a leader.

Why was he here?

Who was this woman?

She no longer had the luxury of selfishness. There were others who depended on her for protection. While she knew Damien would never knowingly put her or the others at risk, she had no idea who the strange woman was. Her magic felt like no other Irina she'd known in over five hundred years of life.

Sari pulled away from him and stood, ignoring the pain on Damien's face and the anger that flashed in his eyes. She would have words with him later, but for now…

"*Yah tichen*," she commanded her staff. *Mend yourself.* The piece Damien had been wielding flew from the ground and joined with its mate. The staff settled in her hand, whole and unmarred. Sari spun and walked toward Mala and Astrid who were holding the slight woman between them. The woman's eyes held fear and not a little anger.

"Take them to the guesthouse," Sari barked in Norwegian. "And put guards on them both."

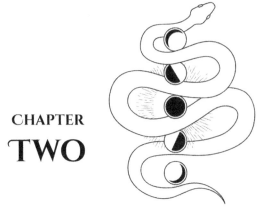

CHAPTER
TWO

"WELL, that went as well as I expected."

Astrid raised an eyebrow at him but said nothing else as she checked his knee. His face had healed, but the knee needed to be looked at. Sometimes joints could mend before they'd been straightened. It had happened to Damien before in battle, and the subsequent re-breaking was something he would pay to avoid.

"Who is she?" Astrid said.

"A brother's widow," Damien said, grateful for the presence of an old friend. "Malachi was killed weeks ago in Istanbul. I decided to bring Ava here."

Astrid and her mate had been stationed in London under Damien's watch before the Rending. Before everything had gone to hell. He found out years later that Marten had been killed protecting a retreat in Ireland while Astrid was working at the scribe house in Dublin as the Irin fought the Grigori there. The healer had disappeared after losing her mate. It didn't surprise him that Sari had found her.

"Why here?" Astrid said. No judgment. Simple curiosity. "You knew she would not react well."

"Ava's magic is unlike any I've felt before. She is one of us.

Mated and marked. But she was raised among humans and has no training. My archivist could find no record of her true parentage."

Astrid frowned. "Unusual. Maybe you need a better archivist."

"Rhys is the best. He's still working on it. Ava needs training. She could hurt someone without meaning to."

"Unlike other singers we know, who fully intend their blows to wound." Astrid finished wrapping the knee. "You still should have known better, Damien. You were looking for a reaction."

"Maybe."

"You got one. Just like you always do. You're the only thing in Sari's life that can make her lose her balance like that. You know that, don't you? Keep the knee wrapped for an hour or so. You know the spells to mend it."

"I do."

"I'm sorry her mate was killed." The healer looked up. "I'm sorry about your brother."

"Others have lost more than I." Damien refused to feel grief. Not when he'd survived and others hadn't.

"Would you like me to break both arms then?"

He blinked. "What?"

The healer wound the rest of her bandages and placed them on the table. "Perhaps your knee would stop hurting if you felt a greater wound."

He couldn't stop the hint of a smile. "Stop being so wise, Astrid."

"Impossible."

He squeezed her hand. "It's good to see you."

"And you." She rose and walked to the door. "I'll explain about the girl. Lie low for a few days. Talk to Orsala, but leave Sari alone for a bit."

Damien stared at the wall where a picture of his mate and some of her sisters hung. They were smiling and laughing on a beach somewhere. Damien didn't think he'd ever seen a picture of Sari laughing.

"I don't know if I can, Astrid."

"Try."

"Why did you fight with her?"

Damien heard his brother's mate as he was finishing in the washroom. The girl had been patient so far. She was a patient kind of person but exhibited the mercurial, almost excessive energy of an Irina too long in isolation.

"Because she needed a fight." Damien stepped out of the washroom. "And I give my mate what she needs."

When Damien and Sari used to meet in London, she exhibited the same erratic power. Ava had been raised among humans and was still trying to get a grip on her magic, which was unlike anything Damien had felt. He was doing his best to help her even if he had to take a beating for it.

He donned the modern clothes he felt most comfortable in: worn denim pants and a short-sleeved cotton shirt. There was much about modern life that he enjoyed, like indoor plumbing and finely woven clothes. He didn't enjoy electric lights. He'd never rested as well once they'd been developed, and he was grateful for the more primitive conditions in Sari's valley.

He took a deep breath, inhaling the scent of damp earth and Sari's magic.

"Where are we?" Ava asked him.

"Norway."

"Yeah, I figured."

Damien tried not to smile. He supposed he was too long out of feminine company. His brothers at the house in Istanbul didn't seem to mind the curt answers he gave. He sat down by the fire and waited for the scent of the smoke to drown the familiar trace of Sari's power that permeated the air.

"We're in the Nordfjord district," he elaborated. "Sari's family has had this property for hundreds of years. It used to be just a small cottage they used for holidays. Very private. Her family was always very private. They liked their own space and never took well to living in retreats. After the Rending, after we lost… so many, she left me and came here. I knew she'd gathered other Irina but didn't know how many."

It wasn't the whole story. But then Ava didn't need the whole story. She had enough to deal with.

She looked out the window at the setting sun, and the rays touched her face, making her skin glow.

How many years did she have? Twenty-eight? Twenty-nine? She was a child in his world. Yet the Creator had seen her mated to one of his own brothers. A fierce wave of protectiveness rose. He hadn't been exaggerating to Astrid when he said she could hurt others without even meaning to. She did need to be trained. But more, she needed to be kept from harm. The honest part of Damien knew that protecting Ava had become about so much more than honoring his brother Malachi.

This young human girl had become every child he had lost. Every Irina under his watch who'd been butchered by his enemies.

She looked back at him. "This is your first time here?"

"No. I came here before. When we were first mated." Waves of memories threatened to drown him. "We spent time here together. I'm one of the few Irin scribes who even knows this place exists. We're safe here; I'm sure of it."

"When was the last time you saw her?"

He leaned toward the fire, enjoying the heat on his neck. "It's been years. We used to try to meet in other places. But it was too… It's complicated, Ava."

"You would abandon your men?"

"Yes."

"Defy the council?"

"Yes."

"I don't believe you."

The memory of her bitter words still made him angry. Sari and her sisters had abandoned everything. The villages. Their seats on the council. The halls of the Library that were once bathed in song. Centuries of tradition and learning had been lost, and without the tempering influence of the Irina, Damien saw the leaders of his race becoming cold, corrupt, and insular.

But even more painful, the singers had abandoned their scribes. Their brothers. Their colleagues. Their sons. Their *mates*.

"Does she really hate you so much?"

Yes.

And yet, even in his anger, he couldn't escape his fierce pride at the memory of their fight, which echoed so many training sessions in the past. His Sari had not held back a single strike.

"She hates me as she loves me," he said ruefully. "Wholly and completely. Sari never does anything by halves."

"Are they all angry? Are all the Irina angry like Sari?"

"No. Maybe. There's not a simple answer."

"Try. I need to understand."

Ava knew about the Rending, but how could Damien explain a two-hundred-year-old wound that still bled? And the centuries of mistakes that led to a horror he still saw in nightmares? And he hadn't seen the worst of it. He'd witnessed Tala's death, but Sari had borne witness to so many losses Damien didn't know how she ever closed her eyes.

"You can see how powerful they are. The Irina, I mean. An Irina singer at the height of her power, trained by her elders, can wield frightening magic. With a word, they can change the course of the wind. Render a strong man weak or a weak man strong—"

"Break a stick in half and then mend it?"

That was a new one. He hadn't seen her do that before.

"All Irina have different powers. Seers. Healers. Elemental magic. Some of that is natural and some depends on how they train. In the past, they used their magic for mostly creative endeavors. Healing. Building. Teaching the young. Scientific discovery. These were always their greatest strengths. The more... martial magics were not valued. The oldest Irina derided offensive spells. 'Male's work,' my grandmother would sneer at my father and me."

His paternal grandmother kept to politics and manipulation, as obsessed with bloodlines as his grandfather had been. She'd scorned battle training as much as she pursued warriors' blood. She'd been pleased by Damien's placement with the Templar order because of their political power, not their battle prowess.

Damien continued, "All Irina knew some protective spells, of course. And many to help themselves blend in with the human world, but it was the Irin scribes' job to protect them. And for our part, we didn't encourage our mates to learn offensive magic."

Thank heaven, he hadn't been able to keep Sari away from it.

"Why would they need it? They had us. And we..." His throat threatened to close on him. "We would never leave them unprotected."

"Except you did."

He tore his eyes from the fire. "We did. And we learned how desperately wrong we were only after we had lost everything."

"Not everything. You and Sari still have each other. Lots of people—most of the Irin—lost their mates."

"I am one of the lucky ones. We aren't exactly a peaceable pair, but then we never have been."

Ava frowned. "Will she ever forgive you?"

"I don't know."

You're the only thing in Sari's life that can make her lose her balance like that. You know that, don't you?

Hope pushed past the bitterness in Damien's chest. "But I'm tired of being patient. And as I give Sari what she needs, so she will give me what I need. If meeting you has taught me anything, it's that there are things in this world that are not as they appear. We lost half of ourselves during the Rending. Then we allowed this wound to fester. We're dying from within, and it needs to stop. Change must happen."

"Do you think they're ready for change?"

He had to believe they were. Had to believe it or he'd go mad.

"I don't know," he said honestly. "But look at you, Ava. You shouldn't exist, and yet... you do. Change has already come. They just don't know it yet."

HE FELT HIS SHOULDERS BURNING. HIS THIGHS WERE ON FIRE.

"Too many days in the car," he grunted at Mala.

His sparring partner raised a single brow but said nothing, tapping his forearm with the flat of her sword and nodding toward the row of staffs laid out along the far wall of the barn Sari and her sisters had turned into a training facility.

"You're a better sparring partner for me than Sari is," he said. "Don't tell her I said that."

Mala's face broke into a grin. *Her shoulders are too narrow for the sword. But she can beat me with the staff,* the woman signed.

"She can beat me too."

I know. I saw.

Damien chose his weapon and turned. The tall warrior he faced carried some of the most ancient blood of their race, her people coming from the Nile basin in Central Africa where the archangel Uriel had once dwelled. Mala's skin was dark and flawless; high cheekbones planed her face. Her hair was closely cropped, her profile regal.

Mala was beautiful. So beautiful Damien's brother Alexander—a scribe so devoted to battle he'd been a warrior-monk during the Crusades—had abandoned their order to run away with her, despite the objections of both their kin. Mala had not even reached one hundred years when Alexander mated with her, a child bride in her clan. The couple had lived in isolation for centuries until Alexander had been assigned to London. Damien had renewed his friendship with his old comrade, and Sari had made a lifelong friend.

Alexander had been killed during the Rending, and Mala had lost her voice, but not before she'd killed a dozen of their enemies. A vicious scar ran up from her collarbone, across her neck, and up her jaw. To Damien's mind, the jarring scar only made her beauty more vibrant and dangerous.

They worked in silence for over an hour, Mala stretching old muscles long out of use and forcing Damien to use skills he'd abandoned. He'd become accustomed to fighting with daggers. Dirty, quick street fights that were over too easily. This practice session was as refreshing as the northern air.

Once she'd beaten him thoroughly, they stopped. His knees and calves felt the sting of her blows, his blood was flowing, and his *talesm* shone with a low light. He stripped off his shirt and dunked it in a barrel of water in a corner of the barn, then squeezed the water over his head. He turned when he felt a towel hit his shoulder. Mala motioned him to sit on one of the benches and took a seat across from him.

Have you come back to end this ridiculous exile?

He frowned. "What exile?"

Your mate's.

He took a deep breath and pressed the towel to his face. "She wants to be here."

No she doesn't.

"Why do you say that?"

Mala pursed her lips and shook her head.

"Mala, if there's something I need to know… Is it Orsala?"

Don't be an idiot!

"Then tell me what's going on."

You're both so foolish, Mala signed. *To have your* reshon *and keep away from her exhibits the most infuriating self-control on the planet. You're both guilty of it, and neither of you will budge.*

"Do you think I don't want her back?" Damien fumed. "Giving her time and distance is killing me."

Then why have you left her alone for so long?

"She couldn't even look at me," he said quietly. "After it happened. Two hundred and fifty years later, and she still won't meet my eyes. We'd meet in London for a week and it would be like tearing open a gut wound, Mala. Every time. That's why I stopped. I'll never give up on her, but she needs to come to me when she's ready."

Mala threw her hands up and clenched them before she started signing furiously. *Wasteful! How you and Sari waste time incenses me. Life is unforgiving and brutal and violent. It has always been so. We hold on to those we love because they are the ones who help us survive it. You of all people know this.*

"That's why I'm giving her time, Mala. After the Crusades—"

After the Crusades, you and all your brothers were walking dead men. Her hands and face spoke fury. *Do you think I don't know this? Alexander healed when he chose to heal.*

"When he met you."

And when did you heal, Damien?

"When I met her," he whispered, closing his eyes. Mala's staff reached out and knocked his knee. "What?"

Don't ignore me. I love you both.

"I know you do." He dug the heel of his boot in the sawdust. "You said she doesn't want to be here."

He saw the coiled tension in Mala's shoulders.

This has gone on for far too long, she signed. *We're isolated here, but we still get news. The scribes' council is out of control. The Fallen powers are shifting. The Irina need to go back, and I'm not the only one who feels that way.*

"Sari?"

It's an awful thing—Mala leaned forward—*to know where you want to go. To know you must get there. And to not know the way. There is no compass for this journey.*

"Since when has Sari needed a compass?" Damien asked. "If there is no path, she makes her own."

I think she's forgotten that, Mala signed. *That's why she needs you.*

"My beautiful one," he whispered in their dream, playing with her hair as she lay on his chest. "My proud girl."

"I am no girl." She sighed. "I have not been a girl for a long, long time."

"You are *my* girl."

Sari said nothing but buried her face in his neck. He put his hand on the back of her head and held her.

"What do you need, *milá?*"

"I'm so tired."

"What do you need?"

"You," she whispered. "I need you."

"I'm here." He pulled her back until her eyes met his. "Command me, love. Tell me what you need and I will give it to you." Damien smiled. "I will fly to the gates of heaven if you wish it."

"Don't leave me."

He stilled. "I will never leave you. I never have."

Her startling blue eyes showed confusion. "But you did."

"Never." He held her gaze. "I am here. I am waiting for you, Sari. All you have to do is come to me."

Her eyes filled with tears. "It won't be enough."

"Sari?"

"There is a hole in me. A hollow well I fear is endless. If I came to you, would it be filled? Or would the emptiness only hurt us both?"

"It is not endless, *milá*. I felt this once too."

"What did you do?"

"I kissed you." He touched her lips with his own. Touched them and left them there. "I loved you, and my proud girl scared the emptiness away."

"That's too simple."

"It's a start." He took her mouth in a longer kiss. "We have to start somewhere."

CHAPTER

THREE

"SO the humans thought you were mentally ill, did they?"

"What were they supposed to think when a little girl told them she heard voices no one else heard?"

At least this Ava had backbone. She would need it. Her heart ached for Ava, but Sari didn't see friends in strangers. And this girl, even mated and marked by an Irin warrior, gave off an energy Sari had never felt before.

One of the first magics the newly hunted Irina developed after the Rending was the ability to conceal their energy. The Irin could sense them, but so could the Grigori. They were soul conduits, hearing the voices of humanity and picking up their energy. In Irin communities, they had thrived with regular contact from their brothers, mates, and sons. Mixed with the human population, they attracted too much attention, grew too manic.

Learning how to conceal and then channel that energy had been the driving focus of the first haven Sari had lived in, the one Gabriel and her grandmother had established in Switzerland. Orsala had gathered some of the oldest singers in Europe with the express purpose of finding magic that could hide their abilities and conceal them from Irin, Grigori, and human senses. They had succeeded, then they had quietly spread their knowledge to the survivors. Over time the Irina became ghosts and legends. For Sari, cloaking her magic had become as automatic as shutting out soul-voices.

But this girl, Ava, had no defenses. The energy that poured off her was dark and tangled. Grief, obviously, but there was something else. She was ready to run. What Sari needed to know was why.

Karen set down lunch, and Sari said, "Eat, sister."

No reaction.

Astrid said, "Please, Ava. Stay and eat with us."

"Fine." Her voice was stiff with suppressed anger.

Sari ignored her and murmured a prayer of thanksgiving for the meal.

Deciding to try a new tack, she said, "I'm glad Damien brought you here. It is not good that you were in the world for so long on your own. You could have easily hurt someone, including yourself. Not to mention, I'm amazed you're not locked up somewhere, rocking in a corner."

"I'm rich enough to avoid padded rooms," Ava said. "So that helps."

"I imagine it does."

What on earth had brought her to Damien? But it hadn't been Damien, had it? It had been Malachi, a scribe in Damien's house. It had been *love*. She remembered herself as a young woman. Would anything have been able to keep her away from Damien? Probably not.

Sari continued, "And then you had to go and stumble into my mate's scribe house."

"He wasn't very happy to have me."

Oh, I bet your appearance tossed him sidewise. Oddly enough, this made Sari like the girl more.

"He's a suspicious old man." *And a proud one.* "The Creator has plans he doesn't always share with his scribes, no matter what they'd like to think. The folly of men is pride."

Astrid said, "And the folly of women is resentment, sister."

"I didn't ask you, Astrid."

Resentment? Why shouldn't she be resentful? Was it folly to guard your heart?

Ava spoke again. "I think Malachi said something similar once. About Damien being a stubborn old man. But… he's still a good man. I can tell."

Astrid caught her eye.

I told you so, the meddling healer seemed to say. *I've told you for years that your mate is a good man and you're lucky to have him, no matter his failings.*

Sari narrowed her eyes at her old friend. *Shut up.*

Astrid said, "It's good that he brought you to us. We can begin your training immediately."

"And what kind of training will that be?"

Magic. Hand-to-hand combat. Magic. Wrestling. Knife fighting. Archery. *Magic.* Staff fighting. Sword training, if the girl had any talent for it. But mostly magic. Sari didn't let an Irina live in her haven without knowing how to defend herself and those she might need to protect.

But no need to make the human girl panic.

"A very thorough training. My grandmother will enjoy meeting such a mysterious Irina."

Ava didn't look pleased. "Oh. Goody."

SHE FOUND HIM SPARRING WITH MALA ON THE EDGE OF THE trees. They were darting in and out of the forest, hacking at each other with sabers, and they were not going easy. Mala had two bleeding cuts on her arm and appeared to be limping.

Damien had a slash across his abdomen and another on his thigh.

And he was loving it.

There were few swordsmen who could match him, but Mala had been trained by her mate, Alexander, who'd been in the same order as Damien during the Crusades. Her fighting style was nearly identical, and Sari could tell both her mate and her friend were enjoying themselves despite the blood.

For the moment, her anger evaporated and she savored watching him. Damien in motion was a pure and violent grace. Like the eagle over the fjord, he glided and struck with equal skill. Centuries of training and a millennia of blood. His family had bred Mikael's line for war, and her mate was the epitome of their success.

He was muscular, but lean enough to be quick. Tall, but balanced. Though they were covered, she knew the lines of his *talesm* stretched up his left arm, over his chest, and down his right side, covering his arm, shoulder, and torso. The family marks his father had scribed down his back were as fierce and fine as the mating mark Damien had tattooed over his own heart.

Mine is the fire. Mine is the blood.

Mine, her soft touch and her sharp tongue.

When he saw Sari standing on the edge of the forest, he held up a hand and Mala stepped back, sword pointed down.

Damien turned to her. "Is it urgent?"

"I can wait for Mala to finish you off."

Mala signed behind Damien's back. *No, sister, that's your job.*

Sari signed back. *Tart.*

Frustrated much?

Unaware of the teasing behind him, Damien stripped off his drenched shirt, and Sari was forced to conceal her reaction. Nothing in the world compared to Damien in the flesh.

He'd always run hot, and she'd always enjoyed seeing him sweat. He wiped the dampness and blood from his face.

Mala signed, *Roll your tongue back in, or take him home and work out some of the bitchiness.*

Sari said, "Is he tiring you out, Mala? Finished so soon? Maybe I need a new weapons mistress."

Damien turned and frowned. "What?"

I'm tired of both of you, Mala signed, laughing. *I'm finished fighting for today. Damien, talk to your mate. Or toss her skirts up. It'll make both of you more pleasant to be around.*

"I don't wear skirts anymore," Sari shouted as Mala walked toward the barn.

Damien leaned against the trunk of a linden tree, his shirt still dangling from his fingers. "Not that I don't appreciate the view of your thighs, but I do miss your skirts." He eyed her legs. "Opportunities always seemed to present themselves when you were wearing them."

"You must be forgetting corsets. They were in fashion once too."

"You hated corsets and avoided them as much as you could."

"I believe you told me once they were tools of the Fallen, designed to make the daughters of heaven weak and breathless."

"They are," Damien said. "They also made access to your breasts more difficult. That may have been part of my hatred."

It was habit to tease him, even after all these years. In all their centuries apart, she missed the ease and pleasure of his company as much as anything else.

"What did you bring me, Damien?"

He shoved away from the tree and walked toward her, his steps sure and his skin still gleaming in the afternoon light. His *talesm* were black against tanned skin. His muscles rippled as he moved over the rough ground. Every instinct in her reached for him, drawn to his voice, his scent, his taste. She crossed her arms over her chest to keep from grabbing him and following Mala's suggestion.

Damien stopped in front of her. His gaze dropped from her eyes to her lips.

"Me," he said. "I brought you me."

Sweet heaven, she could almost taste his mouth on hers.

"I'm talking about the girl."

"I know. She's wounded. Grieving. Bereft of her *reshon*. Unsure of her place in the world without her other half."

I brought you me.

She closed her eyes, and he gripped her chin.

"No," he bit out. "Not anymore."

Her eyes flew open before they narrowed. "You are not the watcher here."

"Don't close your eyes to me. You can't pretend I'm a dream."

"You said you would wait for me."

"I have waited. I've waited centuries." He stepped closer, until she could feel the heat from his skin. "Do you think I'm forcing myself on you?"

"Yes."

"I'm not. I'm just crawling out of the box you forced me into. You're not allowed to close your eyes to me anymore. Not allowed to forget us. Not allowed to pretend we don't exist."

"Nothing could make me or any other singer forget the scribes exist."

"I am not talking about the damn scribes, Sari!"

Shocked silent by his anger, she didn't say a word.

"I am talking about *us*," he continued. "Stop pretending we aren't wounded. Fight with me, damn you. Kiss me. Hit me. Shout at me. Do *something*. But stop living this half life. Stop pretending we both died along with our child."

She struck him. Her fist shot out and struck his jaw before she let out a horrified gasp.

"I'm sorry!" she cried. "I'm sorry, Damien—"

He grabbed her and kissed her, taking her mouth with a hunger born of anger and pain. She could taste the grief on his lips, along with the coppery bite of blood where her fist had struck. His fingers tangled in the knot of her hair, tearing it loose and twisting it around his hand as he drew her in.

She was frozen in his arms. Aching to reach out and grab him. Battling the need to run away.

Reshon, his voice whispered in her head. *Come back to me.*

He slowed, easing Sari from anger to longing, teasing her mouth with soft bites on her lower lip before he drew away and tucked her face into his neck. He laid his rough cheek against her temple.

"Sari, Sari, Sari." He whispered her name like a prayer.

"I'm sorry I hit you," she choked out.

"I told you to."

"We weren't sparring."

"Were we sparring the other day in the meadow?"

No. She'd been venting her rage then too. She might have used staffs instead of fists, but she had attacked him before she kissed him.

"Be angry with me," he continued. "I can bear your anger. Heaven knows, I deserve it. But I can't bear your silence."

"What have you done, Damien?"

What are you doing to me? She couldn't face his grief *and* her own. If she allowed herself to think about the past, the grief would swallow her again.

She took a steadying breath and stepped back. "We need to talk about this girl you brought to me."

"Ava."

"Yes, Ava."

"I did come here because of her. But not only because of her."

She focused on the part she could deal with at the moment. "She's dangerous."

He touched his ear. "I know."

And he did know. Damien had told her how Ava's scream when her mate died had caused his ears to bleed and almost put another of his brothers into a coma.

"She's powerful, but it's more than that," Sari said. "Her power is… different."

"I can't sense it as you do."

"It feels different. Trust me."

Damien frowned and nodded over to a group of large rocks where someone had built a fire pit. They sat across from each other and stretched out their legs, toes almost touching.

Almost, but not quite.

"There has been movement among the Fallen," he started. "Jaron has left Istanbul."

"What does that have to do with Ava?"

Jaron was one of the more moderate of the Fallen. If one could call any Fallen moderate. But while the ancient angel was unspeakably powerful, he mostly ignored the human and Irin worlds. He didn't create vast, silent armies of Grigori offspring. He didn't actively hunt Irina. According to Damien and her grandmother, Jaron had parked himself in Istanbul centuries before and watched the world flow by.

"Jaron has some connection to Ava. An interest in her. We're not sure why."

"A connection?"

"He sent her a vision before he left."

"So she's a seer?"

"Possibly." He glanced up, and she knew he was thinking about Tala. "But her visions are not… normal."

"Are any visions normal?"

"You tell me."

Ignoring a question that would lead too close to an open wound, she redirected him back to the angels. "Why did Jaron leave Istanbul? Especially if he's interested in the girl."

"Because Volund wanted the city."

Volund. The very name pitched her stomach. Over decades, Irina intelligence had learned through interrogation and often torture that the Rending had been masterminded by Volund, an archangel who scared even other angels. His appetite for human lovers was voracious. His legions of offspring were some of the most violent and hungry. Volund was a monster who wanted nothing less than the total destruction of the Irin race. That was why he'd targeted Irin women and children.

"So Volund holds Istanbul now."

"His sons killed Ava's mate. But not Ava. Her voice was too powerful."

A dark thought twisted at the back of her mind. "Is her father Grigori?"

It was possible for Grigori to have children with human women. It usually didn't end well, but sometimes both mother and child survived. Oddly enough, some of the most gifted human artists and geniuses over the centuries were Grigori offspring. It was, in Sari's opinion, the only redeeming feature of their race. Occasionally, their angelic blood showed true and created something beautiful.

"I thought she must be Grigori offspring initially, but I don't think so. Her father is a high-profile musician. He has relationships with women and doesn't kill them. And he's involved in her life. Not deeply, but they do have a relationship."

Which would never happen with a Grigori, because they were monsters.

"How do we know he's truly her father? There's something…"

"Strange?"

"Old." It felt right when she said it. "She feels old. Perhaps not a Grigori. Her father could be Irin. A very *ancient* scribe. Something like that."

Damien's jaw tightened. "Her mother is human."

Sari looked up. "So?"

He folded his arms and shook his head. "I'm not saying that an Irin male has never had an attraction to a human woman. We are not saints. I know it's possible, but——"

"Not possible, Damien. *Probable.* Likely even, since the Rending. It's not as if the scribes have many options for partners, do they?"

"An Irin scribe is not going to take advantage of a human woman just because——"

"Who says he'd be taking advantage?" Sari said. "There is a singer here whose partner is human. Orsala doesn't like it, but there's no denying their feelings. She's not taking advantage of him."

"It's not about feelings! I'm talking about biology. Irin scribes are not like singers. We cannot touch humans. We *will* hurt them."

"It's taboo," Sari said. "Not magic. You know how I feel about this. The fact that touching humans is taboo does not mean it's a biological impossibility. Grigori don't kill women on immediate contact. Biologically, they're——"

"The same as scribes?" he erupted. "No, they are not."

Sari set her jaw. "If Grigori can have human children, then so can Irin. It's possible, Damien. And it might explain Ava."

"No scribe would do this." He crossed his arms. "Maybe it's biologically possible, but it would not happen, Sari."

"Why? Because you wouldn't touch a human? Because you'd never allow any of your men to do it?" She snorted. "Are you still so naive, Damien?"

His eyebrows flew up. "You're calling me naive?"

"Yes." She leaned forward. "You may be older than me, but you're still the noble Irin warrior of ages past. This world is not black and white. It never has been."

"You think I don't know that?"

"You think every scribe has a conscience and a code of honor because you do."

He looked away from her.

"Not every scribe is noble. Not every Irin wants the Irina back. Not every one of your brothers would sacrifice himself to protect me or any of my sisters."

"I know I'm no saint. None of us are."

"No, you're *honorable*. And decent. And good."

"Sari—"

"And I love that about you," she continued, even as her throat started to close. "I love your honor. I love your decency. But Damien, the world is not like that. It's a hard, cruel place. People are selfish and weak. We do things…" She choked. "We do horrible things because we think it's the only way to survive."

Damien locked his eyes on her. "There is *nothing* you can do that would make me love you less, Sari."

She gave him a bitter smile. "That's because you don't know what I've done."

"Do you really think I don't know?"

She shook her head. He didn't know. If he did, her honorable mate would be horrified.

"*Milá…*" He held her gaze. "There is no warrior unstained by guilt. We protect. That is what we do. But it's never without cost. You know the things I've done."

She closed her eyes. The screams of Grigori intermingled with the screams of the children and the desperate pleas of an old man. *Release me…*

"Sari." Damien knelt in front of her. "Come back to me."

His hands on her knees anchored her and undid her at the same time. For a moment, she allowed herself to feel.

"I'm so tired, Damien."

"I know, *milá*."

He cupped her cheek but she kept her eyes closed. If she looked at him…

"Don't be kind to me," she whispered. "I can't be kind to you."

"Why not?"

"Because you make me feel."

He paused. "Is that such a bad thing?"

"If I feel one thing, I'll feel everything." She took a weary breath and pushed his hand away. "I need to talk to my grand-mother about Ava. Maybe Orsala can make some sense of this mess."

Sari could tell Damien didn't want to let her go, but he did.

"She's not a mess, Sari. She's a person who needs help. She is the widow of a fallen warrior, and we owe her succor."

Ah, there he was. The protector. The guardian. The commander of men. Loyal to his men, even beyond death. Loyal to a council who'd led to her destruction.

"Until I know who she is and what she's capable of, she's a threat." Sari rose and walked away from him. "I'm sorry, Damien. Call me a cynic if you want, but I no longer have the luxury of trust."

"OUR WOUNDS BLIND US," ORSALA SAID. "WE SEE MONSTERS in the dark, but the monsters are in the mirror too."

Sari sipped the tea her grandmother had poured. "You think she's the daughter of a scribe and a human?"

"From the power she's rumored to have, I think she must be. No Grigori could father a child with so much magic. I don't even know if a scribe would, but it's the only explana-tion that makes any amount of sense."

"I'm sorry I had to ask you to stay away. This girl…" Sari frowned. "She's like an open wound."

Orsala might have stopped her longevity spells and

allowed time to age her, but her eyes were still sharp. Her mind, a silver blade. "Is it the grief?"

"That and the lack of shields. I see a thousand cuts across her mind, and no one has bandaged them. She does need our help. She needs to know she's not crazy, to start."

"She should know that by now, don't you think?"

Sari raised an eyebrow. "Ava has been told her whole life that she's insane. You think falling into our world has helped? She needs shields. Quickly. Maybe once she has them, she can start thinking clearly. Can you imagine not being able to shield your mind from the humans?"

"No. It's as automatic as breathing for all of us."

Sari stared out the window. Her grandmother's cottage was set away from the rest of the haven and against the trees. Orsala liked her solitude—loved being near the forest that reminded her of her mate—but she wasn't forced into it. For Ava, solitude had been a means of survival.

"She's solitary by nature," Sari said. "She won't take help easily."

"She had to be solitary." Orsala's eyes went to the forest. "You think there's more out there. More humans like this girl?"

"I think there has to be. Maybe not as powerful as she is, but do you really think thousands of scribes have been celibate for two and a half centuries?"

"No." She shifted and took a deep breath. "She has magic. It's uncontrollable right now, but the power is there."

All Irin children were born with magic. Genetically, they were half-angelic. But a child born of a human and an Irin would only have a quarter of that blood. As far as Sari knew, that wasn't enough to control magic the way scribes and singers did.

"It could be her father was ancient," Orsala said. "If he was of an earlier bloodline…"

"One of the first generation?" The first generation of

angelic children had been granted far more power and were damn-near godlike. Many human myths of gods and monsters sprang from those days.

Her grandmother shrugged. "It's possible that would make a difference. What other answer makes sense?"

Sari could tell Orsala wasn't convinced. "I'll bring her to you tomorrow, and you can see for yourself."

"I'll start her training immediately," Orsala said. "No matter where she comes from, the poor girl needs to take control of her future even if her mate is gone. He died, but she didn't, and she's going to have a long life in front of her. Best she not wait to start living it."

Sari kissed Orsala's cheek and walked away, but Damien's words wouldn't leave her alone.

Fight with me, damn you. Kiss me. Hit me. Shout at me. Do something. *But stop living this half life. Stop pretending we both died along with our child.*

CHAPTER
FOUR

D
AMIEN could almost hear his mate shouting in her
head. She had not wanted him to go with her and
Ava to meet Orsala, but Damien decided he didn't
care. In fact, he decided the situation amused him. Sari's reaction to him the day before had been more than satisfactory.
They had talked—truly talked—about their estrangement for
the first time in a century.

> *"You make me feel."*
> *"Is that such a bad thing?"*
> *"If I feel one thing, I'll feel everything."*

Damien had always known Sari's icy reactions to violence
or grief had never meant she didn't feel. If anything, his mate
felt too keenly. Some men might have taken that as a sign to
tread gently.

Damien had trodden gently too long.

"So, why does she live so far away?" Ava asked. "Is it
because of the empath thing?"

"Hmm?"

"Orsala. Why does she live away from everyone else?"

"She can shield herself from the emotions around her," Sari said. "But it costs energy she knew she was going to need to read you the first time. So she went to her house. She likes her solitude, but she's often in the main house."

"That's why you haven't seen her," Damien added. "After today, she'll be around more."

"I feel bad she had to keep away."

Sari said, "She doesn't have to do anything. She chose to. It's no responsibility of yours, so don't feel bad."

Ava was still so human in her reactions and manners. Damien could tell that Orsala's isolation bothered her.

"Still, I'm sorry—"

"Don't apologize." Sari interrupted Ava's attempt to make amends. "My grandmother hates it when Irina apologize too much."

Oh, his gentle girl. Damien sighed to keep from smiling; Sari must have heard it.

"You didn't need to accompany her," she muttered.

"I'm paying my respects to your grandmother, Sari. It would be rude of me not to see her."

"She's not your grandmother."

"No, but she's yours. And, unless you've forgotten, I am your mate. Therefore, she's my family too."

"Trust me. I have not forgotten."

Something must have been bothering her that morning. They'd left on relatively pleasant terms the day before. What could have happened? He leaned toward Sari as Ava walked ahead. "Are you sure about that?"

He slid a finger over the soft skin at her wrist. The air between them sparked, and a surge of sexual energy jolted him. Damien caught his breath as the impact traveled from her skin to his.

Someone was frustrated, and thank the heaven it wasn't only him.

He woke every morning with the memory of her taste in

his mouth and his body raging. Dream walks were growing darker and more vague, as they always did when they were in physical proximity. While their basic physical hunger for each other was served through dreaming when they were far apart, their souls were not apart from their bodies. And everything in Damien's body recognized his *reshon* was near.

Their eyes locked for a moment before Sari tore her gaze away.

Ava was losing patience. "You guys are impossible. You should hear yourselves."

"Then stop listening," Sari said. "It's rude."

"Don't you think I would if I could?"

Ava was saved further headaches by their approach to Orsala's house. When they reached it, the old woman was standing at the doorway, holding out her arms with her eyes locked on him.

"Damien!" Orsala called to him. "Oh, my son. I was wondering when you would come visit me."

He wondered if Sari minded that her grandmother had always kept in contact. Orsala and Damien had bonded centuries before over their love of Sari. As the years passed, they'd become more than family, and Damien considered the old singer one of his truest friends.

"Mother," he greeted her in her own tongue, "does the fire still burn in this house?"

"It does, and you are welcome to its light," she answered. "You and your own." Her eyes flicked to Sari, who was pointedly ignoring them. "You came back for her."

"I had to. She never came to me."

"She would have." Orsala patted his hand. "She will." She turned to the human girl, who was gaping, and took her hand. "And you must be Ava. You are so very welcome. Thank you for coming to visit me."

Damien didn't know what Orsala was reading off Ava, but her approval would be the deciding factor on whether or not they could stay in the haven. Orsala was an empath. She could feel honesty and dishonesty in someone's energy. She could read a person more accurately than any singer Damien had ever met, including his own mother, whose political acumen made her a master of character study.

Orsala's empathy was what had made her such an effective elder. And such a wily adversary. The elder scribes had searched for years, but they'd never found her, nor had they found any trace of the Irina she protected.

She finally squeezed Ava's hand and said, "You have a wonderful sense of humor. I can tell."

Inspection passed, Damien noticed Sari's shoulders relax as Orsala ushered them inside where she prepared tea and made pleasant small talk that made him feel at home and irritated her granddaughter.

Orsala finally cut to the heart of the matter. "How much do you know about Irina blood?" she asked Ava.

"I… a little. Not much."

Ava looked uncertain, and Damien was reminded how much Irin history he took for granted. There was so much about their world that must seem strange and foreign to the girl. Something as simple as male versus female magic was a subject she was still trying to grasp.

"I know that Irin and Irina magic is different," Ava said. "Related, but different."

"Two sides of the same coin is the saying, I think. We speak the same language they write. But unlike us, Irin can grab the magic. Hold on to it with their writing. We can't do that."

Ava nodded. Malachi must have explained that much to her. "Has an Irina ever tried?"

Damien smothered a smile. Oh yes they did, and his mate had the marks to prove it.

"Yes. Some try," Sari said. "It doesn't work for us."

Orsala was quick to add, "No more than an Irin speaking

magic works for them. We are different. We were designed to be."

"And you just end up with messy tattoos and no extra magic," Sari said.

Damien couldn't help himself. "They're not messy. I actually think they're rather attractive, my dove."

Had he just called her his dove? He could almost see an assault spell working its way to her lips. Damien couldn't find it in his heart to care. He was goading a reaction from her. It was the only power he had.

Sari bristled but held in her magic. *"Don't* call me 'my dove.'"

Orsala continued lecturing Ava about Irina magic as Damien watched Sari. With the force of her physical presence so near, it was easy to forget how keen her mind was.

She was beautiful, yes. Her golden hair fell in waves down her back, and her skin was smooth and tan from the summer sun. But her mind and spirit were always what had called to him most. He loved watching her talk about subjects she was passionate about.

"The songs were never meant to be written," Sari said, prim as an academy instructor. "The act of writing them diminishes the power of their meaning."

"I'm not going to get into this argument"—Damien couldn't stifle his smile—"my dove."

"Stop calling me that!"

"Will you both stop?" Orsala snapped, switching into the Old Language. "Or are your petty differences more important than this girl learning about her history and her people? You are embarrassing yourselves, fighting like this. Are you still nursing from your mother's magic?" Continuing to glare at them, she switched languages. "So while I am working with Ava and teaching her beginning spells, you two will continue to research her background. We have records too. And you can speak to Candice."

Candice? Did he know a Candice? Damien didn't think so.

Sari was clearly opposed to this plan. "But—"

"Candice's father was a historian and genealogist," Orsala said to Damien. "One of the first in the Americas, so it's possible she knows something about the families Ava might have come from. Once I get a feeling for her blood, you'll have more to go on."

Was Orsala on his side? He knew Sari's grandmother had wanted them to reconcile for years, but she'd always stayed far away from what she called "family meddles."

"And you want us to work together?" Damien asked. "Are you sure?"

"I am quite positive. Why don't you both finish your tea and start right now?"

Sari said, "Together?"

"Yes. In fact, just take your tea with you and leave Ava and me alone."

Well, this should be fun. Or painful. Possibly both.

He held out his hand. "Shall we, my dove?"

Sari was muttering curses under her breath when she stomped out of the house.

Damien smiled at his favorite grandmother. "So good to see you again, *matka*."

"Don't thank me yet, *Damjan*. You have a long way to go."

AND DID HE. THE MEETING WITH CANDICE COMMENCED immediately after lunch when Sari pointed him toward the library in the main house and left him there. A singer he assumed was Candice came in a few minutes later with several thick, leather-bound journals. She was slightly built, blond, and smiling.

"Hello," she said. "You must be Damien."

He rose to greet her. "I'm sorry we haven't met before. Let me help you with those."

"If you can take these"—she cheerfully handed them over —"I'll get the others."

"Others?"

"There are forty-six," the small woman said. "The majority of the early American records. Mainly from Raphael's line, which was found among the Native American and Norse American Irin. And then the minor angels that followed Rafael, of course."

"But Rafael's lineage was lost," Damien said, staring at the book in his hands. "There are only scattered remnants of his writings in the council archives. How did you come by these?"

"I was the only one left." Candice smiled wistfully. "After." For a moment, the mourning collar she wore around her neck was visible in the late-afternoon light.

She'd lost her mate. And the rest of her family too. Damien wondered how many of the other singers in Sari's haven were as alone.

"My father's journals," Candice continued, "and the journals of his brothers, came to me. It was quite the undertaking to bring them here when I fled the United States, but Orsala and Sari knew they were important."

Damien was in awe. A treasure had jumped into his hands. "I thank you. It should have fallen to one of my brothers to carry this burden." Yet another failure of his brethren. Irin scribes were the keepers of written record. It was their gift and their responsibility. "Heaven will bless you for preserving this knowledge."

"You are welcome to it." She blinked a sheen away from her eyes. "I wonder if you might… Would you take them to Vienna? When you go? There is no real use for them here. I would like to keep my father's personal journal, but all the rest…"

An anchor weighing her to the past. What must it have been like? To be alone with nothing but the writings of your ancestors to keep you company.

"I would be honored, sister." Damien bowed toward her. "I would be honored to carry these records to the Archives. I promise I will keep them safe."

"I know you will. Sari and Orsala both think very highly of you."

Orsala he knew, but...

"Sari?" He smiled. "Does she speak highly of me? You're the first to tell me so."

"No," Candice said. "I said she *thinks* highly of you."

"And how do you know that?"

"It's in her eyes when she speaks of you," Candice said. "Sometimes you don't listen to the words someone says. It's more important to read their eyes."

DAMIEN WATCHED SARI WHEN SHE WAS READING. HE'D ALWAYS loved watching her read. It wasn't her favorite activity. It was too still for her taste. But she did it when it was necessary. Her lips moved along with the words she was reading. Her fingers played in her long hair. She couldn't be completely still.

Feeling his eyes, she glanced up. "What is it?"

"We're not going to find records of her here."

"Why do you say that?"

"Because as far as Ava knows—and as far as Rhys has been able to check—Ava has neither Native American nor Norse blood in her. And all Irin native to the US can track their line to one or the other. We could do a DNA check, but we're not going to find the information here."

"Maybe her family immigrated."

"Then they wouldn't likely be in *these* records." He tapped a stack of more leather-bound journals. "Would they? They'd be in the modern ones that have been digitized."

Candice piped up from the corner. "I agree with Damien. I don't think we're going to find her records here."

Damien needed to freshen his mind with a topic that didn't remind him of the massacre the Americas had faced during the Rending. Almost all the native Irin families had been decimated by the Grigori. The Norse American Irin on the northeastern coast had fared a little better, but not by much.

"Candice, why did you come here?" he asked. "Aren't there havens in the Americas now?"

Candice glanced at Sari, who nodded before the singer answered.

"There are. My mate has distant family here. Some of the scribes in the Oslo house. So I wanted my daughter to be closer to what was left of her people." Candice smiled. "Perhaps at some point, some of them might find mates and have children of their own. It would be the closest she has to cousins."

Damien hadn't known about a daughter. If she was young, then Candice hadn't been widowed during the Rending. "Were you and your mate living in a haven in the Americas?"

"No, he didn't trust them."

Sari said, "Many don't."

"Yes, but in retrospect…" Candice shook her head. "We should have gone to one."

"Looking back is worthless," Sari said woodenly. "We cannot change the past."

"But we can learn from it," Damien said.

"What?" Sari put down the journal she was reading. "What can we learn from the past? Expect the Grigori to hunt us? Not to trust the scribes? Not to trust anyone? Strike before you are struck?"

"You seem to have learned those lessons well," Damien said.

"I had to."

"I know."

Silence descended on the library, and Candice made no excuse when she rose and left them alone.

"We *can* learn from the past," Damien said again. "We can't continue like this."

"It seems as if some of my sisters agree with you," Sari said. "Try to keep this between us, but there is talk among the havens about trying to reform the council. Unless we get some kind of representation in Vienna—"

"You and I."

"What?"

He leaned across the table. "You and I, *milá*. That's what I am talking about. Forget the havens and the council for a moment. *You and I* cannot continue like this."

She reached across the table and grabbed another journal. "I'll talk to you about this when I'm ready."

"You told me yourself you were tired."

"Tired. Exactly. I don't have the energy to deal with politics and still—"

"Hate me?"

She blinked. "I don't hate you."

"Don't you?" He could not keep the bitterness from his voice. "You blame me."

"Am I not allowed my anger?"

Heaven above, yes. He deserved every bit of her anger, along with that of her sisters. The problem was, the anger wasn't helping her survive anymore. It was eating his mate alive.

"Anger drains you," he said softly. "It's a lesson I learned a long time ago."

Her eyes burned. "Does it? I've found that it feeds me."

"But then you feed it, and it grows. Eventually, Sari, it *will* consume you."

She walked over and leaned down to Damien's ear. "Only if I don't find meat to feed it," she said. "You'll have to live without me for a while. I'm going hunting."

SARI LEFT THAT NIGHT. AND DAMIEN DIDN'T SEE HER FOR weeks.

CHAPTER

FIVE

S HE waited, her back pressed to a wall in the dance club, music pumping like the blood in her veins. It was every club in any city she'd ever been to. They all smelled the same. They all sounded the same. The humans all pretended as if they were daring. They weren't. In the vast span of history, Sari found modern humans to be absurdly bland.

A small crush of them walked past laughing, then turned the corner and the hallway was empty again. Except for her. Except for the door leading to the basement rooms where she'd seen the Grigori and the human girl stumble. Sari was waiting. There was only one now, but there were two more out on the dance floor, drawing humans like flies to honey. Soon they'd lure their prey away, and she could strike them all.

A lone figure walked down the hall. Sari could feel the rhythm of the newcomer's heels tapping as she came to a halt beside her. A hint of familiar magic cloaked in carefully concealed power. The tall woman leaned back and rested her shoulders against the wall beside Sari.

"I didn't know you were hunting here."

Sari waited for a group of girls to squeeze past before

answering her sister Renata. "I thought you were on your way back to the haven."

Renata was tall, dark, and striking. The pair of them were almost equal in size, but while Sari had never been slight, Renata could pass for one of the supermodels who posed for magazine covers now. Yet Renata was no pretty face. She was a wildly dangerous, on-edge, revenge-driven Irina hunter.

"No reason not to have a bit of fun before I head home to mother." Renata looked her up and down. "I didn't expect to meet her in a club."

Sari ignored the implied question. It was no business of Renata's why Sari needed to spill blood.

"I count one in the basement," she said. "And two on the floor."

"One in the basement and five on the floor," Renata said. "Or there were when I walked though."

That was a noticeable increase from just fifteen minutes before. "Is there something I don't know?"

"I don't know what information you have. Volund is in Göteborg."

"How sure are you?"

Renata raised a cool eyebrow. "My source died loudly. I believe he told me everything."

A Fallen archangel in Göteborg. Twelve hours from Bergen. Only three by plane. Damien and his black knife could be within striking distance of the angel who had master-minded the Rending within a day. The hissing whispers of her ghosts liked the idea.

"Don't," Renata interrupted her thoughts. "He has a veri-table army of pretty boys around him. Even I'm not that crazy."

"Damien is at Sarihöfn."

"Well, that explains why you're here."

Sari decided to ignore her. "Damien still has his knife."

"Are you sure?"

She turned her head. "Why wouldn't he have it?"

"There are rumors that a heavenly blade was lost in Istanbul recently. I don't know the details, but it could have been his."

"Well, shit."

"My thoughts exactly."

Sari felt them. She angled her head and opened her senses. Grigori soul voices scraped along her mind. She tugged Renata's sleeve, and they faded back into the hallway, waiting for the monsters to come. Waiting for them to make their laughing way down the stairs with the women dangling on their arms. Sari listened carefully but could hear no telltale creaking on the stairs. If they were concrete or stone, the women were in luck.

Next to her, Renata's breath picked up. She wound a black Kevlar-lined scarf around her neck and whispered under her breath as Sari buttoned up the black leather jacket she wore. The collar was reinforced with Kevlar and a fine steel mesh. Grigori always went for the throat first.

Listening to the voices sink underground, Sari and Renata waited a few more minutes before they went for the door. Once inside, they paused on the landing. Sari turned and locked the door. The stairs were concrete covered in industrial carpet, no doubt designed to absorb as much sound as possible from the club above. Lights glowed in the basement lounge, but the stairwell turned and their view was blocked.

Nodding at Sari, Renata drew a knife from her coat, a seven-inch black steel blade; her silver-coated stiletto would be tucked in easy reach. Sari carried nearly identical weapons. One knife to fight with. Another to send their souls to judgment. In this modern world, knives were more practical than swords.

Grigori carried no weapons unless they were expecting scribes, but it was a mistake for any Irina to underestimate them. Even those power drunk on human souls could be dangerous opponents. In the centuries since the Rending, Sari had made it her mission to learn as much about her enemy as she could. If she'd known more—known how to harness her own magic effectively—she could have done more to prevent the slaughter of her retreat.

Grigori were direct sons of the Fallen, and their natural magic was powerful. But they were untrained in formal magic. They did not scribe spells on their body as the Irin did. They could not speak incantations of power.

But Grigori were also fast and inhumanly strong. They were vicious and had nothing to live for save survival and their own indulgence. They were selfish creatures who cared nothing for their brothers, abandoning them or even throwing them in the path of an attacker so they could escape.

Sari listened and waited. The sounds of seduction and pleasure turned her stomach, but she held her peace until it was obvious the six men were occupied. Raising a finger, she began to walk down the stairs. She paused on the landing and peered around the corner.

The lights were dim, but the room was crowded. Couches and chaises lined the walls. One alcove was entirely taken up by a round bed where a man lounged with two women writhing on top of him. The other Grigori were similarly entangled with their prey.

Sari gripped Renata's forearm before she could walk farther. She squeezed until her sister caught her eye.

No humans, she mouthed.

Renata frowned.

No humans, she mouthed again firmly.

Renata rolled her eyes and lifted one shoulder. *Fine.*

Sari leaned close and whispered, "We go in fast. Clean up later."

Renata nodded. With so many humans, there would be no way of taking each Grigori quietly. The women would scream.

But they would live, which was more than they'd had going for them before Sari arrived.

The next second, Renata was gone and Sari ran after. Renata took out the monster guarding the door—his clothes were already falling in a dusty heap—before she moved to the left. Sari went right.

"*Domem man*," she whispered to the first Grigori she saw.

The man froze where he lounged, his neck straining, but nothing else moved. The girl straddling him stopped her ministrations and grabbed his shoulders. She blinked and swayed but said nothing.

"Irina!" the Grigori hissed between clenched teeth.

Sari shoved the shocked—and likely high—human girl off the man's lap, yanked his hair back, and slit his throat in seconds. Pounding music masked the grunts of pleasure that were quickly turning into dying groans. But she didn't have time to plunge her silver stiletto into his spine and release his soul. No, too many other monsters crowded this den.

The first shocked cries came from a blood-splattered girl straddling one Grigori's legs. Her lover was limp below her, his throat cut but his mouth still trying to work. Renata stood behind him, a shadowed figure holding a dripping blade.

"Help! *Heeelp!*" the girl screamed a moment before Renata punched her jaw, sending the girl flying to the ground and silencing her.

After that, any hope of stealth was lost.

Humans ran screaming, some heading straight upstairs with no thought of clothes, only to be trapped by the door that Sari and Renata had locked behind them to contain the mess. Other girls scrambled for the corners of the room. The three remaining Grigori shoved through the mass of panicking females, searching for their attackers and kicking aside those humans who were already passed out.

"*Ya fasham!*" Renata shouted, throwing one off-balance and into a wall.

"*Shanda man,*" Sari said under her breath, directing her voice at a powerful Grigori who shoved two human girls into a wall as he raced toward her. The spell caused him to stumble, but he was stronger than the others.

"*Ya domem.*" She held up her hand and he froze.

His lip curled up. His neck muscles strained. "You… can't hold me… bitch."

"Yes." Sari brought her black knife up and sliced his neck so deeply the blood poured like a river down his chest. "I can."

He went limp, though her magic held him upright.

"Sari!"

She spun just in time to see one charging toward her, tackling her legs and slamming her to the floor before he rolled to his feet and stood over her.

For a brief, panicked second, she was the woman curled on a dirty floor, bloody and beaten by these cursed sons of the Fallen. She screamed, scrambling to her feet and lunging at the monster who'd knocked her down. No finesse. No strategy. She was pure fury and animal instinct.

The Grigori wasn't expecting Sari's wrath. Or her weight. She was no slip of a girl, nor did this creature outweigh her. She knocked him to the ground and grappled until she had him pinned under her body, one knee high in his crotch, the other leg holding him down.

Sari whispered no magic. She raised her arm and slammed a fist into the Grigori's finely arched cheek. She felt the bone shatter beneath her punch, so she drew back and did it again. And again. His head lolled to the side and she let go. Gripping his hair, raising her other fist to smash the opposite cheek in.

"Sari!" Renata's voice cut through the deafening and satisfying crunch.

"Stop playing," her sister bit out. "These humans will figure out how to open the door in minutes."

"Clean up," Sari said, spitting blood from her mouth.

The Grigori below her was dead weight. She turned his neck to the side and drew the silver-tipped stiletto from a pocket near her left breast. The breast that had swollen with milk, even after this one's brothers had killed the child in her womb. She drew the knife and plunged it into the base of his spine. Then she stood and went to the others in the room; they were still clinging to life but immobile from blood loss.

Sari turned each head to the side and plunged the silver knife in, ignoring the pleading eyes of the one she'd cut first. She didn't wait for the young Grigori to dissolve before she went to the second, whose chest was a river of blood. His eyes screamed his hatred, even as the light went out. His face turned gold, and he vanished under Sari's bloody hands.

Within minutes, all the monsters were no more than dust. She and Renata took turns drugging the women on the stairs. Most of them were drunk, high, and suffering from Grigori feeding anyway. When they woke in the empty lounge, the whole episode would be another bad dream.

Sari and Renata climbed the stairs back to the club and walked arm in arm through the surging mass of humans.

They were practiced and efficient. Cleanup had only taken fifteen minutes.

...YOU FEED IT, AND IT GROWS. EVENTUALLY IT WILL CONSUME you.

Sari let Renata drive back to the haven. She stared out the window as Renata babbled about the play she'd seen in Paris and the nightclub in Budapest where she'd tracked a nest of Grigori back to their house and killed them in their sleep. She joked about a persistent lover. Her thoughts about adopting a dog to keep at the haven. They drove through the night, and eventually Sari fell asleep.

She found him in her dreams. When he enfolded her in his arms, Sari let the quiet tears come.

"*Milá*, you must stop."

"I can't. You know I can't. Nor more than you can stop."

"Rest then. Or come with me so you do not hunt alone."

She let him hold her as she cried out the pain and the exhaustion. Her mate held her and kissed her forehead, her cheeks.

"Come to me," he whispered. "I wait for you. You do not walk alone."

THE HAVEN GREETED RENATA LIKE THE PRODIGAL DAUGHTER that she was. Everyone in Sarihöfn knew she'd been called back, but none of them mentioned it. Orsala organized a sing for Renata's return and to formally greet Ava, who'd been working for weeks to tame her magic. As the evening sky darkened, Sari's house filled with people. There were few reasons to celebrate in their small commune. Irin children only celebrated birthdays until age thirteen. Mating ceremonies were few, and Midwinter holidays were still months away.

Sari tried to greet the occasion with the same spirit as the others, but Damien's presence was an open wound. Since he'd come, she couldn't ignore the ache in her spirit or the emptiness in her bed. Even his presence that night seemed designed to torment her. The warm brown shirt he'd worn brought out the gold flecks in his dark eyes. His step was light and his voice soothing. Everything in her yearned to go to him and indulge in the luxury of his presence.

"Why are you avoiding him?" Renata asked, leaning

against a counter in the kitchen where Sari was making spiced wine.

"Who?"

"You did not just ask that."

Sari cut her eyes to Renata. "Did you see Maxim when you were on the continent? How is he? Are you over your ludicrous excuses yet?"

Renata rolled her eyes. "Fine. Keep your secrets. But you should know the man is hunting for you, and he's got better instincts than both of us combined."

"Maybe once. Not anymore."

"Don't fool yourself," Renata said. "Sometimes I wonder if you see him at all."

"Don't be ridiculous." She stirred the wine. "And don't pretend you know my mate better than I do. It's presumptuous."

"Predators don't roar before a hunt, sister." Renata pushed away from the counter. "Some of the most dangerous don't roar at all."

As if they'd planned it, Damien sauntered in moments after Renata left.

"Your hunt went well," he said, crossing his arms and leaning against a wall, watching as she poured the wine into a crock made for warming.

"Is that a question?"

"No. Renata said you took out a nest of seven."

"Six."

"Hmmm." He frowned. "She said seven. Perhaps she marked a kill before she joined you."

"Six or seven. That's a few less to prey on the humans in the city."

"Renata told me Volund is close by."

Sari paused. "Did she say where?"

"No. Should she have?"

Her shoulders relaxed. If Damien knew Volund was

nearby, he would report it to the council. The same council that had sent him after more than one angel in his time. Whether he made it out alive was irrelevant to the elder scribes. He was theirs to command, and the knowledge had always infuriated her. But there had been nothing she could do. They would call and he would answer.

That was assuming he still had his heaven-forged blade.

"Do you still have the blade?"

"No."

She spun. "What? Why? What happened?"

"I didn't lose it," he said softly. "Nor was it taken from me."

"So what happened? Are the elders now demanding control over the spoils of war?" She hated that knife and everything it represented. But her mate had bought it with blood, killing an angel before most scribes had earned their first battle scars.

"I asked to store it in Mikael's armory in Vienna. Living in Jaron's territory saw little need for it. The Library Guard will return it if and when I have need of it. I have their word."

It also made the Elder Council less likely to call him for assassinations if he didn't carry that blade with him. Yet Damien had never been one to avoid danger. If anything, he plunged into it. There was something more to this. Something he was holding back.

Sari asked, "When did this happen?"

"Why do you care?" His voice took on an edge. "Do you have need of it?"

Her face reddened. "You know I cannot wield it."

There were specific magics needed to wield a black blade. Magic that had never been taught to the Irina. The spells a scribe worked on his body were intricate and layered, often inscrutable to anyone but the one who had written them. The deep magic that allowed an Irin scribe to command a blade forged in the heavenly realm would be hidden within *talesm* tattooed over centuries.

In contrast to Irin spells, Sari's spells were blunt instruments scraped together in desperation. Ancient Irina singers of Mikael's line once sung battle magic so potent, legends said a single voice could turn an army. There were songs written about them, great sagas of their frightening power.

But most of that magic had been lost.

The Irina had civilized. Modernized. Turned their attention to the burgeoning disciplines of science and art. And slowly they'd been marginalized. Forgotten.

Until they were tame. And then they were dead.

Damien slid closer, glancing at the doorway, which had remained miraculously empty. Magic at work? Or just her grandmother and Renata? Sari would bet on the second.

"I gave up the weapon..." Damien paused. "If you ever called for me, I wanted no tie to the council to hold me back. I could not take such a weapon from the meager arsenal the elders had after the Rending. But I did not want to be beholden to them if you called."

Sari's breath fled. He'd given up an object of extraordinary power so that he could come to her if she called.

"You would abandon your men?"

"Yes."

"Defy the council?"

"Yes."

She hadn't believed him. A wave of anger rose up and choked her, but this time the anger was directed at herself. She'd called him a liar. Spat in the face of the sacrifice he'd made, though she hadn't known he'd made it.

"Why didn't you tell me?" she asked.

"Would it have made a difference?"

Yes.

She said nothing, but he saw the truth in her eyes. It would have made a difference. Knowing his loyalty lay with her —*only* with her—might have changed everything.

Damien let out a strangled laugh. Then, shaking his head, he walked away.

CHAPTER

SIX

DAMIEN had to leave the kitchen, or he would have screamed. One act—minor in his own mind—might have healed the breach between them over one hundred years before. He walked into the night, striding toward the barn lit with tiny lights to celebrate Ava and Renata. Groups of friends and a few small families were already trickling into the barn. Laughter and light called him, but Damien stopped and stood in the dark.

He'd never told her. He'd never realized it meant so much. Sari had always distrusted the council, but it had never occurred to him that his loyalty to her and to their union was in question.

"Are you sure? I don't think—"
"The council has demanded it, milá. *I don't have a choice."*

A hundred small memories batted at him, each as damning as the last.

"But why must all the Irina go? Don't the watchers have any say?"
"This is a ruling from Vienna, Sari. I am not an elder."

"The elders have mandated…"

"Council protocol says…"

"This is what I do." He'd left her after their first night together. *"Do you understand? This is* always *what I will do."* He'd abandoned her, warm and vulnerable in his bed, to follow the dictate of a council half a world away. He'd abandoned her and her sisters in a retreat away from his protection, then commanded his men to do the same.

Why shouldn't she have thought his first loyalty was to Vienna? His every action had spoken that truth, even if she had always been first in his heart.

He turned when he heard footsteps. Orsala joined him in the shadows.

"I am a fool," he said.

"No more than we all can be." She put a hand on his shoulder. "The sing is about to start. Come. I think the two of you need healing tonight more than anyone else here."

He could feel the magic growing in the air, like the heady perfume of lavender in the summertime when the fields bloomed near his father's castle. Songs drifted on the wind, caressing the land that hummed with Sari's power.

"I have been blind," he whispered. "Proud. Stubborn."

"And so has she."

Damien turned to the black forest and breathed out a soundless scream of frustration. "What do I say?" he asked Orsala, wishing his mother, as blunt as she could be, was with him. "I don't know how to fix this, *matka*. I never did."

"Words are useless. Truth is not gentle. Show her," Orsala said. "Tell her everything. Stop trying to shield her and don't wait for her to ask. *Show her.*"

Show her what? That she was his heart? The pulse of his blood? The only hope of joy he clung to?

Damien walked into the barn and took a place near the

side door. He couldn't bear to sit with the happy families and laughing friends. He spotted Ava sitting near Astrid and checked to make sure she was well. But though the girl looked uncertain, she didn't look scared. Only curious.

He let his eyes fix on Sari, who was sitting at the front of the room with Orsala, Renata, and an older woman Damien was guessing was the chief archivist. Not attempting to hide his stare, he noted that his mate continually sneaked glances at him, though her eyes never fixed as his did.

Show her.

Orsala stood and greeted the assembly. "We are here to celebrate a new sister among us and a sister returned home. As is our custom, we welcome our sister Ava with the songs of our fathers. It is with our voices we remember, with our ears we understand..."

Sari and Renata started a harmonic hum that was soon joined by the other Irina in the room. The communal magic drifting in the air found focus and began to pulse and flow. It stroked along his arm, teasing his *talesm*, then twisting away, the curl of energy like laughter against his skin.

Silly scribe, it seemed to say. *You cannot capture this power with ashes.*

The hair on his arms rose as the chief archivist began the Song of Uriel's Fall, a creation story about the first of the Forgiven to fall to earth, enchanted by the beauty of a human queen, Anat. It was a song of joy and power that fell into despair when Uriel returned to the heavens. Anat remained, struggling to care for her children, the first of the Irin race. The angel returned, but not to stay. He blessed his children with the magic of long life, protecting them and Anat, who reigned into old age with her children around her.

Legend or history? It didn't matter to Damien. It was Irina history told in Irina song. It grew and stretched to the voice that sang it, changing and molding itself over time, new with each voice, yet still the ancient story.

MEMORIES

Through the tapestry of singing, Damien heard Sari's magic, a voice unique through all time. A voice that, once silent, the universe would never hear again. A treasure. A gift.

Reshon, his soul whispered.

Created for him as he was for her.

Show her.

Damien let his heart pour through his eyes. Focused on his mate as the song grew louder.

Let the whole assembly see how he adored her. How he longed for her. His mating marks were living silver and Sari's a gleaming gold. Their eyes met across the room. His soul broke open as he willed her to see his need for her. His joy in her song and his longing for her presence.

Her gaze met his and locked. For a moment, she sang only to him.

> Now rest in the power of heaven, my love
> Forgive me for my absence
> I long for the jewels that live in your eyes
> And the golden touch of your hand

He held out his hand. Sari rose and came to him. The magic grew louder and stronger as a single voice rose above the others. He recognized Ava, her magic threaded with darkness and a power unlike any other.

In that moment, Damien saw a great circle rising in the sky, a sun of twisted gold and silver. Behind the sun, a thousand stars hidden by the glow of the swirling star that lit the heavens. A thousand stars waiting to be seen. To be heard.

He and Sari existed in the vision. They were both a part of it. One with the twisting star in the center of the sky. Rising. Growing. Poised on the precipice of change and wholly dependent on each other to survive.

Sari breathed it in as he did, resting her cheek against his chest. Their hands met, palms together as their fingers knit and held.

"Make love to me," she whispered.

"Yes."

In a daze of raw emotion and pure magic, she led him out the side door and to her house, up shadowed stairs and into her bedroom. He saw nothing, noticed nothing except her. The skin revealed by moonlight. The waterfall of golden waves down her back. Damien had lost the ability to speak.

Show her.

He took her mouth gently. Urgently. Swallowed her needy gasps and lifted her from her feet. He brought her to the bed and laid her down as he eased off the last of her clothes. His eyes could not take in the beauty of his mate laid before him, her body lit gold as if the sun and stars lived beneath her skin, her hair spread behind her like feathers.

He took off his clothes, his eyes never leaving hers.

"Who said"—he crawled up the bed, fingers spreading her tresses across the pale sheets—"that angels don't have wings?"

His heart was light with joy.

She reached out and grasped his shoulder, drawing him down to her. Damien rested on his forearms, her breasts pressed against his chest and his legs between her thighs. He felt her heat against him. The teasing scent of her arousal and magic filled the air.

"We don't have wings," Sari whispered, reaching down to grasp him. "But some of us have swords."

His mouth fell open at the pleasure of her hand. "*Sari.*"

"And songs."

"Your voice," he panted, "is the most beautiful sound in the world."

She arched up and whispered, "Your touch brings me to life."

He thrust his hips, sliding between her fingers and into the welcoming heat of her body. Her neck arched back, and she closed her eyes with a gasp.

"Eyes," he said.

"Don't stop." She lifted her legs and wrapped them around his hips. "Never stop."

He wasn't going to. But…

"I need to see your eyes." He paused and put a hand on her cheek. "Sari."

With a shivering gasp, she opened them and stared straight into his.

"I need to show you," he said. "You have to see."

Her eyes shone as she nodded. Sari placed both her hands on his cheeks and drew him closer, never letting her eyes leave his even as he made love to her.

A gift. A moment of grace.

Damien didn't ask why. He took her gift, poured his heart into his eyes, and did everything he could to show Sari that she was everything.

THEY MADE LOVE TWICE MORE THAT NIGHT. DAMIEN DIDN'T sleep. For long hours he held her, feasting on her touch and the weight of her body spread across his. He had no need to dream. His dream lay in his arms for however long he could keep her. He'd shown her his heart, but did he dare show her his pain when hers felt so much greater than his?

As the dawn light turned a familiar pearly blue, he spoke. "Our daughter would have been born this time of year."

Sari froze but did not pull away.

"I know you thought it was a son. But I always dreamed of a daughter."

"Why are you speaking of this now?"

He couldn't read her voice. "The better question is, why haven't we spoken of this earlier?"

She rolled over, not leaving his arms but turning her back to him. "It was a long time ago."

"We never talked about it. Not once. It was as if she never lived."

"She didn't."

He reached down and pressed his hand to her belly. "She *did*."

Sari was silent for a long time. When her voice finally came, Damien thought it might break him.

"Don't make me speak of this," she whispered.

"Then don't speak." He pressed his forehead to her temple. "Let me speak."

She didn't move. Not an inch.

"I miss her," he said. "Every day. The year she would have turned thirteen and sung her first blessing, I was a wreck for months. I traveled to Jerusalem and sat on top of the Zion Gate, watching the pilgrims come and go. I saw a girl who would have been our daughter's age traveling with her parents, and I broke down weeping. I went to the desert after that."

"To the Rafaene house?"

Encouraged, he continued. "They didn't ask questions. I wasn't the only one there."

She said nothing more.

"I didn't lose our child," he continued. "Not as you did. But I *did* lose her, Sari. Or him. Do you know how happy I was?" He felt her tears on his arm. "I was over seven centuries old when you became pregnant. I'd lost hope of ever having a family. Then I met you. And you were… so startling. So unexpected. When I discovered you were with child, I thought, I do not deserve this happiness."

"Don't say that."

"I didn't deserve it. I don't. But that joy was given to me

for a brief time, and I treasured it, even if it ended in tragedy. Because she did live. And she was loved deeply."

Her chest was heaving, her eyes dripped with tears, but Sari cried in silence.

"I still miss her, *milá*. I need you to know that. I still think about her. I still—"

"Damien, please."

"I need you to know that I have not forgotten her. That I never will."

Her body was still beside him. Her voice, when it came, was a whisper. "Please leave."

Every instinct in him begged to stay. For her comfort, and for his. Damien closed his eyes and pressed his forehead to the back of her shoulder. "Are you sure?"

"I want to be alone."

She'd let him say more than he thought she would. Damien placed a soft kiss on her shoulder and released her.

Sari immediately fled to the attached bathroom, shut and locked the door. He dressed in silence and made his way back to his cottage just as the sun broke over the horizon.

DAMIEN SUSPECTED HE'D MADE A HUGE ERROR, ORSALA'S advice or not, when Sari refused to meet his eyes the next day. And the next. In fact, though Sari had stopped sniping at him, she completely avoided spending any time alone. He'd been afraid she'd leave the haven again, but she didn't. She just didn't talk to Damien.

"Ava's magic," Orsala said after she'd dragged him to her cottage for tea. "I want to talk to you about it."

"About the darkness?"

"You've seen it too?"

"Felt it." He paused and thought, trying to tease out the

memories of his sister's magic from the intensity of his night with Sari. "It's not evil, but it feels…"

"Dangerous."

"Yes."

Orsala sat and ran a finger along the edge of her mug. "I think, for now, we watch and wait. She's still grieving, and that might be part of it."

"Did you see anything like this after the Rending?"

"No."

And that had been the most intense period of grief any of them had ever experienced.

"Then probably there is something different about her. About her magic." *About her blood.*

Orsala seemed to understand what he had not said. "I thought she was of an ancient line of Irin at first, but… Is it possible?"

"That her magic is of the Fallen?" He shifted in his seat "Anything is possible, *matka.* We know her mother, but her father is a mystery. Her magic is…"

Indescribable. Damien didn't know how to classify what Ava had done at the sing. No seer he'd ever met had been able to show others a vision as Ava had.

Orsala paused. "I don't know what to think."

"I think things are changing. I don't know how or why. But the impossible has become real. A woman with no connection to our race has been marked and mated to one of our blood. Her magic is unlike any other. Perhaps this is a sign from the Creator, or perhaps it's something else."

"If there are more women like Ava out there, more women who have survived in the human world…"

"Trust me when I say every Irin scribe with no hope of a mate or family will think of this," Damien said. "I *have* a mate and I thought of it. If there are more Irina out there—women who can join our race—every scribe in the world will be looking for them."

"But we don't know enough about her." Orsala shook her head. "As I said, she's not evil, but there is something different. Her heart is good. It's filled with incredible sadness right now, but her heart is a good one."

"So we watch and wait," he said, taking a gulp of tea and wishing it was spiked with whiskey. "It's the only thing we can do."

Orsala rose to refill their cups. "What happened with Sari? You were together after the sing and now she'd not speaking to you."

"I talked to her about the baby," he said. "She asked me to leave. I was not shocked."

Orsala's face went blank. "Well, no one can ever say you avoid the thick of battle."

"We never talked about it, *matka*. Not once."

"This is Sari. She doesn't talk about any of it."

He huffed. "Do *any* of the singers?"

"Do the scribes?"

"Yes."

Orsala blinked. "Really?"

"Orsala, there is a generation of Irin scribes with no mates. No children. And no hope of either. Of course they want to know why." He tried not to let his frustration get the better of him, but there was anger too. "I have two scribes in my house who were babies when their parents were killed. This world, this twisted reality, is the only life they've ever known. Irina are myths to them. When Malachi brought Ava to the house, you'd have thought they saw a ghost."

He glanced out the window at the small row of houses on the edge of the haven. Set back in the trees, they were populated by rogue scribes and the mates they refused to leave behind. Men who had abandoned posts and assignments when their singers needed to flee. To the Irin Council, they were rogues. To Damien, they were an example of what he should have done.

"You don't have many scribes here," he said, "but you do have them. The few children who are born see mates and families around them. The generation of scribes that were abandoned by the Irina have never known what it is to live in a world where they aren't isolated and alone."

"We did what we thought was right," Orsala said. "We took the children we could find."

"And you left many behind."

"What were we to do, Damien? Take children away from their fathers? We could never do that."

"I don't know!" He raked a hand through his hair. "But I wish we were not judged for the sins of our fathers."

"Were they not your sins too?"

He turned toward Sari's voice. She was standing in the door, black sunglasses protecting her eyes.

"Grandmother, Karen was hoping you could help her with a recipe. I was sent to find you." Her head angled slightly toward Damien. "And now I'll be going."

No. Dammit, *no.*

Damien followed her, fed up with her avoidance. He reached out, but she turned and raised a hand.

"*Ya sala domem.*"

He halted at the spell. He could feel his body straining against her magic. She wouldn't be able to hold him long, but if he were an enemy, it would be enough for the advantage.

"A new spell. I approve," he managed to say. It felt as if he were talking through mud.

"I'm so glad you do."

"What have I done to earn your ire this time, my dove?"

"The sins of your fathers? But none of your own?"

"I know my sins better than any other," he said. "I have lived with their consequences for centuries."

"So have we."

"I can admit it when I'm wrong," he said. He stretched his

shoulders up as he felt the spell ease. "It was never my intention—"

"Intentions don't matter when the outcome leaves you dead." Sari backed away from him, walking farther down the path. "That's another lesson we learned."

"The scribes learned lessons too, you know." Damien spoke quietly. "We learned what it means to lose our hearts. To lose our minds. We learned what it is to be alone."

"Alone, maybe. But alive."

"Do you know how many surviving warriors took their own lives in the decades after the Rending?" Damien said, his anger building as her magic waned. "Two in ten. Twenty percent of our men were unable to carry on. And it wasn't only grief, Sari. It wasn't only those who had lost mates and children. It was *guilt*. It was shame. That we had been blind to the plans of monsters. That we had never conceived of that level of brutality."

"You should have."

"You think I don't know that?" he yelled. "That they didn't? They *killed themselves* because they failed. Is that not punishment enough in your eyes?"

Sari blinked back tears. "What do you want me to say? That I grieve for them? I do."

"They didn't want your *grief!*" he said. "We only ever wanted your forgiveness. But we knew we didn't deserve it."

"Damien—"

"I see them in my sleep," he continued, the pain rushing back to the surface. "I see the blood and the dust and the smoke from their fires. Because I failed them too. I failed you. I failed Tala. I failed our *child*." He felt tears on his cheeks, but he did not wipe them away.

Show her, Orsala had said. He'd show her. He'd show her every black thought and twisted shame. Then she could rip him to pieces if she wanted. It was the least he could offer after killing her sister and her babe.

"After I failed my mate, my child, and my sister," he continued. "I failed my men. Because I was their watcher and I didn't see. It wasn't their fault they weren't in the village to protect their families. It was *mine*."

She took her sunglasses off. Her eyes were bloodshot. She looked like she hadn't slept in days. "The Rending was not your fault," she whispered. "We all should have seen the signs. I was a warrior too."

"And I was your watcher. In the end, it was my responsibility. What good is a watcher who does not see? He is nothing. *Nothing*."

"I never said that! Don't put words in my mouth."

"You're not the one saying it. I am."

"Damien—"

"I don't blame them, you know. The ones who killed themselves. I can't blame them. Not when I'm the one responsible for their deaths."

"No." She rushed to him, wiping the tears from his cheeks as if they didn't have the right to touch him. "Damien, no."

"I failed them all, Sari." He grabbed her wrist and pulled her hand away. "I failed you, and you won't forgive me. I don't blame you."

Damien turned and walked into the forest, losing himself in the trees and leaving Sari behind. She did not call him back.

CHAPTER SEVEN

S ARI sat staring at the empty bed in her room. She hadn't followed Damien. She needed to calm down, and he needed to know she was thinking about what he'd said.

Tala's death.

The council's inaction.

Why did the wound still ache *so badly*?

She had never doubted Damien's sorrow. Never doubted his pain. But the well of guilt that consumed her mate was something he *had* hidden from her. Knowing Damien, she shouldn't have been surprised.

Sari was as angry at herself as she had ever been with him. She knew there was no way any of them could have known. They had all been taken unaware. He was no more responsible for the Rending than any other scribe.

"We only ever wanted your forgiveness. But we knew we didn't deserve it."

How could she forgive Damien when she couldn't forgive herself?

She rose and wiped the tears that had fallen down her cheeks. She'd been still for too long. All she needed to clear her head was a good bout with a training dummy. She strode out the door and headed for the barn.

Maybe neither of them deserved forgiveness. Maybe that wasn't the point. What would happen if, instead of fighting for her own forgiveness or withholding it from her mate, she just gave in? Accepted it. And him. And moved forward.

Renata fell into step beside her while she walked toward the barn. "I want to talk about Ava."

"Reni, I can't right now."

"Because you're fighting with your mate?" Her friend snorted. "You both need to get over it."

"Get over it?"

Renata usually wasn't so flippant.

"Yes," she said. "Get over it. It's not Damien's fault the Grigori are bastards."

"I know that."

"And it's not his fault your sister died."

Sari stopped. "You don't know anything about that."

"I know what Orsala has told me about her, and I know she was a seer."

"So?"

Astrid must have been drawn to their raised voices. She walked over to them, her hands in her pockets and her collar raised against the whipping wind. "What are you two arguing about? Renata, it wasn't only Sari who wanted you back. All of us thought you needed a break. So stop—"

"That's not what we're talking about," Renata barked. "Sari, if anyone could have prevented the Rending—anyone at all—it was the Irina seers. If they didn't see the signs, why on earth would the watchers have seen? Why didn't the elder singers see it?" Renata crossed her arms. "I have more anger for the elder singers than anyone else. They are the ones who allowed the council to isolate us. They are the ones who scoffed at martial magic. If anyone is to blame, it is ourselves."

"We were following the leadership of our elders!" Sari said

"So were they!"

"So we all blame ourselves?" Astrid asked in an acidic tone. "Excellent. Now we can all go punish ourselves and be miserable. Honestly, isn't there anyone who would just rather blame the Grigori?"

Sari and Renata turned to the healer.

"We all lost," Astrid continued. "Every single one of us. There was no one unwounded by the Rending. Even scribes in isolated libraries who'd taken vows of silence and celibacy felt the loss. And then we did exactly as the Grigori wanted. We turned on each other!"

Renata said, "Astrid—"

"Wouldn't Volund be pleased?" The healer continued to rail. "I'm no better than anyone. I have blamed the scribes. Blamed the council. Blamed myself. Meeting Ava has reminded me that there *are* honorable scribes in our world. Beyond the council. They are waiting for their partners and sisters. If we hide in our safe havens and do not join them in this fight, then we have allowed the Fallen to win."

Renata said, "It's not as if we do nothing. We have killed as many Grigori as the scribes."

"So why do we hide?" Sari said. "Why do we keep this a secret? It's not a secret from the Grigori. They can spot an Irina assassin on sight. We only keep it secret from the scribes. As if what we do is shameful."

Renata said, "I have no shame in it."

"Then why are we hiding?"

Renata had no answer. But Astrid did.

"Because we're afraid," she said. "Because we are still afraid."

SARI WATCHED THE SMALL COTTAGE WHERE DAMIEN AND AVA were staying from her vantage point on the porch of the main house. The lights glowed, and she could hear the faint sounds of laughter. Her friends were there. Karen and Bruno. Renata and Astrid. They had welcomed her mate and their new sister to the haven with an openness that Sari lacked.

Perhaps the hospitable part of her had died in the Rending. Perhaps it had never existed at all. She was not a creature of the hearth and the home, despite the earth magic that ran in her veins. She was made to protect. Made for war. Once, Damien had loved that about her.

Mala stepped out the front door and came to stand in front of her. *Go to him.*

Sari shook her head. "He's enjoying his night. He needs a good night."

His tortured confession still haunted her. She did not fear her mate taking his own hand to harm himself, but self-destruction could come in other forms. Perhaps he would go to the council and offer to bear the heaven-forged blade again. Perhaps there was one battle from which he would simply not return.

Go to him, Mala signed again. *He needs you more than he needs peace.*

Sari laughed then, a pained sound that cracked the night air. "Do you know how often I have wondered what the heavens were thinking? One *reshon* in the world, and I was chosen for him."

Mala said, *As he was chosen for you.*

Damien was a scribe among scribes. Battle-tested and honor-bound. The finest of Mikael's blood. The hope and pride of his family. She heard his low murmur cross the space between them and wondered what stories he was sharing.

"Any singer would be honored to mate with such a man," she said softly.

If you won't go to him, then you need to go to Renata, Mala signed. *Our contact in Bergen called. There were three Grigori spotted there.*

Not unheard of, but coming on the heels of Renata's return, Ava's appearance, and her mate's presence, it seemed significant.

So go, Mala signed. *Tell Renata and let her hunt closer to home. She's getting on my last nerve.*

Sari nodded and descended from the porch, crossing the space between her mate's cottage and her home. She knocked on the door, surprised to see Ava, not Damien, answer.

"May I come in?"

Damien appeared in a flash, standing behind the small woman holding the door. "Sari?"

It was only then that she remembered his words: *When you are ready*, milá. *When you can find forgiveness in your heart for me, come to me. Knock on my door, and I will always open it. Always. Come to me when you are ready to take me back.*

Oh damn.

Damien's mouth hung open.

Panic stole her breath for a moment. No. She hadn't meant… There was still so much to talk about.

Damien's eyes were ablaze with the most painful emotions she could have seen on his face.

Hope.

And incandescent joy.

Panic fled and peace whispered in her ear, *It is time.*

Enough.

Sari knew that nothing could keep her from him when he looked at her as he did. No anger, no pain, no fury was worth the loss of this man's joy.

And they were surrounded by five of their friends.

"Sari!" Renata called. "Come in! Wine or coffee?"

She had to do something. She stepped into the house. "*Kaffe*, thank you."

"Of course."

It was Ava who finally closed the door after Sari moved into the cottage and took a chair Bruno dragged to the table for her. Karen set a cup of coffee in front of her, and Sari drank it mechanically.

Moments later, Damien sat across from her, shock gone, a wicked teasing happiness in his eyes. The corner of his mouth lifted because he thought she had surrendered.

The fact that she had did nothing to soften her mood.

"My dove, what brings you here—*to my door*—tonight?"

If he hadn't called her "my dove," she might have resisted the urge to antagonize him. She sipped her coffee as if her body wasn't already rioting. "You know, this is my land. My guesthouse. So technically, I don't think this is your door."

"I believe that's what they call 'splitting hairs.'"

Astrid said, "Well, this is entertaining, but I do think there might be some larger purpose to this visit than just coffee and cake."

Trust Astrid to understand when her emotions were in chaos. "There was a group of Grigori spotted in Bergen."

Damien's mood shifted immediately.

"How many?" he and Renata asked.

"Three that we know of. But I'd not be surprised if there were more. There's an Irin couple who lives there, among the humans. No children. They watch for us."

Renata said, "I'll go."

"I'll go too," Damien said.

"No," Sari said, surprising herself. Damien and Renata would work well together. But...

She could not see him leave again. Not when nothing had been resolved.

"This is our territory," Sari said. "Renata will take care of them."

Damien obviously thought her pride was getting in the way of her sense. "Sari, this is no time for—"

"Besides, I'd like you and Bruno to start doing patrols

around the perimeter of the haven. Orsala has sensed some outside magic, and she wants us to be careful. Some protective spells written on the trees would be appreciated."

It was true. The fact that Orsala had asked Bruno to do it and mentioned nothing about Damien was something she didn't need to share.

He was still irritated. "Fine. And Bruno and I will start patrols. It's only three Grigori. I'm sure Renata can handle that on her own anyway."

Renata teased him. "You just wanted to steal my fight."

"Obviously."

Sari glanced at Ava, the woman her grandmother told her was a seer. She saw nothing of Tala's skill or confidence about her, but who knew what might be lurking behind that inscrutable facade?

"I don't suppose you've seen any threats?" she asked.

"Uh... Should I have?"

"You're a seer."

"I'm not very good though."

Well, at least false pride wasn't an issue.

Bruno's laugh was cut off by his mate.

"No, really," Ava continued. "You can ask your grand-mother. I was trying to do... the thing I did the other night at the sing. And I couldn't. So I don't know if I'll see any trouble coming. If there is any coming."

The girl didn't know visions didn't work like that.

Not like that.

"The house. The house, of course. I know where it is. The clothes are mine. I can see them there, but this time everything is silent."

I know where it is.

The clothes are mine.

Empty clothes. Tala foreseeing her own death, though she could have no idea what it would mean.

The visions didn't work like that.

If only they did.

Sari wanted to be angry, but she couldn't. Tala couldn't have known. And neither could Damien.

Ava was still stuttering and confused. "Is there… some trouble coming?"

Renata answered her. "Trouble is always coming. I'll take care of it."

Sari warned her out of habit. "Don't be too eager. We don't want them to know they're close to anything important. Draw them away from the city if you can."

"And try to find out who they belong to," Damien added. "I know Grigori in the territory generally belong to Volund, but we had some surprises in Istanbul. Powers may be shifting."

Sari glanced at Renata. She hadn't told Damien about Volund.

"Powers are always shifting," Sari said.

"Change is constant." Damien locked his eyes on her. "And healthy."

"According to you."

"You can't stop this," he said for her ears alone. "You never could."

No, she never could. Her need for him was an addiction. "I can try."

The problem was, she didn't really want to succeed. And he knew it.

"You shouldn't."

Ava wasn't completely oblivious to the tension in the room. "Well, obviously we're not talking about Grigori anymore."

No, they weren't. Damien still stared at her and Sari couldn't look away. This night would change everything. He'd shown her his scars. She'd never tried to hide hers. If she took him back tonight, it would be forever. She would allow nothing less than his complete loyalty. To her. To the Irina.

And that might mean his precious council would have to go to hell.

Renata said, "I want to take Ava to Bergen."

Was she crazy?

"Absolutely not." Sari was shocked when she heard Damien's voice echoing her own. "You don't think she should go?"

"No."

Sari stood. She had to do *something*, and bolting from the room wasn't an option. "But she'd be a tactical advantage. I've heard about her range."

"She's too young. And untrained."

"She'd be with Renata."

As Tala was with you.

"She would still be vulnerable."

Because she was not a warrior. Renata and Mala had both been in awe of the range from which the girl could hear Grigori, and Sari had considered taking over her training to make her more field ready, but she was still a long way from prepared.

Once, Damien wouldn't have cared about that. He would have been convinced he could protect her.

As he'd been with Tala.

"Wait, I'm confused." Ava broke in. "Are you arguing for or against me going with Renata?"

Everyone shushed the girl, but Sari couldn't take her eyes off Damien. "Are you telling me it wouldn't be worth the risk? To have an intelligence advantage like her skills in the field—protected and at a distance from combat—are you telling me you wouldn't risk that?"

His voice was quiet. For her ears. "I wouldn't risk it. I wouldn't risk her. Not anymore, Sari."

She knew he was telling the truth, but the tears came anyway. "But… it makes the most tactical sense."

"*Milá*, I learned the hard way. Not everything is about tactics."

Tala would have made the same argument Sari had. She was an asset in the field. She would be able to help in the battle. Damien could protect her because she wouldn't put herself in danger. She was a *tactical advantage*.

Her stubborn, infuriating, brilliant sister.

You're not really angry with him, Tala's voice whispered to her. *You're angry with me.*

The next minute, Damien grabbed her arm, dragging her out of the house and into the cold night, leaving their audience behind before Sari broke down sobbing. Damien put his arm around her shoulders and hurried them into the trees.

When they were surrounded by the forest, she shoved away from Damien and shouted, "I'm so angry with her!"

Damien frowned, then his eyes lit with realization. "I know, Sari."

"She shouldn't have gone to the city."

"And I shouldn't have taken her."

"She shouldn't have left me!" Sari's chest felt as it were being ripped apart. "Everyone left me, and I wasn't strong enough!"

"It wasn't your fault." Tears shone in his eyes.

"I couldn't protect them. I wasn't fast enough." She sobbed. "I heard the children screaming, and I didn't know what to do!"

"That's not true." He stepped forward and grabbed her shoulders. "You killed at least a dozen Grigori that day. Maybe more. I talked to the survivors, Sari. Your protection let them escape. Children lived because of you. Families survived because of you."

"Not enough." She broke against his chest. "None of it was enough."

He wrapped strong arms around her and held tight. "I know."

"And I blamed you."

"I deserved your blame. And Tala wasn't here to take it."

"I'm sorry, Damien. I'm so sorry."

"Don't." He held her, his arms like iron bands around her. "I'm sorry I didn't see the risk. I'm sorry I was so arrogant. So horribly, horribly wrong."

"I know Tala insisted."

"I should have sent her back. Should have hidden her at the house and made her stay there. I should have told Gabriel. Should have broken protocol, even if she reported me to the council. Sari, I should have—"

"No more." She pressed her tearstained face to his shoulder and put her arms around his waist. "No more, Damien."

They stood in the silence of the forest, clinging to each other. The night was cold and the wind was turning bitter, but Sari felt none of it. She only felt his arms around her. His cheek pressing against her brow. Her mate. Her warrior. Her Damien.

"Our war is never over," he said in her ear. "It never will be. But can we be at peace, *milá*? I think I could face a host of the Fallen if there was peace between us."

Reshon. Mate of my heart.

I choose you.

She raised her head and kissed him.

I choose this scribe.

"We go forward from here," she said. "We forgive each other and ourselves. If we grieve, we grieve together. If we fight, we fight together. Yes?"

"Yes." He took her mouth and owned it.

Sari sank into his kiss, which was laced with the taste of coffee and cinnamon and spice. He groaned and backed her against the trunk of a nearby tree, wedging his knee between her thighs. His mouth traced down her throat. She threw her head back and gripped two handfuls of his hair.

"If I asked you to abandon your house"—she panted—"would you?"

He bit her throat. "There will be another who can lead them."

"Defy the council?" She reached down and slid her hands over the strong plane of his back.

"I think"—he palmed her backside and squeezed—"a little rebellion would be good for them."

She closed her eyes and gave in to the intoxication of his touch. "And if I asked you to run away with me?"

Damien drew back and his grin lit the night. "Sari, *my dove*, you would never run away."

SARI TOOK DAMIEN BACK TO HER ROOMS WITH NO INTENTION of ever letting him go again. They would fight. They would argue. But as he watched her disrobe in the darkness, his clothes already abandoned on the floor, she knew she had come home.

"I love the curve of your bottom," he said, sliding his palm around from the front to the back. He curled his fingers into the hard muscle and pulled. "I love everything about you, but nothing in a dream walk can compare with your bottom in the flesh." He gave it a sharp smack as a wicked grin crossed his face.

She laughed. "You love everything, do you? Even my temper?"

"Even that." He slid his hand from her bottom up her back, pulling her over to straddle him. "Sing to me."

No sweeter magic. She felt her mating marks light. His glowed silver in reaction.

"What do you want me to sing?"

"My mating song." Damien put her hand over his chest,

over the mark he had scribed there with her words. "Once more, *reshon*."

She nodded and drew his mouth into a long kiss. He sat up and hugged her body to his, their flesh pressing together. He tasted her skin and teased her breasts, circling them with light touches until she was mad with want. Sari reached down and felt for him, guiding his length into her body as he groaned. His mouth became ravenous.

"Sing to me." He bit her shoulder. "Sari, sing."

"I choose you," she began.

> "Through ages you have come to me,
> And I choose you.
> Because you wandered many roads alone
> And this body has bled and shed blood in
>   honor,
> I choose you."

Damien braced his arms and powered into her, shoving away the bitter memories of the past. He loved her with a ruthless focus as she panted out the last verse of her vow.

> "The one who sees me and challenges me,
> My warrior, my lover. Friend, protector, help-
>   meet, mate.
> As iron sharpens iron, I will ever be your own.
> I choose you, my love."

When she came, it was with his name on her lips, crying her pleasure into his mouth, but he did not cease. He flipped her over and entered her again, one hand squeezing the bottom he loved so much as his lips pressed hungry kisses to her spine. Reaching up, he twisted her hair in his hand and pulled her mouth back to his.

"Mine is the fire," he whispered.

"Mine is the blood.
Mine, her soft touch and her sharp tongue.
She that wields a strong hand
And a gentle embrace
Is my lover.
My own.
Mine is the need and the desire.
My witness, her song.
Daughter of heaven,
Beloved of my heart.
My Sari.
My own.

"I love you," he panted as her body began to tighten again. "I love you more than my own life."

"I know." Tears came to her eyes. "I know, *reshon*."

"You are everything that is heaven to me."

"I love you, Damien."

The tension exploded, and this time Damien followed her, groaning his pleasure into the curve of her neck, holding her to his chest as he collapsed and curled his body beside hers.

"I never want to be parted from you again," he said. "Not for a month. Not for a week, *milá*. Two hundred years has been more than enough."

"Then we won't." She kissed the fingers knitted between her own. "We won't."

CHAPTER
EIGHT

D AMIEN woke in the middle of the night, his mate sleeping beside him. In the weeks since their reunion, they had not slept apart. Not even when Renata and Mala took Ava to Bergen. At the end of the day, the girl had wanted to go. Sari, much to Damien's surprise, had given her permission.

Sari was no elder scribe to lock a singer away from battle.

They were not, nor had they ever been, a peaceable pair. Though flowers bloomed around the old farmhouse, Damien and Sari still fought. Her magic was running high, and the earth responded with profusions of wildflowers that sprang from her happiness. But it must have known them both, because nearly all the delicate blooms that emerged rested in a small nest of brambles.

Mala and Ava had returned from Bergen, but Renata had made some excuse to go to Oslo. Something strange had happened, and the hunt had not gone as expected. Nevertheless, all three woman were unharmed.

Yet Damien could not sleep.

I've brought something dark here.

Ava had warned him when she'd returned from Bergen,

shaken and trying to hide it. He could not refute her fear. There was a shadow hovering over Sarihöfn. Whether it was the long northern nights or something else, he did not know. A darker shadow hung over Ava, and Damien didn't know how to help his sister fight the darkness in her spirit that seemed to grow each passing night.

Sari woke with a gasp beside him. "*Ya kazar man.*"

The spell caught on the air and flew toward the window, cracked to let in the night air.

"Sari?"

"Someone has breached the perimeter. Someone with magic."

Leaping from bed, he had his shirt, boots, and knives ready before she was able to rise.

"How many?"

She shook her head and rubbed her eyes. "Not many. They're resisting my wards and coming from the northwest."

"They'll be in the forest. What are you waiting for?" he asked. "Where are your shoes?" It hadn't rained yet, but the mud would be thick under the trees.

"By the front door." She pulled on her clothes and tied back her hair, reaching for the staff in the corner.

"Should we wake the others?" he asked as they rushed down the stairs.

"I don't know."

"We wait until we see who is it. It could be harmless."

"They found us," she muttered. "How did they find us?"

Damien said, "If these are Grigori, we will find them and kill them."

"If these are Grigori, we will have to move the haven."

Because there would be no way of knowing who they could have told.

"Hunt first," she said. "They will be no match for both of us."

She slipped on her shoes and a dark cap before Damien

could find a coat. It was too cold to fight in shirtsleeves, even for a northern native like Sari. Damien had fought in far colder, but he knew the risk of rushing into battle. When they left the house, they were warm and eager for the hunt.

Despite the danger to the haven, his heart soared. Hunting at his mate's side had ever been a thrill to him. He was proud to belong to a warrior, and her skills had only grown sharper with time. She was a shadow running over the land. The earth beneath her was steeped in her magic and her grandmother's. No doubt, her mother's had touched it as well. Ancient power tugged at him, recognizing her claim over his body.

When they reached the trees, he pulled her back and held up a hand, tracing a finger over his *talesm prim* and activating his magic. Sari waited as his power rose. Spells for hearing and clarity. Spells to enhance his vision and increase his reaction time. And, finally, a spell to enhance his sense of smell. In the space of seconds, Damien's magic roared to life, and he knew exactly who and where they were. The scent of sandalwood was unmistakable.

They were Grigori. Damn.

"This way." He jogged carefully, knowing she would be behind him.

He smelled them before he heard them. He heard them before he saw them.

Two figures crouched in the shadows with long-range night vision goggles pointed at the training barn. These were no mere stumblers. They were dressed in combat gear and carrying rifles. A sharp whistle let Damien know one of the Grigori had spotted them.

"Damn," Sari whispered. "They heard us."

The Grigori melted back into the trees. They were well trained, but they were not Irin.

"One apiece?" he asked.

She nodded, took off her gloves, and sank her hands into the ground. Whispering under her breath, she rose and ran into the darkness as Damien pulled out his hunting knife. He closed his eyes for a moment, aware that the shadows were deceiving. It was the worst kind of light for him to see in. The moon was full, so the shadows were sharp under the trees, making it easy for anyone dressed in black to conceal themselves. He used his nose and his ears to track the Grigori through the forest.

The man knew he was being hunted. He darted in and out of the shadows, heading back toward the road. No doubt, if he reached it before his friend, the other man would be on his own. Information was more valuable than Grigori life.

He heard the crack of Sari's staff against a tree and forced himself not to turn. She could take care of herself and a single Grigori opponent. He came to a halt in a small clearing, confused by the scents.

The snap of a twig had him looking up just as the Grigori dropped from the branch, knife aimed at Damien's neck.

He dropped and rolled to the side, coming to his feet just as the man came to his. They circled each other, waiting for a weakness. Damien could have charged him—his *talesm* would deflect almost any knife strike except from a heaven-forged blade—but he wanted to take stock of this monster. He was better trained than most.

"Questions, bookkeeper?" the Grigori taunted. "We tracked them from Bergen. Your women are not as elusive as they think."

Mala had come from Bergen. They hadn't found the haven through Mala.

"Bookkeeper?" he said. "That's a new one."

"That's what you do," he said. "Live in the pages of books, trying to resurrect your glorious past."

"Is that what your keeper told you?" Damien said, intrigued by how much the monster was talking. They usually didn't say much. He kept circling the man. He had found the weakness in his stance, but he was curious how much the man would reveal.

"I have been trained by Volund himself." He couldn't help but boast. "First of the Fallen. Keeper of a guardian's blade."

Guardian's blade, was it? That was something he'd have to look up. He remembered no mention of a "guardian's blade" in Irin texts.

"It doesn't matter what sword your master wields," Damien said softly. "In a few minutes, you will be dead and the haven will be gone. So if you've called anyone, they're wasting their time."

A flicker in the man's bravado. He had called someone. Undoubtedly, they were already on their way. From where, Damien did not know, but he had no time to waste.

The man smiled one last time. "Bookkeeper, you don't know who I am."

"No. It is you who don't know who *I* am." Damien lunged forward, dropping his knife and grabbing the Grigori's raised left arm. Twisting the man's arm around his own neck in a chokehold, Damien reached for a second knife with his left hand. One deep plunge in the kidney and the man slumped. The knife fell from the Grigori's fingers, and his head fell forward. Releasing his arm, Damien took out the silver-tipped dagger in his right pocket and stabbed it into the man's neck.

"I am Damien of Bohemia," he whispered. "May your soul be judged fairly for your deeds."

The dust rose, but Damien did not choke on it. A gentle breeze blew it from his eyes, and he turned to see Sari leaning against a tree at the edge of the clearing.

"Yours must have been more talkative than mine."

"He belongs to Volund, and he already called someone," Damien said. "We need to begin the evacuation immediately."

"THIS IS MY FAULT." AVA SAT AT THE KITCHEN TABLE, RACKED with guilt as Damien watched Sari and her sisters sort out the evacuation of the haven.

Damien said, "No. You did nothing wrong. Mala is sure you were not tailed from Bergen. This is from some other crack in our defenses. It was… surprising. But we had become too complacent. It was probably inevitable after so much time. There have been so many who have used Sarihöfn as a refuge over the years. No magic is impenetrable. And with the Grigori becoming more aggressive, we should not be surprised."

And Sari had warned them in time. Bruno was monitoring the roads to make sure no unexpected company arrived. Orsala's wards were in place. There was no panic, only the sad melancholy of friends who knew they must part. This was not the first time a haven had been breached. This would not be the last.

Damien watched Sari delegate tasks to each person who came to her, making sure the families with children were prioritized. Only an hour after they'd killed the Grigori in the woods, those families had already been evacuated, which told Damien that escape plans must have been set in place long before.

"Fatima and Lionel have already made plans to go to the Caribbean. They're simply moving up the timeline." Sari leaned over a table, scanning a list that Astrid had given her. "Sorted. Sorted. Not. Karen, find out where Marie is headed. If she's going to meet her mate, I don't need to know where, but I need to know she has a plan."

"Yes, Sari."

"And find out if she made arrangements about the fund. If she's going to be offline for a time, she needs to let her associates know."

"Got it."

Marie, Damien was guessing, was one of the computer-savvy Irina who managed money. He knew that in the modern world, it took an enormous amount of coordination and funds to hide so many. Papers and deeds needed to be forged regularly. Money had to be carefully managed because, though they'd had much time to acquire it, singers in hiding also had to spend an enormous amount.

Yet all this happened with a smooth rhythm that told Damien it had been coordinated and rehearsed down to the smallest detail years in advance.

She could rule.

Oh, yes, she could. She'd be quick to anger but slow to judge. She would see every angle before they could be argued away. More, she had passion. If the Irina needed anyone, they needed someone with passion. Sari needed to go to Vienna, yet he knew his mate had an instinctive aversion to politics.

"What will they do about money?" Ava broke into his reverie. "And the farm?"

He'd asked the same thing only an hour before. "There are humans Sari trusts who will take care of the farm. And they have saved money for hundreds of years. They will give money to families and individuals as they need it. They have enough."

Not much extra, but enough.

"I have money. More than I need. If any of them—"

"Keep your money, sister. They will be fine."

"They've planned for this."

"Yes. After the Rending, we knew no place would be safe forever."

They watched cars and vans pull away for hours as, one by one, the singers and scribes of Sarihöfn scattered across the globe.

He told Ava, "We'll stay here a few days with Sari. We're still deciding where our family will go. Sari and I have different ideas about what should happen now."

He wanted nothing more than to keep his mate and her

grandmother safe. At least for a time. He had bolt-holes and contacts all over the world. It wasn't that he wanted to isolate her forever, but the thought of plunging back into battle when he'd just gotten her back did not appeal to him on any level.

Ava asked, "And me?"

"You're coming with us, of course. That we all agree on. You still have many lessons with Orsala. And you're part of our family."

Ava didn't look as if she believed him. "I'm not sure I'm a very safe person to be around right now."

"Good!" Sari strode into the room. "Then my plan it is, Damien."

"*Milá...*"

"I know you want to go someplace safe and hidden, my love, but I cannot agree."

It wasn't as though he didn't know her capable of battle. He just wanted to enjoy peace with her a little bit longer.

Sari spoke to Ava. "I have taken care of my sisters. I have sheltered those who needed it. I have been peaceful too long. Give me an enemy to bloody my hands on."

Peaceful? She called hunting a half dozen Grigori down in an Oslo nightclub peaceful? Damien frowned at his mate, but she ignored him.

He cleared his throat. "The Irina need—"

"We know what we need." Now Karen was interrupting him. "And that is not to have others dictate to us. Bruno and I can take care of those who need shelter. There is a house that belonged to my mother outside Prague. It has been empty for many years. Bruno and I will create a safe place and let you know when it is ready. I am not a warrior. And my Bruno knows this. But your mate is, Damien. And you know that."

Damien threw up his hands and let them make their plans. At the end of the day, this was Sari's evacuation.

Mala signed to him from across the room. *Sit down, Watcher. Let someone else take responsibility for once.*

They're not in the mood to listen to me anyway, he signed back.

Why do you think I'm sitting here and letting them do all the hard work?

Will you come with us? he asked. *We could use your help in Vienna.*

Is that where we're going?

She'll decide on it eventually. Maybe I'll suggest we avoid it to hurry that decision along.

Sneaky.

I know what motivates her.

I need to go with Astrid and Karen. At least for a while. But I'll keep Vienna in mind.

Damien nodded. *Good.*

Mala clapped at Sari to get her attention. *I'll accompany Karen, Bruno, and Astrid. Make sure the others are settled before I return to you.*

Sari told the room, "Mala will go with them, as well, at least for a time. Has anyone been able to call Renata?"

"Candice was trying to call her mobile," Ava said. "She's not at her apartment in Bergen. She might still be in Oslo. Candice and Brooke are going to the scribe house there with Chelsea. Her mate is stationed there."

Damien's mate was glorious when she was in her element. And her element, he realized with a smile, was command.

Sari moved next to her grandmother. "We always knew this place could not last forever. Change has come. We are ready. Now let this quiet war end."

IT WASN'T UNTIL DAYS LATER, ON A QUIET CAR RIDE TO OSLO where they were going to meet three of his brothers who had traveled from Istanbul, that Damien understood just how much their whole world had changed. Ava and Orsala slept in back while Sari told him the news that had them rushing to the city days before they were meant to depart.

"Ava," Sari said. "Damien, she's even more than we thought." She had slipped into Old Orcadian, which was as close to a secret language as they had.

Damien frowned. "What are you talking about? What's wrong?"

"The call from Renata, the one that made me rush us to Oslo?" Sari seemed to stutter.

"*Milá*, what is it?"

She glanced over her shoulder. "Damien, her mate is alive."

Damien pulled the car over before he swerved into traffic. Luckily, none of the passengers woke. "That's impossible."

"It's not. Malachi is alive."

Damien was stunned that the pain was still so strong. He had lost so many brothers-in-arms he could no longer count them. But Malachi's death and Ava's grief were still raw, bleeding wounds that reminded him too much of his and Sari's past.

"Sari, whatever someone told Renata, I saw Malachi die. I know he is—"

"Alive," she said. "According to Maxim, who is both your brother and his. Renata went to see the man herself because she didn't believe him."

Damien said nothing. Maxim was so far from fanciful he was a card-carrying member of the cynic's society. Yet he had told Renata that Malachi was alive?

"How does Renata know it's him?" Not that Maxim would commit such a cruel deception, but Damien had to know. "Had she met him before?"

"She's seen pictures. Ava had pictures from—"

"Of course." Ava was a professional photographer. Of course she'd have numerous pictures of her mate. She must have shown Renata at some point.

Hope and reason warred within him. "How can this be?"

"We know her power is different."

"Are you saying *she* did this?"

"Malachi doesn't remember much. But he remembers Ava's voice commanding him to come back."

"*Commanding?*" He realized he'd shouted it. Looking over his shoulder, he saw Orsala stir, but Ava and Mala were still sleeping. He put the car back in drive and continued. "What do you mean, commanding?"

"She used magic. She probably didn't even know she was doing it. But she used the Old Language. *Vashama canem.* Return to me."

"Return to me," he repeated. "The mourning cry. She spoke it and he returned?"

"Damien, her magic—"

"Is not evil." He glanced at her. "She's not evil, Sari."

"I know you like to think of the world as black and white, evil and good, but can we accept that it's not that simple, Damien? Our sister is not Irina," she whispered.

"I know what she does is not traditional magic, but—"

"Damien, no Irina would seek to bring anyone back from death. It is anathema to us. To ask for any soul to leave heaven when that peace has been granted them would be forbidden."

"But is it impossible?" he asked. "Clearly not. There has to be a will behind the magic, Sari. You and I both know it. Perhaps we think it impossible because we know it is forbidden."

"Or we think it impossible because it is," she whispered. "For us. Perhaps her magic is not from the Forgiven at all."

Damien fell silent.

"The Fallen don't teach their offspring magic," he said after two more exits had passed.

"They don't. And an Irin scribe could never mate to a human with Grigori blood," Sari said. "And fallen men don't return from the dead."

Yet suddenly all those things were possible.

"If it is truly Malachi," Damien said, "if he is truly alive and Ava was the one to do it, then everything has changed."

"I know."

Damien took her hand and held it in his own. "Your quiet war has ended, my love. What this war is, I don't think any of us can know."

CHAPTER
NINE

THEY met with the scribes from the Oslo house, and it had never been more apparent to Sari that the Irina needed to return. The young men of the house were in awe of her singers and even more taken with Candice's daughter, Brooke. Some of them, their watcher told her, had never seen an Irin child.

They've come back. Do you think they've really come back?

"What have we done?" she whispered to Damien in the quiet of their room. "They're like little boys."

"Most of these men never had mothers," Damien said. "Wait until you meet Leo, Maxim's cousin. He is both the fiercest and the most gentle man you'll ever meet. Ridiculous around women."

"Of course he would be," Sari said. The scribes did not socialize with human women. What would be the point when prolonged contact would only hurt the humans? "The boys here, they were so excited to think that we'd returned."

"This is a young house." Damien took a deep breath and pulled her closer, drifting toward sleep. "Other than Chelsea's mate and a few of the older men, none of them have seen singers."

Tears came to her eyes. Her sisters had become myths in their absence. Sari had known it would be a long road to bring the Irin race back together, but she'd had no idea just how rough it would be.

Damien was almost asleep, but Sari could not quiet her mind. "*Reshon*, I'm going down to the library," she whispered, kissing him.

"Not too late," he murmured. "Malachi in the morning."

"I have not forgotten." She slipped out of bed, covering him with the blanket before she pulled one of Damien's sweaters over her comfortable leggings and shirt.

She passed the library, intending to get a glass of water from the kitchen, but she halted when she saw the watcher of the Oslo house, Lang, leaning over a map spread on the large wooden table.

"Good evening, Watcher," she greeted him.

"A good evening to you, sister." Lang's smile was polite, but weary.

"I had intended to read for a while, but I don't want to disturb you. Perhaps I should find a book and—"

"Please." Lang waved a hand. "Take anything you like. You won't disturb me. I'm accomplishing nothing here; I simply cannot sleep."

"I know the feeling."

He nodded. "It sounds like reports of the evacuation have been favorable."

"I'm only waiting for word from a few yet. The rest have checked in."

"Remarkable."

"We have had practice in hiding."

A tinge of bitterness to his smile. "I know."

"Did you lose your mate?"

"No. I had been pledged…," he said. "We were not yet mated. She left after her village was attacked. I believe she is still alive, but I have no idea where she is."

And though Lang looked as if he still longed for his lost lover, Sari had no intention of asking after her or even inquiring about her name. It was an unspoken rule of the havens. Those who wanted to be found were found. Those who wanted to hide were given their privacy. No one had the right to expose another.

"You have tended your fire well," she said. "I have been a watcher's mate for many years. I know a well-run house when I see one."

"Thank you." His cheeks tinged red. "I was worried you would think my men untried boys by their reactions earlier. They are fine warriors, each one of them, and will protect your sisters who shelter here as if they were the last Irina on earth."

"Damien tells me we have made ourselves myths and legends," Sari said. "I can hardly judge them for our absence."

He nodded, then turned back to the map.

"What are you looking for?" she asked.

"I don't know." He frowned. "Grigori attacks in the city indicate an increased presence, but I cannot find a pattern to their attacks. We don't have anyone stationed at the house right now who can hack into the police computers."

"Ask Rhys, Damien's archivist. He's very good on computers. If my sister Marie were here, she could do it, but she's meeting her mate somewhere in Southern Europe right now."

"I'll ask Rhys first," he said. "Thank you for the advice."

She examined the map. "You have some marked."

"A few I've been able to confirm, but I know there are more."

"And this is an increase?"

"Yes." Lang glanced at her. "You seem... familiar with strategy."

"I wasn't simply a watcher's mate, Lang. I was one of Damien's warriors in London and Paris."

"Truly?"

"Trained by Damien of Bohemia himself. But my sister Mala is more dangerous than me in the field."

"I look forward to seeing her fight."

"Only since you are fighting on the same side." Sari leaned over the map. "I may be shit at polite conversation, but I'm quite good at chess. Now tell me more about the attacks you know of, and let's see if a new pair of eyes can tell us anything."

HER EYES WERE BLOODSHOT WHEN DAMIEN FOUND HER BEFORE dawn, but an edgy, irritable part of Sari had eased. Damien came into the library, kissed her cheek, and handed her a cup of coffee.

"You stayed up all night." He eyed the notes she'd scribbled on sticky notes at the edges of the map.

"I know," she said. "I'm sorry." She sipped the coffee. "But can you call Rhys? We need him to hack into the police computers."

"You will be his favorite person today. That's like handing the man a new toy."

Lang rubbed his eyes. "You have meetings this morning, and I have monopolized your time. My apologies, Sari."

"I'm going to go take a shower," she said to Damien. "That will wake me up. When Rhys gets here, can you—"

"I'll have Lang brief me," he said. "We need to leave for Maxim's soon. Maybe after we've confirmed… Maybe after, you can try to grab some sleep."

She nodded. Damien started walking away, but she grabbed him and whispered, "You know, I'm far better at planning attacks than reuniting lost lovers who think their mates are dead."

"I am glad your romantic heart beats only for me," he said, kissing her nose. "But you're not getting out of this." His eyes softened. "And I need you with me when I see him. If there has been some mistake or deception…"

"I'll be there," she said.

He pulled her into an embrace. "One of my lost come back to me," he whispered. "I cannot conceive of it, *milá*."

Sari tried to think of how many of Damien's brothers had been lost in battle over his eight hundred years of life. She couldn't imagine it. To have even one returned to him felt like a gift, no matter what the circumstances.

"I'll be ready to go in a few minutes," she said. "I'll try to sleep later so I don't hit Ava." The girl's morose attitude was starting to get to Sari. Not that she could blame Ava for it. She only hoped this revelation went according to plan.

NOTHING, OF COURSE, WENT ACCORDING TO PLAN, ESPECIALLY Ava trying to flee the apartment before she could even see her miraculously resurrected mate. But by the next evening, when the reunited pair walked into the Oslo house, Sari wasn't quite as worried as she had been when she and Damien left them that morning.

It helped that, for the first time in her memory, Irin scribes and singers were standing around a field map, strategizing over how and when they'd go after the nest of Grigori that had descended on Oslo.

"I've still got a call to London for help," Lang, glancing at Malachi and Ava as they hovered on the edges of the room, talking with Orsala and Rhys. "But I'm thinking about calling them off."

Damien said, "If we wait too long to strike, there could be even more."

"Is that a deterrent or an incentive?" Sari asked.

Both the men stared at her.

"I'm just saying. If we wait and there are more of them, we'll still defeat them. But we'll have rid the world of more Grigori. That's not a bad thing."

"Your confidence is encouraging." Damien kissed her forehead. "But I have a tendency to side with Lang on this. These numbers are disturbing. If we wait longer, victory is not assured."

"I disagree."

"Let's ask Rhys about it," Lang said. "Once he runs the numbers, I'll feel more comfortable making a decision to wait or strike."

"Fair enough," Sari said. "It is your house, Watcher."

Damien narrowed his eyes. "You know, she was never this agreeable with me."

"Do try to follow what I'm trying to say, Leo." Rhys's annoyed voice broke into their banter. "The red is a confirmed attack and kill. The yellow is for attacks that were stopped, but the Grigori wasn't eliminated."

"So many," Sari said, walking over to study the map that Rhys had marked up. "Lang, this is far more than average, correct?"

"Yes. Activity has picked up over the past year, but the majority of these attacks have been in only the past couple of weeks."

Damien asked, "Do we think there any chance this increase in activity and the exposure of Sarihöfn are not related?"

No.

No one said it, but it was obvious they all thought the two were connected.

"There are few coincidences in the world." Malachi's deep voice caused Sari to turn. "It's possible, but I don't think it's likely."

He was a curious creature to her. He reminded Sari of her mate, but the Turkish scribe was far more raw and untested. It was clear he adored his mate, but just as clear that he wasn't quite sure what to do with her. Insecurity marked his steps when he drew closer, but Sari could tell it was not natural to him. He had the bearing of a man very sure of himself who'd been planted in a completely unknown world.

"Tell me more about Volund," Malachi asked.

Yes, what was the mastermind of the Rending up to these days? Sari leaned closer.

"As far as we know, Volund still has one of his primary bases near Göteborg," Lang said. "Which gives his soldiers easy access to the continent and a steady stream of tourists, whom his men usually target. He's been building in power for centuries. We believe he took out the major power in Russia in the 1920s, and he appears to have connections with the lesser Fallen in Spain and France."

"Have you talked to Maxim about what he's heard?" The question came from Leo. Sari had already warned the giant scribe that Damien had stolen her heart long ago. He was as sweet as Bruno, but far more innocent. And lethal.

"Your brother has been an unexpected font of information over the past few years. I don't know who he knows—"

"It's better you don't ask," Damien said. "I never did when he was in my house."

No wonder Maxim and Renata constantly circled each other. It sounded like they were two of a kind.

Lang returned to the topic of Volund instead. "The sudden absence of Grigori last summer fits what you and Maxim have said about him making a move in Istanbul."

They continued debating what the Fallen could be planning. Then Malachi turned the world upside down when he mentioned Ava seeing Jaron in a dream.

Damien's temper spiked. "When? At Sarihöfn? Was he able to find you there? Is that why—"

"I don't know." Ava's guilt was written across her face. "I haven't remembered the details of my dreams about him until the one last night, though I'm fairly sure I've seen him before He was… cryptic."

Sari grabbed Damien's hand, trying to calm him down. "It's not her fault that she can't remember," Sari said. "We both know how obscure visions can be."

"She is not Tala," Damien said.

"But she is a seer nonetheless."

"—talking over the vision with Malachi to try to make sense of it," Ava was saying, "but a lot of it is confusing. I… I can try…"

Malachi said, "Tell them. Show them. There is no shame in trying."

Though she clearly didn't want to. Sari could hardly blame the girl. It was obvious she hated being the center of attention.

"I can try to sing you the vision so you can see what I saw."

The scribes present looked confused. Orsala looked excited.

Sari asked, "Like you did at the sing? That was amazing."

Lang asked, "What is this?"

Damien leaned over to him and tried to explain what Ava could do, but Sari knew by the excitement in the room that all Lang's men were eager to see the pretty singer show them herself.

A young scribe spoke from his place at the edge of the room. "Would you sing for us, sister? Would you?"

She was nervous, but resolute. As the girl began to sing, Damien took Sari's hand, holding it as Ava's strange magic filled the room.

Only it was more.

Immense.

And frighteningly powerful.

She glanced up and saw Malachi's arms encircling Ava's waist.

This is bigger than us. The sudden certainty almost knocked her over. *Bigger than them.*

So much bigger than anything we have seen before.

Sari knew in that moment that whatever was coming would change everything.

Ava's song filled her mind.

Two eagles, circling and attacking each other.
The sky, the sky. Sprayed with a thousand hidden stars.
Concealed behind a blood-red sun, the stars waited in silence, glowing with subtle power.
But the eagles didn't look up. They kept fighting.
Hot blood sprayed down on Sari's skin. She could hear it. Feel it.
She heard wolves growling at her feet. Jackals laughing in the bushes.
She was alone, but she wasn't. All the animals watched as the fierce birds ripped at each other, screaming in rage.
But no one watched the stars.
A plummet to the earth.

A piercing pain in her chest before a voice filled her mind. Enormous and elemental, she knew she was hearing the voice of an angel for the first time in her life. Sari wanted to weep from its frightening beauty. She wanted to beg it to keep speaking. She wanted to cover her ears and hide.

I will tear the threads of heaven to return. And you will help me, Ava.

The world went black, and the next thing Sari felt was Damien patting her cheek.

"*Milá?*"

"I'm fine." She blinked awake. "What happened?"

"Malachi went a little crazy."

"You would have too if one of the Fallen talked to me that way."

He lifted an eyebrow, but he did not disagree. "What did you see?"

"What did *you* see?"

"A vision of two eagles fighting. The Fallen. Jaron and Volund, I think. There is a battle coming between the angels." His face was grim. "One that we seem to be drawn into, no matter how I'd like to sit back and let them kill each other. It seems I'll need to retrieve my knife from Mikael's armory after all."

"Did you see the stars?"

He frowned.

"The stars behind the sun," she said. "The stars, Damien. Didn't you notice them?"

"*Milá*, no."

How could he not have seen? They had called to her, begging for someone to see them.

The room was still in chaos, everyone shouting to be heard. Rhys's voice broke through Sari's internal confusion.

"*That* was different," he said.

"It was similar to the vision she shared with us at Sari-höfn," Sari managed to say. "But this one was far more violent and powerful. I would guess that having Malachi back is multiplying her power."

Lang said, "Two birds… Volund and Jaron?"

Damien said, "I think it's clear that some war is between them now."

Much debate over the meaning of the vision followed, but in the end, it was Lang's decision about whether or not they would track and kill the Grigori in their nest. Break protocol to go after the monsters where they rested.

It was Lang's decision, and with a cadre of scribes and singers around him, the Watcher of Oslo defied council mandate and asked Sari, Damien, and all their friends to join him in battle.

HER MATE FOUND HER IN THEIR ROOM, SHARPENING HER KNIVES and staring out the bedroom window. They were waiting to hear from Maxim and Renata. When they did, they would attack.

"What are you thinking?" he asked.

"We need to go to Vienna," she said. "I know… I know you have concerns. But this battle—whatever is happening with Ava's sudden appearance in our world—this is bigger than us." *The stars were waiting to be seen.* "We need to be there, Damien. We must reform the singers' council. I know this is what I am being called to do."

Damien sat on the floor and stretched his legs out beside hers. "I may have been thinking the same thing."

"But you were arguing with me about going to Vienna only yesterday."

He shrugged. "You like to argue with me."

Sari narrowed her eyes and set her knives down. "Were you fighting with me about Vienna just so I'd be more determined to go?"

Damien said nothing, but Sari saw the glint in his eye.

"You scoundrel!" she said, laughing as she tackled him to the floor. "What kind of mate are you?"

He kissed her and rolled over so he had her body pinned down. Sari enjoyed the delicious weight of him as he began to kiss her.

"I'm the best kind of mate for you," he said, nudging up her chin to bite her neck. "The kind who gives you exactly what you need."

"Do you know what I need right now?"

"I can guess."

He settled more firmly on her, and Sari felt the length of him grow hard between their bodies.

"You're a keen strategist, Damien of Bohemia."

"My mate is a warrior," he murmured against her skin. "She expects nothing less."

CHAPTER

TEN

L ANG had tried to argue with Sari, but his objections
were ridiculous. The singers who stood with the
scribes of Oslo and Istanbul in the cold Oslo dawn
were as battle-tried as Lang's men. Sari and Renata. Chelsea,
who stood with her mate. Even Orsala had come, the old
woman bearing her staff, a silver blade at her waist.

Malachi and Ava had slipped off down an alleyway while
the others were debating. For what, Damien did not know. But
he trusted his brother. Malachi would not have left without
reason.

Damien counted heads and didn't like the numbers. Seven
Oslo scribes had come, leaving five back at the house to guard
the Sarihöfn Irina still sheltering there. Four of his own men,
along with himself and four trained Irina. Sixteen warriors
against what Maxim and Renata thought were around sixty
Grigori crammed into a four-story apartment building. At
least they had the advantage of surprise.

"If we spread throughout the house and attack en masse,"
Sari was saying, "then they will not have time to react."

"There are four stories," Max said. "Six rooms on each
floor if the buildings nearby are similar."

"That's twenty-four rooms and sixteen of us," Rhys said. "Where's Malachi and Ava?"

"Don't worry about them," Damien said. "I don't want any of us fighting alone."

"Then we partner up," Lang said. "Four people—two sets of partners—on each floor, working in tandem. We lose some element of surprise, but we watch each other's backs. Work as silently as you can for as long as you can. We'll be detected at some point, but let's kill as many in their beds as we are able." He directed his words to his men. "Do *not* wait for them to attack. I know we are going against mandate in this mission, so I am giving you the order. *Strike first.* Kill them quickly. Kill them as they sleep if you can."

Lang's men nodded, and not a single one looked troubled by their rebellious commander.

"They're sleeping now," Damien said. "If you want to go, we should go."

They silently paired up. Mated pairs together. Renata and Maxim stayed close. Orsala quickly joined one of the younger scribes and walked forward with Damien and Sari.

"We'll take the bottom floor," Damien said quietly. "Clear it and move up. Orsala, can you and…" Damien frowned when he saw Orsala's companion. "What's your name?"

"Andrew, sir."

The boy looked so eager Damien wondered if he'd ever seen battle. But Orsala had chosen him, and Damien trusted her judgment.

"Orsala, can you and Andrew guard the door? Make sure none leave the house?"

She nodded.

"If there are humans and they try to escape, I'm depending on you two to contain them."

He could have used her more in the battle, but the old singer's magic would be the most effective near the door.

Sari said, "By the time we move up, we'll have lost the element of surprise."

"Then it's a good thing you like to fight." He glanced down. "You brought your staff."

"And my blade." She smiled. "Why limit my options?"

He'd forgotten how much he loved fighting at her side.

The group was small but moved swiftly. As they approached the house, he saw all the Irin males touching their wrists to activate their *talesm* as they whispered prayers before battle. The Irina pulled out black scarves and twisted them around their necks.

"Kevlar lined," Sari said. "Standard issue for all singers now."

To protect their voices and their magic.

"I do love technology sometimes."

"So do we."

Damien felt his magic ripple over him. He leaned over and pressed a flash of a kiss to his mate's mouth. Their power touched and sparked before he pulled away, smiling.

Maxim bent and picked the lock, then he and Renata slid into the building silently. Lang motioned for two of his men to follow. Pair by pair, the Irin force entered the house and spread out. Damien, Sari, Orsala, and Andrew were the last to enter.

The common room on the ground floor was littered with beer and liquor bottles, which acted like small booby traps as they picked their way through the detritus. Andrew and Orsala went right. Damien and Sari to the left. The smell of sandalwood, marijuana smoke, and sex filled the air. The Grigori of Oslo had been to the party and come home to enjoy their ill-earned rest.

Sari cracked open the first door. Two beds had been crammed in the room. Two sleeping Grigori soldiers lay on one, the other was occupied by a single man. Still another stretched on the floor. All blond and beautiful. All wearing the distinctive glow of angel blood in their skin. In sleep, they were beautiful creatures. When they woke, their soul-hunger would kill.

It went against Damien's every instinct to kill an opponent in his sleep, even monsters. The Grigori were predators, and his people were outnumbered. Killing them in stealth made the most tactical sense. And yet…

He looked down when Sari squeezed his hand.

I know, her eyes seemed to say.

I love you, he mouthed.

"*Ya domem,*" Sari whispered to the man on the floor as Damien slapped a hand over the lone sleeper's mouth. In sync, they turned and stabbed the Grigori in the back of their necks, silver knives striking like lightning. Within seconds, two were dead, leaving only the pair on the bed.

Damien held a finger to his lips, but it was only out of habit. Sari was as silent as the grave. Damien took the first with one quick plunge of the knife as he lay sleeping on his belly. Sari whispered her paralyzing spell again, freezing the man before she flipped him over and killed him. Damien didn't even think he woke.

"I really wish that spell worked for me," he said.

"It's very useful."

They moved to the next room. There were three Grigori there, and they dispatched them just as neatly. They were walking to the third room when Sari's eyes flew to his. She looked up a second before Damien heard it.

A muffled yell.

Eyes flew open. Voices rose.

"Irin!" one of the Grigori hissed. "Brothers!"

Sari's staff flew out, knocking the rising men back to the bed as Damien's knife went to work.

WELL, THAT HAD ALMOST GONE ACCORDING TO PLAN, SARI thought.

As she tossed the groggy men around the room, Damien tackled them and pinned them to the ground, killing each one before they could reach for weapons.

And there were weapons. A veritable armory of illegal firearms and knives were stored in the corner of each room. If these were Volund's men, he was not skimping on their supplies. Some plan was definitely in the works. Sari only hoped their actions that morning would foil it.

"Sari!" Orsala called from the hall. "The ground floor is clear on our side."

"Go to the door," she called. "Guard it while we go upstairs."

As she and Damien ran upstairs, Sari could tell there were far more than sixty Grigori soldiers in the house. They poured into the hall, overwhelming the Irin scribes who fought them.

"Damien!" She nodded to the left where four men came bursting out of a bedroom.

She tripped the first with her staff, stomping on his neck when he fell.

"*Ya fasham!*" she cried, ducking out of the path of a throwing knife as she aimed a spell at another Grigori. The man stumbled, the unbalancing spell knocking him into a wall. Damien caught him around the neck and twisted, stabbing his silver blade into the man's neck as the dust began to fill the air.

Sari dragged the man she'd tripped to the end of the hallway, pulling him up and finishing him before she felt movement at her back.

It was instinct to duck and spin. Her staff held out, she caught the charging Grigori at the knees while Damien grabbed his hair and pulled him off her. Within seconds, his dust was joining that of his brothers.

The whole building was in chaos. Irin and Irina fought in

the halls, trying to avoid being drawn into dark rooms where an unknown number of Grigori lay in wait. Sari heard something downstairs and cursed under her breath. Not waiting for Damien, she ran down and charged into a dark room they'd cleared before only to find four men with guns pointed at the door. She fell to the ground a moment before they fired. One bullet clipped her leg, but she didn't stop to feel it.

"*Shanda vash!*" she cried. Magic filled the air and caught the Grigori off guard. They had been expecting a scribe. "*Ya domem man!*" Sari couldn't aim the magic. She couldn't even see them. She simply pushed the most powerful paralyzing spell she knew into the room, hoping if it didn't freeze them, it would at least slow them down.

The pained grunts and lack of gunshots told Sari she'd been at least partially successful.

"Damien, guns!" She couldn't have her mate charging in unaware. *Talesm* as strong as his could deflect a low-caliber firearm, but she had no idea what these men were carrying. A thumping against the wall outside.

"You just had"—he was so fast she could barely see him as he ducked in the room and threw two knives across the room —"to charge in"—two more knives and Sari heard guns clatter to the floor—"without me!"

"I didn't know they had guns!"

"Because we didn't see piles of them in the other rooms, did we?" Damien stalked over to the four men pinned to the wall by Sari's magic, knives through various parts of their bodies. "Honestly, Sari!"

"Yell at me later," she said, pulling out her knife and dispatching two Grigori before Damien stabbed the others.

"Are you bleeding?"

"A scrape. It's fine."

"It better be." He stalked out the door without looking, only to have a Grigori burst out of the closet and leap on his back. Damien bent down and tossed the man over his shoulder with one heave, tumbling him into the hallway where he bashed the man's head on the ground.

Another Grigori darted from the closet and ran after Damien, not seeing Sari still standing in the room. He leapt on her mate's back, and Sari ran after him, using her staff to flip the Grigori off. Damien turned the first one over and plunged the stiletto in his neck, then snapped his fingers at Sari. She kicked over the next monster, and Damien dispatched him too.

He rose to his feet, Grigori dust coating his shoulders, and stalked toward his mate. He caught the back of her neck and pulled her to his mouth, claiming her with a ravenous kiss.

"Mikael's blood, we're good together," he said with a fierce grin.

Sari laughed and ducked into the dark room, determined to check the closet to see if any more Grigori were lurking.

DAMIEN WATCHED HER FIGHT THROUGH THE WANING GRIGORI forces. They had lost one scribe that he had seen. The man's partner had been cornered, fighting off three Grigori attackers while another leapt on his brother before anyone could get to him. He'd been gone in seconds, the knife plunged into the young scribe's neck.

"No!" Sari said, running after the Grigori. Damien held her back as the scribe's partner sliced through his opponents with a short sword, sending them writhing to the ground before he ran after his brother's murderer.

"Let him take his vengeance," Damien said, walking over to the half-dead Grigori the young scribe had gutted and kicking them over to expose the back of their necks. With three quick stabs, the Grigori were gone, their souls joining the dust rising in the room.

He was bloody and tired. There had been more knives than guns—clearly, the men were trying to avoid detection from the humans—but enough guns had fired that Damien knew the human authorities would be called and called quickly.

They needed to finish this and run.

"Do you hear that?" Sari asked him, her eyes pointed up.

"What?"

"The wind."

The stairwell filled with the sound of it. Gathering and growing. Churning wind, as if a vortex sat above them. It filled the building, sucking the dust of the Grigori and the dead Irin up in a fog of gold. Damien closed his eyes against it and reached for Sari, pressing her face into his chest as the air grew more and more violent.

A giant rush of air up the center of the building, drawing dust and blood and empty clothing.

Then everything stopped.

Everything.

"Heaven above," Sari whispered when she lifted her head.

Damien's mouth hung open. The wind had frozen. Truly frozen. Dust and drops of blood hung in the air as if gravity had been suspended. Sari reached out and gathered a handful.

"What is it?"

Damien's eyes lifted. The building was old, the stairwell circling up the building, open to the landings on each side. A column of gold light shone through from the roof, though when Damien glanced outside, he saw nothing but black churning wind surrounding the building.

"Something is happening on the roof," he said.

The scribes and singers around them were also frozen. The battle had stopped. The last of their opponents routed. No one moved as the horrible evidence of battle hung before them. All the Irin stepped toward the center column of light, heads pointed up. For a moment, the blood, the dust, the light —everything was suspended in time. And then…

A black shadow from the bottom of the building shot up, taking everything with it. It threw the remaining Irin back against the walls as it ascended with a roar.

Then everything was silent.

"WHAT do you think it was?" Sari asked Damien when they'd finally returned to the house.

They'd bathed and changed into soft linen clothing as was traditional for healing and prayers. Damien held her leg, wrapping a bandage over what remained of her wound. The bullet had gone clean through the muscle, which was mostly healed. Between hers and Damien's magic, the leg would be useable by morning.

"Angels," he muttered. "Damn meddling fallen angels."

"I don't understand Jaron's fascination with Ava."

"Don't you?" Damien raised an eyebrow. "Think about it, Sari."

"You think one of Jaron's sons is her father."

"Why else would he be so taken with her?" Damien asked.

"But her magic—"

"Is too powerful to be Grigori offspring." He nodded. "I know."

"So what is she?"

Damien gently pushed her back on the pillows and stretched out beside her. "I would be a heretic," he whispered, "if I told you what I think."

Sari smiled. "You're a rebel already, my love."

"Then I suppose we can rebel together."

"Tell me," she said.

Damien rolled to his back and gathered Sari to him, stroking her hair and speaking quietly. "The vision Ava sent us," he began, "was not the same for everyone."

"What do you mean?"

"I asked the others. It was mostly the same, but there were different details in each one. Different… angles. You saw the stars when no other saw them."

"The stars hidden behind the blood-sun?"

He nodded.

"The Irina."

He tapped her cheek. "Why would a Fallen angel send Ava a vision about the Irina? The Fallen care nothing for the Irina except for wanting them dead."

"So what could he have been…" Sari's breath caught when she realized what Damien was saying. "It's impossible."

"Why?"

"Because…" Because they hadn't seen it. Because they hadn't looked.

A thousand stars hidden behind a blood-red moon. A thousand voices waiting to be found.

"Whoever said," Damien whispered, "that the angels only had sons?"

"You don't think Jaron is Ava's grandfather," she said. "You think he is her father."

"The only reason he couldn't be is because the Fallen do not have daughters," Damien said.

Sari pushed up and looked into his eyes. "The Fallen don't have daughters. Irin cannot mate with Grigori. And dead men don't come back to life.

"Except when they do."

Sari couldn't think of anything to say. The revelations

Damien spoke of rocked the foundations of her world. And not only of her world, but of the entire angelic race.

"If what you think is true, this changes everything."

He nodded. "Everything."

"Do we tell her?"

"No."

Sari frowned. "Why not?"

"I don't think she's ready to know it. Not yet. If she was, her father would have told her."

"Damien…" Her voice was choked. "What does this mean? For us? For the Grigori? If we accept Ava—"

"We accept that not all Grigori are inherently evil," he said. "I know."

"But they are," she said, unable to stop the tears. "They killed us. Slaughtered our babies. Tore our people in two."

"I know."

"How can we accept anything but their destruction?"

Damien pressed her face to his chest. "*Milá*, I don't know. I don't know any more than you do. But I know Ava is not evil. So if Ava is possible, then anything is."

Sari closed her eyes and remembered the stars in her vision, remembered the distant, desperate light trying to break through the darkness. Their desperate light hadn't felt evil either. It had felt lost. Forgotten.

"Shades of grey, remember?" Damien said. "We thought our world had hundreds. Perhaps there are even more than we can imagine."

◆ ◆ ◆ ◆ ◆

"You're going to Vienna?" Ava asked her.

"We are." Sari paused packing her bag. "But I promise to keep in touch."

Her suspicions about Ava's parentage were at the forefront

of her mind, but she believed Damien was right. The girl wasn't ready to know yet. She was still so unsure of her place in their world, and Sari would never have her doubt it. She was also unsure of her mate.

Though they had reunited, Malachi's mind was still fractured. He had little to no memory of anything but Ava. And his *talesm*, the spells he'd drawn from childhood, had disappeared, leaving his magic untapped and weak.

"We're going to Germany for a while," Ava said. "His grandparents had a home there, and he's hoping…"

"It's a good idea," Sari told her. "Perhaps with familiar things around him, he'll be able to remember more."

"That's what I was thinking too."

Ava was fragile, and Sari couldn't help but think of all the other girls like her who might live in the shadows of the human world. Daughters of angels with power they didn't understand, abandoned by their sires and cursed to wander among humans who had no concept of their worth.

"I'm going to Vienna to reform the Irina Council," Sari said. "We need to come back. And when we do, we'll need our seers."

Ava still looked unsure. "I don't really know what I'm doing," she said. "I only see what Jaron sends me."

"And that is a power that no other Irina has. Learn to use it."

The girl nodded, but Sari could tell she was still unsure.

"We need you, Ava. Our world needs you." That much, Sari was sure of. What she didn't know was what that world would look like when this battle was over. "Will I see you in Vienna someday?"

Ava nodded, and Sari smiled.

"Good."

EPILOGUE

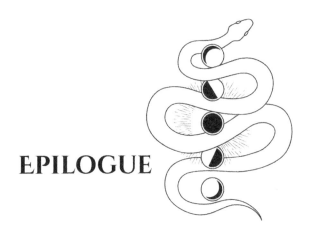

Vienna

H E watched her, triumph surging in his chest as his mate pulled away from the linen-clad warden of the Irina gallery. He saw her whisper something before she strode down the steps and walked fearlessly onto the floor of the Irin Library as others only watched.

It was a palace of ancient learning. The heart of Irin power. And not a single singer sat among those wielding it on the floor.

Damien could hardly breathe as Sari strode to the center of the room and lifted her voice.

"I am a singer of Ariel's line," she proclaimed loudly, "and I request an audience with the Irina Council."

But there was no Irina Council.

And his mate was going to change that.

"I am an Irina singer!"

Sari lifted her voice, and Damien thought her forefathers must have heard her in the heavenly realm. A beam of light shone through the stained-glass windows of the Library, hitting her linen robes and making them glow gold and red. Dust and blood. She was a warrior. *His* warrior. But also a warrior for her sisters.

He burned with pride that she was his.

"A daughter of Ariel's line," she continued. "I request an audience with my representative on the Irina Council. Where is my council? Where are the elder singers who speak for me?"

One brave elder stood.

"Daughter," he said. "I'm sorry, but your council has fled."

"No. My council was attacked."

Another elder stood. "Your council is in hiding."

Sari took a step toward him. "My council was protecting itself. Protecting its daughters when the scribes did not."

Damien heard the muttering and whispering around him, but he could not take his eyes from the woman commanding the floor.

"And they do not trust us to protect our sisters even now?" the second elder said, an oily smile taking over his face. "Does the Irina Council not trust us to protect our own mates? Our daughters?" He wasn't speaking to Sari, but to his audience, the Irin scribes who watched. "We *want* to protect them, and yet they hide."

Sari walked back to the middle of the room where the star of the elder singers' desks had once sat with honor. Now those desks lay abandoned, unused and forgotten, pushed into the corners of the room.

A million hidden stars, struggling for the right to shine.

"And I *want* to speak to my council," his mate said again.

"I'm sorry." The elder's smile said one thing as his words said another. "But your council is no more."

She raised her hands, his glorious mate, and her magic filled the room. Old magic. New magic. The two twined together as the scribes' gallery stood frozen in silence.

There was a low rumble, then with a mighty crash the seven desks of the elder singers slid to the center of the room, pulled by Sari's elemental power. Papers and dust went flying. Furniture shifted as people ran to escape the desks' path.

Sari stood motionless in the center of the floor, eyes traveling to meet the gaze of each elder as the massive wooden desks settled into place in the ancient star-shaped pattern around her.

Damien released the breath he'd been holding.

And Sari said, "It's time."

End of Book Three

VISIONS

THE IRIN and Irina are together again. Society is being rebuilt. But what do you do when the foundation of your world has crumbled? Where do you go when all the boundaries have been redrawn? For Damien and Sari, charting a new path into the future means confronting the demons of the past. They've forgiven each other, but can they forgive themselves?

Through ages you have come to me,
And I choose you.
Because you wandered many roads alone
And this body has bled and shed blood in honor,
I choose the one who sees me and challenges me,
My warrior, my lover. Friend, protector, helpmeet, mate.
As iron sharpens iron, I will ever be your own.

—Sari's Song

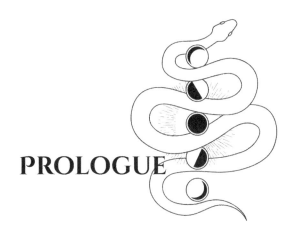

PROLOGUE

S ARI woke screaming. *"Where are the children?"*

They were on top of her. Clinging to her legs and throat, their teeth like knives against her skin.

They dissolved in front of her, empty clothes falling to the floor as gold dust rose in the air, mixing with the steam of the ritual bath.

Their blood ran in rivulets between her thighs.

Sari flinched as heavy arms came around her. Darkly inked arms. Familiar arms. She was covered in sweat. She wasn't sure what was a dream and what was reality. His arms felt real, but so had the children.

So had their teeth.

"Sari."

"Where are they?" She heard their little voices crying in her mind. "They're dying."

"Sari, wake up."

She closed her eyes and felt something crawling up her legs. The terror closed her throat as her heart took off at a gallop. "They're killing us!" she choked out, trying to squirm away.

"Sari!" A hand wrapped around her braid and tugged hard. "Wake up. *Now*."

The pain jolted her out of the dream's grip. She blinked tears out of her eyes as her breathing slowed and evened.

"I'm with you." A low voice began a familiar litany. "We are in Cappadocia. You are safe in the scribe house. Your grandmother and Mala are here. There are no children. No Grigori."

But there was someone missing. "Where is Tala?"

He pressed his forehead to her sweat-soaked temple. "Wake up, Sari," he whispered in her ear. He shifted until she was lying against his chest. "Please, *milá*. Your *reshon* is here."

Reshon. She lifted the shields that guarded her mind and heard him. A voice attuned to hers. His soul rested against hers, bracing her spirit and carrying her when she stumbled.

"Damien?"

He let out a breath. "I'm here, sweet girl."

Sari said nothing. She turned and wrapped her arms around his waist, pressing her cheek against the mating mark on his chest and anchoring her physical self in his presence. Damien brushed his fingers up and down her back and allowed Sari to hang on to him.

It had been two years since the Battle of Vienna.

Three since the battle in Oslo where she and her sisters had slaughtered their last nest of Grigori.

In the time between, the revelations had come hard and fast. Their sister Ava was not the fallen angel Jaron's daughter, but she was a granddaughter, descended from one of the hidden stars Sari had seen in Ava's vision. Thousands of daughters born to the Fallen and abandoned to the human world, killed, or abused by the brothers who should have protected them.

A few rogue Grigori whose sires were dead had been able to break away and protect their sisters, the women who called themselves *kareshta*. The silent ones. Their discovery had rocked the foundations of the Irin world and led to a massive battle that killed four of the Fallen, including Jaron and the hated Volund.

It was a battle that only added to Sari's nightmares.

Hundreds of dead lived in her mind. Not only those of the Rending, but the broken bodies of the Grigori children who had attacked them in Vienna. It didn't matter that they were tiny vicious monsters bred to attack the Irina, whose martial magic did not affect children—she dreamed of them all.

Every night she closed her eyes, and they attacked her again. Only this time there was no relief. No magic could shield Sari from her own actions. There would be no rescue from dreams.

Damien held her tightly. "Rest, my love."

"I won't be able to sleep anymore." She sat up and brushed hard at her cheeks, willing the flashes of memory away. "Go back to sleep. You have training with Mala tomorrow. I'll go to the library."

"Sari—"

"Please." She pressed a kiss to his mouth. "Please. I need time alone."

The memory of the dead was devouring the peace she and Damien had found. Sari knew joy again. She laughed and loved. She knew the touch of her mate and the comfort of her adopted family, many of whom had moved on and started new lives. Many of her sisters had found mates. Borne children. Found purpose and place in the Irin world again.

But her own guilt stalked her in the darkness. Made her rise screaming in the night when she could no longer bear it.

And it was more than the children. Sari also felt the weight of her actions against the Grigori through the years. How many had she killed in her thirst for revenge? Sons of the Fallen who might have only been trying to survive? Some might have left sisters behind.

She had killed without mercy. Hunted relentlessly. Tracked

the demons who had killed her sisters and slain their children, believing the lie that history had taught them.

The Grigori were evil.

They hunted without conscience.

All deserved to die.

But they had been wrong. And the burden of that knowledge was slowly eating Sari alive.

DAMIEN COULDN'T SLEEP WITHOUT SARI BESIDE HIM. HE ROSE and walked to the ritual room, deciding to add to his morning prayers and meditation since he'd be getting no more rest.

The ritual room in Cappadocia, like everything in the old scribe house, was carved into the soft volcanic cliffs of the region. Hundreds of years before, the first scribes had come and built there, lured by the dry air that was perfect for a library and scriptorium. It had been a center of Irin learning ever since and a haven for travelers.

Evren, the chief archivist, had welcomed Orsala as a friend and colleague, pleased to have such a renowned singer in their company as the Irina gradually rejoined their brothers and mates in Irin politics and society.

Damien and Sari had returned to his watcher's post in Istanbul, though they were as often in Cappadocia as they were in the city. Orsala didn't need them close, but Sari had a difficult time adjusting to her grandmother's absence.

He entered the ritual room and nodded to an older scribe in the corner who was tending the fire. He stood before the main wall and traced his fingers over the inscribed glyphs of the Old Language that had been carved and worn by countless hands. He moved left to right, following the line of the invocation and murmuring prayers for peace and blessing for his family. His mate. His mother. His father who had died in battle.

Gathering a slate, paper, and quill, Damien knelt in front of the fire and began to write a favorite passage from the Epic of Kairav, the tale of a warrior scribe's journey to return to his mate. It had been a favorite of his when he was a child and one of the first long passages he'd learned to copy.

A movement in the corner caught his eye. Damien turned to see a scribe kneeling and joining him before the fire. There was something about the man that was so familiar he couldn't help but stare.

Smiling, the man said, "We have met before, brother."

"Indeed, I think we must have, but I cannot remember when."

"I am somewhat changed since the last time you saw me," the man said. He wasn't tall, but he had a warrior's build. He was dark-haired and deeply tan. His *talesm* had the style of local writing, and Damien suspected that Cappadocia, if not home for him, was very close to it.

The memory hit him.

"You are Evren's son," Damien said. "The Rafaene scribe who helped my brother and me in Vienna."

"I am." The man's smile grew. "My name is Bernal. It is good to see you again, brother."

"Your time as a Rafaene has come to an end?" Rafaene scribes were mainly warriors of Rafael's line. As healers, they suffered more than most from their actions in war. They were permitted to take regular respites, but for seven years at the most.

"I cut my time short," Bernal said. "I felt needed in other ways."

Damien couldn't help but remember his mate's screams that night. "There is much need for healing within our people."

"There is."

He said nothing more. Sari's wounds were private.

"Tell me," Bernal said. "Did you achieve your objective in Vienna?"

Damien's purported mission had been to break into Mikael's armory and retrieve weapons for his men to fight against the Fallen. His true objective, however, had been to retrieve his own heaven-forged blade. With rising angelic activity and so many power vacuums after the death of Jaron and Volund, Damien wanted the knife back. What he didn't want was for the council to know he had it.

"I did," he said. "Your actions helped greatly in our battle against the Fallen and the Grigori that day."

Bernal smiled as if he knew he wasn't being given the whole story. That was fine with Damien. He had no need to spill secrets to anyone but Sari and wasn't concerned if the scribe knew it.

He rose and nodded to Bernal. "Perhaps I will see you in the meeting hall, brother. Right now I must go to my mate."

Damien burned the passage he'd transcribed in the ritual fire and watched the smoke rise through the carved-stone chimney in the center of the room.

> Though she reside across oceans,
> I will return to her.
> Though my love may scorn me
> And my men flee
> Still I will journey on.
> For my home is with my beloved
> And my soul will have no other.
> My home is in my lover's arms.
> With her, I find rest.

♦ ♦ ♦ ♦ ♦ ♦

Damien left the ritual room and found Sari in the library as the blue light shone through the high windows of the room. She sat on the ground in the corner of a hallway, her back against one wall, staring at a tiled mosaic one of the Greek scribes had created two hundred years before from the shattered remains of his village. It told the story of the Rending in vivid detail. Shards of pottery and broken staffs made up much of the material used. A piece of a doll's face. A delicate earring. Charred wood and broken glass were mixed with the tile.

Damien sat next to Sari and took her hand. She squeezed his but said nothing. He often found her here, but it wasn't anger he saw on her face that morning. Only deep sadness.

"Why do you come here?" he asked.

"To remember." She laid her head on his shoulder. "To try to remember the rage."

Damien said nothing.

"But I can't," she continued. "Not anymore. Perhaps rage and guilt don't make easy companions."

"You protected your sisters," Damien said for the thousandth time. "Likely saved countless human lives by—"

"Not without cost." She took a deep breath. "Not without innocents lost, my love. We both know it is not possible."

"What must I say to you?" He tipped her chin toward him and forced her eyes away from the mural. "I know this guilt. It's the guilt of every honorable warrior after a battle. Innocents are killed, no matter how much we try to avoid it, because evil hides behind the good."

Her eyes blinked back tears. "I envy your hierarchy now. Did you know that? There is comfort in knowing you were following orders. Obeying protocol."

"So others can bear the blame?" Damien pulled back. "Obeying orders is no excuse for dishonor. The Irin Council must take responsibility for its actions. And lack of them."

"But don't you see, Damien? We made our own rules. Or

had none." She swallowed hard. "We had no mandate to follow. We had no excuse."

"You did what you thought you had to in order to survive."

"I see their faces." She covered her eyes. "Every night. When will they go away?"

Never. Damien didn't want to say it, but he still saw them. Still saw innocents' blood staining the streets of Antartus. Still saw the red spray across a field of silk flowers. The blank eyes of Grigori children who had known no other life than being slaves of the Fallen.

"We go forward," Damien whispered. "We give the dead their peace. The dead do not care that we mourn them. They do not care that we rack our bodies in grief. We move forward, Sari. That is how we honor them. We live. We survive. And we change our world so that future generations do not have to make the decisions we did. We change this world so that our children may have peace."

CHAPTER

ONE

S ARI was ready to murder. "You said that Konrad would oppose the measure."

"He was planning on it." Gabriel leaned back in his chair in the library of Damien and Sari's town house in Vienna. "But new information revealed to the council has put him in a difficult position. And I can't say I disagree with him."

Gabriel was her brother—would always remain her brother—but he was also chief secretary to the elder scribe Konrad, one of the most powerful and influential leaders in Vienna.

And he was pissing her off.

"What new information?" Sari asked.

"A new report from the watcher in Hamburg came in. He can't ignore it, Sari. Two scribes mated to *kareshta* within months of their appearance at the scribe house? These women know no magic. They have no training or education. What is their status?"

Damn eager scribes. Couldn't they have practiced a little more patience? "The *kareshta* are… mated to Irin scribes. Why should their status be any different than any other Irina?"

"You know why. These unions are one-sided. The women have no idea of their responsibilities as mates. They have no idea about our world or our traditions. They might be true unions of the heart or these women might be desperate. No one would blame them. But they could also be a security risk, and you know it."

Because unless their angelic fathers were dead, any offspring of the Fallen, Grigori or *kareshta*, was little more than a slave to their sire. Free will was not an option. Most Fallen ignored their female progeny, but there were some cunning enough to use their daughters as spies.

"Gabriel, we have debated for months," Sari said. "The Irina Council is opposed to forcing the *kareshta* into any kind of registry. The council does not have the right to—"

"The Irina Council is not unanimous. And most acknowledge that the scribes' council has the right to police their houses," Gabriel said.

"They only belong to the elder scribes because they kicked the Irina out!" Sari replied, her temper rising. "They are not *their* houses any more than the Library is *their* Library."

"You know what I'm talking about."

"Language matters, Gabriel. Words matter. You, of all people, should acknowledge it."

He looked away, knowing she was right.

Sari had no patience for the doublespeak of politics. She wasn't an elder and had no desire to be, but she had become the de facto representative of the haven guardians around the world, most of whom still distrusted the Irin and Irina Councils. Almost all of the Irina havens were still operating, allowing her sisters a safe place as the political landscape constantly shifted. Sari was there to make sure that their interests were acknowledged. She was a leader, but she was not a politician.

"I'm not disagreeing with you," Gabriel said. "But women and children are appearing out of nowhere. We have no history for them. Some have no human documentation at all. They were born in seclusion, and most of their mothers are dead. The majority have no idea which of the Fallen sired them. There are reasons this is necessary, Sari."

"They are not cattle," she hissed. "Not livestock to be tagged and herded."

"No one will be treating them as such!"

"You say that now," Sari said. "But what of the time when sympathy for their plight wears thin, Gabriel? What will happen when a daughter of the Fallen wants to disappear? What if she grows tired of our world? What might happen if a scribe and his *kareshta* mate need to go into hiding? Registries last forever. Pictures last forever. We no longer live in a world where information disappears."

"The Rending will not be repeated." Gabriel's eyes were black flames. "But not everyone is a warrior, sister. They are asking for protection. For shelter. Would you have us bare our necks to the shadows?"

"And would you have me bow to the whims of old men who would lock me away for my own good?" Sari countered. "These women don't know enough to make any choice yet. They need safety and knowledge before they can make any decision."

Gabriel tugged at the back of his hair, his usually unflappable demeanor tested by Sari's stubbornness. "Heaven knows you won't stop teaching them magic, no matter how the council protests."

"They need to be able to protect themselves. And the havens do not answer to the council."

"And so we put ancient knowledge in the hands of our sworn enemies!" he shouted, rising to his feet. "Women who could be spies. Women who could be feeding knowledge to the Fallen. We hand them this power and hope for the best?"

"All we're teaching them is how to block the voices," she said. "Protect themselves as well as they can."

"Are you that foolish, Sari?"

She rose to meet his anger. "You think I don't know the risks?"

"I think you see every lost sister as your own!" Gabriel's face was flushed. "And they're not, Sari. They are not Tala. Not Abra. Or Diana or any of the countless others we lost. These women are the offspring of very powerful enemies. And we have no idea where they come from or where their loyalties lie. Even Kostas's faction is not so forgiving as you."

"Kostas is a paranoid rogue Grigori who sees angelic infiltration everywhere. He won't even accept children unless he knows their sires are dead by his own hand."

"And he's probably smarter than we are," Gabriel said.

"They're *children*."

"I know," Gabriel said, stepping closer. His voice dropped. "But they're not *our* children."

The truth sat heavy in her gut.

"You and I know better," Gabriel continued, "than to assume innocence just because a face is young."

Her eyes met his. "Then what do we do? They need to belong to someone."

"I don't know." He let out a long breath. "Some days I don't think I know anything anymore. But Sari, compromise must happen."

"I do not see a compromise on this issue," she said. "The *kareshta* do not belong in your record rooms on some kind of secret list."

"How can we help them if we don't know who their sires are? How can we make sure they have some assurance of self-determination?"

"How can we help them"—her voice rose again—"when a councillor who said he would be their ally turns his back on them over one troubling report?"

"That is political reality, Sari. Konrad does not answer to you."

"Konrad doesn't even listen to me," she scoffed.

"Trust me," Gabriel said. "Everyone listens to you. They don't have a choice when you spend most of your time yelling. You are the thorn in the side of every councillor who disagrees with you, scribe and singer alike."

Sari thought she was supposed to be offended by that, but she just couldn't find it in her to care.

HER MATE FOUND HER IN THE BACK GARDEN. DAMIEN HAD been at the Archives all day. He spent most of his time when they were in Vienna working on a translation of Old Slavic battle songs from his grandmother. He was translating them into the Old Language, curious if any contained martial magic that could be recovered for the Irina.

He worked in the Archives, corresponded with his men in Istanbul, and avoided politics like the plague no matter how much his family tried to draw him in. Though his father had died in battle one hundred and twenty years before, his mother, the *praetora* of the region where Damien had been born, had never loosened her grip on power and politics. Katalin was as ruthless as she had ever been.

And she still disliked Sari.

Damien came and knelt beside her as she dug her hands in the soil. The garden was the only thing that gave Sari peace in the city. Well, the garden and her mate. The former was overgrown—they'd returned to Vienna only the week before —but it still recognized her song. The latter shifted her until she was leaning against him, still pulling weeds as she sat between his legs.

"Hello, *milá*." He brushed her hair to the side and kissed her neck. "How is our brother?"

"He's well."

Damien kept away when Gabriel visited. Though the two could see each other in passing without Gabriel going into a rage, the relationship had never healed. Sari didn't know if it could. Her brother covered his grief with work and political machinations, but he had never recovered from Tala's death. And though Gabriel could acknowledge Tala's part in putting herself at risk, Damien was still the easier target.

"He gave me some news that was not welcome," she said. "Konrad has withdrawn his objections to the *kareshta* registry movement."

"Hmmm."

"That is not a surprised 'hmmm.'"

"No, it's not."

"Did you see this coming?"

Damien paused before he spoke. "I know the number of women who come to the house in Istanbul," he began, "and I also know that angelic presence is very low in my city."

"Because of Jaron."

"Because Jaron didn't take many human lovers, and he didn't allow many minor angels in his territory. But Jaron is gone, so that will likely change."

"And?"

"And just in the past year, three women have come to our house looking for sanctuary. Three in a very quiet city."

"And we sent them to Sirius."

Sirius was part of Kostas's faction, and the rebel Grigori was even more passionate about the women and children under his care. He had a keen mind and solid judgment. In fact, he reminded Sari very much of Damien.

"We send them to Sirius," Damien agreed. "But not every watcher has a Sirius close by. And Kostas is very secretive about his resources. He won't talk to many aside from you, Max, and Ava. So what do the other watchers do, my love? Where do the women go? Who teaches them about our world and makes sure they pose no threat?"

VISIONS

Much as she was loath to admit it, Damien had a point. "The Irina should be teaching them. I'm not as foolish as Gabriel seems to think. I don't believe they should be taught powerful spells unless we know we can trust them. But I *do* believe we have a responsibility to at least teach them shielding."

"I agree. But who will teach them?"

"There should be Irina in every scribe house," Sari said, pulling more weeds and wishing she had something bigger to take her aggression out on.

"And there, my love, is the sticking point." Damien leaned forward and rested his chin on her shoulder. "Do you think the Elder Council wants to admit they need the Irina? Not only back in the Library, but in every scribe house in every city around the world? Think about it. Any Irina who took such a posting would have to be powerful enough to teach and train the *kareshta*. Not only matrons and builders and healers. *Martial* Irina. In every scribe house."

Her back went up. "And is that a bad thing?"

"To a council that has wielded absolute control for generations without answering to anyone? Absolutely. They see the martial Irina as a threat. Women who took the law into their own hands and fought under no one's authority before the restoration of the singers' council. No rules. No protocol. It will take time for attitudes to change."

And Sari had to admit that most Irina trained in combat would buck at the thought of obeying a watcher's commands. She was one of the few who had operated within the hierarchy before the Rending, and even that had been tempered by being a watcher's mate. She couldn't imagine Renata following orders. Or Mala. So who would take these positions?

She took a deep breath and leaned back into Damien's chest. "I hate this."

"There are no easy answers, Sari. We do the best we can."

Move forward. That's what they'd agreed on. Move

383

forward to make a difference. To create a better world. No looking back.

But why did it have to be in Vienna?

"I hate politics." She sat up and started yanking out weeds again. "I hate councilors who change their minds. And singers who can't make up their minds. Factions with no leaders, and coalitions that exist solely to reject every reform proposed."

Damien knelt beside her and began to pull weeds. "Don't forget the polite speech."

"Double-talk."

"Endless compromise."

"Fluid principles." She ripped a stubborn dandelion out by the root.

"Covering your ass before looking out for the greater good."

"Campaigns!" Sari yelled. "When no one is supposed to be bloody campaigning!"

Damien laughed and grabbed her around the waist, tackling her to the grass before he kissed her.

"We are not politicians, my love."

Sari huffed. "I hate being bad at things."

Damien laughed harder.

"But I'm shit at politics," she said, his laughter making her smile. "I'm utter and complete shit at it. All I want is to walk into the Library and bash them all about their perfectly coiffed heads and kick their linen-covered asses. Maybe break some things."

"I think you already did that."

"Well, I'd like to do it again."

His laughter fell away, and Sari closed her eyes as Damien traced a line along her jaw.

"They need you," he said quietly. "Whether they appreciate you or not. They need you kicking their asses instead of kissing them. They need your passion. Your principles. Your unwillingness to bend."

She sighed. "I know compromise is necessary."

"There are plenty in Vienna willing to compromise," he said. "What is needed is others who will hold them accountable."

"So you approve of my obstinate disregard for political subtlety?"

"My love"—he kissed her nose—"I revel in it."

SARI WAS CHATTING ONLINE WITH ONE OF THE HAVEN guardians in Canada the next day. Several e-mails from Gabriel had told her everything she needed to know about the *kareshta* registry vote and the status of the motion. The council was still stymied, but this time it was by a few of the elders who didn't want *kareshta* to have any political status or protection at all... unless they were mated to Irin scribes.

It was an extreme position, but it had split the coalition enough that no mandates would be handed down in the near future. For the moment, watchers would retain control over how they dealt with the women and children who came to them.

Sari was hoping that if enough of the watchers tapped Irina resources in their area to help them deal with the new *kareshta*, then the registry might become a moot point. Local singers and scribes could deal with each case individually, without the need for intervention from Vienna. It would also move more Irina into scribe houses and back into mainstream Irin society.

She heard a key rattle in the door.

"Sari?" Damien called.

"In the library." She signed off from her session with Abigail's daughter and closed the computer. "Why are you home already?"

She expected a teasing reply about missing his mate, but Damien said nothing. He wasn't the most talkative of men, but his silence that afternoon unnerved her.

"Damien?"

He walked into the library and leaned against a bookshelf. "I received a letter from Katalin today."

Sari frowned. "I didn't see anything in the mail."

"She sent a messenger."

Sari rolled her eyes and decided to sort her own mail, which had been piling up for a week. Her mate's mother could be singularly aristocratic, old-fashioned, and paranoid. "What did the letter say? Did she ask if I was dead yet?"

"Please don't joke about that."

Sari looked up. "You're in a mood."

Katalin had been appeased by Sari's connections when Orsala was on the council, but she was still obsessed with bloodlines, and Sari suspected that—should she meet a tragic end—Katalin would waste no time in trying to breed Damien to a singer with Mikael's blood.

Or breed him to any singer. Damien's mother had been more than clear about her desire for grandchildren, a topic that Sari and her mate were currently avoiding.

"What did Katalin want?" she asked absently, sorting through the mail and mentally bracing herself for the children discussion again.

"She wants us to come for a visit."

The letters dropped from her hand. "A what?"

"A visit." Damien didn't look any more thrilled than she did.

"To Řekaves?"

"Yes."

Sari paused, unsure of what reaction Damien might be expecting. "Do we have to?"

"When has my mother ever specifically requested that we come to visit her?"

Sari blinked. "Never."

Sari and Damien had never been invited to his mother's home even though the old castle where Damien had been born, raised, and trained as a warrior was only a little over four hours away by car. They had met his mother in Vienna twice. Once before the Rending and once in the past year after the Irina Council had been reformed. Both meetings had felt more like diplomatic visits than family dinners. Sari had briefly mentioned the possibility of Katalin becoming involved with the new council only to receive an unblinking, glacial stare.

Katalin of Vértes did not become directly involved in politics.

If Damien's mother was requesting a visit, she had a reason other than meddling in Damien and Sari's life.

"I think we must go," he said. "She would not be asking unless it was important."

Sari nodded, watching Damien as he read the letter again. It was written on thick linen paper with black ink calligraphy. Katalin didn't use a computer or a secretary for her letters, Damien had once told her. If you received a letter from the *praetora*, it was written in her own hand.

"Damien?"

He looked up. "Yes, *milá*."

"We'll go. As soon as you like. I don't have any meetings this week that can't be postponed."

"Thank you."

"You don't have to thank me," she said. "How long has it been?"

Damien looked up. "How long has what been?"

"How long has it been since you've been home?"

"Home?" Damien laughed, walked over, and kissed her, tossing Katalin's letter on the pile of Sari's mail. "I'd hardly call Rěkaves home."

She smiled. "How long has it been, Damien?"

He stopped and stared out the window that looked into the back garden. "I went home briefly in 1890."

"When your father died."

"Yes." He paused but said nothing more about his father. "Before that? The last time I lived in my mother's home was at the end of the thirteenth century."

Sari blinked. "So long?"

"I was only there for a few years before I left for Paris with the rest of the order." He crossed his arms, but did not turn to her. "I went to Orkney after Paris, and you know the rest."

Sari tried to imagine being so distant from her roots. Though she'd traveled, most of her life had been spent in Northern Europe and Scandinavia. Sarihöfn was home.

Damien turned and caught her expression. "Don't look at me like that, *milá*. I am not a wanderer to be pitied."

"But where are your roots, Damien?" The earth singer in her was dissatisfied with his response. "Where do you feel most at home? I can't imagine, *reshon*."

"Sarihöfn. London. Istanbul. *You*." He walked over and kissed her cheek. "You are my home, Sari. I can wander the world for the rest of my life. The only home I need is you."

CHAPTER
TWO

D AMIEN used the hands-free calling on his phone
to speak to Malachi while Sari caught a nap on
their way north.

"So while we're seeing more activity from new Grigori,"
his first lieutenant was saying, "none of it is organized. Those
we do track down are either low-level irritants or connected to
Kostas in some way."

Damien's ears pricked at the mention of the rogue Grigori
commander. "Are his men hunting in the city?"

"Some. So far everyone we've encountered has checked
out with Sirius."

Kostas was the leader of a faction of free Grigori, and
Sirius was his second-in-command. They were sons of the
Fallen whose angelic sires were dead and who chose to lead a
more disciplined life. They did not hunt human women,
though a few of Kostas's men were in consensual—if precar-
ious—relationships with humans.

Most of their focus was on hunting fallen angels. They
also found and cared for *kareshta* and Grigori children who had
not yet been corrupted. The more Fallen they killed, the more

Grigori had free will. It was one of the reasons Damien had allowed the Grigori commander to take some of the heaven-forged blades from Mikael's armory during the Battle of Vienna. To his knowledge, Kostas and his men had tracked and killed two Fallen since then, though they were only minor powers.

"Use caution when dealing with them. I don't know how disciplined their command structure is," Damien said.

"I suspect it is even more strict than ours."

Because though a Grigori could live life without killing humans, it was still rare. They did not have written magic to control their need for human souls, nor did they have mates who fed their energy as the Irin did. The few who managed did so because leaders like Kostas kept them on a tight and brutal leash.

"How often do you speak to him?"

Malachi asked, "To Kostas? Rarely. But Ava has regular contact with his sister, Kyra, and Sirius and I have exchanged phone numbers."

"Keep me informed if anything looks like it's changing."

Istanbul, his post for centuries, had always been a quiet one. Jaron, who had controlled the city for most of Damien's term as watcher, had not allowed his sons to run rampant, nor had he hundreds or thousands of them as other fallen angels did. There was a brief spike in violence after Volund had taken over, but that had calmed when Jaron and Volund killed each other in Vienna. For the most part, Istanbul was a peaceful part of the Irin world, well able to allow him and Sari to travel.

"Can you spare Leo right now?" he asked Malachi.

"I can." The man paused. "Is there something I need to be aware of?"

"I don't know yet."

"I thought you and Sari were in Vienna."

"My mother called us to Rěkaves, her castle west of Prague."

"Going home for a visit?" he asked. "So why are you asking about Leo?"

"I have a feeling this isn't a simple visit," Damien said. "My mother does not do simple visits. She has some task for me."

"You have Sari. And a veritable army of Mikael's warriors in your mother's training, if rumors are correct."

"They're correct..." He rubbed his jaw. "But I don't know them. I don't trust them. Or my mother. So if you could spare Leo, he would be welcome to join us."

Malachi thought. "I can spare Leo. Max is here and grumbling about not having enough to do lately. So I'll just double up his patrols. Do you want me to ask Mala as well?"

Damien's ears perked up. "Is Mala there?"

"She and Orsala came for a visit with Ava and the children."

He smiled. "And how are your tiny terrors?"

Malachi groaned. "Still not sleeping. Well, I should say that Geron sleeps very well. Until Matti wakes him. The poor little man has no rest from his sister."

Sari grumbled at the talking and turned toward Damien in her sleep, a frown marring her face.

"Geron will have no rest from women," Damien said, smiling at his sleeping mate. "It's best he learns this early."

"I'll be sure to share this wisdom with my infant son. Out of my mate's hearing, of course."

"Good." Damien smiled. "They are treasures, brother."

"They are." Contentment laced Malachi's voice.

For the first year, nightmares had been Malachi's constant companion. His feelings about children had been as conflicted as Sari's after the battle. Ava's pregnancy and his children's birth had healed the cracks in his soul. Ava and Malachi were family, and Damien was relieved to witness their peace.

"So Mala is here," Malachi continued. "And restless. If you'd like an extra hand, I'm sure she'd enjoy getting out of the scribe house. She's quieter, but she's worse than Max about being bored."

"Send them both," he said. "I'll find something for them to do. If nothing else, they can train with my mother's men for a time. I know Mala would enjoy it, and Sari would enjoy having her sister along."

"Consider it done. I can't imagine Mala objecting, but I'll let you know if she doesn't want to leave Orsala right now."

"Thank you."

"Safe travels."

He fumbled with his phone, trying to keep his eyes on the road and still hit the damnably small buttons to shut the thing off. Sari reached out and took the phone from his hand.

"Let me." She took it and shut it off, putting it away in the center console.

"Sorry we woke you."

"Why must you both yell on the telephone?" she said with a yawn. "They are not bullhorns."

He grimaced. "I am still uncomfortable with this human magic."

She laughed, but it was true. Technology had many benefits, but Damien was still becoming accustomed to the rapid pace of change.

"What were you talking about?" she asked. "I only caught the last bit about the children and Mala."

"Malachi should be brought to the Watchers' Council," Damien said.

"What?"

"Sorry, I was just thinking aloud. He should be nominated for promotion to his own house. He's more than ready."

Sari thought for a long while. "I don't know if he is."

"He's more than capable."

"But his children are young," she said. "And we are away

as much as we are in Istanbul. In practice, he *is* a watcher. He shares those responsibilities with you."

"But he does not have the title."

"I don't know if he wants it." She rubbed her eyes. "Not yet anyway. Sharing those responsibilities with you allows him and Ava to travel for her work and to visit her family. When their children are young, that is probably more important than a title."

"Hmmm."

"Talk to him about it, but I suspect he is happy where he is."

Damien took her hand. "You are wise, my mate."

"I know. You're very fortunate to have me."

He grinned. "Malachi is going to send Mala and Leo to Rěkaves."

"Why?"

"Because… it's Katalin. Who knows what she has planned?"

"Hmmm."

"I see you don't disagree with me."

"I would never disagree with you about your mother," she said. "I do wonder if you're being too cautious."

"I just don't understand why she's asking us now. We've been in Vienna regularly for almost three years."

"True. But you told me yourself time moves more slowly for her."

Katalin of Vértes was a medieval Irina born in the middle of the tenth century. When she was trained, the Elder Council was a power more theological than political. Most practical decisions in the Irin world were made by families with lines that traced directly back to the Forgiven. Katalin and Damien's father, Veceslav, were a political mating designed to unite two of the strongest lines of Mikael's descendants. Damien was their only surviving child.

Katalin was *praetora*. The undisputed leader of Rěkaves

and Mikael's house now that his father had died. To say that she lived in another time was an understatement. While the rest of the Irin world had modernized and power had coalesced in Vienna, Rěkaves and the surrounding area had remained locked in feudal tradition. The council left Katalin alone because Mikael's house continued to produce the most-skilled warriors of the Irin race.

Damien reached for Sari's hand. "There is something else going on," he said. "I know it. The only question is, how forthcoming will she be?"

DAMIEN PULLED ONTO THE ROAD THAT LED TO THE WARDEN'S house at the edge of Rěkaves land and slowed as he wound through the trees. Sari rolled the window of the borrowed Range Rover down, and he inhaled the familiar scent of pine and woodsmoke. Within a few minutes, he saw the wood-and-stone warden's house and the large barn where vehicles were stored. He parked the Range Rover in front of the barn and took a deep breath.

"We'll take horses from here," he said, pocketing the keys to give to the warden.

"No road?"

"Katalin despises anything with a motor," he said, opening his door and walking around to open Sari's door.

"How medieval," she said with a smile.

"Very."

The first flashback from his old life came when he knocked on the warden's door and an older scribe opened it a second before he bowed deeply.

"Sir," he said. "We did not expect you so early."

"We left Vienna before dawn. Please don't…"

But the man was already straightening. He didn't look Damien or Sari in the eye when he said, "I will have the groom fetch your horses immediately."

Damien let out a defeated breath and held out his keys. "I leave my vehicle in your care, Warden."

"I will have it fueled and washed in case you need it, sir."

"Our luggage is inside."

"I will have it brought to the castle immediately."

Sari was suspiciously silent as the scribe led them out to the barn and the stable behind it. Within moments, Damien and Sari were led to a pair of Arabians, a black stallion and a chestnut mare, already saddled and ready for their riders.

"Kazimír." The groom handed the stallion's reins to Damien. "And Draga." Sari took the mare's. "The finest from our stable, sir. Chosen for both of you by the *praetora* herself for your use during your stay."

"Thank you, brother."

Damien saw the smile flirting at the corner of Sari's lips as he greeted the horses and the groom left them. "Just say it."

"You're—as Ava would say—kind of a big deal here, aren't you?"

Damien let out a sigh and mounted the stallion. "It's a thirty-minute ride to the castle," he said. "Let's enjoy that time in silence, shall we?"

Sari let out a delighted laugh and swung on top of her mare. The equally spirited Draga leapt ahead, Sari urging her to a canter up the road. Damien kept behind her, scanning the familiar meadows and forests of his youth. Not much had changed in this corner of the world. His mother saw to that. He breathed deeply and enjoyed the fresh air and the controlled power of the animal beneath him.

He patted Kazimír's neck. "You're a fine one, aren't you?"

The horse gave a proud toss of his head.

"Care to stretch your legs?"

The stallion tensed beneath him, sensing Damien's shift in mood. He leaned forward and urged the stallion to a gallop, passing Sari and racing up the hill. Knowing his mount knew the roads better than he did, Damien closed his eyes for a moment and let the horse carry him, let himself fall back into the ancient rhythm of man and steed, a partnership that had often been his only company on long and lonely journeys. He pulled Kazimír to a halt at the top of the hill and looked out over the castle where he had been born.

A single white tower dominated the skyline across the valley, the ancient structure rising from a hill in the center surrounded by rolling meadows. A narrow river cut through the land, curving around the central hill and feeding the fields and orchards that surrounded it. Ancient stone walls encircled a Gothic castle Damien's father had renovated in the thirteenth century. He knew modern improvements had been made, but the heart of the castle remained as it had always been, as unchanging as the line of Mikael's blood who had built it.

As he watched, a banner rose over the central watchtower. A red dragon on a black field, gold thread catching the light in the sun.

Meros ni she-ar.
Meros ni gharem.

By the time Sari reached him, the banner had already risen and was flying in the wind, and watchmen were gathered on the walls. Damien watched her reaction as she caught sight of his childhood home for the first time.

"Heaven above." Her mouth dropped open. "That's…"

"Rěkaves. The river house. Seat of Mikael's *praetores*." Damien lifted an eyebrow and smiled at his mate. "Welcome home, *reshon*."

THEY FOLLOWED THE RIVER ROAD THROUGH THE VILLAGE AT the base of the castle, Damien nodding politely to the residents who came out to greet him. It was an Irin village, mostly consisting of families who had made their home here when a son or daughter was taken into Katalin's training. By the early twenty-first century, generations of farmers and tradesmen from all over the world had made the community unique in Damien's knowledge. Because Mikael's blood ranged over the earth, faces from Europe were as common as those from Asia, Africa, and the Americas, along with every combination one could imagine. Though the language was modern, accents were diverse.

"I amend my earlier statement," Sari said as they rode through the village. "You're not *kind* of a big deal, you *are* a big deal."

"I'm not here very often."

"Did you know it would be like this?"

He deftly avoided the question. "You never know what to expect from the *praetora*."

He wondered what Sari's reaction would be when they were greeted at the castle. From the warden and groom's welcome, Damien had a feeling he knew what was coming.

As they rode up the hill, he heard the massive iron gate opening. The sound of hoofbeats on stone and wood against metal. As they crossed the threshold, the drums started. The castle grooms came forward to take their horses as Damien and Sari were led up a walkway built into the castle walls. He took her hand and gripped it, surprised at the way his heart beat with the drums. It was instinctual. Elemental.

It was in his blood.

When they reached the top of the central watchtower, they turned, and Damien saw the open courtyard spread below them, clear but for the drummers lining the walls and his standard hanging from the ramparts. He stood next to Sari, his face impassive as the drumbeats picked up.

"What is this?" Sari whispered.

"Our welcome."

Low chanting came from an arched doorway, deep voices that echoed a moment before Mikael's warriors burst into the sunlit courtyard. Two staff bearers—a singer and a scribe—leapt over each other, engaged in the martial dance of the *sabetes*, the staff fighters, as their brothers and sisters circled them, stomping their feet and pounding their staffs on the ground.

The fighters' skin was bared from the waist up, silver *talesm* and gold mating marks alive in the open air. It was an acrobatic battle display of sweeping movements and choreographed strikes.

The drums beat on and the chanting did not stop. A chorus of staffs struck the ground in unison as the warriors' chanting rose.

"*Meros ni she-ar!*"

Bang. Bang. Bang.

The staff bearers fell back and the *karebes* broke through, their silver swords beating against leather-clad shields. They stepped with ceremonial solemnity as two pairs of swordsmen stepped forward and engaged in a dance as thrilling as it was lethal. One pair fought with short sword and dagger, the other with Eastern sabers.

"*Meros ni gharem!*"

Blades struck against shields.

Damien glanced over at Sari, who appeared rapt with wonder at the martial display. It was *Sabet e Kareb*, the staff and the blade, the traditional martial greeting of Mikael's warriors. Damien could feel the drums in his chest, the rhythm rising through his feet as the men and women fought. A single misstep and any of the combatants could be seriously injured. Damien knew from experience those blades were not dull.

And through the clashing of metal, he heard her. The beat of the drums could not drown out the hoofbeats of his mother's war mount.

Katalin rode into the courtyard astride a powerful chestnut mare, leading a company of riders armed with pikes, long axes, and sabers. She rode tall and straight, her russet hair flying loose behind her as she held her battle-ax high. She galloped around the courtyard, striking a series of targets thrown in her direction, each colorful wooden disk shattering as her weapon found the mark.

The drums and the chanting. The staff strikes and the ring of metal hitting shield. And over the warriors of Rĕkaves hung the heavy fog of magic. Damien could feel it in the air, hear the songs of the singers rising and the snap of ozone as blade struck blade.

Katalin held her ax out to the side, halting in the center of the courtyard, her chin lifted as her dark eyes rose to Damien's. She wore no finery to greet him, nor would he have expected her to. She was clothed in leather breeches, tall riding boots, and a blood-red shirt the same color as the dragon in Damien's standard. A braided gold torque encircled her neck.

"Warriors of Mikael's line," she called in the Old Language. "What do we claim?"

As one, the scribes and singers spoke, and Damien couldn't keep from joining their chorus.

> "Meros ni she-ar.
> Meros ni gharem.
> Meros ni silaam achokab!"

Ours is the blood.
Ours is the bone.

Ours is the vengeance of heaven.

As one, the scribes and singers surrounding Katalin turned toward Damien, fell to one knee, and shouted, "*Ave, praetor!*"

Sari slowly turned to Damien and said, "I think we need to talk."

CHAPTER
THREE

T HEY were shown into Katalin's receiving room after the greeting in the courtyard, solemn servants nodding and serving wine and refreshments before they took their leave.

"So you're the *praetor*," Sari said without preamble. She grabbed a handful of grapes and a glass of wine before she sat on one of the low chaises near the fireplace. It was summer, but the stone walls of the castle still attracted a chill. "How long?"

"For around one hundred twenty years or so." Damien did not sit. He wandered around the large room lined with book-cases, chests, and wardrobes.

From the informality of the setting, Sari knew that this was Katalin's office, for lack of a better word. This was not a cozy family room or a formal sitting room with art on the walls. Swords and axes hung on one wall, polished but well used. Boots were lined up on a rack near the door. A coat was thrown over the back of a chair piled with stacks of papers and books. It smelled faintly of lavender, wax, and oil.

The only decoration was a large oil portrait of a hawk-faced man whose profile told her it must have been Damien's father or grandfather.

"You've been *praetor* of Mikael's guard since your father died," she said.

He ran a hand through hair still tousled from their hard ride to the castle. "There is always a *praetor* and *praetora*. Once my father died, the title came to me, whether I wanted it or not."

She cocked an eyebrow at him. "You've been neglecting your duties?"

He gave her a withering look. "Do you really think Katalin needs my help?"

Sari shrugged. "She called you here. You tell me."

"She never approved of my taking a watcher's position with the council. She thought I'd serve for a while before coming home." He ran a finger along a line of books. "Put in a hundred years or so to cement political connections in Vienna as my father did, then return here."

"And mate with a nice girl she'd chosen for you?"

"I don't think niceness would be a deciding factor," he muttered.

"But you didn't."

He huffed out a breath and finally turned toward her. "My father and mother were both still living. I wasn't needed here."

"But your father is gone."

"And I'm still not needed."

Sari munched on the grapes, feeling intimidated by the surroundings and forcing herself to ignore the twisting in her stomach.

"She called you here," she said. "Had the warriors greet you in formal fashion, displaying their prowess, and then call you their *praetor*. I think you need to be prepared for anything, my love."

"Can you really imagine the two of us living here with Katalin?"

No. She cleared her throat. "You are a scribe well acquainted with duty and tradition, while I am a Northern ruffian from a land that has never acknowledged any Irin nobility. I honestly don't know what to think or how we'd get along here."

"You and Katalin would butt heads at every turn," he said.

The door swung open and Katalin strode in. "Don't assume, my son. It was your father's failing; don't let it be yours. It's what got him killed, you know."

Damien refused to look at his mother. "I am not willing to live my life caught between my mother and my mate," he continued as if Katalin had never arrived.

Sari said, "Hello, Katalin."

"Sari, please don't get up." Katalin sat at her desk.

"I wasn't planning on it."

"I trust you've been taken care of."

"The warden said our bags would be brought to the castle immediately."

Damien crossed his arms over his chest. "Katalin, why have you called us?"

"Welcome home, *praetor.* I trust the guard meets your approval." She kicked her booted feet up on the end of the desk and leaned back. "How do you find your castle?"

"*Your* castle is in excellent condition, *praetora.* The village also appears to be flourishing."

"The harvest last fall was an excellent one, and the brewery is now shipping all over the country," Katalin said, glancing at Sari. "Your mate would be well met. There are several skilled earth singers working in the village."

"My mate would be better suited to—"

"Your mate is quite capable of speaking for herself," Sari said. Turning to Katalin, she continued. "Thank you. I might tour the land. It would be refreshing to be among singers of my blood. The warriors' greeting was impressive."

"Yes." Katalin's eyes flicked to Damien. "Has my son never told you of *Sabet e Kareb?*"

The staff and the blade? Yes, that fit the martial dance they'd been greeted with. It was a jaw-dropping display of power and skill that Sari knew was designed to intimidate an opponent. She imagined ancient armies greeted on the field of battle by the whirling staffs and striking blades of the dancers. They probably pissed themselves.

No need to let Katalin know she'd been completely taken aback. "Damien failed to mention how impressive it was in person."

While Sari knew that Europe, Asia, and Africa had once been controlled by ancient Irin families, she'd had no idea how formal it all was. It reminded her of human nobility. In the northern lands where she'd been born, no such dominance occurred. Power and responsibilities were shared by all the families. Wealth was dispersed and singers of every line were in positions of authority.

Here, she could see the stark delineations. Katalin ruled. Servants bowed. She had no doubt that those servants were singers and scribes who hailed from bloodlines other than Mikael's. Řekaves was a palace—a temple—to warriors' blood.

"Katalin, why did you call us here?" Damien asked again.

Sari could tell by his voice that her mate was losing patience. So, apparently, could Katalin.

"There is a Fallen hunting in Prague," she said. "I called you here to kill it."

His eye twitched. "You assume that I can."

"My son," she scoffed. "I don't care what rumors float about. I know you wield a heaven-forged blade, and I know you have it in your possession."

"Why?"

"Because you are, whether you like it or not, your father's son."

Damien said nothing for a few long moments.

"Why don't you have one of your warriors kill the Fallen?" he asked. "You have the finest warriors of Mikael's line if what I saw is any indication. And those scribes and singers are only initiates."

Heaven above. Sari coughed so she didn't choke on a grape. Those were the *initiates*?

Katalin raised her chin. "I do have the finest warriors in the world."

"And Prague is within your domain."

Her eyes flashed. "It was. Until the petty council demanded my singers retreat from combat."

"Gabriel's fist." Damien rolled his eyes. "Not this again."

Katalin rose. "They treat Mikael's daughters as serving girls. They are happy to have any scribe from Mikael's house, but my singers are shunned? They do not deserve my help! Let their bumbling boys in the scribe house defend the city if they don't want my help."

"Still this?" Damien shouted. "That policy died with the Rending. It's been two hundred years, and you're still angry."

Sari bit her tongue. She kind of thought Katalin had a point, but she wasn't going to say a word.

"I'm unwilling to help them when they try to dictate the terms," Katalin said. "If they want my help, they can petition me like anyone else. And I will choose who I send, not some blustering bureaucrat in Vienna."

Sari thought the Irin Council petitioning Katalin was about as likely as Damien learning modern dance. She poured herself another glass of wine.

"So why did you call me here?" he asked. "To hunt this Fallen? If it is within Prague's territory, then let Prague hunt him."

"They do not have the skills."

"Then hunt him yourself, *praetora*, and forget about your

petty rivalry. The death of a Fallen is more important than politics."

Katalin answered only with silence. Something about her expression must have pricked Damien's interest because he stepped closer.

"Well, that is unexpected," he said. "I amend my earlier assessment. You do need my help."

"Veceslav's blade is still in the armory."

"But Father was always stingy about sharing the magic needed to wield it, wasn't he?"

Katalin's lip curled. "You know I cannot carry it."

"No singer can," Sari said, aware of how much that knowledge must have stung the fiercely independent woman in front of her.

Damien said, "Father did not pass that knowledge to any of the guardians here?"

"No. He taught you. Veceslav was traditional. Some magics were only to be shared by those of our house. It was always assumed that if something happened to him, you would return."

"He never asked me to do that. Neither did you."

Katalin lifted her chin. "And if I had?" She glanced at Sari. "Your mate left you, yet you remained with your house."

Sari set down her wineglass and leaned forward, narrowing her eyes.

"What happened between Sari and me is not your business, *praetora*," Damien said. "We are here. We are together. And we will help you kill this angel. That is all you need to know."

"GRIGORI CAN WIELD HEAVENLY BLADES WITH NO TRAINING AT all," Sari said, thinking aloud from the bath as Damien undressed in the attached bedchamber. "Do you think it's because they're first generation? Is the potency of their blood what allows it?"

"They can carry them," Damien said, leaning in the doorway, clad only in his pants. "But they cannot command them. A Grigori using a heaven-forged blade is as effective as any Irin soldier using it untrained. He will lose it as often as he kills with it. And he might just kill himself. The blades... They have a mind of their own."

Sari laughed. "They're not sentient."

"No, but they have... personality." He frowned. "I don't know how to explain it. They're objects of magical power. They have will that has nothing to do with us."

She flicked water in his direction. "So you say. I cannot refute it."

"It's not a gift, you know." He cocked an eyebrow at her. "To carry one."

"I know." She took a deep breath. "But it is power."

Damien frowned. "Why haven't the Prague scribes called for help from the council?"

"Maybe they have."

"Then why hasn't it been answered?"

"Politics? Simple disorganization? You have to admit that council hierarchy broke down after the Battle of Vienna. I think they're still scrambling to regroup."

"Perhaps." Damien didn't sound convinced.

"You should ask Bruno," Sari said. "He and Karen still run that safe house on the outskirts of Prague."

"I'll call him in the morning." He didn't move from the doorway. "There are too many warriors here. I noticed during the *Sabet e Kareb*."

"It's the oldest martial academy in Europe, Damien. I'd expect there to be many warriors here."

"But there are too many. In times past, a warrior was called from Rěkaves almost as soon as he'd achieved mastery.

My father and mother's students became watchers, Library guards, special hunters. Now I see more lingering in the castle guard than I have ever seen."

Sari frowned. "Why? Is she out of favor with the council?"

"Yes and no." He took a deep breath. "Katalin has always had a… tenuous alliance with the Elder Council. They have no power over the *praetores* of Mikael's house, and that irks them."

"The village here, was it unaffected by the Rending?"

Damien nodded. "My mother and father's warriors never left the valley unguarded. In fact, many of the singers from retreats near Prague fled here for protection. It was one of the few stable places during that period."

"So Katalin protected her people when the council failed," Sari said.

"And she never lets them forget it." Damien rubbed his jaw, and Sari tried not to be distracted by the flex of his biceps. "My mother occupies a position of tremendous political power, but she never becomes directly involved. My father's mother was much more active politically. Katalin is a warrior first and always. She's also an aristocrat on a continent that has eschewed them."

"She's out of touch."

He nodded. "She always has been. But that never affected the students here. Now I fear that it has."

And that bothered her mate. Sari tucked the idea away to mull over when she wasn't naked and in the same room as her lover. She lifted one long leg up and hung it over the edge of the tub, drawing his eyes.

Damien walked toward her, unbuckling his pants. "That, my love, is a very large tub."

She wiggled her toes. "It's warm too."

He stripped his pants off and leaned over to kiss her long and hard. Then he climbed in, sloshing water over the aged stone floor.

"You're making a mess," she said as he used his teeth against her neck.

"I don't care." Damien hooked both hands around her waist and drew her body forward, lifting her breasts out of the water before he put his mouth on them. "After all," he muttered against her skin, "it's my castle."

She let her head fall back and tangled her hands in his hair, content to let him play lord of the bathtub. She had no objections, especially when he was doing marvelous things to her breasts. The tension of the day had left him in a mood. One she was happy to let him work out on her body.

Flipping her over, Damien pulled her to straddle his lap. As she sank down, he grabbed a handful of her hair and dragged her mouth to his. He was rougher than usual, his grip harder as he held her hips.

"Damien." A low groan left Sari's throat when he tugged her hair, arching her body back before he latched his mouth to the heated flesh of her breast.

"Yes." He scraped his teeth along Sari's skin. "My name, *reshon.*"

"Damien," she whispered.

"Who is your mate?"

"Damien."

She could feel the rise of pleasure at his hands. His mouth drove her to the brink of release, and his commanding words undid her. The hand in her hair loosened, and she opened her eyes to meet the tightly leashed violence of his desire.

"Who is your lover?"

"You are," she said.

"Who do you choose?"

Unable to speak when her body shook with release, she fell forward, bracing herself on his black-inked shoulders and pouring her cries into his kiss.

"Who is your mate, *milá?*" he asked again, whispering soft kisses against her lips.

"Damien." Her heart raced, and her body was weak from pleasure. Something had roused in him, a fierce, possessive need to claim her.

He hadn't finished. Nor, she realized, did he intend to. At least not in the bathtub. Sari clung to his shoulders as he stood, her legs wrapped around him. Damien stepped out of the bathtub, oblivious to the water that splashed across the floor. He made his way to the massive bedchamber warmed by a large stone fireplace. The bed fit the room, a wide four-poster platform with thick velvet curtains and an eiderdown mattress. Damien tossed Sari on the linen sheets before he crawled up her body, the air crackling with barely leashed magic.

He bit the inside of her thigh and muttered, "Again."

SARI AND DAMIEN LEFT THE CASTLE THE NEXT DAY TO DRIVE into Prague. The house Bruno and Karen ran served as a safe haven for traveling Irina and a few scribes they trusted, along with *kareshta* who needed a temporary place to hide. It lay south of the city in the middle of a dense forest.

The location was ideal. They were close enough to Prague to be easily connected while still isolated enough to be private. Astrid, Sari's healer in Sarihöfn, was also living there, though she made noises about moving. Candice and Brooke had been living there until Candice accepted a position in Vienna at the Central Archives. The two had moved only six months before.

"Sari!" Karen waved and ran down the porch steps when she saw them. "I can't believe you finally came to visit me."

"It hasn't been that long," she said as she climbed out of the car. "Has it?"

"Two years," Karen said. "Before Vienna. Shame on you, sister."

They embraced. Karen had always been the best of the Irina, in Sari's opinion. Fierce in her love and stubborn in her protection, she was the ideal mother. Sadly, her only daughter had been killed in the Rending. It was a loss that no one could bear to speak of with either Bruno or Karen.

"Damien!" Karen hugged Damien too. "Bruno will be back in a few minutes. He just went to the market in the village. You're at Rěkaves?" She put an arm around Sari and led them into the house. "Why on earth are you at Rěkaves? I didn't know Damien was in contact with his mother."

"I am," he said quietly. "Karen, do you know about the Fallen in Prague?"

She fell silent for a moment.

"Has the council finally responded?" she asked. "*They* sent you? But I thought…"

She didn't need to finish the question. Bruno was one of the few scribes Damien had trusted with the knowledge that he carried a heavenly weapon again. If Bruno knew, Karen did.

"I have my blade again, sister," Damien said in a low voice. "But the council does not know it. Katalin called for me."

"Katalin?" Karen scoffed. "Since when has her royal highness deigned to protect any outside her little valley?"

"She waits for the council's call," Sari said.

"She waits for their groveling," Karen said. "The watcher here sent a petition to Rěkaves months ago after he hadn't heard back from Vienna. She ignored him. He must not have groveled enough for her liking."

Had Katalin refused the watcher because she couldn't be bothered or because she didn't have a warrior who could wield a black blade, Sari wondered. If it was the latter, Sari could hardly imagine Katalin acknowledging the weakness. Far better to have other Irin leaders think her callous rather than ill-equipped.

Bruno banged in the door a second later, raising his enormous voice to greet their guests. "Look who is here!" he roared. "And me without my ax."

"I'm glad of that," Damien said, rising to embrace the giant man. "I get enough threats from my mother. It's good to see you, Bruno."

"And you."

They spent a few minutes chatting about the mundane things of life. Roads and fuel prices. The odd weather that summer and new beers that were available. Mutual friends and new children.

After a few minutes of conversation, Sari decided to change the topic. "Why has the council been slow to respond to the Prague watcher?"

"About the Fallen?" Bruno asked. He and Karen exchanged a look.

"The local watcher is vocal," Karen said. "Has become a bit of a squeaky wheel."

"And?" Damien asked.

"And he's asking for help. Not only with the Fallen, but with the increased Grigori activity in the city."

"So there *is* Grigori activity."

"Yes. But not… typical."

Sari said, "Is any Grigori typical anymore?"

"A few," Karen said. "But I know what Bruno is saying. These Grigori are not thieves and murderers, as Volund's sons were. Neither are they good men or trying to protect anyone but themselves, as Kostas's men are doing. The council knows about them but has decided it's more expedient to put out fires instead of looking for the spark that keeps igniting them."

"And these Grigori don't seem to kill the humans they take," Bruno added. "They seduce them, yes, but they have learned to feed without killing. Maybe they fear the scribes and their new mandate?"

"Maybe they fear Kostas," Damien said. "He's only a few hours away."

"True," Sari said. "Or maybe they're taking advantage of the situation. For many scribes, offensive action against the Grigori or the Fallen is still foreign. If they can play on that, let it be known that they do not callously kill humans, then they can operate more freely."

"Whatever their motives," Damien said, "They are being spawned by one of the Fallen, and that Fallen is seducing more girls, breeding more children. He has to be stopped."

"Have there been any *kareshta*?" Sari said.

"Yes." Karen's eyes were sad. "They met with Bruno, but he had to send them away. We didn't know what else to do. Brooke and Candice were still here, and they freely admitted that their sire was not dead. We could not allow them to stay."

"It's a problem everywhere, sister." Damien squeezed her hand. "Do not let guilt consume you."

Sari asked Bruno, "Do you know the angel's name?"

He nodded. "They call him Aurel. He's not an archangel. I think his power lies in the middle of the range. Definitely no Volund or Jaron, but more than a nuisance. Whoever kills him will have to wield a black blade and be backed by an efficient and competent company of warriors."

Black blade. Efficient and competent warriors. Sari was beginning to see why Katalin had decided to call Damien.

"Does he have any allegiance?" Damien asked. "Is there anyone he answers to?"

"Svarog," Karen said.

"I thought Svarog was dead," Sari said.

"He's not," Bruno said. "He was allied with Volund, but according to Max, he backed out of the Battle of Vienna. Left his people and his territory intact."

"And swept up territories that had once belonged to his rivals," Karen added. "Svarog is no fool."

"And this Aurel answers to him?" Sari asked.

"Yes."

Sari watched her mate, wondering what he was thinking. It was exactly the kind of twisted scenario he tried to avoid. Give him a clear target and a clear objective in battle, and Damien was a golden god of war. Give him value judgments and murky council politics…

"Well," Damien said quietly. "It appears that I'll be the one hunting this Aurel. Perhaps Svarog as well. So any information you can give me will be more than welcome."

CHAPTER
FOUR

THE following night, Damien returned to Prague, this time on his own. He'd left Sari and his mother alone. Hopefully everyone had all their limbs when he returned.

So far, the women had been resisting the urge to antagonize each other. Or perhaps they'd joined forces. After all, though Katalin was an aristocrat to the core and Sari fiercely independent, they both hated the Elder Council and politics in general.

Maybe shared enemies really did make friends.

Quite separate from politics, Sari was enjoying watching Mikael's singers train. The regimen Katalin oversaw was ancient and more detailed than any other instruction for martial Irina around the world, though much was familiar to Sari because Damien had trained her. Sari was still hoping to pick up some new wisdom and hopefully some martial spells he didn't know while Damien hunted with his brothers in Prague. Leo and Mala had arrived that afternoon from Istanbul, finishing a two-day drive that had left both of them itching for a hunt.

"Leo?" Damien called as he opened the door to Karen and Bruno's house. "Karen?"

Mala was the first footstep he recognized. She skipped down the stairs and captured his neck in a quick hug before she darted outside.

"Karen?" he called again.

"In the kitchen!" she shouted from the back of the house. "I'm trying to feed the hordes."

Damien found his way back and slapped his brother on the shoulder. Leo was eating at the table, devouring a loaf of bread with butter as Karen stood over the stove, stirring a pot.

"So good," Leo mumbled. "Mala refused to stop for food."

Damien chuckled. "I don't believe you."

"It's true." He gulped down a mouthful of bread with a drink of milk. "She would stop for gas and tell me to get something from the little market." Leo looked horrified. "That's not food in there."

"This one eats more than Bruno." Karen was smiling, but she looked almost frazzled. "I didn't think that was possible."

"Karen is a jewel among singers," Leo said. "I knew she'd take care of me when I arrived." He scowled at Mala when she came through the door and sat at the table. "Unlike this one."

He complains too much, Mala signed. *And always hungry. I think he would have stopped five or six times a day.*

"That's not excessive!" Leo shouted. "I eat six times a day at home. Do you think this body runs on candy bars?" Leo flexed a massive bicep. "No. No, it does not."

The scribe was six and a half feet tall at a minimum. Damien was tall, but Leo and his cousin towered over him. Maxim was slightly leaner than the massive Leo, but only slightly. And yet both men were surprisingly stealthy hunters. Max was pure shadow that had Damien wondering whether the young scribe had learned some of the tricks his old brother Otto had known. A keen scribe could combine spells to make himself almost disappear.

It wouldn't have surprised Damien one bit. Maxim was quiet about it, but Damien used the young man's dubious connections to gather information. Long before the *kareshta* were revealed, Maxim had contact with Grigori. He had sources and traded information. Had he crossed lines under Damien's command? Undoubtedly. But if Damien didn't ask, then Maxim didn't tell.

Leo, on the other hand, was the Irin equivalent of a rapidly moving tank. No one expected a scribe of his size to be fast, but he was. He was so fast that he was almost always underestimated in battle. Before a Grigori knew what was happening, he was on the ground with a stiletto in his spine. Then Leo would move on to the next one. He was as deadly as he was sweet.

"I hear we're going to hunt tonight," Damien said.

Leo nodded and spoke around a mouthful of bread. "Max called around. Gave me a name and an address. Said he's the one to follow if we want to find Aurel."

"Good to know," Damien said. "Any word from Kostas on this lot?"

No, Mala signed. *But Sirius was concerned. If Aurel's among Svarog's faithful, Sirius says there are likely to be children nearby. Svarog keeps his offspring close at hand.*

"Affection or distraction?" Damien asked. He knew better than to trust that Grigori children were mere innocents caught in the crossfire.

Distraction, Mala said. *Though Sirius claims that Svarog cares for his children better than most. At least the males.*

"The females?"

Cast off, not killed. Mostly left in the human world.

"I see." But he didn't see. How any creature could abandon their young was inconceivable to the Irin, for whom children were rare.

His thoughts drifted to Sari. Would Damien ever feel comfortable bringing up the idea of children again? He felt as if he should wait for her. But knowing and accepting that meant acknowledging that Sari might never want another child. Never want to experience the vulnerability of motherhood again.

If Sari had never been with child, Damien could have told himself that it didn't matter. But she had been. For a few brief months, he'd felt the utter and overwhelming joy of fatherhood. He could no longer pretend that being a father was something he was ambivalent toward. He wanted it more than anything except his mate.

Yet Sari might never be ready. And Damien could not blame her.

DAMIEN, BRUNO, AND LEO WERE HARDLY INCONSPICUOUS IN the human bar that evening, but according to Leo it was the best place to find the Grigori named Christopher, who had the habit of adopting an Australian accent to lure backpackers and wanderers who flooded Prague in the summer. They didn't have a picture, so they'd have to keep their eyes and ears open. When Grigori wanted to attract humans, they could turn on the charm and have them flocking in droves. But this one, according to Max's source, preferred the inconspicuous approach.

"Possible," Bruno muttered from the shadows.

Damien watched the blond man who fit the rough description. He was young and attractive, but Damien immediately dismissed him.

"No."

"He matches. And he's approaching that group of girls."

Damien flicked a thumb along his jaw. "Acne scarring on his chin. Not Grigori."

Grigori were more perfectly formed than humans and Irin. They did not get acne. They did not get disease. Sons of the Fallen were perfect physical specimens who reflected the glory of their angelic sires even if their power was less.

"How about that one?" Leo said. "Coming down the hall."

Damien glanced over his shoulder. The three scribes were hidden in the shadows. It was the only way to escape notice. They'd thrown light jackets over their *talesm*, but Grigori were still adept at spotting Irin. They had to be in order to survive.

"Possible," Damien said. There was something about the man...

The human girl with her arm around the young man's waist looked up at him with an adoring—nearly infatuated—gaze. They walked to the bar and stood, waiting to order drinks.

"If it's him, he's taking his time," Bruno muttered.

It was possible the man was Grigori. He was certainly handsome enough and exuded the charisma that other sons of the Fallen did. But Damien wasn't positive, and he wasn't going to terrorize an innocent human and his date.

"We should have brought Mala," Damien said. "Irina can read soul voices. She'd know for certain."

"We'd attract too much attention," Leo said.

Because while three gruff men built like wrestlers had a difficult time blending with the general populace, the addition of a statuesque African woman with a ferocious scar on her neck would make stealth impossible in the middle of Prague. Mala was waiting for them in a nearby square.

"There," Bruno said. "Look at his hand."

The man had slipped his hand under the woman's shirt, just at the waist. His fingers appeared to be stroking and teasing her skin, but Damien saw her mouth fall open and her eyes close. The touch of a Grigori was intensely pleasurable to humans, as erotic as it was deadly.

"He's *feeding* from her," Leo said. "In public."

"Smart," Damien said, rising to his feet and slipping on his jacket. "But he won't take it too far with this many people around. Leo, go to the back door. Bruno, keep watch. I'll wait for him in front. Remember, we don't want him taking off. We need to make sure the girl is healthy and get information from him. That's all we're doing tonight."

- - - ✦ - - -

DAMIEN WAITED ACROSS THE NARROW ALLEYWAY. THE BAR WAS on a side street from Old Town Square, one of the countless pubs that catered to tourists and backpackers in the beer-loving capital of the Czech Republic. It was the perfect place for the Grigori to hunt. He'd already contacted the watcher of the Prague house, who was busy with an uptick in Grigori attacks and was more than happy to have a few extra scribes lending a hand, even if Damien was vague about the true purpose of their mission.

It was only fifteen minutes later that the Grigori and the woman stumbled out of the pub. Alcohol had combined with Grigori feeding, making the woman totter as her date kept one arm around her. No doubt the other patrons thought she'd simply drunk too much. Damien, however, could see the early effects of Grigori draining. Wide pupils. Pale skin and flushed lips.

Bruno walked out a few feet behind them.

"Christopher!" Damien called.

The man turned and caught Damien's eye. In a split second, he'd dropped the woman and shot down the alley like a rabbit, headed for the square and the crowds that would be filling it on Friday night. Damien charged after him, dodging pedestrians and keeping an eye on the blond head of the Grigori. He ran quickly but couldn't get clear of the crowds of boisterous humans without attracting attention.

"Damien?" Leo called.

"To the square!"

Leo overtook him and the humans got out of his way. Whether it was the murderous look on the giant's face or the sheer size of him, the crowds parted. Within seconds, Leo had zeroed in on the fleeing Grigori and was reaching out—

Just as the man took a tumble to the ground, tripping face-down on the staff Mala had extended to catch his ankle. Christopher went down hard and loud, drawing the attention of the humans around him.

Mala melted back into the crowd as Leo made a show of helping the man up, locking his arm around the Grigori's neck.

"Let's get some food in your belly, Chris!" Leo said, laughing. "Too many beers, yes?"

"No..."

Christopher's face was pale and drawn. He looked around in panic, but no one paid attention to another drunk tourist in Old Town Prague. Leo muscled his way through the crowd, his massive arm locked around the Grigori in what looked like a friendly hug, following Mala while Damien and Bruno strolled the same direction.

"Like an elephant, that one." Bruno stuck his hands in his pockets.

"If an elephant ran like a cat."

"He'd be an excellent rugby player, you know."

"Yes. But he makes an even more excellent soldier."

MALA REVIVED THE MAN WITH A SLAP ACROSS THE KNEES WHEN Leo's chokehold got a little too aggressive. There was no permanent harm done, Damien thought as he pulled up a chair across from the Grigori. He'd been duct-taped to a chair and wore a terrified expression.

"Your name is Christopher, is it not?" Damien asked.

No answer.

"My name is Damien of Bohemia," he said. "Have you heard of me?"

He could tell by the man's eyes that he had.

"You've heard the stories of me, yes?"

"You killed Camissares," Christopher whispered, his fake Australian accent slipping. "One of the ancients."

"I did."

Camissares hadn't been one of the most powerful of the Fallen, but he had been ancient. An ancient murderer of children. He'd preyed on young girls and had delighted in watching their bellies swell with his young before they withered away, leaving his angelic spawn to be raised by a veritable army of their half siblings. Damien hadn't known about female Grigori children then. He shuddered to think what the monster had done with his own daughters. Probably killed them, as many of the Fallen did.

Damien had been glad when the order to stalk the angel had come. Camissares's sons had stalked the eastern roads, taking multitudes of those running to or away from the holy lands. Killing him had been a challenge and a reward.

"So you know, Christopher, that I am a respected scribe," Damien said. "When I tell you that your sire is marked for death, you should believe me."

"Aurel?" Christopher said. "Aurel is marked for death?"

What Damien saw in the Grigori's eyes confounded him. Anger. Desire. Anticipation. Rage. The Grigori hated and loved his sire, just as so many of his kind did. Without his sire, a Grigori would be hunted, but he would also be free.

"Aurel is marked," Damien confirmed. "And if you'd like to live, you can tell us where he lives."

"That's all?" Christopher said. "I don't have to fight him with you?"

"Why would you ask that?"

"There are rumors that Grigori fight on the same side as Irin now. In some battles, we are forced to fight our sires and are used as bait."

"The only Grigori I have fought with have chosen to fight at my side. Is that what you want? To fight the angels?"

"I want to be left alone. I don't want to fight at all."

"Want to be left alone to hunt human girls, you mean?" Bruno asked. "We didn't find you meditating, did we, Christopher?"

The man paled again and his eyes flicked to Mala. "I have to. You know that. You'd do the same thing if you didn't have your women."

Leo leaned forward. "You kill them, though. You don't need to."

"I don't kill all of them. Not if I can help it. But you kill all of us. So who's really the monster?"

HE'D CALLED SARI WHEN THEY CAPTURED CHRISTOPHER. BY the time Damien finished interrogating him, she had arrived. The Grigori had agreed to drive with Damien out to where the fallen angel, Aurel, made his home. It was an isolated house set on a curve of the Vltava River. According to Aurel, numerous Grigori guarded the road, but the angel had no way of guarding the river itself.

Damien didn't particularly like boats, but when Bruno found one to borrow, it seemed like the best option for gathering information. They set off from a small private dock downriver and made their way up the curving Vltava and away from the lights of the village along the riverbank.

It was pitch-black on the water, but Bruno didn't seem to mind. His spells for night vision were particularly keen.

Damien sat in the stern of the fishing boat with Sari at his side.

"He says the angel doesn't watch the water," Damien said.

"Do we believe him?"

"No. Maybe."

Sari tapped her foot impatiently.

"You know this is a scouting expedition only," Damien said. "We're gathering information. Forming a plan."

"I brought the camera."

"If we go in now, the angel—"

"Damien." She turned to him. "Do you really think me an untried youth?"

He squeezed her shoulder. "I think your heart is even bigger than your spirit, *milá*. That's why I'm telling you now that the Grigori said there will be children."

She froze. "At the house?"

"We knew it would be a possibility."

He watched her carefully. Sari's reaction to Grigori children was rarely predictable. She alternated between irrational fear and pity. The few children they'd come across since the Battle of Vienna had caused her to retreat into herself, and those had all been harmless girls or boys seeking shelter in scribe houses.

Aurel's children could be another matter entirely. Like the children in the Battle of Vienna, they might be trained to attack. They could be vicious or unstable or frightened by someone invading their home. There was really no way of knowing if they were innocent or dangerous.

She squeezed his hand. "You're right. We did know."

"If we kill this angel—"

"When we kill him."

"When we kill this Aurel, his children will be free."

"Which presents new challenges," Sari said. "I know this. But try not to get ahead of yourself, my love. First we kill him. Then we deal with the survivors."

The boat chugged up the river for a few more miles, passing the house that Christopher pointed out, then Bruno cut the engine and the lights, letting the boat drift downriver as they got out the binoculars and cameras that Sari had brought. Christopher was tied up and stowed belowdecks while they made notes about the lay of the land and the buildings they could see. Bruno had agreed to take him to Kostas's men in Budapest the next morning, but until then, the Grigori would be at their mercy.

The house wasn't one of the historic buildings that dotted the small river towns but a starkly modern multistory complex that led up the steep riverbank and took advantage of the view. It resembled a hospital to Damien's eye. One long building lay closest to the river, and he saw guards patrolling a hallway that ran the length. They didn't carry firearms that he could see. They did carry knives.

He handed the scope to Sari. "The building along the bank, what do you notice?"

She took a moment. "Doors. Lots of them. It looks like a hospital or... an apartment building of some sort. They're numbered."

"I noticed that too." He also noticed when her shoulders tensed. "What is it?"

She handed him back the scope without a word. Damien looked through it and immediately saw what had unnerved Sari. A child, a beautiful boy that Damien would place around four years of age, was walking down the dock that led out of the low apartment-style building. He was holding the hand of the guard and chattering. The guard appeared amused. Indulgent, even.

A door opened and slammed, drawing his attention.

"Damien, are you seeing this?" Leo asked quietly.

"Yes."

A woman strode down the long hallway, her eyes searching out the windows. She paused, then something made her shout. She walked to the doorway, and Damien saw that she was hugely pregnant. Her dark eyes were black in a moon-pale face, but he could tell she had once been beautiful even if she was now wasting from the child she carried. She walked out the doorway and toward the guard and the boy.

She was unafraid. In fact, Damien would recognize the look on her face anywhere. It was the expression of a woman who'd been frightened and angry at the same time, the familiar look of a parent who couldn't find her child.

She bent down and took the little boy by the shoulders. It was then that Damien saw she wore long, opera-style gloves. They went over her elbow and disappeared beneath the light summer robe.

"Sari." He handed her the scope. "You have to see this."

She watched silently for a few minutes. Damien couldn't see well, but it appeared that the figures were retreating.

"She's wearing gloves," Sari said. "Did you see how she touched him? She knows what the children are."

"The boy," Bruno said. "He was the image of her."

"Do you think he belongs to her?" Leo asked. "Grigori mothers rarely survive their children. *And* she's pregnant."

Damien sat back and looked at the house. It was more than a house. It was a compound. A dozen guards that they had seen. More that he knew were unseen. Staff to clean the buildings. Gardeners to tend the immaculate landscaping.

"Other Grigori are here," Damien said. "Females maybe? Who can help the mothers…?"

"What are you muttering about, old man?" Sari asked him.

"This is more than an angel with a few mistresses," Damien said. "He has apartments for them. Staff to help care for the children, I am guessing. The guard was taking care of the child. Then he stepped back immediately for the mother when she called him."

Leo asked, "What are you saying? This Aurel is one of the Fallen. He sends his sons into the city and surrounding villages to feed from the women there. That mother was *dying*. You could see it on her face. She—"

"We're not changing the mission. Aurel must die," Damien said. "However… this operation just became much more complicated."

MILENA

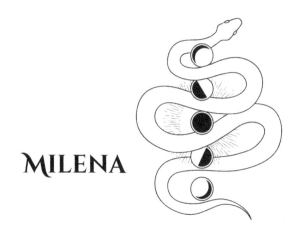

M ILENA watched the lights of the boat as it turned and putted downstream. It was a fishing boat, one of the many that made their way up and down the river every morning and evening.

But she'd seen no lines dropping in the water and more than one quick flash of a lens pointed toward Aurel's house.

"Milena?" Tomik had picked up Vaclav and was carrying him back to the children's house. "Is everything all right?"

She felt the baby in her belly kick at his brother's voice. She had just found out that morning. A boy, Aurel had told her with a smirk. She was going to have a boy for the monster. Just like her sister, Stefana, mother to the little boy Tomik carried in his arms.

"I thought I saw something on the river."

"William and Benes are watching tonight. Nothing will come ashore. It's probably just a fisherman. Maybe a curious tourist. It's not as if Aurel's house blends into the landscape."

"You're probably right." She reached up and rubbed Vaclav's little back, sliding her glove-covered hand under his sleep shirt to feel the warmth of his skin. It was the closest she could get without harm.

When she'd come in search of her sister, she'd had no idea she'd find an irrational shadow of the bubbly former athlete. They looked and acted nothing alike. Milena was the serious daughter. Stefana, the fun party girl. But they had always been close. Fun or not, Milena knew her sister would never be out of contact for so long unless something was wrong. Curious snooping had brought her to Aurel's attention. The rest was unpleasant history she tried not to think about.

She chose to focus on the children.

Stefana was gone, her vibrant beauty fading like a withered rose in winter. She'd lost her grip on the last threads of her life only weeks after Vaclav had been born, all the while worshiping the monster who had killed her. Vaclav and the other little ones were all Milena had left. She trusted Tomik's care for the children, but Milena was only another human, one of the nine who had come and gone in the five years she'd been with Aurel. Come and gone, usually because they'd given birth to children and could not bear to part with them. Those who had girls survived to bear another child, usually a son who slowly killed them.

Milena couldn't explain it. But then there was much she'd stopped trying to explain. She only knew that the opera gloves Tomik had secretly bought for her were not a fashion accessory. They were the only thing that allowed her contact with the children who'd come to see her as a mother when most of theirs were gone.

"Milena?"

She turned toward William's voice. "Is everything all right?"

She knew by the look on his face why he'd called her.

"Still?" She curled her lip in disgust and put a hand on her belly.

"There's already a girl up there," William said. "He may just want… an audience."

Milena fought back the urge to vomit. She'd thought

becoming pregnant with the monster's child would stop his interest, but sadly she'd made herself too annoying to Aurel.

She'd managed to satisfy him without becoming pregnant for three years until finally her luck ran out. Her body's stubborn refusal to get pregnant had made her noticeable to the man, and his triumph when she'd finally gotten with child was matched only by his smug satisfaction. He called her several times a week. At first it was to rape her again. Then to make her watch him rape others.

Oh, Aurel wouldn't call it rape, and neither would most of the women. But Milena had seen through whatever strange spell he used. Her mind had never been under his power, not even when her body couldn't escape.

Her baby—Milena refused to give him any ownership over her or her child—was due in another month, and she was almost as thin as Stefana had been when she'd had Vaclav. If she managed to survive her child's birth, caring for him, even with Tomik's covert help, would be impossible.

Milena had no joy in motherhood, only desperation. She loved her son. She adored her precious nephew. She loved all of them. But a clock was ticking inside her. She had to escape or she would die.

Then all of them would be at the mercy of the monster.

CHAPTER
FIVE

S ARI watched her sister spar with Katalin, staffs crashing together as the two women fought. Mala shifted to the right and paused, her feet dancing lightly over the packed earth. Katalin was a patient opponent, the stillness of her stance concealing lightning-fast reflexes. Both women had stripped down to undershirts, and their arms were red with welts and scrapes. Sweat dripped off Mala's face, and Katalin wiped her brow.

The feral expression on both their faces belied the friendly challenge the *praetora* had offered. "Sparring" might have been the intention, but the result was a pitched battle of staffs that had drawn the attention of the entire training courtyard.

Sari leaned against the wall and watched. Mala was the only one of her warriors who could occasionally best her with a staff, and that wasn't often. Mala also appeared to have a slight upper hand in the match.

Was it smug to enjoy knowing she'd be able to beat Katalin? Probably, but she was fine with it. Especially since the thinly veiled barbs had not ceased since their arrival. Sari did her best to ignore Damien's mother, but it was difficult at times, especially when the subject came to children.

The finest of Mikael's line. The legacy of his forefathers. That was how Katalin referred to her son. Like one of the Arabian horses she bred, Katalin expected Damien to continue the legacy to which she'd dedicated her own life. And that legacy included children.

"There are some magics that only belong to our line."

She was talking about the magic that allowed Damien to command a heaven-forged weapon, but the implication was clear.

Sari was not of Mikael's blood. She was a mutt. Her father, a blend of Chamuel and Mikael's magic. Her mother of Ariel's line. Sari took a bit of her magic from both, nothing like the centuries-driven breeding of Damien's family.

And yet, looking around, Sari had to admit that Katalin's methods were effective. Barbaric, but effective. The warriors she'd seen training were skilled, quick, and disciplined. They were trained and drilled in not only the ancient martial arts but also modern disciplines from all over the world. Sari saw krav maga and Brazilian jiujitsu. Judo, dagger fighting, and tahtib.

Mala and Katalin continued to beat each other, each gaining taps on the other, though the "taps" often drew blood. After twenty straight minutes of fighting, Katalin finally raised a hand.

"Draw." She grinned and reached her arm for Mala's, who grasped the offered forearm. Both singers bowed over their clasped arms before they released. "Well met and challenged, Mala."

Mala signed and Katalin looked for Sari.

"She said thank you for the match," Sari translated. "She has only had clumsy scribes to duel with since I've been gone."

Katalin laughed and spread out a welcoming arm. "Please. Make use of the facilities here as you like and work with my warriors. They would do well to learn from you."

As I can learn from them, she signed. *Perhaps one of them can teach me a trick to best Sari, as she's the only singer who can beat me senseless.*

Katalin's smile did not falter, but Sari was fairly sure her eye twitched.

"You have no mate?" Katalin asked.

Mala shook her head and signed, *I lost my Alexander during the Rending. He was in the same order as your son. Most of my blade training is from him.*

Katalin nodded as Sari translated.

"An old discipline, but a thorough one. I can see the Egyptian influence in your staff fighting though. Your mother?"

And my father.

"You are of Uriel's line, correct?"

Mala lifted her chin and nodded.

"If you have the desire to mate again," Katalin said, "let me know. I have numerous warriors who are looking for mates. Your children would be magnificent."

And with that, Katalin walked off and the crowd dispersed, not a one even blinking at Katalin's statement, though Sari could see more than one of the males glancing at Mala with clear interest.

Mala's eyes were saucers. *Did she just say that?*

"Yes, she did." Sari couldn't decide if Mala looked more surprised or offended.

I am not a breeding mare. I don't even know if I want children.

"If it helps, she sees everyone that way. I suppose you should be flattered to even be in the running for one of 'her warriors.' Especially without a drop of Mikael's blood in your clan."

Mala curled her lip.

"It's a compliment, sister." Sari couldn't stifle the laugh any longer. Luckily, Mala began to smile.

She's something else. I think she's trapped in the thirteenth century.

"You think she's that modern?" Sari asked. "You might be giving her too much credit."

Can you imagine being her child?

"No. I've never been able to imagine it. The concept of *reshon* is foreign here. All marriages among Mikael's house are arranged."

No wonder Damien ran to you.

"He ran away." She smiled. "He didn't run to *me*."

Of course he did. Mala winked and walked away.

SHE STARED AT HIM AS HE READIED FOR BED. IT WAS, SARI realized, the little things she had missed the most during their separation. The feel of his body next to hers in bed at night. The sound of him humming as he readied in the mornings. So much of their lives were lived for other people, but in their quiet moments, he belonged to her.

His broad shoulders stretched. He'd spent most of the day in the library with Leo, poring over the pictures they'd taken of Aurel's compound and diagrams Rhys had secretly procured from the architectural firm that designed the house.

"Do you want me to rub your back?"

He let out a low, rumbling sigh. "Please."

Scooting back in the giant bed, she made room for him between her legs. Damien crawled toward her naked, leaned back, and kissed her jaw before he sat up.

"Thank you, *milá*."

She put her hands on the ink-marked shoulders. "You're tense."

"The compound is well designed. Leo and I agree that we'll need at least a dozen men to breach the defenses if we're to retrieve the women and children safely. I'd like you and

Mala to go over the rough plan we made if you have time in the morning."

"We do." She dug her fingers in and felt him tense a moment before his muscles gave way under her hands. "Mala sparred with your mother today."

"Who won?"

"Neither."

Damien laughed.

Sari continued, "Then Mala told Katalin that I was the only one who could best her. The *praetora* developed a sudden twitch under her left eye."

"I'm familiar with that twitch. It's the same one she's had since I was a child who didn't obey."

She stroked her hands along the ridges of muscle that lined his spine. "Was she a firm disciplinarian?"

"Yes." He cocked his head. "But she never struck me. It wasn't done in my family. It was seen as a sign of temper, and temper was to be controlled."

"Always?"

"Always. Rage could be let loose in battle, but even then, it could not interfere with clear thinking."

"No wonder you found my family so unruly."

He chuckled quietly. "If I did something to displease her, Katalin made me muck the stables, which was not one of my jobs. The groomsmen knew me well by my tenth year. I became good friends with a few of them."

Sari smiled. "I like this little rebellious boy you speak of. And your father?"

"If I disobeyed him, he laughed. Then he made me polish the armory."

"The whole of it?"

"I didn't disobey him very often."

Sari smiled. "I think your father knew how to discipline you more wisely."

"Yes, but Katalin got more labor out of me. So who had the better strategy, hmm?"

She kissed his shoulder and leaned forward, working strong hands down his muscled arms.

Damien took a deep breath but didn't speak.

"What is it?" she asked.

"Do you want a child?"

Sari froze, her hands on the sensitive skin inside his elbow. Before she could pull away, Damien crossed his arms and grabbed her hands with both of his.

"I need to know," he whispered. "I need… If you don't, you don't. But I need to know."

Your children would be magnificent.

Sari banished the thought of Katalin's voice from her mind. "I don't know."

The tension in his shoulders did not ease.

"I avoid thinking about children," she confessed. "You know why."

"I do."

"But here… in this place, surrounded by your history and the legacy of your family, I know—"

"My desire for a child has nothing to do with legacy or history"—his voice was harsh—"or bloodlines or any other nonsense my mother is obsessed with. *I* want a child. Our child. But if you cannot—"

"I can have children," Sari said. "According to Astrid, there was no permanent damage."

"You interrupted me," he chastised gently. "If you cannot bear the idea of having more children, I do understand. But it is something that I want. Maybe… I need it."

Sari closed her eyes and rested her head on his shoulder, her hands still clasped in his.

"You need it," she whispered.

Because the man in front of her, the mate she adored, was built to be a protector. Built to guide and teach and love. He had never sought the power that had been offered to him. Never taken the mantle of leadership his family had demanded.

"You are my home, Sari. I can wander the world for the rest of my life. The only home I need is you."

Not a castle or a territory. People were his home. The lives and loves he protected, his legacy.

Her heart seized in fear. The thought of bearing another child, of allowing her heart and her body to be so vulnerable again, almost undid her.

"Sari." He let go of her hands and turned into her arms. "Sari, speak to me. Was it too soon? Whatever you decide—"

"I'll try." Had her voice ever been so small? She hated the sound of it.

"No." He wiped a tear she didn't realize had fallen. "I shouldn't have said anything. I'm impatient and—"

She cut him off with a bitter laugh. "Who has ever accused you of impatience?"

Damien said nothing, but he wrapped his arms around her and eased them down to lie in the bed. He pressed a kiss to her temple. "It was too soon."

"Damien"—she sniffed—"it was always going to be too soon."

He said nothing.

"I'm never going to be..." She took a deep breath. "I'm never going to be an easy mate. I'm never going to be the woman who dotes on her mate and her home. I thought once that I could be content in domesticity, but I wasn't. I was miserable at the retreat. Miserable out of the fight. I didn't want to admit that for the longest time because it felt disloyal to all who had died there, but it was not my home."

"I know."

"And even now, I feel as if I'd be giving up a part of myself to bear a child and raise it. But I do not want to deny you something that is so important to you. You'd be a wonderful father, but I don't know if I would be a very good mother."

"Sari, in what house do you think I was raised?" he asked, shaking her a little. "If you are not healed enough to bear the thought of a child, then I can accept this. Some wounds leave scars that last forever. But what do you think I expect of you as a mother? Baking and mending? Who do you think raised me?"

"Katalin. And clearly she was the epitome of warmth and love."

He burst into laughter. "Indeed."

"No child deserves to be neglected. No child deserves to question his worth."

"My mother…" He sighed. "She was not the ideal nurturer. Nor was she a monster. We are who we are, Sari. And though you might have a temper fit for the battlefield, that passion also warms my bed and my heart." He kissed her cheek. "You love me. You love me ferociously and fearlessly. You would sacrifice anything for those you love. Our child would know this. Any child of ours would know the ferocity and fire of her mother's heart. You might drive a child to distraction, Sari, but she would *never* feel unloved."

SARI WAS STILL THINKING OVER WHAT DAMIEN HAD TOLD HER the next day as she and Mala looked over the plans Damien had drawn up.

A dozen warriors, Mala signed. *Maybe more.*

"That's what Damien was thinking as well."

We come from two sides. She pointed at the road and the river. *One team to take out the Fallen, another to remove the women and children from the equation.*

Days of observation had given Sari and Damien better

intelligence about the numbers inside Aurel's compound. There were three human woman—all pregnant—and at least ten children. Most were boys, two were girls. They ranged in age from toddlers to the oldest child, who looked to be around six years old. He was most often seen with the guards assigned to the children, and Sari guessed he was approaching the age when he'd be removed to a different location.

"The children might resist," Sari said. "It may seem strange to us, but Aurel's compound is their home."

The women could resist too.

Sari put her hands on her hips. "We drug them if we have to. The priority is making sure they're not harmed."

And their guards?

"We'll have to make that judgment call on the ground. My instinct is to kill them all, but if they've been protecting the women and children—"

Removing their familiar protectors could backfire. Mala paused. *If they are true protectors, they will not object to our mission.*

Sari pursed her lips. "Solomon's baby? Let another have them so long as they're not harmed?"

We try reason. Make it clear we mean the women and children no harm. If they still resist, we take them out. If their loyalty is to the women and children, we let them live. Mala frowned. *In a sense, these Grigori are prisoners too.*

"You're being very reasonable about this," Sari said. "About this new way of things."

The majority of the Grigori are evil, she signed. *Some are good. The majority of the Irin are good. Does that excuse those who are evil? There is no single truth in this world. That much I have known since my family disowned me.*

"They were wrong to do it."

From their perspective, they were right. Mala smiled. *Their customs and traditions were set down centuries before Alexander and I met. They were set down for good reasons. We ignored them because we fell in love. Yet I would not have given up my mate for a thousand lifetimes of peace*

439

in my mother's house. I have lived in competing truths for years. I'm quite comfortable with them.

"We'll all have to become comfortable with competing truths if we're going to survive this new world," Sari said, glancing up as Katalin entered the room, grabbed a large tome from a lower shelf, and exited without saying a word. "How do you think she'll do?"

Not well. But maybe she'll surprise us both.

"Not likely." Sari leaned her hands on the table and let the layout of Aurel's compound sink into her visual memory. "We can't get anyone on the inside, can we?"

The woman you saw the other night?

She shook her head. "There's no way of knowing if we can trust her. She clearly cares for the child, but she might care for Aurel too. If she tells him or lets anything slip to one of the guards, the whole operation is compromised."

We have a bigger problem than that.

"What?" Sari frowned at the satellite images of the road leading up to the compound. There were numerous cars in the images. A coincidence, or was the road frequently traveled? A busy road might make the initial approach easier, but it would also mean any guards at the gate were always on high alert.

Mala rapped on the table to get her attention.

"What?"

What the hell are we going to do with them?

"The gate guards? I'm thinking we bypass them entirely. We deal with the perimeter gate another way and take them out from the back. I want to scout a bit and find out how dense this forest—"

Not the guards at the gate. The woman and children. The ones we're rescuing? What are we going to do with them once Aurel is dead?

"Oh." She frowned. "Well, I need to call Ava about that."

Ava?

"To get Kyra's number. I figure if anyone is going to have

an idea what to do with thirteen women and Grigori children
—and any guards who might be attached to them—it would
be Kyra and her brother."

Do you have her number?

"No, but Ava does. That's why I need to call her."

Mala shook her head. *She won't give it to you. She promised
Kyra. But she can pass a message along.*

Sari huffed out a breath. "Kostas is still that paranoid?"

There's a saying about that. Mala raised an eyebrow. *It's not
paranoia if they're actually trying to kill you.*

CHAPTER
SIX

"FIREARMS." Damien walked to the front of Katalin's desk and started taking various small arms out of a backpack and lining them up. "You need"—two nine millimeters—"to be training your people"—a Russian submachine gun—"with guns." The last thing he set down was an eighteenth-century flintlock pistol. Heaven knew where that relic had come from. "Honestly, Katalin. This is what the watcher in Prague has recovered just in the past few months."

His mother curled her lip. "Disgusting invention. When did the Grigori start carrying them?"

"I would guess sometime in the past three hundred years." He put his hands down on the desk. "This is no longer an option."

"Bullets rarely kill scribes." She waved a hand. "They are clumsy weapons."

"They kill us if they sever our spine in the right place."

She frowned. "But they can't—"

"They'll kill us if they manage to hit an artery and we can't get to a healer quickly enough. Or if our magic is weak-

VISIONS

ened. Or if a Grigori gets their hands on some of the high-tech rounds the humans are inventing."

She sat up straight, her back like a steel rod. "Mikael's warriors do not hunt with guns."

"They do if they want to step into the twenty-first century. Hell, the nineteenth might be an improvement, Katalin."

"Noisy." She rose to her feet. "Dirty. Clumsy. They attract too much attention from the humans, and I refuse to—"

"You cannot be this ignorant," he erupted. "When I was drilling the men yesterday, only three of them had any firearms training and that came from their parents. This is not the twelfth century, *praetora*. Grigori still prefer blades to bullets, but that is changing. And while bullets rarely kill us, it is possible and becoming more and more probable every year. Further, your singers do not have *talesm* for body armor. By limiting their training, you limit their usefulness."

That got her attention.

Katalin narrowed her eyes. "What do you suggest?"

"I suggest a full training program for firearms. Sniper training for those who show aptitude. Even the playing field for your people when it comes to guns. Even if the Grigori don't use them often, they do use them. And ignorance can kill."

"Who would do this training?"

He racked his memory. "I can think of four instructors in Europe, including one of my men in Istanbul. One in Kazakhstan. Two in North Africa and three in South. And that's not counting the Americans, who are acknowledged experts when it comes to anything with rifling. Malachi would know who to contact."

"And you?"

"What about me?"

Katalin raised a bored eyebrow. "Now who's being ignorant?"

"I am not an expert in anything to do with firearms. I'm competent, but nothing like a true master."

His mother paused before she sat down. "I will bow to your wisdom on this decision because it is fitting that you innovate the training regimen based on your experience, *praetor*."

Damien shoved away from her desk. "I have never claimed that title."

"That means nothing to me or any other warrior here. You are *praetor*, whether you want it or not."

"That is not the life I have chosen."

"It is the life chosen for you. The honor and responsibility of your blood. Who will train these men and women if something happens to me? Our bloodline preserves a martial tradition handed down for millennia. Is your stubborn refusal to acknowledge it supposed to mean anything to me?" She shook her head. "You selfish child."

"Amazing," Damien said. "It seems that after nine hundred years, I have finally become immune to your manipulations, Mother. No one is keeping you from choosing a successor from one of the hundreds of students you have trained over the centuries. No one but you."

Katalin rested her chin in her palm. "Is it so abhorrent to you? This legacy we've built? It is for you as well. I have resigned myself to your mate. She has—at least—a little warrior blood and a fine spirit for battle. Eventually you will have children if she can get over—"

"Do *not*"—Damien's voice dropped to a growl—"mention children to Sari."

Katalin's mouth twisted into a bitter smile. "Does Sari think she is the only one who has ever lost a child? We birth them. We lose them. If we are very lucky, one survives. That is life and she hides from it."

"Whether Sari and I have more children has nothing to do with you, Mother. And if you think I'll let you browbeat my mate, you are very much mistaken. No more veiled insults. No more leading questions. That subject is not your concern."

Katalin rose, fury painted across her face. "Yes," she hissed. "It most certainly is. *You are my son.* My only living child. Your birth was the culmination of centuries of sacrifice and magic from two ancient lines. Do you really think I will see that die out because—"

"We are more than our blood!" Damien took a steadying breath. "And Sari is more than my mate. She is my *reshon*, Mother. You have never understood that."

"She makes you *weak*," Katalin spit out. "If you had mated a warrior of Mikael's line, you would have already taken your place here. You would have picked up your father's shield and carried his banner. *Meros ni she-ar, Damjan.* No legacy survives without sacrifice."

"You're not wrong about our legacy," he said quietly. "You and Father taught me more about leadership than any teacher in over nine hundred years. I know sacrifice because you practiced it."

He saw his mother's shoulders relax. Her eyes softened toward him.

"But you *are* wrong about Sari." Damien was weary of Katalin's belligerence, but he would not relent on making his point. Anyone with eyes could see his mate was more than a match for him. "The Creator himself chose that singer as my *reshon*," he said quietly. "Are you more wise than heaven?"

Katalin had no answer.

"You will let her come to whatever decision suits her about bearing a child. And it will be in her own time. *If* we have children, they would be blessed to have a grandmother who would love them as fiercely as you would. But that will never happen if you are at odds with their mother. Think about that, *praetora*, when you think about your legacy."

THE TENSION BETWEEN DAMIEN AND KATALIN WAS SO THICK at dinnertime Sari had taken his hand under the table and held it throughout the meal, knowing how her touch anchored him. He picked at his food. Most of the dishes at the table were childhood favorites Damien guessed his mother had ordered from the kitchen as some kind of conciliatory gesture.

He tried not to think of it. Not when his own guilt was picking at his conscience. He wanted to believe his bluff from earlier in the day. Wanted to believe that his mother's words about tradition and legacy meant nothing. He would be lying. The more time he spent at Rěkaves, the more he realized how much he was needed.

Sons and daughters of warrior blood still petitioned Katalin for training. From all over the world, Irin parents brought their children to Mikael's *praetores* for training. And that training—while still brilliant—was verging on irrelevant because Katalin had not incorporated or accounted for the new realities of the Irin world. Firearms were only one example.

Many of the men and women he'd spoken to had little idea who or what free Grigori or *kareshta* were. Few had any idea what the current mandate was and even less knew that much of that mandate depended on the watcher of each house. Fully trained Irina were waiting for calls from the Watchers' Council, not knowing if their skills were needed or welcome in the new Irin world.

And while singers only made up a quarter of new petitions for training, they were disproportionately represented among the trainers because Irina warriors were not welcome in the scribe houses. Some trained singers stayed in the valley. Others left for havens around the world. Most had drifted into the human world.

Sari squeezed his hand under the table, snapping Damien's attention back to the present conversation. His mother, as usual, was interrogating someone about their bloodline.

"But surely you have some idea what your line is," Katalin said to Leo. "You said your grandfather came for you."

"Eventually," Leo said. "But… I don't think anyone ever asked about our bloodlines. They were just happy we were alive. They thought Max and I had been killed with our village. When our grandfather arrived, he took us until our training at the academy in Kiev. He wasn't a talkative man. He rarely spoke of the past."

"But how did you survive?" Sari asked. "If your parents were killed, your aunt and uncle—"

"We have no idea." Leo gulped from his pint of ale. "We were only three when we showed up at the scribe house in Vilnius. It was almost a year after the Rending."

"So someone saved you," Katalin said. "Cared for you for a year—which a human could not do—then dropped you off at a scribe house?"

Leo shrugged. "Yes."

"An Irina," Sari said. "It must have been an Irina who survived, then fled and couldn't take you. Or thought your family was at the house and wanted to reunite you."

"Probably. Max and I never looked into it."

Damien was betting that Leo hadn't, but Maxim surely had. A mysterious benefactor would irritate the man too much. Leo's cousin was surprisingly good at finding answers when dead ends appeared. How he did it, Damien didn't ask.

"Well," Katalin said, "it is evident to me that you are of Mikael's line, though not directly. The blood is still very strong but diluted, I'd guess, by Chamuel's line. Nevertheless"—she looked pointedly between Leo and Mala—"a strategic mating would be a benefit to your offspring."

Leo's jaw dropped and his eyes went wide. Mala's signs were hard and fast.

Damien, if you want me to leave your mother unmaimed, tell her to stop trying to breed me like one of her mares.

Sari was the one who spoke. "Katalin, let's leave the breeding talk for the stables, shall we? Besides, I'm fairly sure that Leo is a sentimentalist like Damien and me."

Katalin rolled her eyes.

Leo said, "Sentimentalist?"

Damien said, "Because you want to wait for your *reshon*."

Leo blushed but didn't look away from Damien. "Oh. Well, I don't think that's sentimental." He looked at Katalin. "It's strategic."

Katalin raised a dark eyebrow, her smile amused. "Oh?"

"A *reshon* is a mate chosen of heaven," Leo said. His face was still red, but his voice was strong and sure. "She will be a singer created to meet my soul. Surely, *praetora*, no one could prove a better or stronger mate than one chosen by heaven."

Damien's desire to laugh in his mother's face was overwhelmed by his pride in the quiet sincerity of Leo's words. He squeezed Sari's hand. *No one better or stronger.*

He leaned over to Sari and whispered in Norwegian, "I need you to think about why our path led us here. To Řekaves."

Sari's eyes went wide. "What?"

"I need your counsel on this."

"What are you thinking, Damien?"

He couldn't judge her thoughts from her voice. Sari had taken on the even tone she used when she wanted to conceal her feelings. She might have been surprised or angry. She certainly wasn't pleased.

"I am thinking… Our path has been in shadow. But it may be becoming clear. And I need my mate's counsel when she has thought on this."

Sari nodded slowly. "I can do that, *reshon*."

"Thank you."

"I can't promise you will like my thoughts."

He smiled. "That's why I need them."

THEY DIDN'T SPEAK OF IT ANYMORE THAT NIGHT. AFTER dinner, Katalin joined Damien, Sari, Mala, and Leo in the library to talk about the plan they'd been working on.

"How did you find such detailed blueprints?" Katalin asked.

"Computers," Damien said, spreading out satellite images he'd found online.

"The computer?"

"The Internet can provide much useful information."

"But some false." Sari tapped on one photograph with a marker. "This guardhouse is no longer here. It's been moved off the road. We should expect that some of these paths aren't accurate either."

Leo said, "The basics don't appear to have changed. The guardhouse at the main road is the same."

Mala tapped on the table. *The dock is longer. Aurel has added to it.*

"He's added to it, or some of his sons have," Sari said. "Remember, they appeared to be invested in the children's well-being."

Mala said, *And they took care with the human women too.*

Leo said, "Given the option, they might join Kostas if their sire is dead."

"We can't assume that," Damien said. "For now, we treat them as hostile."

Sari said, "Agreed."

"Katalin, how many soldiers can you give us?" Damien asked. "We need quiet feet and flexible minds."

"I'll talk with Desmond and Natalya in the morning," she said. "They'll know."

Damien tended to agree. Desmond and Natalya were his mother's right and left hand at Rěkaves. Both were extraordinarily competent, and Natalya was an expert archer. Damien had his eye on her for sniper training.

"Katalin," he said, "I'd like Natalya to join us if you can spare her."

Sari said, "Good thinking. Position her at a good vantage point and have her cover the dock. Two or three more archers would be ideal and would give us backup with the children."

"Agreed," he said. "In fact…" Damien was distracted by some kind of commotion at the castle gate. Pounding steps heralded a man bursting through the door.

"*Praetora!*" the man panted. "Grigori on the road!"

"What?" Katalin shoved away from the table. "Where? How did—?"

"How many?" Damien asked quietly. "And how did they approach?"

The pale messenger said, "Two. They're coming on horseback down the main road. One has the warden held at knifepoint in front of him."

"Two?" Sari asked, glancing at Damien. "Coming down the main road?"

Katalin said, "Once the archers have them in sight, they'll be taken care of. Calm, Edmund. Your father will be fine."

"Tell the archers to hold," Damien said. "If this man meant us harm, he'd obviously not be using the main road and coming in clear view."

Katalin spun on him. "You do not have the right to call off my archers." She turned back to Edmund. "The archers will fire."

"They will not." Damien strode from the room. He headed toward the front door, his mother on his heels.

"Damien! Grigori do not enter this valley. I don't care who this man thinks he is, but—"

"He will enter this valley if he is an ally, Katalin. He'll enter this house if it's who I think it is."

"You are not in command!"

"Are you so foolish?" He didn't stop walking. He had to get to the main guardhouse. And get the roster and contact number for all the guardians who stood on duty regularly. "Our relationship with the free Grigori is tenuous at best. I'll not have you putting an arrow through this one's brain. Not when he's one of the few sane ones in the lot of them."

"Damien!"

He didn't stop. Damien pushed the doors open and jogged across the courtyard. Within minutes, he was in the main guardhouse.

"Weapons down," he said a moment before Katalin came barreling behind him.

"Do not lower your weapons!" she shouted. "Keep them in sight."

The two archers on the wall didn't turn. Their bows were raised and ready, but neither had drawn. Both were wearing top-of-the-line night vision goggles. Damien noted their relaxed stance and mentally added them to the sniper-training list.

"Kevin," one said softly. "Please deal with this."

Kevin stepped between Damien and Katalin. "*Praetora*, the intruders are sighted, though both remain waiting just outside range. Scouts have not reported any other incursions, though they continue to call in. The perimeter is being double-checked."

"He is an ally," Damien said. "Call them off and lower the gate."

"Grigori do not enter this castle," Katalin said. "Unless their head is mounted on the point of my ax."

"Katalin, this man is coming here to help."

"We do not need help from any Grigori."

"I suspect the second rider is his sister," Damien contin- ued. "She is one of the *kareshta*. Rarely among humans or Irin. Sari specifically asked for Kyra's help, and Kostas would never allow her to travel alone."

"He has Fritz at knifepoint!"

"Because you are already trying to kill him," Damien shouted. "Do you think he didn't anticipate your welcome, Mother? Kevin, tell the men to lower their weapons. I will ride out to meet him myself."

Katalin glared at him. "Kevin, ignore my son."

The guardian sounded acutely uncomfortable. "*Praetora…*"

"Kevin," Damien said, "I'm going to ride out to meet this man and his sister. I trust that the captain of the Rěkaves guard will not allow me to be skewered."

"Kevin, bar the gate. No one leaves the castle."

His temper spiked. His mother thought to hold him captive? *In his own castle?*

Damien stepped closer, his eyes never leaving Katalin's. "Kevin, lower the gate and saddle a horse for me."

"Bar the gate," Katalin said, her voice sure. "And tell the archers to fire when the Grigori is in their sight."

Kevin said nothing, but Damien noticed the man hadn't moved. He stood at calm attention, eyes darting between Damian and Katalin.

"They do not answer to you," Katalin whispered. "I am their *praetora*."

"And I am their *praetor*!"

Katalin smiled, and Damien could hear the clanging of the gate as it swung closed behind him.

The lock clicked.

Praetor.

"And so you are," Katalin said softly. Raising her voice, she said, "Kevin, saddle the *praetor's* horse. Ready the castle guard to receive these… Grigori. They are under the *praetor's* protection until such a time as they become a threat."

"Did you orchestrate this?" he asked quietly, hating her in that moment more than he ever had before.

"Did I orchestrate your Grigori friend showing up unannounced, taking my warden captive, and holding him at knifepoint?" Katalin asked. "No. But neither am I one to let a strategic opportunity pass. I am your mother, Damien, and I didn't read you fairy tales in your cradle. I read you *The Art of War*."

CHAPTER
SEVEN

"KYRA." Sari embraced the nervous woman who was led into the library. "I'm so sorry about the… welcome. Damien's mother is very, very old-fashioned."

"Please, don't worry about it." Kyra gave her a soft smile. "I told Kostas we should have called. He's in the main hall talking to Damien and your mother-in-law."

Kyra was just as tall, thin, and ethereally beautiful as Sari remembered her. She was the daughter of Barak, an angelic ally of Jaron's who'd been slain in the Battle of Vienna. Sari had always thought that Kyra, with her luminous skin and gold eyes, looked like a fairy princess.

Sari said, "I hope your journey was uneventful otherwise."

"It was fine." Kyra waved a hand. "I don't live very far from here in fact. But please don't ask me specifics, or Kostas's head might fly off."

Sari laughed. Kyra didn't look any different, but two years of peace from the soul voices that had tormented her early life had given the woman a peace and assurance she'd lacked when Sari and Ava had met her. She was still soft-spoken but didn't seem as shy, though her eyes were darting over Sari's shoulder nervously.

"Kyra," Sari said, turning to the others in the library. "I don't know if you remember—"

"Leo," Kyra said, faint color rising in her cheeks. "And Mala. It's good to see you again. Both of you."

"Yes." Leo looked like he'd swallowed his tongue. "You look... well. Not that you looked ill before."

"I'm not. Ill, that is. I mean, I'm well. I'm... better."

"That's good."

"Yes."

Leo and Kyra stood across from each other, nervous as sheep. Mala's eyebrows rose, and she shot Sari a barely contained smile.

They're adorable.

Sari signed back, *They're clueless.*

Doesn't mean they're not adorable.

Before Sari could fling Kyra into Leo's arms, the door burst open and Damien came striding in, Katalin at his side and Kostas at his back. Two of Katalin's guards trailed the dark Grigori, but he paid them no attention.

"Sari, thank you for waiting. We had to come to an agreement about protocol while Kostas and Kyra are here."

Kostas went to stand next to his sister, subtly drawing her away from the others in the room. Sari wondered if he was aware of his actions or whether the overprotectiveness was so automatic that it acted like instinct.

"Damien has assured me that Kyra will have the freedom of the castle." He offered Sari a grim smile. "I, of course, have guards."

"I do agree with Katalin on this matter," Damien said. "The guards are more for your protection than ours."

"Keep telling yourself that if it makes you feel better." Kostas looked around, surveying the room until his eyes fell on Mala. "I remember you."

Mala made no attempt to greet Kostas. Though Sari knew that Mala believed in the new order and respected the free Grigori, the reality of confronting the specter of those who'd not only taken her mate but robbed her of her magic was another thing entirely. Mala met Kostas's eyes with cool regard.

"Hard to forget that face," Kostas murmured under his breath before he turned to Sari. "Ava tells me you hunt Aurel?"

"We do."

"He owes some fealty to Svarog," Kostas said. "Are you certain you want to attract that angel's attention?"

Damien turned to the men standing at the door. "Leave us. Close the doors and wait outside. I'll call if you're needed."

"Yes, *praetor*," both answered at once.

Sari noticed that the exasperated grimace on her mate's face that usually accompanied the title had disappeared. Damien didn't correct them. He turned away and waited for them to close the door, his face set in a stony mask.

She had a sinking feeling in the pit of her stomach.

Damien said, "Sari, Mala, Leo, and I were going over the plan before you decided to take Fritz captive."

"There's not a scratch on the man." Kostas walked over to the photos and plans spread on the library table. "You've done your homework. Do you have anyone on the inside?"

"No. We have no idea if we can trust any of them."

"You can't. Not yet anyway." Kostas cocked his head and tapped on a photo. It was taken in the early morning, a small child in what looked like purple pajamas curled in the arms of a guard who walked her up and down the dock. "But judging from these pictures... I'm guessing there are some of Aurel's men who have loyalty to the children. This is a girl."

Damien looked up. "Is that significant?"

"She looks to be around three years old. She's alive and being cared for. Yes, it's significant."

Kyra said, "Angels who don't kill their female children rarely care for them. They leave them at hospitals or orphanages. The girls don't cause harm to the humans, so leaving them doesn't attract attention."

Kostas said, "And *kareshta* rarely make good soldiers. Still, this indicates…" He tapped the photo again.

"Affection?" Sari asked. "Is an angel capable of that?"

"No," Kostas said. "I'd say it indicates possession. He likes to control his offspring whether he has use for them or not. And added to that is a guard…" He paged through more of the pictures. "More than one. *Guards* who are also caring for the children. They could be allies, but they're probably not."

"Why not?" Sari asked. "If we're trying to free them from Aurel—"

"Remember," Kyra said. "You are the bogeyman to those children. You are the ones who would steal them away. Kill their protectors. In those little ones' eyes, *you are the bad guys.*"

Sari heard Katalin curse long and low, but she didn't have time to think about Damien's mother or the leaden feeling in the pit of her stomach when she'd heard the word "*praetor.*" There were human women and vulnerable children who were more important than her personal dramas.

"What do you suggest?" Sari asked.

"Women only to get the children," Kostas said. "You have female warriors obviously." His eyes went to Mala. "Use them to get the children. They will be expecting scary men with tattooed arms. They won't be expecting women."

Damien crossed his arms. "And?"

"Whatever educated guesses you've made regarding security for the little ones, toss them out. Removing the children safely could be harder than killing this angel."

Sari hadn't finished undressing for bed when Damien entered the room. Before he said anything, he came and put his arms around her from behind and rested his chin on her shoulder.

"How angry are you?" he asked.

"You've accepted the *praetor*ship."

"Yes." He didn't move.

Sari let out a long breath. "I'm not angry yet. I'm processing."

"I could make excuses about how she backed me into a corner, but I'm not going to. I've been thinking about it for days."

She'd known. Of course she'd known. When he'd drilled the men with Katalin's weapons master. When he'd walked the castle walls with Natalya.

"Sari, talk to me."

She groaned and let her head fall back into his shoulder. "Damien."

"Malachi is ready to take over in Istanbul. We both know it. If you can't stand the idea of living here, we can live in Vienna and I can travel here when I'm needed."

"Don't be ridiculous. You can't revamp the training regimen without being here."

"*Milá*—"

"And I won't live separately from you. That is not an option."

His arms tightened around her waist, and Sari knit her fingers with his.

Damien said, "You're making me feel very selfish right now. I should have consulted with you sooner, and I should not have let Katalin outmaneuver me."

"I can agree with that. She played you expertly. You're getting rusty, old man." She turned in his arms. "But Damien, there is not a selfish bone in your body. You've avoided this for one hundred and twenty years because you know how difficult it will be."

"It will be difficult."

She laid her head on his chest and listened to his steady heartbeat. "And even if you were being selfish, you're overdue for your time, my love. If this is something you feel you must do, then I am with you."

"Katalin is not going to change."

"I don't expect her to. We'll fight often."

They stopped talking for a while, and Sari let the quiet resolution she felt from her mate sink into her own mind.

She could live here. It was close enough to Vienna that she could continue to be involved in the political reforms, but being in Řekaves would also allow her to take an active role in training new warriors in the reality of this new world.

Would she have liked to have more time to think about it? Probably not. The more time she had to think about big decisions, the more anxious and belligerent she became. Damien had bent for her needs too many times to count. She was due to bend a little for him.

But hours later, after her mate was sleeping soundly, Sari still couldn't rest. She wrapped herself in Damien's coat and left their chamber, seeking cool night air and a clear head. She walked into a deserted courtyard, but the shuffling feet and murmuring voices of the guardians on the walls drew her eyes up. She climbed to walk along the battlements, the night guard nodding to her in respect.

Halfway around the walk, she smelled cigarette smoke and followed it to Kostas, who was staring over the wall and into the black forest on the west side of the valley. His two guards stood away from him, one watching while the other closed his eyes and leaned against the wall.

"I'm annoying them," he said.

"Because you're not in your chamber?"

"Yes. And neither of them smoke."

"You shouldn't either."

He sucked on the end of the cigarette and let the smoke trickle from his lips. "I've never known a Grigori to get cancer, have you?"

"I haven't known that many Grigori."

Kostas grinned. "At least not many that weren't at the end of your sword."

The guilt reared up and bit her. Kostas must have seen it on her face.

"Don't," he said. "We're not worth feeling guilty over."

"I probably killed some of your brothers who were only trying to survive." She closed her eyes and remembered a dirty street in London. "In fact, I know I have."

"Do you think we're not all murderers? We are. I guarantee that you've saved more human lives than the Grigori lives you've taken, singer."

Sari said nothing, suddenly wishing the taste of tobacco brought her any kind of comfort.

"Is that why you're doing this?" Kostas said. "Taking these children?"

"We're saving them."

"Are you?" Kostas took another drag. "Have you even thought of what you're going to do with them once you 'save' them?"

"That's why I called Kyra."

He gave her a bitter laugh. "My sister has had enough trouble served to her. She doesn't need additional worries."

"Then why did you bring her here?"

"Because your mate did me a favor once," Kostas said.

"And I don't forget favors. Especially when they're freely given."

"If Damien did you a favor, he expects no recompense for it. That's not who he is."

"But it's who I am." Kostas took another drag. "I do not like owing people. So I will help you free these children and help you figure out what to do with them. They're only a few, after all."

A few, maybe. But they were a few who would soon be out of the Fallen's hands and given some hope of a future.

"You realize there are far more, don't you?" Kostas asked with a smirk.

Sari nodded.

"Are you going to save them all, Sari of Vestfold?"

Maybe. Maybe she was going to save them all. Maybe she couldn't, but she'd damn well try.

Sari met Kostas's eyes and let the ghosts that tormented her rise up to meet the bitter Grigori leader. He met her look, and the cynical smile fell from his face.

"I don't think you can comprehend how many children I have watched die, Kostas, son of Barak," she said quietly. "I don't have the luxury of cynicism. So if I want to save these children, then I will. And I'll save the next ones. And the next. I'll save them or I will die trying. That is my penance for failure. What's yours?"

"Killing the Fallen. As many as I can until the day I die. I don't have longevity spells, so I don't have all that much time left."

For the first time, Sari noticed the marks of age around his eyes. There were no traces that a human would notice, but Sari could see the bone-deep signs of exhaustion with life. The average Grigori had a set lifetime unless an angel was feeding them power. Kostas had already lived well past his allotted time, and Sari didn't feel like asking why.

Sari nodded at him. "Then we understand each other, Grigori."

She turned to go.

"Rest well," Kostas called.

Sari paused.

"No hidden meaning." Kostas looked back to the forest. "I know how well I sleep. I truly hope you rest well, Sari. We'll get your children tomorrow night."

CHAPTER

EIGHT

D AMIEN nodded to Leo, who moved through the dark brush as silently as a hunting cat. One archer covered them from a vantage point across the river while two others had their eyes trained on the dock where Sari, Mala, and Kyra would land with three other singers from Mikael's house. Hopefully the distraction Damien and Kostas would provide at the gate would draw their guards away.

Aurel's compound was built in three tiers and surrounded by decorative electrified fencing and electronic sensors. The lowest level near the river was the women and children's apartments, a long narrow building surrounded by gardens and lawns. A cheerful play area for the children, but also one that left no cover to hide. All the riverbank was landscaped to provide maximum visibility. Guards patrolled it regularly, and Leo had seen motion sensors along the riverbank.

The second tier was farther up and contained the Grigori quarters along with the armory and training areas. It wasn't a large force—Aurel had another compound where his sons were trained—but it was enough to keep the grounds and his personal home well covered.

The third tier lay south of the other buildings on the rise of a hill. As angular as the others, this building made no attempt to blend with the hills but towered over them. A large covered walkway surrounded the property on the second level. There were no exterior stairs.

That was Aurel's home. To breach it, Damien would have to enter it from the ground floor, putting himself at a disadvantage since they had little idea what the interior contained.

The black blade was strapped to his thigh, heavy and hidden beneath tactical pants that would rip away easily when he needed to draw.

A buzz against his leg. He shielded the light from his phone when he checked it. Sari and her sisters were in place.

Damien pointed at Leo, who moved into position with five scribes from Rěkaves, their *talesm* covered even though the night was warm. If everything went according to plan, the scribes, singers, and Grigori children would be fleeing together, and they didn't want to terrify the little ones.

Spreading out along the perimeter fence, Leo and his men disappeared into the brush. Damien looked at Kostas and nodded.

SARI KNEW THE MOMENT THE ALARMS HAD GONE OFF. GRIGORI flooded from the house and ran up the hill. There were still two positioned along the riverbank, but hopefully the alarms sounded the same. Sari had decided there was no way to avoid tripping the sensors, so the best idea was to trip them all at once. Mala and Kyra rowed the boat toward the dock, and Sari ducked as the boat slid under. Securing it with rope, the six singers stepped out of the boat and waited.

There was no shuffling. No sound of alarm. The only sound was the steady sound of the river and the creaking wood of the dock. Mala ducked out from under the dock and moved toward the shoreline. They were all clothed in black, and Mala moved like a panther up the grass. She crouched low, dug something out from behind a rock, then tossed it in the river.

Camera, she signed.

Any others?

Not that I can see. Move now. I'll immobilize the guards.

No kill unless necessary.

Mala nodded and disappeared into the night. Sari and Kyra moved toward the children's apartments. When they encountered the electronic lock, she stepped back and let one of the Rěkaves singers step forward.

The singer slid a keycard in the lock. The card was attached to some electronic device Rhys had sent from Istanbul. Within a few moments—like magic—the door clicked open and they slipped inside.

Another siren, but this one worked to their advantage. Children walked out of the rooms, rubbing their eyes and yawning, only to gape at the black-clad women they encountered. Sari did a quick head count.

Two girls she could see, holding the hands of small boys who might have been their brothers. Six boys of various ages. The Rěkaves singers spread down the hallway, weapons concealed, to check the dark rooms.

"Vaclav, get back here!"

The woman's voice didn't stop the small boy from darting into the hall. It was the boy Damien had seen on the dock. Tiny Grigori children surrounded her, and Sari felt her skin begin to crawl. She had to stop herself from shouting at Kyra when the woman knelt down to eye level with the boy.

"Hello, Vaclav," she said. "I'm Kyra."

"Vaclav!"

Two gasps from the end of the hall pulled Sari's attention

from Kyra. Two pregnant women stood at the end of the hall; one was holding a sleeping girl, one hand on her swollen belly.

"Vaclav!"

Another human voice, but this time coming from her right. "Who the hell are you?" the voice asked in English.

The pregnant woman was holding a gun and pointing it at Sari. It was the woman from the dock, the one wearing opera gloves.

"I'm here to get you out of here. To help you and the children," Sari said, glancing at the gloves the woman still wore. "You know they're dangerous."

"What?" one of the women at the end of the hall said. "Why would we want to leave? Aurel takes care of us. Tomik takes care of us."

"Gabina, shut up," the woman said. "How can I trust you? Maybe you just want to get rid of them. Tomik said the babies aren't wanted in the world. That they'd be taken away." She glanced at Kyra but didn't lower the gun. "Woman, get away from my nephew. Vaclav, come here."

"We want to keep them safe," Sari said.

"See her?" Kyra rose and stepped closer, pointing at a little girl holding her brother's hand. "I *am* her. My brother protected me. Took me away from my father. She's not the only one."

Sari could tell the woman with the gun was still a long way from trusting them.

Kyra knelt down by the girl.

"Stay away from her!" the woman shouted.

"What's your name?" Kyra asked.

"Zuzana."

The woman's attention wavered between Sari and Kyra. "Get back. Don't touch her."

Kyra kept talking. "I'm like you, Zuzana."

The little girl's eyes were suspicious. "What do you mean?"

Kyra whispered, as if sharing a secret. "I hear voices too."

The little girl blinked. "I didn't tell anyone. Not even Milena and Tomik."

"It's okay. There's nothing wrong with you. But I can teach you how to make them stop."

"You can?"

One of the Rěkaves singers at the end of the hall tapped her wrist at Sari. "No word yet from the guardhouse. If the *praetor* hasn't neutralized the threat, we won't be able to hold them off. The boat will be coming in five minutes. We need to move."

IT WAS MUCH HARDER, DAMIEN DECIDED, TO IMMOBILIZE opponents without killing them. Zip ties and duct tape were marvelous inventions, but they took a lot longer. A dozen men were tossed in the guardhouse, and they still hadn't seen the last of them.

"Go," Leo said. "Take the men. I'll hold here with the rest. I can eliminate any stragglers. You and Kostas go to the house."

One of the men started shouting behind his duct tape; his panicked expression struck Damien as more than concern for his sire. He knelt down by the oddly familiar man.

"If I take the tape off, do not yell."

The Grigori nodded vigorously.

Damien ripped it off. No sooner could the man's lips move than he was speaking.

"There are women in the house with Aurel. He keeps them there until they become pregnant. I know who you are, but they're human. You are pledged to protect them, son of the Forgiven. They are innocent."

Damien narrowed his eyes and realized why the man seemed familiar. He was the Grigori guard who had been on the dock with the children the other night. "What is your name?"

The Grigori hesitated. "We're not allowed to speak our names to outsiders."

"Some magic?"

The man nodded.

"Can you tell me what is in the building down by the dock?"

The man's jaw clenched. "No," he ground out. "But know that heaven will judge you if the innocent pay for the guilty's crimes."

Damien glanced at Kostas, who nodded. The Grigori pulled the man up and tossed him toward one of the Leo's men. "Hold this one. Damien and I are going after an angel."

"I can't wait much longer," Sari said. "You cooperate, or we'll put you out."

The woman hissed and firmed her hold on the gun pointed at Sari. "You will not drug children. You said you were here to help them."

"Milena," one of the pregnant women down the hall called, "what is going on?"

"Gabi, Belinda, go back in your room. Shut the door and wait for Tomik or William. Children, go back into your room. Tomik will be here soon."

The pregnant women turned to go, and Kyra shot to her feet, holding the little girl she'd been talking to.

"*Zi yada!*"

The little girl started crying when the women fell to the ground. Kyra turned to the woman the others had called Milena.

"What have you done to them?" she screamed as the children all began to wail.

"Listen to me, human." Kyra marched up to Milena, who lowered the gun as soon as it was pointed near a child. "The women are fine. We are here to help you escape this angel."

"Angel?"

Kyra grabbed the gun out of her hand and handed it to Sari. "Yes, *angel*. He's a monster, isn't he?"

"Yes." The woman looked defeated. Hell, she looked on the verge of falling over.

Kyra continued. "These children and you are innocents. I was once like them. We are taking you away from here, saving your life, and getting help for these babies. Are you with me, or do I need to knock you out too?"

The woman's eyes were tortured. She didn't look at Kyra, she looked at Sari.

"How do I know? How do I know I can trust you? I cannot trust anyone. Not with them."

Gritting her teeth, Sari knelt down and picked up a little boy who was sniffling and staring at the women Kyra had knocked out.

"Please believe me," Sari said, stroking his dark hair. "I would never harm a child."

The child stopped crying at her touch. He nuzzled into Sari, wrapping his arms around her neck and clinging to her. Sari swallowed the lump in her throat and held him tight. The screams in her mind died back as she focused on the vulnerable little boy in her arms.

"I would *never* harm a child."

DAMIEN DIDN'T WASTE TIME TRYING TO BE COVERT. IF THE angel didn't know they were coming at this point, he was an idiot and he'd be easy to kill. The Rěkaves scribes fanned out and covered him as he and Kostas breached a narrow door in a utility area on the far side of the house facing the electric fence.

Damien grunted when the sting of electricity coursed through his body. "Doorknob is wired."

Crude but effective. Especially for human intruders.

"Let me guess," Kostas said. "There's some mystical spell that will allow me to enter this place even though it'll be painful as hell. But don't worry, it won't kill me."

"No." Damien picked up a two-by-four that had been stored in the utility area. "Just electricity. It'll kill us both."

He used the two-by-four to ram down the door. It took four tries, but the hinges gave way.

"I see we've abandoned stealth," Kostas said.

"The alarms didn't give that away?"

The question was, would Aurel already be gone? Angels couldn't fly, but some could transport themselves. If Aurel had fled, he'd be returning with more of his men. His children, those Sari was rescuing that moment, would still be under his control. Damien didn't want to think about what the angel could make them do. Or what that could do to his mate.

The utility door led to what looked like a basement. Locked rooms were along one wall, but Damien heard nothing behind them. Still, they'd have to be checked later.

No movement on the stairs.

"I don't hear anything," Kostas whispered as the scribes moved to the main floor. They spread out and searched the rooms, but no one was found. No Grigori. No women. No angel.

Damien was near rage. If they could not find Aurel, they would have to abandon the children. There was no telling—

"Wait." Kostas put a hand on his arm. "I hear something."

He calmed the rush of his blood and focused his senses.

"I hear it too."

It was a quiet, whimpering sound.

"Dear God," Kostas said. "Please tell me he doesn't have a taste for children."

There was no stopping the man. Kostas bolted up the stairs before Damien could shout at him to stop. He was through a door and flung across the room as Damien ducked. He came in low and rolling, drawing the large hunting knife at his waist. Not the black blade. Not yet…

"Bastard!" Kostas yelled from the ground. "Let her go."

Aurel was in human form, lying naked on the bed, a young woman between his legs. He had a silver knife at her throat and a thin line of blood trickled down her breast.

Damien tried to meet her eyes, but she was frozen in panic. The whimpering had come from her. She was staring at the body of another girl across the room. That one wasn't moving. Her blank stare told Damien she would never move again.

"Who are you?" Aurel asked. "Which house are you from?"

"No house sends me," Damien said calmly. "Let the girl go. What need have you, a son of heaven, for a human to shield you?"

Aurel chuckled. "Pretty words say court training. Are you one of Katalin's warriors, then? You're better than most, but you're still not better than me."

"Do you think so?" Damien was taking stock of the angel. If he'd been able to transport himself, he'd already be gone. The fact that he was using the girl meant he didn't have the confidence to fight even two scribes on his own. Or Aurel had so much confidence that he wanted to toy with Damien and Kostas. Not atypical behavior from one of the Fallen. They were easily bored creatures.

"Let the girl go," Kostas said, lurching to his feet. He was leaning against the wall, but he was standing.

"No." Aurel swirled the blood in circles on her skin. "I like her here. Besides, your little attack came at an… inconvenient time. I'm modest."

"I doubt that." Damien glanced out the window to see the river in the distance. There was someone running across the grass. "We're getting rid your children, you know. Even if you kill me and my brother, they will all be gone."

Rage flared on the angel's face. "They're mine!"

"They'll be dead soon."

Aurel tossed the girl off the bed and stood, his form growing to seven feet tall and broad as a barn door.

Not scared then, Damien thought. Bored. Damn.

He raised the knife, but it was no match against the angel's voice. Aurel roared, and the force of it flung Damien back into the wall, pinning his hand over his head. The roaring went on. It was a feral howl and a thundering train. The cry of a storm and a felled tree. The sound was elemental. He wanted to clutch his ears and curl up in pain, but he was pressed against the wall with no hope of escape.

The angel's gold eyes glowed in the darkness. The human girl screamed and scrambled to the corner. Damien heard the other scribes trying to climb the stairs, but the voice of the angel held them back.

Then, as suddenly as the sound came, it died. Damien opened his eyes to see Aurel with an arrow lodged in his temple. He looked confused. Another flew through the window and pierced his neck.

"Go!" Kostas yelled.

Damien drew the black blade and stumbled across the room, every muscle and bone screaming. One of the Řekaves scribes ran into the room, launching himself at the angel's knees as his brothers drew their weapons.

With a crash, the angel fell forward, crushing the scribe who'd tackled him, arrows still piercing his neck and his temple.

"*Praetor*, the blade!"

The scribes pinned Aurel down as he struggled. Kostas crawled over and yanked the arrow at the angel's temple to the side. Then he shoved a fist in the monster's mouth to try to keep him silent.

Damien crawled over the massive form and straddled Aurel's back.

"I need his neck!" he yelled.

Kostas roared in pain but shoved his fist to the side to expose the neck.

"Bastard!" he screamed. "He's biting off my hand!"

Damien plunged the knife in Aurel's spine as Kostas yanked his hand back, his fist closed around the massive tongue he'd ripped from the angel's mouth. A screaming sound filled the air.

"Get back!" Damien yelled, pulling at Kostas's shoulders. The hand the angel had bitten was dangling at an odd angle. The angel had turned the Grigori's hand to raw meat. Damien didn't know how Kostas had pulled out the monster's tongue.

They crawled away from the angel as its skin turned black. Fine cracks appeared, riddling its giant body, rapidly gaping wider as a fiery red glow emanated from the center of its chest. It looked as if the angel was melting from the inside, his skin breaking apart from the heat.

"Grab the girl," Kostas said. "Get out of here!"

The screaming wind became louder. None of the Řekaves scribes moved toward the girl.

"For God's sake!" Kostas yelled. He tucked his wounded hand into his side and crawled to the traumatized woman. He was trying to lift her just as Damien reached them both.

"I've got her," Damien yelled. "I've got her. Run!"

They made it down the stairs just as the room exploded.

CHAPTER
NINE

S ARI held the boy against her chest as they made their way downriver in the fishing boat. They left the wreckage of Aurel's house behind, left the bound Grigori who'd wanted to stay. Only Tomik had wanted to come with the women and children. Milena trusted him, so Damien had allowed him to board the fishing boat headed for Prague and Astrid, who would take a look at Kostas's injuries and see if his hand was reparable.

"He's never been held," Milena said. Zuzana had curled into the woman's side with Vaclav resting against Zuzana.

"What do you mean?"

"Lucas." Milena nodded to the boy in Sari's arms. "He never trusted Tomik. Or any man. I think he witnessed Aurel do something horrible to his mother. She didn't waste away like most of them. One morning, she was just gone."

"And she left her baby."

Milena nodded. "He wouldn't let Tomik or William pick him up, and I can't hold them like that. So he's never been held."

Sari's heart threatened to break open. The finely held control almost snapped. "How old is he?"

"A little over two."

Sari clutched him tighter and had the satisfaction of feeling Lucas sigh against her chest, his chubby cheek pressed to her skin. He was sleeping.

"Do you want the baby?" Sari nodded to her stomach. "If you don't, I understand. We can take care of him for you. He won't harm either me or my sisters."

Milena put a hand over her belly. "You're not taking him from me. I've figured out how to care for them. If he can drink formula—"

"There's no reason he shouldn't be able to."

"Then he's mine. I don't care who his father is. He's my child."

Sari shifted the baby on her chest. "He's making you sick. You know that, don't you?"

"No." Milena shook her head. "He makes me brave."

The fierce look in the woman's eyes humbled Sari. She imagined the first mothers, human women who sacrificed so much for their beloved children. What must it be like to know that the very thing you loved could kill you? And still they fought. Still they loved. No wonder the first mothers were venerated in ancient songs.

"What are you going to do with us?" Milena asked.

Sari looked around her. Three unconscious human women, one wary rogue, and fourteen Grigori children. Grigori children at her feet. Leaning against her. Crawling in her lap as she held a baby. It was a scene from one of her nightmares.

Except that it wasn't.

Her mate stood at the helm, talking with Natalya, the archer who'd sent the arrows into Aurel and given the scribes the chance to kill the angel. Leo and Kyra tried unsuccessfully not to stare at each other. Kostas was pale from pain and blood loss, his hand wrapped in thick bandages and held to his chest. But Mala guarded him as he talked with Tomik, who was rubbing his temple and glancing at Milena. The scribes and singers from Rěkaves draped the children in blankets and poured them glasses of milk, asking their names and tousling their hair or rubbing their cheeks. Any sign to show that they were safe and among those who could care for them.

All Sari could picture was a giant castle and an empty courtyard that echoed with the sounds of war. How much better if they rang with the sounds of war... and laughing children?

"We're taking you home," Sari said to Milena. "My home. Your new home if you want it."

Milena put a hand on her belly. "We don't have anywhere else to go."

• • • ✦ • • •

"You have got to be joking," Katalin hissed. "I told Damien he could store the Grigori here until he found a place for them. You are not adopting all of them like stray dogs."

Sari put her hands on her hips. "Call them dogs one more time, Katalin. See what happens."

It had been weeks since the Grigori children had come to Rěkaves. As far as Sari and Damien were concerned, they were there to stay. Katalin, on the other hand, had different ideas when they'd told her she'd become a grandmother.

Damien put a steadying hand on Sari's shoulder.

"Mother," he said, "this is not an option. Sari has offered the women and children sanctuary. This is her home, and the offer will not be rescinded."

"This is *my* home!"

"And ours as well." Damien slid an arm around Sari's waist. "Or have you forgotten who is *praetor*?"

Katalin bared her teeth. Sari managed to contain a smile.

How do you like your manipulations now, Katalin?

Sari might have felt smug, but the powerful singer was seconds away from erupting.

"Aurel was a singer," Damien said.

Katalin blinked and closed her mouth. "He was what?"

Sari turned. "A what?"

"A singer, Mother. He didn't have fire. He couldn't transport. His power was in his voice."

Katalin frowned.

Sari said, "I don't understand."

"Magic. His magic was in his voice. He pinned me to the wall with one scream. That's why Kostas tore out his tongue."

Sari really wished she'd been there to see that.

"Why does that matter?" Katalin lifted her chin. "Each of the fallen have different strengths."

"True. And this one has three daughters who have been given sanctuary with us." Damien released Sari and stepped toward his mother. "Think about it, Katalin. First-generation angelic blood. Have you seen their eyes? Pure gold."

Sari saw the gears start to turn in Katalin's head. She was glad she'd kept silent.

While Sari knew that Damien's heart was soft for the Grigori children, Katalin had not held them as they cried in sadness for the home they'd lost or the mothers they still missed. She had not bathed the children and played in the bubbles as Mala and Kyra had. She had not held Lucas every night, rocking the little boy until he fell asleep in the nursery where Damien had once slept. Katalin had not fed them bread from the kitchen or tucked them into bed as Damien and Leo did.

Perhaps that softening would come in time, but for now, Damien needed to reach his mother on a level she would understand.

Martial advantage. Potential power.

"Think of the magic they could command," he continued.

"We will raise them. You will train them. Think of the power they might wield with their voices alone."

"The boys," Katalin started. "They won't have spoken magic."

"No, but they're still first generation angelic offspring. Imagine the potential, *praetora*. Imagine the sheer power they will have as the first generation from even a minor Fallen like Aurel. Now imagine that power trained by Mikael's house."

Katalin narrowed her eyes. "The first sign of evil I see from them—"

"Will likely be fights with their brothers," Damien said. "Or playing in the armory. They are no more evil than I was at that age."

Heaven above.

Sari's thoughts turned to childproofing the castle. She winced.

Luckily, Damien and Sari had a wealth of willing babysitters. Most of the initiates at Řekaves were enamored with "the *praetor's* little ones." The children scarcely went anywhere without three or four of the guard following along.

Shouting erupted in the hall outside. Then squealing and laughter as tiny feet rushed past, followed by more tiny feet. Then a silence Sari had learned to dread. She ran out the door and nearly collided with Milena.

"Are you okay?" She held out her hands.

"Thank you," Milena said. "But it's me. So clumsy. I can barely walk without falling over."

"Why are you on your feet?"

"Vaclav," she said, her face pale. "I heard him shouting and—"

"I'll go check," Damien said, pushing past his mother. "Katalin, the matter is closed. If you want to argue with me later, I'll be in my office."

Sari watched Damien run toward the sound of a metallic crash that echoed down through the castle.

"I am so sorry," Milena said. "He's never had this many toys. Not that armor is a toy, but—"

"Has he always been interested in weapons?" Katalin said, crossing her arms and watching Milena.

"Vaclav?" Milena looked to Sari, who nodded for her to go ahead. "Well, yes. I'm afraid so. He's seen Aurel's sons practicing since the time he could walk. His favorites are bows and arrows, but anything that can be used to hit is also popular. There are eleven brothers, you see. All within a few years of each other. Anything and everything is a weapon with the boys."

"And the girls?"

Milena smiled. "It's hard to tell. They mostly keep to themselves. It must be the… voices that Sari and Kyra have talked about. They are better here."

"They would be…" Katalin muttered, her eyes focused down the hallway. "Perhaps I should go help Damien with the children. He has no experience with small ones like that."

The next moment she was gone, and Sari stared down the hallway, her mouth agape.

Milena said, "They're good children, I promise. They're just rowdy. And I thought it best to be honest if we're going to stay here."

"You're staying." Sari squeezed her hands and led her into the library. "And you have no idea how much you just helped make that easier. Now let me see if the baby wants another song."

They'd been experimenting with Sari singing to the child in Milena's womb. The contact, along with Sari's voice, seemed to feed the boy and leave Milena less exhausted. It wasn't a cure. The child was still taking a toll on his mother's body, but it seemed to help like nothing else did. Sari had started to sing to the other women as well. All three were adapting to life in the castle, but Sari had only truly bonded with Milena, whose fierce, protective heart spoke to her.

As Sari sang, Milena drifted to sleep in the warm room, her shirt pushed up and her belly exposed. When she was finished with the song, Sari pushed Milena's shirt down and covered her with a light blanket, but Milena continued to sleep.

Do you want to be a mother? Milena had asked her the week before.

I don't know. To be that vulnerable again…

Sari had children now. She had a house full of them, and there were more out there, waiting to be saved. But should the heavens grant her another child, how could she not be thankful? Milena was human—a biology student in another life— far more vulnerable than Sari had ever been. And yet she'd never given up. Never lost hope or the warrior's spirit that had made her a champion for her baby, her nephew, and every other child under her care.

"He makes me brave."

DAMIEN WAS SINGING THAT NIGHT WHEN HE PREPARED FOR BED. There was a deep contentment in her mate that filled something in Sari's own soul. It had been a good day.

There would be no permanent damage to the suit of armor in the great hall, and Katalin had decided it was a good learning opportunity to teach the children about each piece of armor, what it did, and how it had developed over the ages. Along with its history, Katalin decided to invite Desmond to teach the children about Irin and human uses for armor while introducing them to corresponding spells that could mimic the affect.

The children had been blessedly silent for an hour, and Sari suspected that ideas of banishment were far from the *praetora's* mind.

Astrid had patched Kostas back together and forced him into a week of bedrest, but his left hand was missing a pinky and two knuckles that were beyond her skill to save.

The day after his release, he'd left Kyra with Damien and Sari so he could travel to Prague and visit a rogue Grigori there, letting that man know Aurel's sons were now free and some might be open to living a more honorable life. He'd taken Leo with him, much to Leo's disappointment.

"Do you think Kostas knows about Leo and Kyra?" Damien asked, brushing his hair and tying it back. It was down to his shoulders, and beards were remaining in fashion. Sari was immensely pleased.

"There is no Leo and Kyra," Sari said. "That would mean one of them would have to actually do something to make a 'Leo and Kyra' happen."

"Poor Leo," Damien said.

"Poor Kyra. She's the one who has to live with a hundred overprotective big brothers."

"We could use her here," Damien said. "There's more than enough room in the castle. She has a keen understanding of the little ones, and she's an excellent teacher."

Kyra had already taught the little girls spells to guard their minds from the voices.

"I'm open to asking her," Sari said. "But you realize that Leo is going to have to go back to Istanbul soon. Especially with Malachi assuming the watcher's position."

"I know. Ava may have left a frustrated rant on my voice mail today about that."

"She's probably still sleep deprived. She'll forgive you. Eventually."

Damien wiped his face and slung a towel around his neck. He walked to Sari, who was sitting on the dressing table.

"Hello, *milá*." He spread her knees and stepped between them. "You look very happy tonight."

"I am."

"If it's anything I've done, tell me. That way I can repeat it." He nibbled along her jaw.

"It's not anything you've done," she said. "It's just who you are."

He drew back and cupped her chin in his hand. "I need no soft poetry when I have your words."

"And I need nothing but you."

"That's all?"

She paused. "If heaven blesses us with a child, I would be well pleased."

His eyes warmed and his hand slipped down to grasp her hips. "Should Uriel bless us with a child, I would treasure her. But my Sari, I am content either way. We have children. More than we know what do to with."

"And more may come."

"I hope they do," he whispered, his eyes alight with mischief.

Sari laughed. "You love it."

"Yes." He slipped his arms around her waist and hugged her tightly. "I love them already, Sari. How is it possible?"

It was possible because Damien's heart was as big as the North Sea. The children saw it and flocked to him, clinging to his compassion and gentleness. His honor and fierce protection. Even Lucas, who trusted no man, was beginning to trust Damien.

"This world of ours is changing," he said.

Sari nodded. "But it is a good change."

"I have wandered a very long time, *reshon*." Damien drew back and looked into her eyes. "And seen more than I ever imagined. War and peace and terrible beauty and loss. And now I've come to the last place I ever expected to find peace and found more than I could imagine. But I need to know: are you truly content here?"

"It's like you said, Damien. Sarihöfn. Istanbul. Vienna.

Rěkaves." She kissed him. "When we are together, we are home."

"A singer blessed me once. She prayed for me to find a mate as warlike as myself."

Sari threw her head back and laughed. "A blessing or a curse?"

"There have been a few times along our path that I didn't know that myself." Damien couldn't help but smile. "But there is such beauty in your violence. Like the eagle over the fjord, Sari. Do you remember?"

Her breath caught at the memory of a night so long ago. A night when Damien's passion had first touched her. The night she had fallen in love with the warrior who changed her destiny.

"I remember." She blinked away tears.

"You have loved me." He kissed her lips. "And since I am a very wise scribe, I clung to it. Through battle. Through loss. Through the darkest night, *milá*. Through the ages, I clung to it."

"I love you, Damien."

"I have treasured it. Because within your love, I have never felt more alive."

Sari grabbed his hair with both hands and brought Damien down for a kiss.

"Even if we live a thousand years," she said. "A thousand years, my love."

"We've had six hundred together." Damien picked her up and carried her into their bedchamber. "Four hundred more isn't too much to ask."

THE END

Please continue reading for a preview of Leo and Kyra's story, The Silent: Irin Chronicles Book Five.

PREVIEW: THE SILENT

KYRA sat cross-legged in front of the fire, breathing in the incense and focusing on the door in her mind. It was a small door, growing smaller every day. Behind it lay the soul voices of humanity.

Her gift. Her torment.

The voices had once battered her mind, rendering her incapable of normal human interaction.

> Emetsam tarrea.
> Ya emetsam tarrea.
> Emetsam tarrea me.

The whispers grew quiet.

Emetsam tarrea.

Kyra reached out in her mind and closed the door, imagined pressing her palm against it and holding it until the pressure in her mind eased. Then she took a deep breath and released it slowly, grateful for the silence that followed.

Kareshta. The silent ones. Daughters of Fallen angels and human women. They were her sisters, her friends, and her burden.

Kyra breathed in and out, tasting the damp sea air on her tongue along with the spice of the incense and the scent of orange blossoms coming from the orchard outside the farmhouse above the sea. Her eyes were closed as she focused on keeping her breath steady and her body still. She wore the loose sundress she always wore to meditate and prayed the beam of morning light she felt across her back wasn't burning her pale skin. Her thick hair was piled on top of her head, and dark tendrils brushed across her neck, moved by the warm breeze rolling down the hills.

She, her brother, and their charges lived a nomadic existence. This retreat was in the mountains near the Bulgarian coast. It was isolated and remote. The neighbors either had no curiosity or her brothers had dissuaded them from inquiring, but no strangers had ever come to visit.

In the months and years that had followed the Battle of Vienna—the great struggle among the Fallen where her father had finally sacrificed his life—many of Kyra's sisters had sat with her, practicing the mental discipline that would allow them to mingle among humans. One by one, they had left.

The *kareshta* who had longed for the world had learned the necessary spells and fled. Some to Irin scribe houses in the major cities, eager to find among the sons of the Forgiven mates who could protect them in their strange new reality. Others took human lovers or struck out on their own, longing for a taste of the life that had been so long denied them by the angels who had sired them or the Grigori brothers who had guarded them.

And then Kyra was alone.

Some of the *kareshta* who remained had tried to learn from her, but most were unmotivated. They didn't desire community with humans, felt too exposed by silencing their minds, or had psyches too damaged to practice magic. Many were old, far too old to learn new magic, they said. They only wanted peace in their final years.

Then there were the children. The children were the most damaged of all.

While her brother, Kostas, remained in the city hunting minor angels and Grigori who threatened the human population, Kyra resided in the mountains outside Burgas with her half brother Sirius, caring for the weakest and oldest of their family.

She heard raised voices coming from outside her cottage. Sirius and Kostas were fighting again.

"Then you tell her!" Sirius shouted. "*You* tell her she's to remain here, locked away from the world while her sisters—"

"Her sisters are not *my* sister. Not *my* twin. You know why she needs to remain close to me. I have to find a way—"

"She deserves her own life, Kostas. She deserves far more than we can give her, but while she still has time…" Sirius's voice trailed off as Kostas dragged him back inside. She heard a door slam.

And then silence.

While she still has time…

Kyra closed her eyes, and her lips tingled at the memory of a dark corridor and a tall scribe's stubble against her mouth. His scent was in her nose, and her fingers clutched his shirt. His arms were strong around her, holding her as she pressed her ear to the wall of his chest, searching for the sound of his heartbeat. She'd been afraid, *so* afraid for him.

"Come away with me. Or stay here. Just don't leave again. Give this a chance, Kyra."

"I can't."

"Your brother—"

"My brother is not the reason."

"Then what?"

The farmhouse door slammed again, and she heard footsteps on the path to her cottage. Sirius. After one hundred years, she recognized his step. She'd watched him grow from a baby to a boy to a man. Now the tall warrior was the protector of the weakest ones. The ones who remained.

And Kyra.

Sirius knocked quickly and opened the door, only to pause and fall silent when he saw her sitting before her fire.

"Give me a moment," she said quietly.

"I can come back."

"Or you can wait. Patience."

She breathed in and out for five more breaths, trying to ignore the frustration bouncing around the room. Sirius was usually the calm and quiet one, but something her sullen and serious twin had said must have riled him, and Kyra suspected it had to do with her. Sirius was constantly pushing her to be more independent. He'd trained her to fight with daggers when Kostas had refused. She'd learned how to fire a gun properly and even participate in hand-to-hand combat under his instruction.

The baby she'd raised after his mother's death had become her teacher. He pushed, always gently, for her to go into the village more often despite Kostas's objections. He regularly gave her tasks that would put her in the path of a variety of humans, from the local priest to the clerk at the village store. At his urging, she'd even learned to drive a car and taken a drawing class in Burgas.

She turned and motioned to the spot on the carpet next to her. "Come. It'll do you good to meditate a little."

Sirius rolled his eyes a bit, but he came and sat beside her.

"What are you two shouting about, *bata*?"

He couldn't stop the grin. "Should you still be calling me little boy when I'm taller than you?"

"I wiped your nose when you were a baby. I can call you what I want."

Sirius laughed and kicked his feet out, laying his head in

Kyra's lap as he had when he was a child. Kyra put her head on his forehead and let some of the nervous energy that had built up in her mind release against her brother's skin. He'd been working in the sun, and his usually fair complexion had turned a pleasing light brown.

Sirius grabbed Kyra's hand and pressed it to his cheek. "You're upset."

"No, just feeling anxious today."

His forehead wrinkled. "The voices?"

"Not that." She took a deep breath and imagined herself walking among the orange groves, smelling the heady fragrance of the pale cream blossoms. "I was thinking about a visit to Ava in Istanbul."

Ava Matheson was a *kareshta* who had lived as a human for most of her life. She'd had no idea she was the granddaughter of a Fallen archangel; she just thought the voices she heard were the result of mental illness. When she met Malachi, an Irin warrior, she discovered a shadow world where angelic and human blood mingled. Now Ava and Malachi were "mated" in the Irin tradition, and Ava and Kyra spoke frequently by phone or video call.

Kyra suspected a visit to Ava might not be too objectionable as long as "that damn scribe" wasn't there. Ava understood Kyra better than any other person she'd met. She'd lived with mental chaos and didn't take silence for granted.

"It'd be good to see Ava," Kyra said softly. "I haven't seen… anyone outside our family. Not in months."

"What if I had an idea other than Istanbul?" Sirius asked quietly, his eyes closed, and Kyra stroked his cheek.

Her touch, and the contact with his sisters, was one of the reasons Sirius was nearly faultless in his interactions with humans. Offspring of the angels all hungered for soul energy. Irin males got it from their Irina, but Grigori who were starved of soul energy turned to taking it from humans since most weren't raised with sisters. They were slaves to their angelic fathers and would stalk humans like a lion hunting his next meal. Kyra had no illusions about the Grigori. Most were evil. Only a few managed to live an honorable life.

But Sirius had been raised in Kyra's arms. Never had the boy been hungry for love or affection. Instead of a predator, he'd grown into a protector.

"What kind of idea?" Kyra asked. "You know Kostas won't let me travel far without him."

"You could go back to the compound in Sofia."

Kyra shook her head. Two of her half brothers had found mates among the archangel Jaron's daughters. Kostas's men had once protected the women by hiding the *kareshta* for Jaron, but since the angel's death, the women were free and happy to find husbands among Kostas's men. It wasn't mating like the Irin had, but it was something, and the Grigori couples who found each other were happy.

While Kyra was delighted for her brothers, she felt out of place at the compound in Sofia where they lived. Added to that, seeing his men content with wives seemed to have an adverse effect on Kostas, whose simmering anger bled into Kyra's mind, sending her anxiety through the roof.

No, Sofia was not an option.

"If you don't want to visit Sofia"—Sirius sat up and crossed his legs, grabbing Kyra's hands and holding them between his own—"then I want you to listen to me."

She could feel his excitement. "I always listen to you, *bata*."

"And you have to keep an open mind."

"What are you talking about?"

"There is a theory among some of the free Grigori. Others like us. About how to better control our magic."

Kyra frowned. "What kind of theory?"

"Have you heard of Yantra tattooing?" Sirius asked. "*Sak Yant*, to be precise?"

LEO PUT HIS HANDS ON HIS HIPS AND SQUARED OFF AGAINST HIS opponent. She was small, but Leo knew not to underestimate her.

"No."

"Yes!"

Two-year-old Matti mirrored Leo's stance, tiny fists on her hips and her rosy-pink cheeks covered in chocolate. They stared at each other. The tall, blond warrior had faced off against his small rival on many occasions. This wasn't the first time. It wouldn't be the last. Ava and Malachi's children were tiny forces to be reckoned with.

His watcher's children were the first in history—that anyone knew of—to carry the mingled blood of Fallen and Forgiven angels. Their powers were unknown and potentially dangerous.

They were also perilously cute.

"You've already had two cupcakes. You were only supposed to have one." Leo lifted the plate from the counter and set it in the bread cupboard. "Your mother will be angry with me if I give you more, Matti."

"Mad?" she asked.

"Yes, mad. Angry."

"I'm not mad," Matti said. "Hungry. Need mo' cake."

Leo narrowed his eyes at the tiny terror. Her dark curls and sweet face were only a front for a master manipulator. "If you were hungry, you would have eaten your apples."

Matti's twin brother Geron sighed deeply and put his chin on his hands. His face was also covered in chocolate. His liquid grey eyes were pools of pleading, but Leo refused to be moved.

"No cake," Leo said more firmly.

This did not suit Matti well. She raised her voice and shouted, "Baba! I want mo' cake."

Leo pointed at her. "That won't work this time. Your father is in Vienna."

Leo's Irin brother Rhys walked into the kitchen and scooped Matti up in his arms. "What are you doing to the child, Leo? She's hungry."

"She doesn't need more cupcakes. She barely touched her lunch."

Rhys kissed the top of Matti's head. "Poor darling. Why would she eat lunch when there are cupcakes? I wholly agree with you on this, Matti. Hold out for the sweets."

Sensing an ally, Matti giggled. "Reez, more cake. Peez."

Rhys turned to Leo. "She said please."

Leo grimaced. "You're not helping. Aren't you supposed to be working on a new translation of the Hokman Abat?"

The pale British scribe walked to the bread cupboard and reached inside. "Well, I thought I'd take a break and have…"

"Don't do it!" Leo yelled.

"Cake!" Matti squealed. "Want mo' cake, Reez."

Geron lifted his arms. "Lo!" he shouted at Leo. "More cake."

"This is the problem," Leo said, lifting Geron into his arms. "They gang up on you. And they have… chubby cheeks. And they're very, very cute."

"Relax," Rhys said. "You take minding them too seriously. What's the fun of being uncles if we can't make them sick to their stomachs on sweets?"

Matti giggled, which made Geron chuckle. Soon the kitchen was filled with laughter, and Rhys was stuffing more cupcakes in both children.

Leo licked chocolate frosting from his thumb. "If they get sick, I'm blaming you."

"I only gave them one cupcake, you gave them two."

"Three cakes!" Matti yelled, her tiny fist raised in triumph.

"They're frighteningly intelligent," Rhys said. "Developmentally, they're very advanced. Did you see Geron copying Malachi last week?"

Leo nodded. "He's so quiet, but he can already write both old script and the Roman alphabet."

"I wouldn't think a child would have that much small-muscle coordination."

"And Matti..." Leo trailed off as the little girl started to sing and dance around the kitchen table.

It was a childish song she'd learned from one of the Irina, a song intended to teach young girls control over their magic, but Matti had already mastered it. As she lifted her voice, the flowers in the vase on the center of the table bobbed along to the tune, dancing and nodding their heads when she called their colors in turn.

Rhys stared with wide eyes. "I haven't seen children in so long, I don't know what's normal and what's not. But that seems very advanced for her age."

"I'm fairly sure it is."

Leo had no experience with children other than Matti and Geron. His mother had been killed during the Rending, the attempted annihilation of the Irin race, when he was no older than the twins. His father had been lost for years and was never really the same after the loss of his mate. He and his cousin, Maxim, had been lost for a year until they'd shown up at a scribe house in Vilnius. He had little memory of his life before his grandfather had taken him and Maxim in. Leo liked children, but he'd never spent time with any.

But now there was a baby boom in the Irin world. Leo would give anything to join in the numbers of scribes and singers starting their families, but he wouldn't be satisfied with any mate. He wanted his *reshon*. His soul mate. The woman chosen by heaven to be his partner in life. He hadn't practiced patience for two hundred years to settle for anything less.

"What about your own family?"

"I don't know if that is possible for me."

"How do you know it's not possible if you won't give us a chance?"

"Leo, you don't know me."

"Are you sure about that?"

A loud crash broke through his reverie, and Leo spotted the source of the racket in the doorway to the living room. Matti was sitting on a rug that Geron was pulling across the wooden floor. It was unfortunate that a side table was in their way. The glass lamp sitting on it had not survived.

"Oops!" Both children turned wide eyes to Leo before they raced out of the room and up the stairs.

"Come back here!" Leo ran after them just as his phone began to buzz. "Hello?"

"Are you on patrol?" It was his cousin, Maxim. "Are the Grigori hunting in daylight now?"

"I'm on twin patrol," Leo said, pounding up the stairs. The two culprits would scatter, of that he was sure. They had excellent evasion tactics. But where would they hide? And did they have any glass shards in their little bare feet?

"I need you to go to Bangkok," Max said.

"What?"

"Bangkok," Max repeated. "Thailand."

"I know where Bangkok is." Leo pushed open his own bedroom door and walked to the closet. "I'm just not sure why I need to go there."

"I've cleared it with both Malachi and Damien. The scribe house is expecting you."

Leo pulled open his closet door. The first thing he checked was his weapons cabinet. Locked, as expected. One couldn't be too careful. "Matti?" He bent down but didn't see anything under his clothes.

"What are you doing?"

"They broke a lamp. There are probably shards. I haven't seen any blood, but you can't be too certain."

"What are you talking about?"

"The children, of course. What's in Bangkok?"

"What do you think? The usual. You'll meet your contact at the airport."

"I still don't understand—" Leo walked backed to the hall. "Geron? Matti?" He heard giggling from Ava and Malachi's room. "I know it was an accident, but I need to check your feet. I don't understand why I need to go to Bangkok, Max. There's an active scribe house there, and as far as I know they have an excellent reputation. Why is Damien involved?"

"Just get there. I have to go." Max chuckled a little. "And good luck with the little ones."

Another crash came from downstairs.

Leo shoved his phone in his pocket. "You have got to be kidding me."

MATTI GIGGLED AS SHE WATCHED LEO'S FEET WALK AWAY FROM her. She loved her uncles, especially Leo. He was like a giant bear with yellow hair and beautiful drawings all over his skin. His drawings were different than her baba's. When she looked closely, she could see little animals playing in Leo's writing, which made his *talesm* much more fun.

Her uncles played with her every day, even when they were very tired from hunting. Leo never got impatient like her mama or baba, but sometimes he didn't understand her games. She crouched in the closet and turned to the black cat who watched her with gold eyes as brilliant as her own.

Matti pointed at him. "You're not a kitty."

The cat opened its mouth and spoke clearly. "You are very

perceptive, small singer. And very magical to have seen me. Your parents and your uncles do not."

"My name is Matti."

"I know your name. You should be careful not to offer it so freely."

Matti narrowed her eyes. This creature didn't sound like it wanted to play with her. How rude.

"Do you want to know my name?" the cat asked.

"We can play."

"Yes, I've seen your play." The cat hissed words that Matti had never heard before. Special words like Mama and Baba warned her about. At his words, the shoes in the closet began to tap their toes, dancing in the low light from her parents' bedroom.

Matti clapped for the dancing shoes. This was a fun game! It was much better than making the flowers dance when she sang their colors. She imagined making all the shoes in the house dance. Her mama's and her baba's. All her uncles' big boots. She could make them dance down the stairs and into the street. Or up onto the roof where Baba grew his vegetables!

Matti opened her mouth to say the cat's words but felt Baba's magic holding her back. She growled in frustration.

"Soon, small singer," the cat said. "You are still growing into your power. One day I think you will make all of them dance."

Matti played with her toes and watched the cat that was not a cat. "I like to sing."

"I know you do. And I think I should like to hear your song," Vasu said. "One day."

Now available at all major retailers in e-book and print.

ACKNOWLEDGMENTS

I ALWAYS have a lot of thank-yous at the end of a book, but for this one, I want to particularly thank my editing team. The structure of this book, the level of planning of the four linked novellas, and the sheer amount of time and organization it took to put everything together in a story that spans roughly seven hundred years was truly a huge project. They all deserve medals and probably some wine. Maybe chocolate. Definitely a promise that I'll never write this kind of book again. (I promise I'll never write this kind of book again.)

Lora Gasway, my developmental editor, was a champion of sorting through my rambles and brainstorms, as well as being the voice of reason who convinced me that this weird book could actually work. If it didn't, it's probably because I didn't take her advice somehow. (Sorry.)

Anne Victory, my copy editor, is not only a master of sorting through my blatant comma abuse, but is also ridiculously understanding about my last-minute panic attacks about scheduling. She truly had to juggle for this job, and I appreciate every effortless catch on her part.

Like Anne, my proofreader, Linda, has extremely keen eyes and her attention to detail is unmatched. In a fantasy world with jargon and universe-specific language, she has managed to keep track of the proper usage and punctuation for completely made-up words. (I'll start working on the medals.)

Marketta Gray, my continuity beta reader and Irin Chronicles expert, was essential for checking universe-specific detail on a book that overlapped not one, but three previous books. I owe her an enormous debt of gratitude for her thoroughness. Also, some chocolate might be good too.

I do a lot of research for the Irin books, scattered among subjects as disparate as Eastern European medieval weaponry, North African martial arts, and early Scandinavian agriculture. But for this book, I want to give special thanks to Sigurd Towrie, the author of Orkneyjar.com, a website that was especially helpful during the research of the first part of *The Staff and the Blade*. I wish I had been able to visit Orkney before I wrote this book, but reading Towrie's site was a virtual visit I greatly appreciated and a starting point for researching this fascinating place.

Thanks also to Cat Bowen, my expert on all things Slavic. And beer. And gin. There's probably not enough food and drink in this book, but that's my fault.

As always, an enormous debt of gratitude to my assistant, Genevieve, and her organizational abilities which allow me to do the writing I need to do and not worry about the things that will completely sidetrack me. Thanks to my family and friends, who put up with a very cranky Elizabeth for many, many months on this one.

And finally, a deep and abiding thanks to my readers who make all this possible.

ABOUT THE AUTHOR

ELIZABETH HUNTER is a USA Today bestselling author of contemporary fantasy, paranormal romance, and paranormal mystery. She is a graduate of the University of Houston Honors College and a former English teacher. She currently lives in Central California with her family and two canine assistants who allow her to feed them and occasionally snuggle.

She's the author of the Elemental Mysteries, Elemental World, and Elemental Legacy series, the Cambio Springs Mysteries, the Irin Chronicles, and other works of fiction. Her books have sold over a million copies worldwide.

For more information, please visit:
ElizabethHunterWrites.com

ALSO BY ELIZABETH HUNTER

The Bronze Blade

The Scarlet Deep

A Very Proper Monster

A Stone-Kissed Sea

Valley of the Shadow

The Elemental Legacy

Shadows and Gold

Imitation and Alchemy

Omens and Artifacts

Midnight Labyrinth

Blood Apprentice

The Devil and the Dancer

Night's Reckoning

Dawn Caravan

The Bone Scroll

Pearl Sky

The Elemental Covenant

Saint's Passage

Martyr's Promise

Paladin's Kiss

Bishop's Flight

(Summer 2023)

Vista de Lirio

Double Vision

Mirror Obscure

Trouble Play